THREE BRIDES FOR THREE BROTHERS

John, Rick and Derrick Underwood are the most handsome trio of brothers in town and it takes three exceptional women to convince them to settle down. For Jodie marrying John seemed exciting and romantic at the time but the reality of life is proving too much. Rick's marriage to Laraine is filled with love and adventure; their life is blissful – until one day it delivers a cruel blow. Dee is smitten with her husband, Derrick. He does all he can to provide for her so when he's sent away to sea, she knows she will be alright. But suddenly she stops hearing from Derrick – where is he?

THREE BRIDES FOR THREE BROTHERS

by

Elizabeth Waite

Magna Large Print Books
Long Preston, North Yorkshire,
BD23 4ND, England.

British Library Cataloguing in Publication Data.

Waite, Elizabeth
    Three brides for three brothers.

    A catalogue record of this book is
    available from the British Library

    ISBN   978-0-7505-3798-8

First published in Great Britain in 2013 by Sphere

Copyright © Elizabeth Waite 2013

Cover illustration © Gordon Crabb

The moral right of the author has been asserted

Published in Large Print 2013 by arrangement with
Little, Brown Book Group Ltd.

Magna Large Print is an imprint of Library Magna Books Ltd.

Printed and bound in Great Britain by
T.J. (International) Ltd., Cornwall, PL28 8RW

1860735

1

Camber Sands, Sussex

'It isn't fair,' fifteen-year-old Delia Hartfield was muttering to herself as she stomped her way home from school, and this wretched weather wasn't helping. The rain was coming down in buckets and with the gale-force winds blowing in over the rough sea, she was struggling to stay on her feet. Living here in Camber Sands was wonderful when the weather was fine, but on a day like this she wished she lived in a town.

There was to be another school outing and she had had to say she couldn't go because she hadn't enough money. She would be sixteen and leaving school in another two months, but in the meantime she and her twelve-year-old brother were given sixpence a week pocket money and a comic every Saturday. Her mother and father were great, really they were – well, most of the time – but her dad would insist that he kept a roof over their heads, food on the table and clothes on their backs and if they wanted more pocket money they should earn it. That was all right in the summertime, when Camber Sands was flooded with holidaymakers; then there were plenty of part-time jobs going. Last summer she had got herself taken on as a helper to the chalet maids in the big holiday camp that had sprung up in the village since the war had ended. Thirty shillings she'd been paid for three mornings and all day Saturday. Now it was the first week in November and all her earnings had long since been spent.

Delia lifted her head and saw that she was approaching the line of shops, most of which had their blinds pulled down. She puffed her cheeks out, rubbed the raindrops from the end of her nose and did her best to run. 'Phew,' she muttered as she reached cover, pulling a handkerchief from the pocket of her navy-blue gabardine raincoat and wiping her face. It was then she became aware of her surroundings: she had taken shelter on the forecourt of Michael's Ladies' Hairdressing Salon. She allowed herself a quick smile. Three years ago when Michael had first opened his salon, it had been the talk of the village. Men didn't run ladies' hairdressing salons! He had lived to prove to the old dears just how wrong they were. As well as the successful hairdressing business here in the village, rumour had it that he owned two more in Eastbourne and Rye and one very posh salon in London.

At that moment a placard placed in the front of the salon's main window caught her eye and she let out a great sigh of disbelief.

WANTED: a SATURDAY GIRL.

As simple as that! Dee didn't stop to think; she opened the door and stepped into Michael's elegant establishment. Already the rain dripping from her mackintosh was making puddles on the posh red carpet. Her shoulder-length chestnut hair was drenched and water was dribbling down her cheeks, while her feet felt as if they were squelching in her wet shoes. She really did look a sorry sight, and her heart sank as Michael Connelly came towards her.

He had to be here today of all days, didn't he! On the few occasions she had come across him, she had been aware that the very sight of Michael set her blood tingling and her heart thumping against her ribs. In his early thirties, he was tall and well built, always immaculately dressed, his skin lightly tanned and his dark hair sleeked back off his forehead. Dee imagined he would have a host of women more than willing to fall at his feet, because besides his good looks and the well-cut, expensive clothes, he was an absolute charmer. Her own mother came here to have her hair trimmed, and she always came away saying that Michael made every single client feel that she was of the utmost importance. Would that there were more gentlemen like him about.

'You poor thing,' he murmured, his voice full of concern as he observed how very wet Dee was. 'Here, dry your hair,' he said, handing her a soft, fluffy pink towel, 'then you can tell me what brings you here.'

Dee's heart sank. She doubted he would even consider giving her a job, and she had no idea how to put her request into words. She was so out of her depth she could feel herself drowning in her own recklessness. Why oh why hadn't she gone home and waited for a dry day, instead of standing here in front of him in sodden school uniform?

Reading the situation perfectly, Michael took her arm and led her through the salon, making jokes about the weather being absolutely wonderful for fish and ducks. He was careful not to put her in a position where she would have to respond with anything more than a smile, sensing that for the moment she was too shy to speak.

Opening a door, he nodded for her to enter. 'This is what passes as our staff room,' he told her. 'Why don't you take that wet raincoat off and I'll get one of the girls to make us both a nice hot cup of tea.'

Delia couldn't believe her luck; why was Michael being so nice to her? She hadn't even mentioned that she had come into the salon to apply for the Saturday job. She shivered a little at the prospect. Would he really consider letting a schoolgirl work here? Ah well, she was here now and she would have to go ahead with her request; she could hardly get up and walk out.

Within a short time the door was pushed open and a smiling young woman whom Dee knew quite well was standing there, a loaded tea tray in her hands.

'Hello, Dee, what brings you here?' she asked, as she placed the tray on a table.

'I saw the notice in the window and was hoping I might get the Saturday job. I never knew you worked here, though, Jodie.'

'Well you wouldn't have known. I work at Michael's salon in Eastbourne and also in Rye, but he's got two stylists off sick and he brought me over here this morning just to help out temporary like.'

Coming back into the room and hearing them talking, Michael asked, 'Do you two know each other then?'

Judith Underwood, known to her friends as Jodie, laughed. 'It's because of this young lady that I am able to have a halfway decent social life.'

Michael looked bewildered. 'Well perhaps you'd better introduce me, as we haven't got around to that yet.'

'This is Delia Hartfield. She lives with her parents and younger brother in the house next door to my sister-in-law, and she is a godsend because at weekends she babysits for me. My boys adore her. Now, I'll leave you two to have your tea and to sort out why she's here, because I have a lady under the dryer who is almost ready to come out.'

Introductions now complete and the tea poured out, Delia took a seat while Michael remained standing. 'My girls all make a decent pot of tea; it's one of the qualifications I insist on in my salons. Women seem to thrive on endless cups of tea. So drink up and tell me what drove you in here on such a wet and windy day.'

Dee drained her cup and placed it back down on its saucer. 'I was sheltering under your awning and I saw your notice. Please, I would like to apply for the job as Saturday girl.' She almost choked over the request, amazed at her own boldness.

'Well you've started off on the right foot. I certainly don't need references; if Judith Underwood trusts you to look after her children, then that is good enough for me. The wage isn't much, just five shillings, but you might pick up a few tips; it depends on whether you socialise well with the customers or not. Also, if you help the stylists – sweep up, tidy their equipment, that kind of thing – without having to be told all the time, then they'll give you something from their tips at the end of the day. How does that sound to you?'

'Are you saying I have got the job?' All kinds of emotions were hammering in her chest as she waited for his reply.

'Well I am certainly going to give you a trial period. You can start this Saturday, but you must bring a note from your parents giving permission for me to employ you.'

'Yes, I will, thank you so much. What time shall I come?'

'Eight thirty. I probably won't be here, but I have two very nice young apprentices who will show you the ropes and introduce you to my stylists before we open up at nine.'

While speaking, Michael had taken her raincoat down from the hook where he had hung it and was now holding it out for her to put back on. Dee shuddered; it was still very damp. However, she managed to smile up into his face as he held the shop door open for her.

'Goodbye, and thank you again,' she murmured before she stepped out into the rain.

Michael stood for a moment or two watching her go, his mind dwelling on her. What was it about the girl that interested him so much? He had no answer; he only felt that Delia Hartfield was somehow different. Not like any of the other young girls he was acquainted with. She was certainly very attractive, and he had felt a longing to be able to wash and set her hair. Though today soaking wet and bedraggled, her long tresses were, he knew, the colour of ripe chestnuts. There was simply a quality about her that was rare in young girls today, more so since the war years, when females had been called upon to do all sorts of tasks normally only tackled by men.

He smiled grimly to himself. Funny he should feel this way about Delia Hartfield when he hardly knew her. All the same, as far as he was concerned she was different with a capital D, and he had no worries that she would turn out to be a real asset to the salon.

'You've what!' Mary Hartfield screamed, her cheeks turning red.

'Got myself a job,' Delia repeated, shaking all over.

Her mother's lips had begun to tremble on hearing this news. Now she regained something of her composure. 'Where on earth have you been? You look like a drowned rat. Besides, you know your father will never let you take a job. He wants you to stay on at school.'

Delia was shaken to the core by her mother's attitude. She hadn't given her a chance to explain.

'Where is this job?' Mary enquired sharply.

'Wish I hadn't blurted it out as soon as I came through the door now. Give me a few minutes to get out of these wet things and then I'll tell you all about it.' Dee broke off and bent down to take off her sodden shoes. In the last few minutes her mum had almost shattered what she'd seen as a stroke of good luck. Her father wouldn't be able to prevent her taking this job, would he? It didn't bear thinking about.

'Well get yerself upstairs then. Mind you put your uniform on a hanger and hang it on the rail in the bathroom, and while you're doing that I'll put the kettle on. You look as if you could use a cup of tea.'

Dee didn't bother to reply. She wasn't about to tell her mother that her future employer had already given her a good hot cup of tea.

'I suppose one day a week won't hurt,' Jack Hartfield said later that night after he and Mary had listened to Delia's tale of events. 'Have to hand it to our girl, she has shown a bit of initiative. After all, it's not as if she is going to make a career out of hairdressing, is it? I still can't think what possessed her to apply for the job,' he added, shaking his head as he opened his evening newspaper. As far as he was concerned, there was no more to be said.

Mary was picturing Michael Connelly in her mind. There were no two ways about it: he most certainly was an attractive man. She could easily understand why their Dee wanted to work in such posh surroundings, and the few shillings she would earn would give her some degree of independence. Jack was right: it wasn't as if she was going to make hairdressing her full-time career, but perhaps the job would serve its purpose as a stopgap.

Upstairs in bed, Dee was thinking about Jodie Underwood. She had known Jodie for almost as long as she could remember. How she loved being with her and her two boys, Lenny and Reggie. Both lads were really well-mannered, fun-loving little boys. Another reason she loved going to Jodie's house was because of the stories Jodie was always willing to tell. Wide-eyed, Dee would sit for hours listening to her talk about her life. She wasn't a great deal older than Dee, but God knew she had lived life to the full and it hadn't always been easy.

Dee didn't like Jodie's husband, John. It wasn't that he wasn't nice to her or didn't make her welcome; it was just that she didn't trust him and never felt comfortable when left alone in a room with him. She'd always had the feeling that when John James Underwood was home on leave, he acted as if he was God's greatest gift to women.

Jodie had been born in Westmorland during the war, but her family had moved to London in the early fifties and that was where she had met John, who was on leave from the Royal Navy. When he returned to his ship, the two of them began to correspond.

On his next leave, John and his twin sister Ethel celebrated their twenty-first birthday with a party, to which Jodie was invited. Jodie summed up that period for Dee in a nutshell: sixteen and a half years old when she went to the party; pregnant before she was seventeen and well and truly married by the time she was eighteen.

John remained in the Royal Navy, while Jodie took up residence in a flat behind the Honey Pot Tea Rooms in Camber Sands. Ethel lived with her widowed mother, who by now was Jodie's mother-in-law, only a few doors away, and was there to help when Reggie was born, and again less than a year later when Lenny arrived.

During both pregnancies John was serving on the *Victory* and could come home on leave from being in dry dock at Portsmouth. When he was eventually shipped out and Jodie was left alone with two very young babies, she decided she was going to do something with her life. Although she spent every available hour with her two boys, constantly on the beach when weather permitted so that the children soon learned to swim, she spent her evenings studying to better herself. By her nineteenth birthday she had passed several examinations and had certificates to prove that she was a qualified hairdresser. She hadn't left the matter there. With her mother-in-law and Ethel holding the fort and taking good care of her two sons, Jodie travelled far and wide to attend seminars and exhibitions to acquaint herself with the latest trends in hairstyling. Dee never tired of listening to the endless tales she had to tell.

It was about this time, according to Jodie, that her own parents came to visit and to meet John Underwood for the very first time. They had refused point blank to come to the wedding. When they saw the flat where their only daughter and their two grandsons were living, they were shocked. Only days after they had returned to London, Jodie received a letter from her father telling her that he had set up an account for her with his bank and had placed ten thousand pounds at her disposal.

On hearing that, Dee's eyebrows had shot up. 'Why are you still working for Michael Connelly when you could open your own salon?'

'Because, my pet, ten thousand pounds might sound like a helluva lot of money, but when it comes to purchasing a lease on a property in a busy upmarket location, it wouldn't be anywhere near enough. You also have to consider having washbasins installed, a good supply of water laid on and God knows how much electrical equipment, and not forgetting a dozen or so really comfortable chairs. Then I'd need to find the wages each week for staff until I really got established.'

Dee had always listened with wonder and admiration when Jodie told her these stories. Now, having plucked up courage and got herself a trial job in Michael's salon, she was determined that if Jodie's plans did come to fruition, she would go and work for her, because she knew full well she would never receive a better training than she would get under Jodie Underwood. Jodie was set for great things, she was certain of it.

A slight doubt was niggling at her. She hadn't even started her first working day yet; wasn't she letting her thoughts jump the gun just a bit? Oh well, there was no charge for daydreams. She snuggled down deeper into her bed and fell asleep humming to herself:

If you don't have a dream, how you gonna have a dream come true?

2

'Well well well,' Jodie Underwood laughed as she opened the front door of her house in Rye on Sunday morning to find Dee standing there. 'From what I heard last night, there's a lot more to you, young lady, than you let on. A whole lot more by all accounts. Come on in. My mother-in-law has taken the boys off to church, but they'll be over the moon when they get back and find you here.'

'Are you saying that you've already heard how my first day at Mitch's salon went?' Dee asked, feeling surprised at how fast news travelled.

'Well, eight of us went in to Camber for a drink last night, and Babs, Nicky and Karen, who you were working with all day, were singing your praises. Seems you came through with flying colours. Did you enjoy yourself?'

'Yes, I did, and I want to thank you again, because I'm sure you speaking up for me went a long way towards Mitch giving me the job.'

'You're off the mark quickly, calling our Michael Mitch. Not everyone is allowed that privilege.'

'Well he phoned at lunchtime to see how I was getting on, and said for me to call him Mitch but to always refer to him as Michael when talking to the customers.' Dee looked at the twinkle in Jodie's eyes and the wide smile on her lips.

At twenty-five, Jodie was a stunningly attractive young woman with a gorgeous slim figure, her shiny black shoulder-length hair always set in the very latest fashion. She had big brown eyes and a complexion to die for.

Jodie knew what she wanted out of life and never hesitated to grasp an opportunity. That description might make her sound hard and self-centred, but in fact just the opposite was true. Her two boys were her life, and she loved them with a deep passion, yet she still had time for the elderly and would help anyone in trouble. As Dee had grown up, she had learnt that Jodie was the best friend anyone could ask for, but you didn't lie to her and you didn't cross her, because if you did, she wouldn't give you a second chance.

This cottage-style house that Jodie had moved into with her two boys, Reggie, who was now seven years old, and Lenny, not quite six, could have done with redecorating, but that wasn't on John Underwood's list of priorities. Home to him was somewhere to hang his hat and a bed in which to sleep when on leave. The navy had provided him with excitement and travel; he didn't want all the responsibilities that came with being married. As Jodie was fond of telling him, it was a bit late in the day for him to have come to that conclusion!

John James Underwood had not exactly fulfilled her dream of married bliss. She was more than grateful that she received an allowance from the navy for herself and their two sons. She didn't need telling that if it was up to John, they would starve and be up to their eyes in debt. There wasn't a time that he didn't walk through the street door without a tale of some kind to explain why he didn't have any money. He drew his pay all right, but she knew it went in the bookmaker's, in the pub or on the floozies he seemed to love to associate with. Even his own mother had warned her that he had a roving eye, and that he would place a bet on two flies crawling up a wall. The warning had come a bit late. She had boxed clever, thank God, and safely salted away the ten thousand pounds her father had sent her, otherwise John would have gone through that money like a dose of salts.

19

First off, though, she had been so impressed with him. Maybe it had just been the uniform, but the fact that he had volunteered for the navy at the tender age of fifteen was something to crow about too, and she had been proud to be seen out with him. In those early days he had taken her dancing, to the cinema and to the theatre. Once she had become pregnant, all of that had gone out of the window, and in the last couple of years John hadn't made any effort to keep their marriage on track.

Jodie could understand why women were attracted to him. He was a philanderer through and through, a womaniser of the first degree. When Dee had first come to the flat to mind the boys, Jodie had noticed the sly glances he was sending in the girl's direction, and had warned him off in no uncertain terms.

'You stay away from her, John. Delia is far too young for the likes of you.'

'Is she indeed?' he had said, deliberately provoking her.

'Yes, she is. It would be like robbing the cradle.'

Just to annoy her, he had persisted. 'The way you put it makes her sound almost irresistible.'

But that had been one jab too far. Anger had flared up in Jodie. My God, just how low could he sink? Even to contemplate touching a schoolgirl... She couldn't help herself she let rip. 'I'm warning you, John, I've stood for the five-card trick ever since we've been married, but even my patience is wearing a bit thin. I'm telling you now young Dee is like family to me. Touch her and I swear I will kill you.'

John knew that Jodie's temper was at full blast,

20

but he still wasn't going to give in. It gave him a great deal of pleasure to goad his wife. 'Since we've had the two boys, you aren't a bit interested in sex, at least not with me.'

Jodie sniffed loudly. 'No, because half the time when you come home I can smell the tomcats you've been with.'

'Well it's a pity you don't let your mind wander back and enjoy the memories of what we used to get up to. Then again, probably better that you don't, 'cos then you'd know what you're missing. Oh, and when you see Dee, give her my regards, and tell her to come and see me when she's a bit older.'

He really was a right bastard, thought Jodie, but he was a handsome bugger, and for that reason if nothing else he got away with murder. His very size and looks were striking; his hair was thick and black and he had the deep skin colouring that came from always having lived by the sea. Mostly though, at least for her, it was his deep blue eyes that were irresistible. When she had first met him, she had almost convinced herself that he was Irish born and bred. When it suited him, he could lay the charm on almost as if he had kissed the Blarney Stone. The fact that he was married didn't deter the women; in all probability the danger of being caught out only added to his attraction.

Jodie filled the kettle and put it on the gas stove to boil before turning to Dee. 'Seeing as how you seem to have enjoyed your first day at the salon, how about coming out on the road with me once a week before the summer season gets under way?'

'I'm not sure I'm with you.'

'Wednesday I work for myself. I go into rest homes and wash and set old ladies' hair. I also go to some really fine hotels that have permanent residents, most of whom are elderly. Having their hair done appears to do them good, makes them feel a bit younger, at least for a while. Have you finished your exams? Would you be able to get Wednesdays off to help me?'

'No problem, especially if I explained I was on a work project.'

'Well, there you are, then, give it some thought,' Jodie said as she set down the tea tray she had laid and poured out two cups from an old brown china teapot.

Dee did her best to keep her voice calm and steady. 'I don't think I fancy going into old folk's homes, let alone washing their hair.'

Jodie raised an eyebrow. 'Why, don't you think you'll ever be old?'

'Of course I will, but I'd like to live a little first. That's not too much to ask, is it?'

'So you don't even want to come with me and see how the other half live? You would feel sorry for a few, but most of them are quite good fun. You'd be amazed at some of the things that go on.'

Dee looked down at herself. She knew the boys found her attractive, with her long reddish hair and slim figure. She was wearing a baggy white sweater over a red miniskirt and big furry boots; what would the old dears think of her? Would it really matter?

She drank her tea and listened with rapt attention as Jodie told her how determined she was to enter even more competitions and hopefully to

22

pass a few more exams. 'You need as many qualifications as possible to get on in the world,' was
her advice.

'Why are you pushing yourself so hard? You've
got a good job and everyone thinks you've done
really well,' Dee said, meaning every word.

'It's a rough, tough world out there, more so
since television became a fixture in almost every
home. I know it's long hours, but my hard work
will pay off eventually if I keep at it. I have just
got to prove that I have what it takes.'

Dee shifted in her seat and gave Jodie the benefit of her most interested smile. 'I'm sorry, but
you've lost me. What has television got to do with
you owning your own hairdressing salon?'

'Absolutely everything. Mitch is aiming for the
same thing. He has got friendly with some hotshot
producer from the television studios at Shepherd's
Bush, who's assured him that good hair stylists are
as thin on the ground as make-up artists are.'

Television was pretty new, but those who worked
in it seemed a hundred per cent certain that it was
where the future lay. It was funny that Jodie had
brought it up today, thought Dee, because only
recently at school they had been given a paper to
do on advertising. Seemed it wasn't only Jodie
who thought that good prospects might lie in that
direction.

When Jodie's mother-in-law came in an hour
later with Reggie and Lenny, Dee was still in a
state of indecision about whether or not she
should take up Jodie's offer. Fortunately Jodie had
insisted that she stay for Sunday lunch, and was at
that moment engrossed in making two special

23

sweets, the recipes for which she had found in a magazine article. A great cook was Jodie, and her puddings and sweets were to die for!

Marian Underwood was a small woman in her early seventies. She might be getting on in years, always wearing a rather old-fashioned black wool dress, and over it one of her own colourful hand-knitted cardigans, but she was nobody's fool. A pair of spectacles were balanced somewhat precariously on the bridge of her nose, but as most folk knew, very little escaped those sharp brown eyes. 'Hello, Dee, I hear you've joined the wash an' set brigade. Wouldn't have thought it was a job up your street.'

Marian had known Delia from the day she was born, and would agree it would be very hard not to like the young lass. Girls like Delia Hartfield didn't come two a penny. She was from good stock, no doubt about that; her parents were the salt of the earth. Pity Delia wasn't a few years older; she'd have made a good wife for one of Marian's other sons.

Three sons and one daughter she'd been blessed with. Ethel had been married at nineteen and widowed two years later when her husband had been killed in a road accident. Poor Ethel, she swore she'd never look at another man, and for years now she'd kept to that promise. Shame; her good-hearted lovely lass had become an old maid long before her time. Of her sons, so far only John was married. From the day he'd joined the navy at the tender age of fifteen, Marian had read the situation perfectly. The uniform made him feel like a man, but the girls he picked up were all predictable, empty-headed and, on the whole, common. She thanked God he had given Judith more than a second glance.

From the first meeting Marian had sensed something different about Jodie, something unusual. And she had been right. Jodie had turned out tops, a right good mother and a damn good worker who deserved better than she often got from her husband, although Marian was clever enough to keep those kind of thoughts to herself. There had been occasions when she had felt the need to draw her son aside and remind him that he had a wife and two wonderful little boys to consider now. Told him in no uncertain terms that it was time he pulled himself together and shouldered more of his responsibilities. But the same thing always happened. He would turn his big blue eyes up to her with the look he knew would melt her heart. For all his faults, she loved him dearly.

It was Wednesday morning. Jodie put the case containing all her equipment on the seat between herself and Dee. She wouldn't risk putting it under the stairs, even though the conductor had said he would keep an eye on it. She'd spent too much money acquiring all the best scissors, tongs, brushes and combs, not to mention the large trade bottles of shampoo and conditioner.

She'd lost count of the number of elderly folk she had visited in their own homes when she was building up her clientele. Not every house had had a bathroom, or even hot running water, and she'd had many a lady bending over a stone sink while she poured a kettle of warm water over their heads. Now she only left the salon on Wednesdays, when she visited long-term residents of the Golden Sands Hotel in Hastings. Some weeks she also visited two rest homes. From what she earned in the rest homes it was not a profitable project, but the thought never entered Jodie's head to abandon her regulars; over a long period of time these clients had become her friends.

As the bus travelled along Hastings seafront, away from the fishing sheds towards the posh area where all the best hotels were situated, Jodie's thoughts were on the past. Where she was going today was a far cry from some of the appalling rest homes she used to visit when she had first branched out on her own. She'd come a long way since then. Given time she'd fulfil her real dreams, she had no doubts on that score.

'Next stop is ours. You bring the smaller case and I'll carry this one,' Jodie instructed Dee as they both stood up and wound their long woolly scarves around their necks. Once safely on the pavement, they set off at a brisk pace. Only a few yards to go, but the wind was gale force and they lowered their heads as they battled along. Looking away from the sea, the view between the detached hotels was one of a moneyed area. The properties were large, substantially built, with long driveways and beautifully kept gardens.

'We're here,' Jodie said, coming to a halt at a wide opening in a manicured hedge that was at least six feet high. Once through the massive open gates the driveway seemed endless, but Dee was staring ahead and she couldn't resist saying,

'Boy oh boy, this is some hotel, and just look at all the posh motor cars.'

They climbed the wide front steps, where the liveried doorman tipped his top hat to Jodie as he said, 'Morning, Mrs Underwood, right blustery one today.'

'Yes James, you're right. Not many of my customers will be venturing out this morning.'

Jodie had to nudge Dee, who was standing stock still staring at the colourful flower beds and the fountains from which the water spurted high and cascaded down on to water lilies floating in the pools. They each gave a brief nod to the doorman, who was holding open the wide doors. 'Wow, talk about how the other half live,' Dee muttered more to herself than to Jodie.

The entrance hall was like a huge lounge. Dark red velvet sofas and armchairs were positioned comfortably all the way around the walls. At one end of the room there was a brick fireplace, its stacked logs ready to be lit. The heavy floor-length curtains and fancy valances had to be seen to be believed, all deep fringes and tassels.

Jodie knew where she was going, and Dee trailed behind her. Jodie pressed a bell and they stood for a moment looking up at the high ceiling from which hung several huge chandeliers. There was a soft purring sound and the lift arrived. The doors slid open to reveal a cheeky, baby-faced lad who looked no more than twelve years old. 'Morning, Mrs Underwood, an' who is first on your list today?'

'Morning, Sydney. Mrs Grantham, first floor, please.'

'Up we go.' He grinned as he pressed a button. 'See you have an assistant with you today.' Turning to Dee, he winked. 'Right old slave-driver is our Mrs Underwood.' There was no time for more chit-chat, as with only a slight bump the lift came to a halt and the doors were slid open by Sydney. 'Hope to see you again. I love redheads,' he whispered as Dee passed him.

'I bet you do, but you've some growing up to do first,' Dee chuckled.

'We could always try doing it together,' Sydney called after her, but Dee was mindful of the look she was getting from Jodie. Wouldn't do to put a foot wrong so early in her probation. Nevertheless, she had enjoyed Sydney's admiring glances and was more than pleased that today she was wearing her best grey miniskirt with thick black stockings that had a thin seam going from the heel to the top. Pity her mother wouldn't let her wear shoes with high heels; it always had to be low heels or flatties. Still, now she was out earning her own money, she might be able to persuade Mum to bend the rules just a little.

The gold numbers on the door told them that this was apartment number ten. Jodie lifted the black door knocker and gently rapped twice. It was only a minute before the door was swung open.

Mrs Grantham's companion-cum-housekeeper, Alice, was herself about seventy. She was plump, with rouged cheeks and a trace of lipstick, and was soberly dressed in a navy blue dress over which she wore a white apron.

'Hello there,' she said, pleasantly. 'Dorothy is

all ready for you.'

Jodie and Dee trooped after her into the most beautiful room Dee had ever seen. The far wall was almost completely glass, and Dee stood rooted to the spot staring at the uninterrupted view of the sea beyond and the huge waves breaking on the shoreline. The room itself had a high ceiling and expensive thick-pile rugs on the wide polished wooden floorboards. The outstanding feature was not the big, comfortable-looking armchairs but a baby grand piano on which many silver-framed photographs of young children, some on horses or ponies, and various adults were arranged. A big bowl of fresh flowers was set in the centre of the group.

Dorothy Grantham came into the room wrapped in a fluffy white towelling robe, her silver-grey hair hanging loosely down her back. She placed her hands on Jodie's shoulders and gently kissed her on each cheek.

When they drew apart, Jodie said, 'Dorothy, you are looking so much better, I am pleased to say. Thank you for allowing me to bring this young lady as my assistant. I don't know if I told you on the phone, but her name is Delia Hartfield.'

Even in a dressing gown, Mrs Grantham looked elegant. Her hair was pure white at the temples, her cheekbones high, her eyes dark blue, but it was her smile that lit up her face and made her so attractive. 'So, Delia, are you going to watch and learn or are you going to practise on me today?'

Dee glanced at Jodie, who stepped into the breach. 'First time out today, so I think Dee will be taking note but also handing me various things.

She already knows how to tidy up after me.'

Dee for her part was thinking that being taken on by Michael Connelly and receiving so much encouragement from Jodie was the greatest thing that could have happened to her. In just her first day at the salon she had seen the way Michael's staff were with the customers, and she instinctively understood that that was the secret of good business. Even the poorest clients, some who had only come in to have their hair trimmed, were made to feel special in Michael's salons, according to Jodie, and it made her love the job all the more.

On Saturday while Dee had been in the salon, Michael himself had styled only two clients' hair. Both had been young women in their twenties and each had very long, thick hair. Dee had been absolutely fascinated as she had watched. The first thing she'd noticed was that Michael had exceptionally long fingers, which he used to the full, running them through the customers' hair, gently massaging their scalps before he even started work. Dee had watched the faces of the young women, and she thought they were almost purring with delight.

Having shampooed Mrs Grantham's hair and done a little basic cutting, Jodie was now blow-drying the fine silver locks. 'Topknot today, or a French pleat?' she asked, smiling at their reflection in the huge mirror that adorned nearly a whole wall in the oversized bathroom.

'I'm having lunch with Laurie Trevelion, so whatever style you think is most elegant,' Dorothy Grantham answered, smiling softly.

'Bun on top of the head it is, then,' Jodie said as

she began to work the long strands into a plait. That part accomplished, she wound the plait around her own wrist before easing it off and into place on top of Mrs Grantham's head. Hairpins secured the coil, and then Jodie went to work with narrow strands of dark red and jet black velvet. When several strands had been interwoven, she stood back and nodded her approval, but she wasn't finished yet. From her case she produced a length of silver ribbon decorated with glittering particles of diamanté, which she again wove in and out of the coiled hair.

Dee forgot where she was for a moment and let out a loud exclamation. 'Wow! Are they real diamonds?'

Both women, still staring at their reflection in the mirror, were pleased with the end result, and also at Dee's excited reaction. Alice's offer of coffee was refused by Jodie on the excuse that she had several clients to visit today, and she packed her case while Dee washed and dried the instruments Jodie had used. She was on her knees wiping over the tiles of the bathroom floor when Mrs Grantham told her it had been nice to meet her, wished her well and slipped a florin into her hand. Dee was thrilled. On Saturday she had been given a few coppers as tips, and even one threepenny piece, but two shillings!

She was beginning to like this life, and it was getting better by the minute.

The next three apartments they visited were all along the same lines as that of Dorothy Grantham. In the main sitting room the windows were floor

31

to ceiling, giving a clear view across to the seafront. The carpets were thick, the sofas and chairs large and comfortable, with lots of matching cushions. The occupants were all elderly ladies, well dressed, with their faces made up and their lips colourful and glossy. Dee wondered if they had ever wanted for anything in their well-ordered lives. The last client didn't seem to care whether Jodie did her hair or not. She had a light lunch laid out on the table, which was set for three people.

'You shouldn't have gone to all this trouble, Mrs Rayner,' Jodie protested.

'Why ever not? It's my pleasure. I know you always make me your last client of the morning, and I do so love seeing you. I know how you like your coffee, Judith, but how about your young friend?'

Dee was just about to protest that she didn't like coffee at all, but she caught the look that Jodie shot at her so she smiled and said, 'With milk and one sugar please, Mrs Rayner.'

There were salmon sandwiches made with brown bread sliced so fine Dee wondered how the old lady had managed it, and all the crusts were cut off. Dee would have willingly declared they were absolutely scrumptious if she had been asked. To follow there was a Victoria sponge cut and served with a silver cake knife on to a plate of such fine bone china Dee was terrified to handle it. But again the sponge was delicious, filled with strawberry jam and thick Cornish cream. At least that was what Mrs Rayner informed them.

'My daughter lives in Newquay and she sends me a pot once every month.'

Dee was wondering if Jodie got this treatment every time she came to visit, but she knew enough by now not to ask.

While Jodie was in the bathroom shampooing Mrs Rayner's hair, Dee went into the kitchen and washed the lunch things. My God, she had to be careful with this beautiful china; it was like handling fresh eggs. And the kitchen! Well! However she attempted to describe it to her mother, she would never believe her. Jodie had said to come with her and find out how the other half lived; well, she was doing that all right!

'Have you had enough? Do you want to catch the bus and go home?' Jodie was smiling as she fastened the lock on her main case.

'Aren't you coming with me?'

'Well not if you want to go straight away. I'm going to see a very old client of mine who has become a dear friend over the years, but she lives in a warden-assisted home in very different circumstances to what you've seen this morning.'

'I'm in no hurry to get home. If it's all right with you, I'd like to come with you,' Dee said in a tone of voice that told Jodie she meant what she said.

'OK, but we'll have to walk towards the end of the seafront and then catch a bus; the place we're going is in the Old Town part of Hastings.'

Their short journey over, the two wind-swept girls looked up at the building, and it wasn't hard to work out what they were both thinking. Jodie shook her head before saying, 'Old age is a terrible thing, especially for those whose whole family has died. Loneliness must be the worst fate of all. Money can buy most things, as we've seen today, but it can't bring your dear ones back. Come on then, let's go in. The lady we're going to see is Flossie Williams. She's in her late seventies, and believe you me, Dee, she no more wanted to end up in a place like this than fly in the air. The real pity of it is she didn't have any choice. She fought a long battle to stay in her own little house, but with her husband dead and nothing but the state pension, she couldn't afford the upkeep, and now she's here in sheltered housing.'

There was no lift in Flossie's building, and both girls were a little breathless by the time they reached flat number 22. Jodie paused before rapping her knuckles gently on the door.

'Who is it?' A croaky voice came from behind the door.

'Flossie, luv, it's me, Jodie, and I've brought a young friend with me. Aren't you going to invite us in and put the kettle on?'

'Oh, it's you, Jodie. Course I am, but you'll 'ave t'wait a minute while I find me keys. Wasn't expecting anyone, so I 'aven't unlocked the door today yet.'

To say that Dee was horrified would have been putting it mildly. The front door opened directly into the one L-shaped room. It held a wooden-topped table with two high-backed chairs, and one armchair that looked quite comfortable but had certainly seen better days. A single bed covered with a pink candlewick bedspread was partitioned in the corner of the room directly under a narrow window. 'It's what the authorities call a studio flat,' Jodie stated in a low voice.

'It isn't the day for you to do my hair, is it?' Flossie asked, sounding bewildered.

'No. It's next week I come to you, but I will do it while I'm here if you'd like me to. First, though, I've brought you a present.' While talking, Jodie had undone her second case and taken out some screw hooks, a length of curtain wire and a pair of brocade curtains, which she shook out and spread over the floor. Flossie's face was a picture as she stared at the beautiful colours that were now on display.

'Are they for me? Where you gonna hang them? And where did you get them from? They look very expensive.' Flossie's voice was all of a tremble, as if she didn't believe what she was seeing.

Jodie motioned to Dee to get one end of the single bed and help her move it out into the centre of the room. Then, taking one of the tall wooden chairs, she moved it over to stand beneath the window. Climbing on to the chair, Jodie found she could just about reach to fix a hook into the wall above the window frame, and to this she now attached one end of the curtain wire she had brought with her.

Sighing with relief, because fixing the hook into the wall had proved to be a much simpler task than she had feared, she moved the chair to the other side of the narrow part of the room that had held the bed.

'Tell me when I've got it straight,' she called down to Dee. 'I'll hold the wire against the wall and make a mark before I put the second hook in.'

It took several attempts, amid much laughter, with Dee calling out, 'A bit higher ... no, that's too high, bring it down a bit... Slightly to your left, yes, that's it, make a mark.' Finally Jodie had the second hook in place on the opposite wall.

'Dee, you hold on to one end of the curtain while I thread this wire through. I would have liked to be able to use tape and curtain rings, but I wasn't sure these walls would hold the weight. Never mind, eh, Flossie. Once I've got the curtains up, I'll show you some tiebacks I've made for when you want to keep them open and let the light shine through, but when you want to hide the bed say when you have a friend in for a cuppa – you'll easily be able to close them. Now stand back out of the way and Dee and I will hang them up.'

Wonder upon wonder! Jodie sent up a silent prayer of thanks as everything went to plan.

'Oh my God, don't they look beautiful?' Flossie's face was beaming, yet her eyes were brimming with tears as she watched Jodie fix another hook lower down on the wall.

'Here you are then, you fix that curtain back with one of the tie-backs while Dee puts another hook on the other wall, and then we'll be able to stand back and see them properly,' Jodie said.

The basic shade of the material was a fawn colour but it had a golden sheen and all shades of pink interwoven, from the very palest to a deep rose. Jodie was thrilled that the joins didn't show. She had made the curtains from pieces left over from an order that she had done for some wealthy folk who lived in a very large house.

Dee was left wondering how many more strings Jodie had to her bow. She was also thinking that her own mother wouldn't approve of this shabbily dressed woman, and she would be utterly appalled at the accommodation in which Flossie had been forced to end her days. But as Jodie had remarked, Flossie might be poor and lonely, but she had always had a big heart.

Jodie truly believed that if you cast your bread upon the waters it would in time return tenfold, but in this case, just the look on Flossie's face as she let the curtain material run through her fingers was all the repayment she needed. Poor old Flossie didn't have any relatives left alive to visit her, and Jodie felt it didn't hurt her to drop in every now and again and bring her a few bits and bobs to make her feel she was still loved and wanted. Jodie had her own family and a wide circle of friends, and although she was big on family stuff, always would be, she'd never turn a blind eye just because a person didn't have much in the way of worldly goods.

She often wished that John had turned out to be a bit more of a family man, but then nobody had everything they wanted.

Not in this life.

3

'Jolly good,' Dee muttered as she counted up her tips. She was doing well at her job, and working in Michael's salon had given her so much more confidence. Michael had said he was more than pleased with her, and had allowed her to work a few hours each day once the school term was finished, right up until Christmas Eve.

It was now the first week of the new year, a busy one because of the late Christmas parties in offices and restaurants all along the coast from Brighton right through to Eastbourne and on into Hastings. She had graduated up to working in the salons in Rye and Eastbourne. Often Jodie picked her up in her car, and sometimes Michael would toot his horn outside her house at eight thirty ready to give her a lift to work. Dee was really enjoying her job, knowing this must be the best time of the year, a new broom sweeping clean, when folk were determined to look their best and enjoy life. With everyone happy, tips were generous. Working with Michael and Jodie had not only given her a source of income, it had opened her eyes to a social life. And she had signed up to go on two courses at Hastings College, one for basic hairdressing and the second one a course of study into becoming a beautician. Jodie had encouraged her.

'Hairdressing on its own is all right for a little village shop, but if like me at some point in the future you aim to have a prosperous beauty parlour in a decent town, you'll need to know a whole lot more than how to style hair. Manicuring and make-up would be a good start.' This had been Jodie's recommendation, and without any dithering Dee had followed her advice.

The social side of her new life had started off one Sunday afternoon when Jodie had invited her over. On her arrival she had said, 'Don't take your coat off, we're going into Eastbourne. The boys will be fine with my brother; he'll take them to the funfair on the pier. I'm taking you to the afternoon tea dance.'

'But I can't dance, well not properly,' Dee had protested. 'I'm all right doing the twist and that sort of thing, but a tea dance doesn't sound as if it is for me.'

'You didn't know anything about hairdressing until you jumped in with both feet, did you?'

'No, I suppose not. All right then, I'll give it a try.'

The results of that one afternoon turned out to be a whole lot more favourable than Dee could ever have imagined. It was such a jolly, happy afternoon. Chris Mannion, the gentleman who was playing the organ, was well known both by the residents of Eastbourne and by the folk who came here regularly on holiday. The dance floor was packed, but Chris made every other dance an excuse me, so that there were not many wallflowers sitting lonely around the hall. It was just like one huge party, with everyone joining in, calling loudly for their favourite songs to be played. At intervals Chris gave them a break from dancing, during which they got themselves a drink and he played all the old wartime songs, which had the rafters of the hall ringing with happy voices.

Jodie leant over and tapped Dee on the shoulder. 'You enjoying yourself?'

'Yes. Yes I am. I never imagined anything like this went on in Eastbourne.'

'There yer go then, you'll be able to get yourself out and about a bit more rather than staying in Camber Sands day in, day out.'

Cups and glasses were returned to the bar. Chris was back ready to play again, and the second half of the session was about to begin.

Jodie was up and away, light as a feather on her feet and never short of a partner. Twice Dee had been asked to partner a nice clean-cut-looking young man who she thought must be in his early twenties. As he approached her for the third time, he smiled and said, 'This is going to be a square tango, but as it is sequence dancing, all we have to do is follow the couple in front. Would you like to give it a go? By the way, my name is Tony.'

'Pleased t'meet you, Tony, I'm Delia but my friends call me Dee. I don't think you should risk taking me on the floor for this one; a tango sounds quite complicated.'

'Don't be daft. Like I said, it's follow my leader. Come on, at least it will be a laugh, and that's what these sessions are all about. On top of that, it's great exercise and good for the figure – not that you need to worry about that. You look smashing, you've got a real sylphlike figure.'

Dee felt herself blush to the roots of her hair. She wasn't used to receiving such compliments. To say that Tony had pleased her was to put it mildly, but she had no idea how she was supposed to answer him, so in the end she just gave him a broad smile, hoping that he had meant what he said and wasn't just playing Jack-the-lad.

Without any more ado, Tony pulled her to her feet, tossed a lock of hair away from his forehead and with his face now wreathed in smiles led Dee on to the floor. A few stumbles at first, but it wasn't long before she found she was thoroughly enjoying herself.

'Phew, I'm warm,' Jodie said, as she approached their table carrying a tray that held two glasses of orange juice. 'I'm thrilled to see you've been out on the floor. That lad you've had as a partner is Anthony Lewis; his father is the manager of the Queen's Hotel. Did you like him?'

'Yes, I did. At first I was like an elephant, twice I trod on his foot, but he was very patient and he led so well I soon found it easy to follow his steps.'

'Something else new you've found out: you're only as good as your partner when dancing. If you're lucky enough to get a nice tall fellow that hasn't got two left feet, then you are up and away. He has to know what he's doing and be able to lead you.'

'Do they have this dancing session here every Sunday afternoon?' Dee asked, trying not to sound too enthusiastic.

'Yes they do, and if you were to know in advance when you were coming, you could dress up a bit, invest in a pair of dancing shoes. I promise you, once you get over your stage fright, Tony Lewis won't be the only young man lining up to dance with you.'

Dee lifted her head and looked into Jodie's eyes, which were twinkling with merriment. 'Life is only just beginning for you, Dee,' Jodie said smiling, but Dee could hear the serious note in her voice as she added, 'Make the most of it, my love, don't be like me, married with two children by the time I was eighteen.'

It was Delia's birthday. That morning over a lively breakfast she had received cards and gifts from her mum and dad and her brother, but that wasn't all. There were cards from all the girls she worked with, a beautiful set of underwear from Jodie and a pretty bottle of perfume from Michael. There were even a few cards from the customers. Sixteen years old! Now she could really begin to live her life. For this weekend, though, she was going to have to put that thought on hold.

Jodie and a whole host of her friends were going off to a dinner-dance which was being held in Hove, the upper-crust part of Brighton. Jodie had taken charge of the arrangements, and insisted that Ethel, her sister-in-law, was going to join them. 'I'm taking no argument,' she told Ethel firmly. 'You've stayed at home too many times and it's about time you tried living again. There's going to be no trouble about how we're gonna get home; I've sorted out bed an' breakfast at the hotel, though whether any of us will be able to face breakfast will be another matter. And I've booked a minibus to take us there and bring us home when we're ready the next morning. You're sharing a twin-bedded room with me, and yes, I will wash and set your hair for you on the morning of the do.'

And that was why Dee was going to be staying at Jodie's cottage in Rye for the weekend in order to look after her two boys.

It was eight o'clock on Saturday evening. Dee was sitting round the kitchen table with Lenny and Reggie, and Brian, her twelve-year-old brother, who had come to keep her company. They were playing cards and board games as the fancy took them. Crisps, peanuts and bowls of sweets were set in the centre of the table, together with a jug of lemonade, and their loud laughter spoke for itself. Not one of them minded that Jodie had gone off to this dinner-dance. Dee's father would be picking them all up in the morning and taking them home in time for the Sunday roast. It would never do for her and Brian to miss out on that.

'Not when I've been slaving over a hot stove all morning,' her mother would likely shout and storm. In reality Mary Hartfield was thrilled that Delia would be bringing Judith's boys to Sunday dinner. She had watched those two dear little lads grow from the day they were born and had been more than a little upset when Judith had moved away to live in Rye. True, it wasn't a million miles away, but it meant she didn't get to see the boys so often. Along with everyone else in Camber Sands, Mary thought the world of Judith, because in so many thoughtful ways she had worked hard to gain that reputation. Weren't many that would say the same about her husband.

Jodie's hall clock was just striking the half-hour when the doorbell rang.

'No moving the dice,' Dee grinned as she got to her feet and went to find out who was at the door. She got quite a shock. A well-dressed, broad-shouldered man was filling the small sheltered porch.

'Who the hell are you?' he asked, grinning broadly as he eyed Dee from top to toe, thinking that she was one of the prettiest girls he had ever seen, with that lovely sweet face, the mass of reddish hair and those enormous green eyes.

'And I might be asking the same thing of you,' Dee replied hesitantly.

His eyebrows shot up but his smile was lazy. 'I'm Derrick Underwood. I thought my brother John and his family lived here.'

'Oh, they do. Sorry, you caught me on the hop. There is only me, the two boys and–'

'Uncle Derrick!' Both Lenny and Reggie were scrambling along the narrow hallway, each boy eager to be first and all the time repeating their uncle's name. It was the sound of delight and familiarity in their voices that told Dee it was safe to invite their caller inside.

'I'm sorry if I startled you,' Derrick was quick to apologise as he bent down and swooped his two young nephews up into his strapping arms.

'Don't worry about it. I wouldn't have let you in if the boys hadn't vouched for you,' Dee told him, ushering him into the hallway and closing the door behind him. 'I'm Delia Hartfield, and this is my young brother Brian. We're staying the night here because Jodie has gone with some friends to a dinner-dance in Hove and won't be back until tomorrow morning.'

'Very wise of you to be cautious,' he told her as he followed her down the hallway and into the living room.

Having set the boys down on their feet, he spent a few minutes throwing playful punches at them, which they gleefully returned. When their uncle fell to his knees in a comical attempt to show he was hurt by their blows, the boys' laughter became uproarious, more so as he began rib-tickling.

It took a few minutes for peace to be restored. As they took their places around the table, Derrick ruffled Brian's hair and said, 'So, Brian, you're the man of the house tonight, are you?'

'Well I am twelve years old,' Brian said, pulling himself to sit up straight. 'My dad said I had to be here for my sister, but I didn't mind 'cos I like being with Reggie and Lenny, they used to live near us before they moved to this house.'

'Yes, Brian, I know they did. Before I went to sea, I actually lived next door to your family, and my mother and sister still do.' Seeing the look of puzzlement on Brian's face, Derrick laughed heartily and turned to face Dee. 'We met several times when you were a youngster, but we can all be forgiven for not recognising each other because it is four years since I set foot on home soil.'

Dee was carefully studying Derrick's face. She did have a faint recollection of meeting a big man in a uniform with gold buttons, and she had often listened as Mrs Underwood read aloud from the letters that arrived from her eldest son. He seemed to have travelled the whole world.

'Well, Delia, do you recall meeting me in the past?' Derrick was smiling at her, and it felt as if he was reading her mind. When she shook her head, he said, 'It's not to be wondered at, because I certainly don't remember you looking like this. Boy oh boy, Delia, have you grown and blossomed! But then I suppose at your age four years does make a vast difference.'

Dee's eyes widened at his remarks, and she found herself saying, 'Everyone calls me Dee.'

'Thank you, does that mean I can call you Dee too?'

Nodding her head, not knowing what else to say, she turned to the three boys who were seated around the table waiting patiently. 'Time has gone so quickly you must all be feeling hungry. Shall we clear the games away and see about getting a meal ready? Would you like to join us?' she added, glancing up at this big man.

'Depends on what you're offering,' he joked.

'Well I usually fry chips for the boys, and Jodie always leaves us sausage rolls, pork pies, slices of ham and plenty of salad. Will that do?'

'Anything in the house to drink?'

'Plenty. Tea, coffee, lemonade, squash.'

'You have got to be joking,' he said, pulling a funny face which set the boys off giggling. 'Besides, Dee, I wouldn't dream of putting you to all that trouble. Boys, what d'yer say to fish and chips?'

'Proper fish shop fish an' chips?' Lenny questioned.

'Yeah, and I'll bring some sausages if they have them, and pickles, and even some ice cream to have for our afters. How does that sound?'

'Smashing,' the boys chorused.

'OK, you lads clear the table, Dee can put the plates in the oven to get warm, and as you're such a big lad, Brian, would you like to come with me? My car is just outside the door.'

Brian glanced quickly at his sister. He was thrilled to have been asked, but he couldn't go out and leave Dee alone with the two little uns unless she said he could.

46

Dee nodded and her smile was full of approval. She thought it was a kind act on Derrick's part. 'Get your coat on, Brian, it's very cold out there, but only if you're sure you want to go,' she added quietly.

'Yes please, Dee.' He couldn't keep the enthusiasm out of his voice. Just to be singled out and asked to accompany this big man had made him feel almost grown up. 'We won't be long, we'll soon be back, won't we...' He stumbled over what he should call this stranger.

'Course we will, lad, and we'll be bringing a tasty supper with us. Meanwhile, Brian, suppose you kind of adopt me and start calling me Uncle Derrick? If I have to put up with these two young scallywags, I think it might be great to have you as an older nephew. Try saying Uncle Derrick and see how you feel about it.'

'Thank you, Uncle Derrick,' Brian said in the most manly tone of voice he could muster as he took hold of the outstretched hand the big man was holding out to him.

'Right, lad, do the buttons up on that coat and let's get going.'

With the sound of the front door closing, Dee breathed out. 'Jesus wept,' she murmured. The way he had swept in, filling the room, taking charge, his head only just short of the height of the ceiling, it was as if a whirlwind had passed through. He certainly was no ordinary man!

Dee could not have visualised what a merry gathering that fish supper would turn out to be. Derrick had taken complete control, dishing out

47

the food on to the hot plates that Dee had ready, buttering the bread as she cut the fresh loaf, all the while keeping the three boys enthralled with tales of the ships he had been on.

It was ten o'clock before the boys had cleaned their teeth, washed their faces and hands and the two youngsters had each in turn been given a piggyback up the stairs to their twin-bedded room. Tonight Lenny and Reggie were tucked up in one bed while Brian was sleeping in the other. Dee, having said her good nights, had left Derrick with them and come down alone to the living room. She was by now feeling apprehensive. What was Derrick intending to do? Had he been home to his mother's? She thought he must have been, because he hadn't arrived with any luggage. Would he want to stay a bit longer? She wouldn't mind a cup of tea, but she didn't think that idea would appeal to him.

The problem solved itself. Derrick came into the room and made straight for the carrier bag that had served to bring the fish and chips home. From it he produced a pint bottle of brown ale. 'Would you like to share a glass of this with me?' he asked.

'Oh, no thank you. I was thinking of making myself a cup of tea, but you go ahead, I'll get you a glass.'

Soon they were sitting opposite each other, Derrick with a pint glass of beer, Dee with her cup of tea beside her and her elbows resting on the edge of the kitchen table, her chin cupped in her hands. She still couldn't really take in what had happened this evening, and yet it seemed quite all right to be here facing this big, friendly stranger.

'Have you left school yet, Dee?' was Derrick's opening remark.

This rubbed Dee up the wrong way. Did she look that young? Whilst he had been fetching the supper, she had hastily put some make-up on and twisted her hair into a French pleat. 'Yes, I've turned sixteen,' she said. 'I was going on to college but I've decided to take up hairdressing instead. This way I can earn some money while I am learning.'

'I see. My sister-in-law has taken you under her wing, has she? Well, you could have gone a lot further and fared a whole lot worse. Our Jodie knows what she wants and she'll go hell for leather until she gets it.'

Without waiting for Dee to reply, he leaned forward across the table. 'Dee, I'm nine years older than you, but I do feel I'd like to get to know you better, that's if you think you could put up with me.' He reached across and squeezed her hand. 'Take your time, I have twenty-eight days' leave.'

Dee was utterly amazed. All evening she had felt comfortable with him. He hadn't done or said anything untoward, had just been really friendly, and she was grateful for that. She was flattered that he had hinted that he wanted to see more of her during his leave, but at the same time she was bewildered.

She was quite used to lads of her own age making passes at her, and sometimes even trying to kiss her, but they always seemed clumsy and awkward and their attempts to be that bit more than just friendly often made her feel like laughing. She and her best friend Peggy Wilson often compared notes, and they both felt the same way. The boys they had gone to school with had a lot to learn about growing up. This evening had opened her eyes to much wider horizons and she felt as if she had been treated as an adult.

At a quarter to eleven, however, when she finally climbed the stairs to go to bed, Derrick Underwood's parting words were running through her head.

'See yer later, kid,' he had casually called as he strode away down the pathway.

It had rather spoilt her new grown-up concept of herself.

4

It was Wednesday, Dee had just finished a morning session at Michael's salon in Camber Sands. It was now one thirty and she was sitting at home enjoying a cup of tea and a sandwich with her mother.

'You got the whole afternoon off?' Mary was eyeing her daughter critically, finding it hard to believe the transformation that had taken place in the short period of time since Delia had started to work for Michael Connelly. Not only did she look so much more grown-up, she also wore her clothes differently and was certainly using make-up and paying a lot of attention to her hair, never wearing it in the same style two days running. She gets the reddish colour from her father but the silkiness and the thickness from me, Mary was thinking proudly as she ran her hands over her own thick dark tresses.

'Yes, I have Mum, is there anything you wanted me to do?' Dee asked as she nibbled at the shredded spring onions her mum had put on the plate as part of a side salad.

'I thought we might take the bus into Hastings and have a look around the shops, that's if you and Peggy haven't made any arrangements.'

'No, that sounds nice, Mum. I'll treat you to a cream tea in Debenham's. Peggy has gone into Eastbourne for a job interview at the dental board.'

'I like the sound of the cream tea. I hope Peggy gets her job; your father and I thought an office job would have been what you would have gone for, but you've made your own choice.'

'Yes, I have, Mum, and I'm quite happy. Now what time do you want me to be ready?'

Mary looked up at the clock that stood on the mantelshelf above the fireplace. 'Shall we say two o'clock? Don't want to be too late coming back or else the buses will be packed with workers.'

'Suits me fine. I'll just throw these crusts from the bread to the birds and then I'll pop upstairs and freshen myself up.' Dee went from the kitchen into the scullery and opened the back door. Despite it still being winter, the garden was looking really nice, very well kept. That was all down to her father. As well as growing flowers and shrubs, he had an allotment at the far end of the garden where he raised every vegetable available, depending on the time of year. Delia was lost in thought as she stood crumbling the bread when a deep, loud voice made her jump.

'And how is our sixteen-year-old young lady doing?'

Dee looked up. The head and shoulders of Derrick Underwood were clearly visible over the top of the fence that divided Mrs Underwood's property from the home of the Hartfields.

'Oh, hello, Derrick.' She met his gaze and suddenly she was tongue-tied. Why didn't he say something else? What did she want, romantic words? No, of course she didn't. But she did want to know if he was going to treat her as an adult or still as a child. These thoughts had gone round and round in her head ever since Saturday evening. She would have liked to have said something clever or at least witty, but was unable to form any words.

Derrick was regarding her curiously. Suddenly, as though reading her mind, he said, 'If you have a free evening this week, would you let me take you to the cinema? I don't seem to have any mates left living locally, Mother tells me they've all moved away. Tell me if you'd rather not or if you think I have a cheek in asking.'

'Not in the least,' she answered quickly. 'It is a bit unexpected but not cheeky; in fact I think it's nice to be invited.'

'Truly?'

Dee walked towards the fence, reached up and touched the back of his hand which was resting on the top. 'Yes, truly. I'd love to go to the pictures with you.'

'That's all right then. Will tomorrow evening suit

you? I have to go to a gathering tonight, purely business.'

Dee's heart sank. She was sure he would be socialising with lots of smart, glamorous women and she felt green with envy. She had only just met him and she didn't want to lose him to someone else before she'd had a chance to find out what he was really like.

A worried expression had come over Dee's face. Derrick was quick to notice it and smiled to himself. 'How about you look in the local paper, see if there's a film you fancy and I'll pick you up tomorrow evening about six thirty?' He leant forward and caught hold of her hand, squeezing it. 'You'd better tell your parents that I have asked you. In any case I'll come round to your house to collect you, put their minds at rest that every-thing is above board.'

'Why? Whatever makes you think they would be thinking otherwise?'

'Well I am nine years older than you. I can't ex-pect them to trust me with their only daughter straight off. It is four years since I last saw your father.'

Dear God, she hadn't given a thought to the fact that her parents might object to Derrick tak-ing her out. She only hoped they wouldn't go on about how young she was. That would put paid to everything. It would be utterly disastrous.

'I'll see you tomorrow,' he grinned.

On the bus going into Hastings it was freezing, and it was perishing cold even inside the shops. But Dee never noticed. She was already head over

53

heels in love. She might only be sixteen years old, but she knew what she wanted and she let her mind wander. Derrick travelled the world; if he were to fall in love with her, perhaps even propose and end up marrying her, would she be able to go with him? She'd need a passport; better see to that right away, in case he needed her to travel at a moment's notice.

'I don't know what's got into you this afternoon, Delia, but you haven't listened to a word I've been saying. You are away in a world of your own. Shall we go home right now, or are you going to come in to the Co-op with me? I need a new pair of walking shoes.'

'Oh, I'm sorry, Mum.' Dee pinched herself, dismayed at the way she had let her thoughts run riot. 'For God's sake get a grip on yourself,' she murmured beneath her breath. 'You hardly know the man and you've got him proposing to you. Try acting your age and stop being so foolish.'

'Of course we'll go and get your shoes, Mum, and then we'll have a walk around Wallace's. Peggy got a really smart blouse in there last week and it was only nineteen and eleven. She said they had them in several colours.'

Dee tucked her hand through her mother's arm and held her close to her side. She felt guilty. She'd ignored her mum all afternoon and let her mind dwell on Derrick Underwood, and she might well be wasting her time. He was a grown man, had a fantastic job and had been halfway around the world. Why would he be interested in a girl who had only recently left school and had never been further than the south-west of England?

54

'You're doing it again, Delia, off with the fairies you are. I'm beginning to lose my patience.'

'All right, all right, Mum. Look, we're outside the Edinburgh Wool shop. Let's go in; you're sure to find something in there that takes your fancy.'

Mary shook her head. 'The way you're day-dreaming, I can't be bothered. Let's go straight to Debenham's and perhaps over tea you'll tell me exactly what is going on.'

Like hell I will! Dee laughed to herself. If she were to lay bare even half her imaginary thoughts, there would be no way she'd be allowed to go to the cinema with Derrick Underwood, or any other place if it came to that.

The afternoon tea was a great success. Seated at the next table to where Dee and her mother were eating were an elderly couple with two young grandchildren. 'It must be lovely to have grand-children,' Mary whispered. 'More time to enjoy them and you get to hand them back when they get tiresome.'

Now who was daydreaming? But Dee had the presence of mind not to elaborate on that subject. She smiled at her mother as she slid a slice of rich fruit cake on to her plate, then splashed more milk into her cup and poured fresh tea from the silver-plated teapot. 'It is still quite early, Mum. When you've finished your tea, why don't we look in Debenham's shoe department? You might see a pair of shoes in there that you like, and if you don't, we'll still have time to go over to the Co-op.'

Mary had a twinge of conscience. She'd been a bit hard on Delia. Lord knows she used to day-dream enough herself when she was sixteen.

'Well, luv, if you're sure you don't mind. My everyday shoes are really looking rough. I would like to get a new pair, something that is comfortable and not too expensive.'

A few minutes later Mary popped the last morsel of cake into her mouth, stood up and brushed the crumbs from her skirt. 'I just want to visit the ladies' room first. Is that OK?'

Dee smothered a sigh of impatience. 'Of course it is, Mum. I'll come with you.'

Debenham's had loads of fashionable shoes that Dee would have given a lot to be able to afford, but there was nothing there that Mary thought suitable for herself. Across the road and into the Co-op stores, and within less than twenty minutes she had proclaimed that a smart pair of black slip-ons with a nice low heel were exactly what she was looking for.

Making their way to the bus stop, Dee was very tempted to broach the subject of Derrick Underwood having asked her to go to the cinema. She thought better of it. Time enough later when her father was home. She was far more likely to get permission from him. What her mother would be likely to say was another matter.

It was the following evening and the time had arrived, Dee had sat through their evening meal without mentioning that Derrick would soon be calling for her. She had dressed with care: plain navy blue skirt, soft long-sleeved jumper, the palest shade of baby blue, and only two bangles on her right wrist where she usually wore at least four. Make-up she had kept to the minimum, hoping she might get a chance to put more lip-stick on before she left the house, and so far she hadn't even dabbed on any perfume.

She had found the chance to tell Jodie about the invitation. 'You do think it will be all right, don't you? He seems ever so nice.'

'He is. A real charmer, like all the Underwood men,' Jodie encouraged. But not in the way that Dee's parents would approve of, she was think-ing. At times Derrick could act outrageously, and he often drank too much, but she wasn't about to spoil Dee's date. 'Go to the pictures with him if your mum and dad say it's all right, just don't start off by believing everything he tells you.'

A rat-a-tat on the door brought Dee up sharply. She lingered upstairs, letting Brian be the one to open the door. By the time she decided to put in an appearance, Derrick had explained why he was here and had asked Jack's permission to take his daughter to the cinema. Everyone was smiling, and Dee sent up a silent prayer of thanks, ignoring the look her mother was giving her, which said that when she got her daughter on her own, she would want some answers to a few questions.

Dee was thrilled. This big hunk of a man stand-ing in their kitchen looking so handsome and dressed so immaculately was waiting for her. She had been nervous about whether he would actu-ally turn up, but there'd been no need to worry. He was here, looking every inch a gentleman.

'You'll bring her straight home after the film is finished, won't you?' Mary had to have the last word.

Delia wished the ground would open up and

swallow her mother.

'Yes, ma'am.' Derrick smiled. Mary didn't look too pleased, but Jack was already grasping Derrick's outstretched hand and saying, 'You have a good time, the pair of you.'

'Yup, I'm sure we shall,' Derrick said, grinning as he followed Dee, who was already halfway down the passage making for the front door.

He had parked his car right outside their gate, and he quickly strode past Dee, opened the nearside door and handed her into the passenger seat. Then, going round to the other side, he settled in his own seat, opened the glove compartment and took out a box of Belgian chocolates, which he placed in Dee's lap. 'Here's to a very happy evening,' he whispered, as he turned the key and moved the gears.

Dee had been undecided as to what kind of film she wanted to go to, and it had been Derrick's choice to bring her to see *The Dirty Dozen*, with stars such as Lee Marvin, Telly Savalas and Clint Walker. Being a war film, there was lots of noise and explosions, during which Derrick held her hand tightly. When it came to the point where twelve men were risking their lives to blow up a very important bridge, Dee couldn't bear to watch. She buried her face in Derrick's shoulder and he held her tightly. At one point he even gently pushed her long hair aside and kissed the nape of her neck.

When the lights were raised for the interval, he bought an ice cream for each of them. He was certainly arousing her curiosity. She felt flattered that he had taken an interest in her; he was so different from the local lads and she hoped tonight's outing was only the beginning and not just a one-off. She liked him so much, but on the other hand she didn't want to give him any wrong impressions. She had decided she must take things slowly, not daydream so much but try and view the situation more realistically.

Derrick could see that Dee was uncertain how to behave, and it suddenly made him realise just how very young and inexperienced she was. He badly wanted to take her for a drink when the film came to an end, but instead he made a hasty decision to drive her straight home. He felt he had to tread with caution. This was entirely new ground for him, and if his association with young Delia were to be given a chance to progress, he knew he would have to take things very slowly.

Her mother must have been watching from the window of the front room, because as Derrick drew the car into the kerb, she had the door open and was calling for him to come into the house and join them for a nightcap.

Derrick's idea of a nightcap and Mary's were two different things, however.

'Come along, I have got the kettle on. Did you both enjoy the film?'

Derrick sighed. It was a mistake to have put a foot inside this house. He would admit that he liked Dee very much, and he could easily visualise them having a future together, even though she was so much younger than himself, but her mother was grilling him like mad: how was his job going, what part of the world would he be in next, was he expecting more promotion? He declined the offer of a cup of tea. He could hardly wait to say good night and get out of there.

When he had left, Dee turned on her father.

'Dad, why didn't you intervene? It's the first time he's taken me out; he hasn't even kissed me. What did you think you were on about, Mum, asking all those questions about his job and his future? Anyone would think he had asked me to marry him.'

'Delia, you're sixteen years old, you need protecting. We're your parents, we've a right to know if his intentions are honourable. Have you made more arrangements? Are you going to see him again?' Her mother was glaring at her and she kept jabbing at her with her finger. Dee hated it.

'I don't know what I am going to do and I wish you would stop going off the deep end. I am going up to bed now, and Dad, will you please talk to Mum, tell her she's putting the cart before the horse.'

'I'll do me best, pet. You go on up and I'll bring you a nice hot cup of tea.' Then, turning to his wife, 'For Christ's sake, Mary, give it a rest for tonight. Sit down and I'll get you a cuppa as well.'

Dee was slow in taking off her clothes, and had only just crawled into bed when her father tapped on her bedroom door and came in bringing a tray holding a cup of tea and a plate of biscuits, which he set down on her bedside table.

'Oh Dad, you're a darling. How's Mum? Is she still ranting and raving?'

'No, she's having a cup of tea. I'll let her simmer down before I say anything. You mustn't let her attitude spoil your life. You *are* very young, very young indeed, but I think you've got a good head on those shoulders and you'll do the right thing when it comes to the crunch.'

'Oh Dad, thanks,' and with that she threw her arms around his neck and kissed his weather-beaten cheek.

'Good night, lass, sleep well, see you in the morning.'

'Good night Dad.'

As her bedroom door quietly closed, Dee sat up straight and gratefully drank her cup of tea. Placing the empty cup back on the tray, she snuggled down under the bedclothes and let herself relive the whole of the evening. Derrick had been nice, she had felt he was being protective of her, and yes, she did so want to see him again.

She sighed heavily, but before she made ready to go to sleep, she closed her eyes and whispered several little prayers.

5

'Anyone at home?' Sadie Johnson called loudly from the open doorway of Jodie Underwood's house. It was a silly question, because not only was the front door wide open but voices could clearly be heard coming from inside the house.

Jodie put her head round the kitchen door and looked up the passage. 'Oh, it's you, Sadie, come on in and tell us what brings you round here on a Sunday morning.'

Sadie was a right old Londoner, a tubby bottle blonde with rosy cheeks, always clean and tidy, always with a smile on her face. She had five children under the age of ten, all of whom she loved dearly. She made sure they were all polite to adults and was extremely proud of each one of them. The family were by no means well off. Bill Johnson was a coalman who owned his own round, and with just one horse and cart he made a fair living. Mostly by working hard, being down in the railway yards shovelling coal into hundredweight sacks by five thirty in the morning five days a week. Sadie herself had three jobs. Tuesday she cleaned the doctor's surgery in Rye, Wednesdays and Thursdays she worked up the market on a vegetable stall and Fridays she collected football coupons for Littlewoods.

'Morning, Jodie, hello, everyone,' she said, nodding her head to the family gathered in the living room. 'Sorry to call on a Sunday. I did come yesterday but there was no one in. The powers that be have decided to do away with weekly collections for the pools, at least in this area. You'll still be able to do them weekly, but only by post. Or you can have your coupons collected but it will be only once a month. You'll still get your list with all the fixtures on it at the beginning of the season, but you'll have to mark your coupons four weeks in advance. It's up to you, Jodie, do you want to carry on?'

'Will it still be you that will be making the collection?' Jodie asked somewhat cautiously.

'Yes, only instead of it being half a crown a week it will be ten bob once every four weeks, but because you'll be paying in advance you'll get a weekly go at spot the ball for free.'

'Big deal,' two of the Underwood brothers said in unison.

'Have you ever heard of anyone winning a penny on that lark?' Derrick asked with a wide grin on his face.

'Maybe not,' Sadie was quick to respond, 'but your mother has come up a few times on her forecasts. Small amounts I'll admit, but if you don't play you'll never have the chance of a big cheque.'

'You're quite right, Sadie, and I wasn't having a go at you, love. I realise it's a job to you.' Derrick was man enough to climb down.

Sadie smiled. 'I'll forgive yer mate, too big to argue with, you are.' Turning to Jodie, she asked, 'So what yer gonna do, Jodie, weekly by post or monthly that I collect?'

'With you, of course, Sadie. Would I desert a pal? In any case I'd heard all about it from Maggie up in the corner shop. I've filled in my lines and the coupon and a ten-bob note are there on the table.'

'Thanks, Jodie, hope you come up big. Be nice for me an' all, 'cos I get a percentage of anyone's winnings whose entry forms go through me.'

'Do you really?'

'Yeah, only a few shillings, and it's very rarely on my round that anyone seems to have a win.'

'Well I'll be blowed. You pick up my money and then you tell me that!'

They both laughed. 'There's always a first and I hope it's you, Jodie. You deserve a bit of luck the way you work every hour God sends.'

'You're one to talk. I'd have a job to beat you.'

'Then we both must love what we're doing, eh? See you around Camber, I expect.' Sadie waved as she put the ten-bob note into her wallet and set off down the garden path.

Jodie stood dreaming for a minute or two. If, just if, she did come up on the pools, what would she do with a large payout?

She hadn't really got a clue, but wouldn't it be a lark?

All that money!

'So how many of you are coming dancing this afternoon?' Jodie asked, as she plonked several dishes of vegetables on to the table. 'How about you, Mum, would you like to come to Eastbourne with us? You can sit and watch the dancing, listen to the music.'

'Ah, Jodie dear, it's nice of you to ask me, but after your lovely Sunday roast all I'll want to do is what I always do, get me head down and have a good old snooze.'

'Well we're not leaving you here on your own, we'll sort something out. In the meantime, will you all please sit up to the table.' Turning quickly, Jodie went into the kitchen, calling as she went, 'John, have you finished carving the meat?'

'Yes, luv, and this gravy is boiling away like mad.'

'Hadn't you got the sense to turn the gas off beneath the saucepan?' she snapped. Picking up a serving spoon she gave the boiling gravy a good stir and then carefully poured it all into a tall jug, grinning as she said, 'Wouldn't be much good using a posh gravy boat, not with all this lot here today.'

She had ordered the beef from the local butcher in Rye, a rib on the bone, and the meat John was cutting looked good, just a little undercooked in the middle the way Marian liked it. Everyone had a couple of slices on their plates and was now helping themselves to an assortment of veggies, while Jodie rushed back to the oven and came to the table triumphantly flourishing a tray of twelve individual Yorkshire puddings that had risen a good three inches.

Besides Jodie, John and their two boys there was Mrs Underwood and her other two sons, Delia Hartfield being the only non-family member. Silence reigned while everyone was busy eating.

'Are we gonna get any pudding?' asked Reggie, spearing a piece of Yorkshire on his fork.

His grandmother laughed. 'I know what you're really asking: have I made some nice treats? The answer is yes, but you aren't going to get to see them until you have both of you cleared your dinner plates.'

'Grandma is right, if you can't eat yer dinner you don't deserve any pudding.' Jodie was grinning to herself as she warned the boys, but she knew she mustn't let them see that she thought it was funny the way they tried their best to get round their gran.

Eating from then on was a serious business, and when Jodie picked up the empty plates, she was glad to see that the vegetable dishes were almost cleared too. The Underwood men had always been good eaters. Now came apple pie and custard, but Jodie put her foot down about Grandma's second treat, a huge trifle. 'We are not touching that. It can go in the fridge until tomorrow.' The command had been given, and when their mother spoke like that, both Lenny and Reggie knew better than to argue.

'I'll take Mum home,' Derrick announced, and Dee's heart sank. She had so wanted him to come to Eastbourne with them. Her imagination had run riot when she'd thought she might get to dance with him.

Jodie caught the look on Dee's face and could tell at a glance what she was thinking. Oh to be young and imagining yourself falling in love!

It was a month now since Derrick had taken Dee to the cinema, and for a couple of days after that outing Dee had worried that he would never come near her again. She wouldn't have blamed him. Her mother had put him through the third degree! Her thoughts now had her smiling. Three times she had been out with him, once to the theatre, one whole day they had spent in Brighton and another time he'd taken her to London, where they had walked along the Embankment and he'd shown her sights she had only read about. But he had never put a foot inside her house again. Oh, he was friendly enough towards her mother, even bought her flowers, but as he said, he didn't fancy getting cornered again. He and her dad were great pals, though, and that meant a lot to Dee.

'John, are you going with the girls?' Derrick asked, and then, without waiting for an answer he turned to his youngest brother and said, 'What about you, Rick? You fancy tripping the light fantastic?'

John and Richard stared at each other but only

for a moment, and then it was John who spoke. 'Don't want to spoil your afternoon, bruv, but if me and Rick put in an appearance, you won't stand a chance in hell when it comes to partners.'

Richard was quick off the mark. 'Oh John, don't put him off. Even on a Sunday afternoon there's quite a few old fogeys that forgo their afternoon nap and go down on to the pier. A trip round the ballroom with our brother and they'll probably be really chuffed; might even feel grateful enough to give him a second go.'

'What the hell's the matter with you two? Afraid of the competition? You wanna remember that with my good looks you two are way back in the queue.' Derrick spoke with absolute confidence, and everybody in the room laughed, even their mother. She was used to this constant banter and to tell the truth she loved every minute of it when she had all three of her boys around her.

'Derrick, if you meant what you said about taking me home, may we please get going or else I shall fall asleep here and you will have to carry me out to your car.'

'All right, Mother, don't get out of yer pram. Put yer coat and bonnet on and we'll get going,' Derrick answered her, smiling and helping her up on to her feet.

There was what seemed like a mass exodus and suddenly Dee wasn't looking forward to this afternoon half as much as she had been. She watched as Derrick walked his mother to his car, helped her into the passenger seat and then walked round to the driver's side. He glanced back towards the house, saw Dee standing in the doorway and called loudly, 'Save a few dances for me. I'll be there by three o'clock.'

Once again Jodie had watched this exchange, and she laughed openly at the change that had miraculously come over Dee's face. As Dee turned to come back into the house she couldn't help saying, 'Changed yer mind? Going to put some make-up on now, are we?'

Dee was feeling far too happy to be put out by Jodie's teasing.

It was a merry party that eventually set off for Eastbourne. Travelling in the first car were John and Jodie with Reggie and Lenny in the back seat. Dee was in the front passenger seat of Richard's car. Rick, as he was generally referred to, was the youngest of the Underwoods, and looking at him she understood why women would go overboard for these brothers. They certainly were a good-looking trio.

The ballroom on the end of the pier was packed, and although Dee had had three dances, two with Tony Lewis, she had done her best to keep her eye on the entrance. Would Derrick keep his promise?

He arrived at three fifteen, having changed into a smart lightweight grey suit. Dee had redone her hair and changed her blouse for an emerald green one because she knew the colour exactly matched her big green eyes. She had also put some lipstick on and changed her shoes for silver sandals. She went eagerly towards him, acting just like the young teenager she was.

'You look good,' he said.

'Thank you.'

He took her hand and tucked it under his arm, and led her to the edge of the dance floor. 'Chris is just playing a waltz. Shall we?'

'Yes please.' She felt so happy she thought her heart would never stop thumping, but as she put her foot on the first step to go down to the dance floor, Derrick stopped.

'Is something wrong?' she asked. He hadn't moved, and she had to tilt her head up to be able to look at him. He cupped her face between his hands and gently kissed her.

She walked on in a complete daze. She couldn't have said why she had been drawn to Derrick, but she had been, right from the very first moment she had set eyes on him. Now he held her close with a sure arm in the middle of her back, and their feet seemed to glide in time with the music. He was a wonderful dancer. His hold on her was firm, and he led smoothly and gracefully, making it easy for her to follow his steps. Dancing with him was better than she had ever imagined it would be. She loved the warmth of being so close to his body, the way he smelled, the way he made her feel so special. When the music came to an end, she could have cried.

Derrick kept his arm around her shoulders as he led her off the floor, and as they neared the table where Jodie and his brothers were sitting, he lowered his head and whispered, 'Know what I love most about you?'

She couldn't speak, simply shook her head.

'How different you are.'

'I'm not sure I know what you mean,' she managed to say.

'In my travels I've met many women. Some have been nice, but most have seen so much of life and it hasn't always been good, and because of that they have become hardened. With you, Delia, life is only just beginning and everything is brand new. I want it to be me that has the privilege of showing you what is out there in the big wide world.'

Not knowing what to say to that, Delia said nothing. How badly she wanted to scream yes, yes, yes. However, there was no question of her having to make a reply. They had reached the table where Jodie and his brothers were, and for the moment privacy was no longer possible.

Rick had his arm along the back of a chair on which was sitting one of the most beautiful girls Dee had ever seen. In fact she was so smart and sophisticated-looking that Dee felt awkward, out of her depth.

Rick got to his feet and made the introductions. 'Derrick, this is a great friend of mine, Laraine Lawrence. You be nice to her, because she's gonna be around for a long time if I have my way.'

Derrick stretched his arm out and said, 'More than pleased to meet you, Laraine. For once I have to say my brother has shown what good taste he has.'

Laraine laughed softly as she took Derrick's hand and said, 'Pleasure to meet you too.'

Dee felt like a schoolgirl again. This Laraine was everything she herself would like to be. She was tall and slim, with a polished air about her. The dress she wore looked expensive and the belt only emphasised what a tiny waist she had. The last straw was her golden hair, which hung down her back and was even longer than Dee's own hair. It was only when Derrick nudged her that Dee managed to hold out her hand and say, 'Nice to meet you, Laraine.'

'You too, Delia. Jodie has just been telling me how hard you've been working and studying. Well done. With your looks, aiming for the top branch of the beauty business has to be the right thing to do.'

From that moment Dee felt she could come to really like this Laraine. She had treated her as an adult, and that went a long way to smoothing her ruffled feathers.

Derrick felt he knew exactly how Dee was feeling. All he could do was squeeze her hand to remind her that he was still there. This wasn't the time for a declaration, but hopefully all that would come in due course.

Delia was certainly hoping and praying that it would.

6

Almost two years had flown by, and Jodie, Laraine and Delia had become inseparable. Laraine was five years younger than Jodie, yet neither of the two found it a problem that Dee was even younger. She was a good sport, worked hard and was full of ambition, but most of all she was great fun to be with. The three young women found it amusing that each one of them was well and truly entangled with the Underwood brothers. Marian Underwood liked and respected them all, and nightly she prayed that her two single sons would hurry up and marry their girls.

Jodie was the one with the good business brain. Against all the odds and the encumbrance of a philanderer like John for a husband, she had put the money given to her by her father to good use. She now owned two shops, premises she had bought as derelict, run-down failures and turned into goldmines. To her it was like having a small empire, and as she was fond of reminding folk, she had built it all on her own efforts, though on the quiet she would admit that whenever she had needed advice, it had been to Michael Connelly that she had turned. Both he and his live-in partner, Danny Spencer, had always been there in the background, willing to advise but never intruding.

It went without saying that Laraine worked on a fashion magazine. She could wear a sack for a dress, swish a huge scarf over one shoulder and bring it round to tie at the waist, and the effect would be amazing. She turned the head of every man as she walked down the street, and to say that Richard Underwood was absolutely besotted with her was no exaggeration.

Dee still badly wanted to succeed in the hairdressing business, but she was keen to expand her capabilities further. Having finished a six-month course for budding make-up artists and passed with flying colours, she was aiming high. Her mother was cautious about it all, but her wise old dad kept saying, 'Wait long enough and work hard enough and you'll get your wish. Just make sure it's worth the wait.'

Dee felt she was growing up fast. For months Derrick had been on the *Worcester*, a three-mast sailing ship used for training cadets and recruits. This meant he was able to get plenty of shore leave, because the *Worcester* was anchored at Gravesend on the river Thames. Yet after all this time she still didn't know what to think. Her feelings hadn't altered; he only had to stand close to her and look at her intently, and immediately she would feel the colour burn in her cheeks. He held her close and his kisses were gentle, but he never went any further. She might only be eighteen, but she wasn't simple. Often she asked herself, was he playing with her? Did he still look upon her as too young?

In spite of her doubts, she was amazed at how comfortable she did feel when they were together. He didn't rush her at all. He seemed to accept the fact that she was young and had never been anywhere or really lived until he had come on the scene. She was grateful to him for that and for so many other things, for the way he told her about his travels, for the way he looked at life, never tiring of explaining things to her, for the great amount of fun they had, his queer sense of humour that always made her laugh. It really did feel wonderful to have him in her life, though she tried hard not to assume that this friendship would last. She was well aware that sooner rather than later he'd be off on his travels again.

All too soon the bubble did burst. Derrick had his orders and he was leaving. British India Shipping Lines had contracted to take parties of schoolchildren to India, and Derrick had been signed on as second mate, which meant he would be away for some length of time.

For Delia it was a ghastly day filled with tears and regrets.

At about the same time, John announced that he too had received his orders from the Royal Navy. He was being shipped out of Portsmouth and off to Hong Kong, and had been granted seven days' leave before he went. Jodie thought it odd that during the whole of that time he scarcely put a foot outside the front door, and these last two days he seemed to have a permanent smirk on his face, almost as if he had got one over on her. Either that or he felt guilty about something or other, but that couldn't be right. John Underwood never felt guilty about anything; he was a law unto himself and bugger anybody who got in his way.

It was nine thirty and Jodie had just got back from taking the boys to school. This was the one day this week that she was going to be at home, and as John had to report back to Portsmouth tomorrow morning, she had thought they might do something together. She sighed deeply as she took off her coat and glanced around the kitchen. She hadn't expected John to clear the table and wash up the breakfast things, but she had expected him to be up and about. From where she was standing she could see through the open door into her front room. It was only a small room, but she was very proud of what she had achieved in there. There wasn't a lot of furniture, but what there was was good. That was largely down to

Michael Connelly; he knew what auction houses she should attend, and if he himself had picked up a rare bargain that he knew Jodie would give her eye teeth for, he always offered it to her for just the amount he had paid for it. Jodie herself had decorated the walls and ceilings throughout the cottage, with a little help now and again from Dee and Laraine. Curtains, cushion covers and bedcovers she had also made herself.

Why oh why can't he take pride in our home? she asked herself almost on the verge of tears as she walked into the sitting room and drew back the curtains. He treated the place as if it were a doss house. At this moment the room looked for all the world as if he had deliberately picked up his kitbag and tipped the entire contents all over the beautiful Chinese rug. One shoe was in the fireplace, God knows why, and in the seat of an armchair there were several rumpled old news-papers, while an ashtray overflowing with spent dog-ends lay on the floor beside the chair.

What's the point of trying while he's still here? she asked herself as she gathered up the news-papers, picked up the ashtray and made for the kitchen to put the kettle on to boil. Having laid a tray, she lit the gas under the grill and placed two slices of bread on the grill pan, which she then slid beneath the flames. Spooning two heaped spoonfuls of tea into the warmed pot, she waited a minute for the kettle to come to the boil. Was she going to miss John? Would the boys miss their father?

Jodie rubbed her hands wearily over her face. When they were first married, any time spent apart had been torture to them both. She really had believed that they were truly in love with each other. The arrival of Reggie just six months after their wedding day had thrilled them both, and Lenny's birth eleven months later had appeared to complete their little family. Since then she couldn't say that their marriage had been all plain sailing. Far from it.

Even so, she did look forward to him coming home, and it still felt good to have him sharing her bed. She might be leading a very busy life and working too many hours, but it was all a means to an end. At first her aim had been to find them somewhere decent to live and to furnish it so that it was a warm and comfortable family home. Now, as the boys grew out of everything so quickly, she needed to work to keep up with their clothing, put good food on the table and to pay the bills. Shutting her eyes tightly, she let out a deep sigh of despair. If only John would realise that her life wasn't exactly a bed of roses.

Filling the teapot with boiling water, she replaced the lid, covered the pot with a padded tea cosy and set it down on the ready tray. As she started to walk upstairs with John's breakfast, she made a resolution. Today was going to be a happy day. It would be ages before they saw each other again. She might receive the odd letter, and the boys might get a picture postcard now and again, but knowing John as she did, even that was probably presuming too much.

Pushing the bedroom door open with her knee, she could see John's reflection in the dressing table mirror. He was sitting up in bed, a sheet barely covering his nudity. 'Brought you tea and toast. I'll cook you a proper breakfast later if that's what you want, but I thought we might go out somewhere, have a really nice lunch and then go together to meet Lenny and Reggie from school.'

His only answer was a harsh, brittle laugh as he settled his hands behind his head.

Jodie resolved to remain calm. 'Come on, John, it is your last day at home. Might be a while before we see each other again. Let's at least try to enjoy ourselves.'

'Suddenly you've got a day to spare for your husband. You quite sure that all the people who depend on you for their weekly wage can manage for a whole day without you?'

Jodie's eyes narrowed for a fraction of a second – sarcasm she could do without – and then she laughed. 'Jealousy rearing its ugly head again, eh, John? What's the matter, haven't you been the centre of attraction this leave? And that reminds me, you haven't been near your mother, so you can drink yer tea, eat yer toast and then shift yerself, 'cos I'm not taking no for an answer. I'll go and put some petrol in the car and we'll make our first stop at Camber to ask your mum if she'd like to come out to lunch with us. An' don't look at me like that. Just for once I'm calling the shots.'

'I hear what you're saying,' John said, grinning. 'Going to be honoured, am I? Allowed to ride in my wife's new car?' he sneered as he swung his legs over the side of the bed and reached for the tea Jodie had poured into his large breakfast cup.

Jodie had to stop herself from pointing out that she had worked hard for the money to buy the car and that it got her from one job to another without her having to rely on buses. But stop herself she did. She was more determined than ever that today should be remembered as a happy one, and if she could persuade Marian to come out to lunch with them, all the better. John wouldn't show off so much, wanting to be cock of the walk, not with his mother there.

'I'll be about half an hour, John. Please get yerself ready, we don't want to waste too much of the day.' Having almost pleaded with him, Jodie made what she hoped was a dignified exit.

As the door closed behind her, John got out of bed and went to where his jacket was draped over the back of a chair. From the inside pocket he withdrew a cheque and laid it flat on the top of the dressing table. He was grinning as he glanced down at the words 'Pay J. Underwood the sum of seventy-five thousand pounds'. Ever wanting more, he was cursing that this week there had been several correct forecasts and the winnings had had to be shared. Only a few weeks ago some silly woman had won hundreds of thousands of pounds and had gone on TV shouting about how she was going to spend, spend, spend.

By God, though, he had been lucky! Jodie hadn't been at home when the two men from Littlewoods had paid them a visit two days ago.

'Mr Underwood?' one of them had asked. And of course he had said he was. It wasn't until he invited them in and they explained why they were there that he realised it was Jodie they were look-ing for. She was the J. Underwood who did the football coupons regularly every week. Of course he should have come clean right away, but he'd let them go on talking, reminding him that a tick had been marked on the coupon, which indicated that he'd made a request for no publicity, and that they would most certainly respect his wishes. It was not such a very large amount because there were several winners this week, but they would still provide a financial adviser if he so wished. He had listened to it all and then told them he would be guided by his bank manager, because actually he had been too stunned to think clearly.

Coming back to the present, he heard Jodie drive off in her car to fetch petrol. She wasn't doing too badly. Two posh hairdressing salons and her bloody fingers in many a pie with that Michael Connelly and Danny Spencer. But to walk away with all her winnings did seem a bit extreme. His moment of being conscience-stricken didn't last long. How much of it would she share with him? He wasn't going to bank on her being generous. His naval pay was good, but not that good. Out of sight of Jodie and with that cheque in the bank, he'd be in a position to have a whale of a time without having to give a thought to how much he was spending.

His eyes moved again to the cheque. The day after tomorrow he would be on his way out of the country; he didn't need to bank it before he left. He could afford to wait. Take some advice when he got to Hong Kong. Plenty of banks out there; surely he'd be able to open an account solely in his name.

Half an hour later, John was bathed and dressed in civvies and waiting for Jodie in the kitchen. He patted the inside pocket of his jacket where the cheque was concealed. He'd go along with whatever Jodie wanted to do today, make sure that both she and his mum had a slap-up lunch. He watched through the window as Jodie expertly parked her car by the kerb. He knew he was abandoning every scrap of decency by holding on to the money, but a chance like this didn't come along every day, and he'd be a mug not to take it.

John's behaviour that day was almost too good to be true. Marian Underwood looked so pleased when the pair of them walked through her front door and John called, 'Get yer glad rags on, Mother, I'm taking you and my wife to lunch. Jodie suggests we eat in one of the old-fashioned pubs in Rye, but if you've got some other preference, just say so and we'll go there.'

'Well, well, wonders will never cease,' his mother said. She turned to Jodie. 'Is he serious or is he just mucking about?' Her voice held such a strong note of uncertainty that Jodie felt sorry for her mother-in-law. She wasn't going to spoil the day by saying that it had been her idea and not her son's.

'He means it, Mum. Either he's had some back pay due to him or he's come up on the gee-gees, but whatever, don't let's look a gift horse in the mouth. Just get your coat on and let's get going before that son of yours changes his mind.'

Jodie didn't have eyes in the back of her head, otherwise she would have noticed the difficulty that her husband was having trying to conceal his amusement. When she did turn around, she felt she had to ask. 'John, what are you looking so pleased about? Haven't seen you smile so much for a long time.'

He was quick off the mark. 'Come and look out of this window, see for yourself.'

They stood side by side looking out through the long glass French doors at two large black cats stretched out in the weak sunshine. By now John could no longer conceal his mirth.

'Look at them. Do you think they're sunbathing? One black cat is supposed to be lucky; two must mean we're going to hit the jackpot.'

Jodie could think of no answer to that, but after a short while she said, 'What about us, John?'

'Well, we're lucky all the time, aren't we? You're always telling me how blessed we are to have two healthy sons and how well you're doing, but then it was never on the cards that you'd fail at anything you attempted and you've proved that point over and over again without any help from me.'

'I'm ready, and we'd better get going if you mean what you said. I like to eat at one o'clock, not in the middle of the afternoon.' Marian Underwood had done well in a short space of time. She was wearing a brown tailored two-piece costume, with her mink stole draped around her shoulders. To complete the smart outfit she was wearing neat court shoes with a Cuban heel and carrying a leather handbag and gloves all in a matching shade of light brown.

John was grinning from ear to ear as he threw his arms around her and planted a kiss on her cheek. 'It doesn't matter how much you have to drink today, Mother, we've not got to walk anywhere. Jodie is driving us in her new car.'

'Get off, yer daft sod,' was her hasty reply.

Jodie settled herself in the driver's seat with a lighter heart. She dearly hoped that John's good mood would last through to the end of the day and that he might even suggest taking the boys somewhere for a treat when they met them from school later on; after all, it would be a long time before they would set eyes on their father again. As she switched on the engine, she turned her head and smiled at her mother-in-law. She knew the old lady would miss her son, as they all would, but she had decided that the best and only solution was to concentrate on their own lives and let John carry on with his. After all, there was going to be thousands of miles between them for some time to come.

7

It had only been a short while since her two eldest sons had left these shores, and now Marian felt there had to be a reason why her youngest son Richard had come to take her out to lunch. Her hunch had not been wrong. With a very satisfying meal over, Richard sat with his elbows resting on the table, leaning forward and telling his mother that he too would shortly be up and away again.

She should have become used to this. Her husband had worshipped the sea, and had owned his own boat from a very young age. During the winter months he had carted coal from one end of the country to the other, but it was deep-sea fishing that was the real love of his life. She and Albert Underwood had enjoyed a good married life. Blessed with three burly sons who each had salt water in their veins, there had been no chance of her opposing their wish to earn their living aboard ships.

Richard, still only in his mid-twenties, could boast that he was a fully fledged master mariner, and had all his papers to prove that he was legally capable of taking command of any merchant ship. Where was he off to this time? As his mother, she knew better than to ask. He'd tell her all in good time if he wanted her to know, and if he didn't there would have to be a very good reason for him not doing so.

Richard's quick success must have rankled slightly with his elder brother Derrick, not that Derrick had anything to reproach himself for. At an early age he had sat for his second mate's ticket and had followed it up by securing his qualification to become a first mate. One more qualification and he too would be at the top of the tree.

'Are you going to order us another bottle of wine?' Marian Underwood absolutely hated these partings. She knew it was daft and that she really should be used to it by now, but her excuse was that she was getting old and she might die before any of her sons returned to these shores.

'I don't think that's a good idea,' Richard said, laughing outright. 'Mother, you're nearly at the stage where you'll start crying into your glass as it is. What I will do is call the waiter and ask him to bring us a pot of hot coffee, and yes I will remember to warn him that you prefer a pot of black and a jug of very hot milk, is that right?'

'You know darn well it is. Can't stand it when they either bring you stone-cold milk or a fart-arse-sized pot with just a teaspoonful of cream in it.'

'Mother! Will you never change?'

'Son, would you want me to change?' she sniffed.

'Not in any shape or form.' Richard laughed as he beckoned the waiter over and gave him explicit orders regarding their coffee.

When it arrived, he sat back and allowed his mother to pour her own. Once she had done so and taken the first sip, she looked at him and grinned. 'Perfect,' she said.

'In that case, Mother, I want you to listen to me. Laraine has agreed to marry me and we don't want to hang about, so we are getting married at the weekend by special licence at Eastbourne Town Hall and then we're flying out to New Orleans for me to join a ship.'

Very ladylike, Marian lowered her cup from her lips and replaced it in the saucer. 'Oh son, I couldn't be more pleased for you. Sounds a bit rushed, though. Any special reason?'

'If you are suggesting Laraine is pregnant, you couldn't be more wrong. It is just that I have been offered this job with Cunard. My rank on the trip will only be second mate, but it does entitle me to take Laraine on board with me. It will be a honeymoon for us and will give Laraine a chance to see a bit of the world.'

'What about Laraine's parents?' Marian thought

everything should be fair and above board. She didn't want any falling out with her new in-laws right at the start.

'Have you forgotten, Mum? Laraine's mother died a few years ago, but we'll see to it that her father is here for the weekend.'

'Seems as if you've got every angle covered. Don't you want a reception of any kind?'

'Not really, just a nice meal with the family, probably at the Grande, because we're off later that same evening.'

'Have you told the rest of the family?' his mother gingerly queried.

'Would I dare spread the word before you knew our news?' Richard could not resist teasing her.

'Well, you'd better get a move on. A rushed wedding or not, they'll all want new outfits and Jodie's boys will need to be kitted out. I know Derrick has already shipped out, but how about John, will he still be here?'

'No, he won't, Mother. Surely you can't have forgotten that John took you out for a meal last week?'

'No, I haven't forgotten that, but I didn't realise he was leaving so soon.'

Rick knew that John had left Portsmouth the day after he'd taken Marian out, but he thought it best not to pursue the subject. We've all got to get old sometime, he thought, and on the whole their mother was doing remarkably well.

'Well, it does leave me with a bit of a problem. Where do I find a best man?'

'We've got some good neighbours you can call on if need be. Now, on the way home I think we should call in and tell Jodie.'

Richard was having a job stifling his laughter. Did his mother really believe that Laraine would have kept this news all to herself? The three women were like sisters; more so in fact than if they were blood-related. Nothing happened to any one of them that the other two didn't always know about within the hour. But one thing was certain: he wasn't going to be the one to tell his mother that they had known before she had. All the same, he decided to pacify Marian and call in to Rye to see Jodie and his two nephews on the way home. He was hoping against hope that he'd get the chance to have a word on the quiet before Jodie let the cat out of the bag.

Richard let out a sigh of relief as they walked into Jodie's house and his mother made straight for the bathroom. Now he could have a few moments alone with his sister-in-law.

It wasn't long before Jodie was staring at him, a thoughtful frown crossing her face. She had heard the news from Laraine but hadn't realised that the arrangements were so far advanced. She hesitated, not feeling comfortable about voicing her opinion.

He looked concerned. 'You think I'm rushing everyone too much, don't you?'

'Well, yes, I do.'

'I do respect you, Jodie, and any advice you've offered in the past has always been good. As a sister-in-law you are fantastic. I'm only sorry that you seem to have picked the worst of the bunch with our John. He hasn't been the best of husbands or a great father to Reggie and Lenny.'

'Rick, I've come to believe that in this life one

has to take the rough with the smooth. We're still together, John and I, and I wouldn't be without Lenny and Reggie for the world. But it's not me and my life we were discussing; it's your hasty wedding plans.'

'I have asked myself many times how I knew the very first time I set eyes on Laraine that she was the woman I wanted to marry. It was not a momentary feeling either. There was something about her that told me I should hold on to her, and my feelings have never changed; in fact if anything they have deepened.'

'Well, if you're that sure, then go ahead. Just seems a shame that half the family aren't going to be here to attend the wedding. But please make sure of one thing: send a car to fetch Laraine's father so that he is here for the ceremony, and then at the end of the day after you and the bride have left, he can spend a few days at my house if he'd like to and I'll make sure that someone sees him home safe and sound when he's ready to go.'

'You are an absolute wonder, you know that, you're always thinking of others. It will please Laraine no end to have her dad here to give her away. Sorry for the hurry, but thankfully Mum doesn't seem to mind that the wedding is being rushed, and we can always have a church blessing and a big family do at a later date. I grabbed this offer because it will be a great honeymoon for us. Just think about it from Laraine's point of view: flying out to New Orleans to board our ship, then heading for Canada and very soon cruising between various ports in Japan, and all the while I shall be earning a good wage.'

'Rick, please, let's leave it there,' Jodie pleaded. 'You're making me feel so envious. When I listen to you and Derrick, I ask myself why John didn't join the Merchant Navy instead of signing himself up for years in the Royal Navy.'

'Derrick and I have asked ourselves that question many a time, and it must have crossed John's mind on the odd occasion. Bit late now, though.'

'Ah well.' She gave a laugh. 'Let's hope he's having a good time in Hong Kong. Come on through to the kitchen and I'll make us all some tea.' A few minutes later she was placing a steaming cup of tea in front of her mother-in-law and pushing a second cup across the table to Richard. 'Is there anything I can do to help this wedding on its way?' she asked.

He gave a shrug. 'I don't know. When you get chatting to Dee and Laraine, I'm sure there'll be a hundred and one things, but I do know that Laraine will be over the moon because you're going to have her father stay here for a night or two.'

'Longer if he wants. The house feels empty knowing that John is so far away.'

The words were hardly out of Jodie's mouth when suddenly the front door opened and slammed back against the wall with a hefty thud and Lenny and Reggie were flinging themselves at their uncle. Their grandmother too got a riotous welcome, though maybe the fact that she was holding out a Mars bar for each of them had something to do with it.

Later that evening, after Richard had taken his mother home, he decided to stop off in Eastbourne. Having parked his car, he walked out on to the pier. Way out to sea, two small ships kept disappearing into deep troughs then appearing again. In the far distance an ocean-going liner looked stationary against the skyline. The sea had always attracted him and his brothers. They were sailors born and bred, and none of them could ever have envisaged working on land. He only hoped that Laraine would learn to love the life at sea as much as he did.

Coming off the pier, he jumped down from the road on to the beach and clambered over the shingle to where the fishermen's huts were. He walked past several huts and stopped at the last one.

'Hello, Bob, how's the world treating you?' he asked, eyeing his good friend. Robert Collier never seemed to change. He had grown up alongside the Underwood boys and was so similar to Rick that they could easily have been taken for brothers. Weather-beaten complexion, head of thick dark hair, broad shoulders, the sleeves of Robert's navy blue seaman's jersey rolled up to his elbows serving only to emphasise his bodily strength and his bulging muscles.

'Can't grumble, Rick. Great t'see you, bet you aren't gonna be ashore for long.'

'Long enough to get married and take my wife on honeymoon, courtesy of the Cunard Line.'

'Why, you jammy bugger. When's the great day?'

'This Saturday, and with both my brothers at sea, I need a best man. Eastbourne Town Hall, twelve midday.'

Bob Collier stuck out his arm, fingers of his hand spread wide. 'I'd be honoured mate. I'll get

89

me ma t'sort out me best bib and tucker.'

The two men shook hands, then Rick slapped Bob heartily across his shoulders. 'How about nine o'clock Friday night at the Mansion for a drink?'

'Wouldn't miss it. I'll be there. How's yer old lady keeping?'

'She's feeling great. That'll be two sons down and only our Derrick to go. That reminds me, I daren't go home and tell her I've seen you, at least not empty-handed I daren't.'

'Course you can't. Crab or lobster?'

'Make it a lobster if you haven't boxed them all up.'

'Must 'ave known you were coming. Got a nice big one, big enough t'suit yer ma. She'll have a feast, I promise you.'

The two of them talked a while, catching up on each other's news, and when Richard left with his lobster in a string bag, he felt on top of the world.

Everything was working out well.

It was seven o'clock and Jodie had just asked her boys to pack up the cars they had been playing with. When the table was cleared she was going to make them a cup of cocoa each before taking them upstairs to bed. Really her mind was far away, wondering how John was getting on. She would very much have liked an itinerary showing the ports of call of John's ship. To be able to mark off their progress every day, let Reggie and Lenny help, and perhaps even make notes for the boys to take to school so that they could show their mates where their dad was. No such luck. John didn't see the need to keep her informed, never mind his two small sons.

The boys were doing as she'd asked, albeit with a load of noisy chatter and laughter, when there came a knocking on the front door followed by the sound of the key being pulled through the letter box and inserted into the lock. Seconds later the door was flung open and the loud voice of Sadie Johnson could be heard yelling, 'All right if I come through?'

Jodie gave a half-sigh. It was a bit late for Sadie to be calling to collect the football money, and didn't those four weeks fly by? Didn't seem a month ago since she'd last paid Sadie ten bob for the month's forecast. She said as much to Sadie now. 'But suppose I'd better keep doing them. You never know, but sure as eggs are eggs the week I stop would be the week I'd win,' she said with a ridiculously optimistic smile.

Sadie couldn't believe what she was hearing, but she squashed her irritation and muttered forcefully, 'Some folk are never satisfied. There was me expecting ... well, not champagne exactly, but a bottle of stout and a fiver if nothing else.'

Jodie felt every muscle in her body tighten. 'Boys, will you please both quieten down a bit. Leave all that, I'll clear it up in a minute. You two go upstairs, wash yer face and hands and put yer pyjamas on, then you can come back down again and we'll have that cocoa. Come on now, shoo, before I change my mind.'

The boys looked at one another but did as they were told, leaving the two women alone.

'Shall I go first?' Sadie asked timidly.

Jodie nodded her head.

'There were several winners. Three weeks ago it was. Payout wasn't that big. I do know that two of our directors called here. I was actually shown your cheque and given my commission.'

'Then how come I haven't even heard that I had a bloody win till now?' Jodie was on the point of screaming, and Sadie felt like joining her. It didn't help when Jodie suddenly asked, 'Can you tell me who the cheque was made out to?'

'That's the point, Jodie, it was to J. Underwood, and your John having all his wits about him saw his chance and must have taken it. Our directors probably asked if he was J. Underwood and of course he was well within his rights to say that he was! Did he not mention it to you at all?'

'Not a word.'

'No sign even that he was feeling over the moon?'

'Now you come to mention it, the last couple of days that he was home he was acting sort of shifty, and on the very last day he really pushed the boat out. He took me and his mother out for a slap-up meal without too much complaining, and he gave the boys half a crown each instead of the usual sixpence. Daft old me, clever enough after the facts are laid bare. The very next day he was up and away and he won't be back for at least eighteen months. Fat chance that he'll have any of the money left by then. By the way, just how much was my payout?'

That was the question Sadie had been dreading. She took a deep breath. 'Like I said, there were several winners...'

'Never mind trying to soften the blow. How much was the cheque made out for?' Jodie's voice was such that Sadie knew she couldn't fob her off any longer.

'Seventy-five thousand pounds.'

Jodie's jaw dropped and she stood there with her mouth wide open.

Sadie went into the kitchen, filled the kettle and put it on the gas to boil. Then she got down on her knees and rummaged in the cupboard under the sink. She had been hoping and praying that she might find a bottle of whisky or something else that she could pour into a cup of tea. But no such luck.

By the time she carried the tea tray into the living room, the boys were downstairs looking like two pink-faced little angels and Jodie had her temper under control, her tears of rage wiped away. She managed to say, 'You pour our tea, Sadie, while I go and make two mugs of cocoa and find some chocolate biscuits, because I think I know two little boys who would like that.'

As she stirred the chocolate powder into the mugs, she vowed to herself, I *shall* live to have my day with that husband of mine. Half a crown to each of his sons out of seventy-five thousand pounds! Good job he was thousands of miles away, or else she would have strangled him with her bare hands.

8

Laraine Underwood, as she now was, stood on the balcony of the hotel gazing at the exotic plants. There had never been a time in her life when she had stopped to think about what she was doing, or the consequences her actions might have for others. Now, as she looked back over the last few weeks, she was certain that everything that had taken place had been with God's blessing. Today she was beginning a whole new life. Here she was in the United States of America, a married woman, about to board a ship and sail to places that she'd only ever seen on maps.

For the moment, though, she was letting her mind wander back to her wedding day. From the minute she had opened her eyes on that eventful day, there hadn't been a second when she wasn't being pampered. Jodie had styled her long golden hair into a glamorous style, weaving fresh apple blossom into the French pleat at the back of her head and giving her a fluffy fringe which had lain across her forehead beneath her ornamental headband.

Dee had worked on both her toenails and fingernails, completing the look by painting them all a very pale shade of pink. Chloe Goldsmith, a Jewish friend of Marian Underwood, whose husband owned warehouses all over London, supplying only the most exclusive shops, had brought several wedding dresses down to Jodie's house for Laraine to make her choice. What a night that had been! It had taken ages before there had been a unanimous decision. The one she had chosen was simple, with straight lines. Without flounces or frills, it showed what it was: perfection personified.

Everything had been one great big rush, but no expense had been spared. Laraine had lost count of the times she had been photographed. At times she had felt like a puppet as she reacted to their commands, to smile, turn this way, look over her shoulder, lift her head higher. What a pity she hadn't got to see any of the photographs yet, and she couldn't help wondering where she might be when the mail did catch up with them.

'Who's daydreaming, then?' The sound of Rick's voice as he came out to join her on the balcony made Laraine jump. He reached up and touched her face, and his dark, searching eyes looked at her with such love that she felt the sting of tears spring to her own. 'How does it feel to be a married woman?' he whispered.

'I couldn't find the words to tell you if I tried.'

'Oh Laraine,' he murmured, folding her into his arms. Then, lowering his mouth to hers, he kissed her more tenderly than he had ever kissed her before.

Three days, just three short days since she had become Richard's wife, and things had already changed so completely that she couldn't even begin to understand the fate that had brought her such devoted love and such a different way of life.

With all the hullabaloo of Laraine and Richard's

wedding, Jodie hadn't had time to think about the way John had so skilfully diddled her out of seventy-five thousand pounds. That was not to say that every single minute she wasn't well aware of that fact. During the day she really did concentrate on other matters, yet still, in her mind, she could see the cheque that she'd never even set eyes on. What she couldn't have done with even a portion of that money, and as for the boys, it didn't bear thinking about. Would John be feeling any re-morse? Like hell he would! He must have received that cheque at least three days before he went back to Portsmouth. No wonder he had looked so smug. How many times had he taken it out of his pocket and gazed at it in sheer wonderment? Hadn't he even given a thought if not to her then at least to his two boys? Surely he had considered what a difference a sum of money like that could have made to Lenny and Reggie's young lives.

Oh well, life wasn't all bad, and as her dad had been fond of saying, what you've never had you never miss. But the point was, she had now been told about her win, knew about the huge amount of money that had come into this house only to be snatched away by her own husband. No matter which way you looked at it, the whole thing had been sheer robbery. And as she was fully aware, there was not a damn thing she could do about it. John had had every right to claim that he was J. Underwood, and he had made the most of the chance. Pity he hadn't given a thought to what a difference that money could have made to his fam-ily, instead of calculating what it could do for him.

Jodie was doing all right, but it was a hard slog.

The boys constantly needed new shoes and clothes and there had to be food put on the table. Both lads were well into sport at school, and uniforms and sports gear were costly enough, but she did her best. Not only did she encourage the boys to take part in every sport that the school provided, she did her best to be there in the field cheering them on no matter what the weather. She had such a busy schedule that sometimes she felt like she was taking on too much. It was difficult when she knew she was needed in two places at the same time, but somehow she always managed.

One of Jodie's peculiarities was her fear of debt. She toiled over her bookwork, making sure that each shop was more than paying its way. She couldn't understand people obtaining things on credit. To her it was spending money you didn't have. And the thought never entered her head that she should give up her round of private clients. Each lady had become a friend, and besides, the fact was that added together, they were still a nice little earner.

So in general life was good. If she could only learn to curb her temper every time she gave a thought to John. Was he living the life of Riley out there in Hong Kong? Had he had the audacity to walk into a bank and open an account in his own name?

There you go again! Asking yerself daft questions when you know damn well you're not going to get any bloody answers. Focus on the things you can do something about instead of daydreaming about what you'd like to do to John. And remember, God has a way of repaying his debts without any money!

With Laraine off on her honeymoon, that left only herself and young Dee to go out and about together. Dee never seemed to have any money to spare, but she certainly was not a spendthrift. She had learnt at an early age the value of a pound and her time would come, Jodie was sure of that. She certainly deserved success, because she had not sat about on her backside but had enrolled herself at college and become passionate about passing exams and gaining credentials and diplomas. She was also shrewd enough to know that she had to be patient and wait her turn.

It was as Jodie was rushing like mad to see the boys off to school that she heard the rattle of her letter box. Shooing them in front of her down the narrow hallway, she watched as Lenny bent down to pick up the post that had landed on the door-mat.

'Thanks, son,' she said as he handed it to her. She kissed both boys and they tore away up the street.

Turning to go back indoors, Jodie glanced through the post in her hand, telling herself she would deal with it all later. At that moment she noticed the raised lettering on the outside of one of the larger white envelopes: TELEVISION AT ALEXANDRA PALACE. That certainly caught her attention, and she hastily tore open the envelope and scanned the one-page typewritten letter. The gist of it was that they were looking for professional hairstylists and qualified make-up artists to work at Shepperton Studios. The letter was signed by John Boulting, Director.

'My God!' Jodie exclaimed loudly. Was someone having a laugh at her expense? She hoped not. Oh, but what if it turned out to be too good to be true? So what? What would she have lost? The cost of one measly phone call. If it were for real, she'd be able to take young Dee with her; when it came to make-up and nails, Dee was far better qualified than she was. In hairstyling she'd be OK, knowing she could count her commendations with the best of them and had testimonials to prove it.

Suddenly the phone rang, and Jodie nearly jumped out of her skin. 'God, I'm a bag of nerves since John pulled that fast one on me,' she mumbled to herself as she looked at the clock. It was getting late, but she supposed she'd better answer it.

She moved to the other side of the room and lifted the receiver off the wall. 'Hello,' was all she managed before hearing, 'Jodie, is that you?'

'Laraine!' And again her heart lurched, but this time from pure joy. 'What time is it there? Oh, it doesn't matter. Is everything all right?'

'Better than all right, absolutely perfect. I'm aboard the ship, our cabin is huge, and the weather is wonderful. From the little I've seen of it, New Orleans is out of this world. We should all come here on holiday sometime.'

'I wish,' Jodie muttered longingly. 'When are you due to leave the States?'

'We've one more day. I'm going to buy some postcards and send them off to Lenny and Reggie before we leave, and I'll try to do the same from every port of call, that's if I'm allowed to go ashore.'

'Oh Laraine, you are a darling, the boys will love that. If I didn't love you and Richard so much I'd be green-eyed with envy. Don't you want to know how your dad is bearing up?'

'Knowing he's with you, I'm sure he's counting himself very lucky.'

'That's where you're wrong, he isn't with me. He spent the first night here, but then Marian carted him off to Camber Sands. She told him her house is bigger and faces the sea, and that she is the sole occupant. I drove him over there and he looked well contented when I left the pair of them.'

'Did he? That's good.' There was a pause, but Jodie knew Rick was there because she could hear him breathing. Finally he took the phone from Laraine. 'Thanks, Jodie, you always were good at matchmaking.' She could hear his laughter down the line.

'He knows he only has to ring me when he wants to go home, so don't go worrying your-selves about him.'

'I did leave you a ship-to-shore telephone num-ber. If anything untoward happens to him, pro-mise you'll ring us straight away. OK?'

'OK,' Jodie agreed, wondering what the hell Laraine could do if she happened to be in Japan.

'I'm going to pass you back to Laraine now. We both love you and the boys, tell them we will be sending post to them.'

In a state of utter excitement, Laraine took over again, telling Jodie all about the taxi driver who had brought them from the airport to the dockyard and how the whole crew of the ship had turned out to give them a riotous welcome. 'I'd better go now, Jodie, Rick is making signs at me.'

'All right, have a wonderful honeymoon. Bye for now,' Jodie said. But the line had already gone dead.

She looked out of the window as she replaced the receiver on the wall, and laughed as the sun suddenly broke through the clouds – it was as if God was trying to compensate her for being here in England while Laraine was on board a ship that was going to take her halfway around the world. But the way she was feeling at the moment, it would take more than a bit of weak sunshine to raise her feeling to top level. OK, she thought, so I'm jealous. You'd have to have a pretty thick skin or even be a downright saint not to be envious while listening to Laraine.

Hardly had she moved than the telephone rang again. 'Oh my God, at this rate I'm never going to get to work this morning,' she muttered as she picked the phone up once again.

'Jodie, it's only me. I'm glad I've caught you. Michael has asked me to work in the Rye salon for the whole week and I wondered if you fancied my company?'

'Dee, you'll never know how much! Come and stay for the week. And if you're home first to-night, have the kettle on! Must dash now, or I'll never get to work today.'

'Thanks, Jodie, see you tonight,' and the line went dead.

Heaving a hefty sigh of relief, Jodie picked up her case and several bags and looked around the room in panic for a moment until her eyes settled on her car keys. Thankfully she grabbed them and without so much as a backward glance flew from the house and out to her car.

Settling herself in the driver's seat, she reached up and straightened the interior mirror. Then, smiling at her reflection, she said aloud, 'Thank God for small mercies. At least having young Dee to stay with me for the week should brighten things up a bit.'

9

Jodie and Dee were sitting at a small table outside a café in the Lanes in Brighton, fanning themselves with menus and sipping coffee. Above them the sky was the most beautiful shade of blue imaginable, with not a cloud in sight. As Jodie looked up, she thought how tranquil it seemed up there, compared with all that was going on around them. It was the first Monday in August, and therefore it was a Bank Holiday. With fingers crossed the night before, because Bank Holidays were notorious for heavy rain, Jodie had suggested that the two of them spend the day enjoying themselves. So far so good.

Reggie and Lenny had gone on a coach trip to London Zoo. It was an outing organised by the school, and for the first time since their father had left Portsmouth, Jodie had felt it was safe to let them go. Over the last thirteen months both boys seemed to have grown not only in stature but also in confidence, so that Jodie no longer worried when they were out of her sight. She had also been assured that at least four members of the staff would be with the children at all times.

Brighton's Lanes were famous worldwide, for there was always so much to see and do, and today was no exception. Besides the antique shops and the many jewellers, whose windows displayed huge amounts of gold, there were street artists, hawkers and hucksters, with a good sprinkling of cafés from which the aroma of splendid food enticed the day trippers to loiter.

'Right,' Jodie said, 'we've lingered long enough. Have you decided what you want to eat?'

'Well, I rather fancy the seafood platter, but it says here that it's a meal for two,' Dee answered slowly, still contemplating the menu.

'Well that's fine, seeing as how there are two of us.'

'Are you sure that's what you want? You aren't just having it to please me?'

'No, truthfully, that will suit me fine, and there is a salad served with it as well as garlic bread, so yes, let's have the seafood platter.'

'Right,' Jodie said again after the waiter had taken their order, 'let's get down to some serious gossip. Things have been so hectic these past few weeks I've hardly seen anything of you.'

'And whose fault is that?' Dee laughingly threw the challenge back. 'It was you that dragged me off to Shepperton Studios and got us both all the extra work, so you can't start grumbling now that we've no spare time to see each other.'

'Hold on a minute,' Jodie said sharply. 'Are you complaining?'

'No, I am not, you'll never hear me doing that. It's an entirely different life, the glamour, the people we meet and the clothes. I was talking to one of the wardrobe mistresses and she said they often have a chuck-out, and if and when they do, she is going to think of me.'

'Fine, I'm glad you're enjoying it, but you haven't mentioned the most important part, have you?'

'I know what you're going to say, Jodie, you're thinking about the pay. Takes some getting used to, doesn't it?'

'Don't give me any of that old nonsense, Dee. You've taken to earning a good wage like a duck takes to water, or if you haven't then I want to know the reason why.'

'Well, when I first heard what we'd be earning I thought it was marvellous, especially as we could put in a docket for all our travelling expenses as well. But the second time I picked up my wages I went straight up to Central Office and told them they'd made a mistake, they'd paid me far too much.'

Jodie almost choked on her coffee. Having safely replaced her cup on the saucer, she gave a hearty laugh. 'Bet that was the first time any employee had done that. I know what you mean, though, because I queried it too. Double pay for Saturdays and treble pay for Sundays. Great, isn't it?'

'I just couldn't believe it at first, but now of course I think it is fantastic.' They looked at each other and their laughter boiled over. 'More in two days than I earn all week sometimes,' Dee blurted out.

'Money for old rope, some would say,' Jodie added for good measure.

'Derrick isn't too pleased about it though,' Dee murmured as the waiter came to the table with their food.

Both were still a bit hysterical as they sorted out the prawns, salmon and lobster and shared the side salad. By the time the waiter came back with the bottle of white wine Jodie had ordered, they had calmed down, and there was silence as they did justice to the excellent meal.

Eventually Jodie took a deep breath and picked up her glass of wine. 'This studio business has been a proving ground for each of us, hasn't it? But I think you've come through with flying colours.'

Dee smiled. 'You know all the right things to say, don't you? But the truth is I couldn't have done it without you. The first time I had to work on the set was for a period costume film, and when I asked for instructions I was told to use my initiative. Honestly, it felt as if I had been thrown to the wolves.'

'My guess is,' Jodie said, 'that once you got over the awe of having a celebrity sitting in the chair, you forgot all about your nerves and just did your job and did it well, same as you always do and always will.'

'I hope you're right,' Dee laughed. Then, holding out her glass to Jodie, she said, 'Here's to television work.'

When they'd finished their meal, they declined

a sweet but ordered two fresh coffees. With those in front of them Jodie suddenly said, 'Are you going to tell me why Derrick isn't too pleased about you taking on the work at Shepperton?'

Though Dee managed a smile, she couldn't meet Jodie's eyes. 'I haven't had the time to write to him so often.'

'You're not telling me the full story, are you? There's more to this than you are letting on. I don't mean to pry, I just think it's queer that Derrick doesn't like you taking on extra work. Didn't you explain that the pay was so much better?'

Dee managed a smile. 'To start off with I was writing to him three or four times a week, but it got a bit much and I couldn't just tell him about our girlie nights out, could I? Apart from that, there was only my work, but Derrick wouldn't be interested in all of that. So I've dropped down to one letter a week.'

'And?' Jodie wasn't satisfied.

'What do you mean, and?'

'Now come on, Dee, either tell me to mind my own business or come clean.'

'I suppose I won't be able to keep it to myself for much longer, so here goes. Derrick has asked me to marry him.' Dee sighed heavily. 'I can't even bring myself to tell my mum and dad. I'm still only nineteen.'

As Jodie looked at her young friend, who had become the nearest thing to a daughter, she felt such an overriding compassion that she had to swallow hard on the lump in her throat. 'Take your time, darling, I'm sorry I pushed you to tell me. But I thought you were almost in love with

Derrick before he went away, weren't you?'

'More than almost,' Dee tearfully admitted. 'I still feel the same way, or at least I think I do, but it is over a year now, and so much has happened. Even in my wildest dreams I didn't think I would have progressed so quickly in the beauty business. Because of you and your encouragement I have such a good life now. I'm not sure I want to be married. Do you understand?'

'Yes, of course.'

'What shall I do?'

'Carry on just as you are, my love. Keep writing to Derrick, but take your time, make him wait for an answer.'

'But how am I going to explain all of this to him?'

'You'll find a way.' Jodie looked at her watch. 'Look, we don't want to waste the rest of this gorgeous day. I think I am going to ask our waiter to call us a cab, which will take us right down to the seafront again. We might even take ourselves on to the pier, and anyway we have to buy a stick of rock for each of the boys or they'll never forgive us.'

After Jodie had told the driver which end of the promenade they wanted to be at, she sank back into her seat, trying to think herself into a calmer state of mind as the holiday traffic thickened around them, making their short journey very slow. Oh you Underwood men, she was saying to herself. Talk about liking their women young! At least Dee was three years older than she herself had been when John had set his sights on her. What would Dee do? She had a good life and a good profession ahead of her, she had already established that much, but would she willingly give it all up? Jodie felt she knew the answer. She closed her eyes and told herself not to interfere.

Dee herself was in two minds as to what she really wanted to do. Well, it didn't really matter, not today at any rate, she told herself. She had time enough to sort things out in her mind before she wrote her next letter to Derrick. She dashed tears from her eyes, wondering what in heaven's name she had to cry about.

The taxi pulled into the kerb. Dee got out and leant against the railings while Jodie paid the driver. 'If I could only see him, spend some more time together, or just hear his voice,' she whispered aloud.

'Hear whose voice?' Jodie asked as she came towards her.

'Oh, no one's. I was just... I was just...' She couldn't think of anything to say and knew she was in danger of bursting into tears.

'It's OK, I understand.' Jodie smiled. 'You miss him, of course you do, but you don't feel as bad as you did when he first went away, and that is because you've worked hard, filled your time up and succeeded beyond your own expectations. But now you're feeling guilty.'

'Oh Jodie, how is it that you can always tell what I'm thinking? You're right, though, I do feel guilty, as if I have neglected Derrick.'

'That's all right, a bit of guilt won't harm you. Just take yer time. Won't be too long now before Derrick will be back and you can get to know him all over again, and *then* will be the time to decide if he is the man you want to spend the rest of your life with.'

'Meanwhile, what do I tell him? He seems to be in a hurry; he's even talked about bringing a ring home with him. It sounds as if he wants us to be married the minute he sets foot in England again.'

Jodie couldn't help it. She was laughing fit to bust. Typical Underwood! Don't do as I do but do as I tell you. Like it or not, she was going to jump in with both feet. Clearing her throat, she took hold of Dee by the shoulders and stared straight into her eyes. 'Dee, I don't have to tell you how much you have come to mean to me, and I will always do the best I can for you. You have a great life ahead of you, but only you yourself can decide what path you are going to take. Married to Derrick Underwood you are never going to want for anything, but then again, as you've already proved, you can easily make a secure life for yourself.' Jodie let the serious look drop and pulled Dee close, holding her tight for a long moment. But as she released her hold she had to have one more stab.

'Dee, you might like to take me as an example. Remember, I was married and had two children before I was the age you are now. I am not saying Derrick is anything like his brother, but surely it's better to be safe than sorry. By the way, have you mentioned any of this to anyone else?'

Dee shook her head. 'No. To be honest, I didn't think that would be a good idea.'

They both thought about that for a while, then Jodie said, 'With weather like this, we're wasting the day standing here. Tell yer what, we'll go on to the pier and have a race: whoever gets to the bar at the far end first buys the drinks.'

'Lucky old you,' Dee said as she straightened herself up. 'You've got flatties on and I've got high heels.'

'Not much luck there then,' Jodie moaned, 'It's a dead cert I'm paying for the drinks.' And before Dee could say anything else Jodie was off like a shot, with Dee trailing behind her.

At least now they both had smiles on their faces again.

10

October had brought with it blustery showers, and folk were upset that the Indian summer had come to an abrupt end and they'd have to dig out their winter clothes again. Today, however, had started off with brilliant sunshine. Michael had asked Dee to do a fortnight at his Eastbourne salon and she hadn't needed any persuasion. As she alighted from the bus at Eastbourne pierhead, she smiled as strands of her hair blew across her face.

'Oh, it's lovely,' she said aloud, taking deep breaths of fresh air, as she watched the white tips of the waves breaking with a splash on the shingle. As she walked the short distance to the salon, her heart was light. She was so lucky, able to walk along by the sea to get to her place of work, fresh clean air to breathe and a modern, up-to-date salon in which to work. And it was all down to having such good friends. As one of the stylists had told her, you were as rich as the number of friends you had. Well in that case, Dee decided, she was pretty well off.

Eastbourne was a good salon to work in. Just three stylists and two apprentices, all nice-natured girls who got on with each other. At eleven o'clock Brenda, the stylist who was permanently stationed at the salon and therefore regarded as being in charge, had sent Rosie along to the local bakery to fetch five buttered barm cakes. Making sure that at all times there were two members of staff on the shop floor to see to the clients, they took turns to go into the back room and have their coffee and barm cake.

Derrick Underwood walked into the small staff room just as Dee was finishing off a conversation on the telephone with Jodie, and by the look on her face as she put the receiver down and stared at him he knew he had done a daft thing.

'Are you all right?' he asked, as he watched the colour drain from Dee's cheeks.

'Er ... well ... if you'll just tell me that you are for real, then maybe I will be.'

'I am so sorry to have startled you. I shouldn't have come here while you are working. Jodie told me not to, she said to wait until this evening to let you know that I am home.'

Dee's eyes were filled with tears. It was such a shock to see Derrick standing there when she hadn't even heard that he had left India. And the situation was no better for Derrick. He was looking hard at this slim young girl, but really the only familiar thing about her was her long silky tresses of reddish hair and those enormous green eyes.

Everything else was different. Even wearing the white smock that apparently was a kind of uniform, she looked elegant, sophisticated, so grownup. He had tried time and time again over the last twenty-odd months to analyse his feelings for her, but the only conclusion he had come to was that he loved Delia Hartfield with every inch of his being. Almost two years with nothing but letters and a few memories had done nothing to dim what he felt. He was home now and he intended to make her his wife.

Delia was like a shy young girl as she stood only a few feet away from him with her arm resting on the mantelshelf. This wasn't a bit like the reunion he had imagined time and time again when he'd been on a late watch and there had been only darkness and the sea all around him. By now she was supposed to have rushed into his arms and he should have been telling her he was never, ever going to let them be parted again.

He hid his disappointment well. Pulled himself up to his full height, and straightened his broad shoulders. 'I'd better get out of here and let you get on with your work. Will it be all right if I come to meet you when you finish this evening?'

Dee had a thousand and one questions she wanted to ask him. She too felt she should have thrown herself into his arms, told him how much she had missed him, but she hadn't been able to do anything like that. Oh, just looking at him had sent her heart pounding against her ribs. He was even taller than she remembered, his hair was just as thick and dark, his skin still smooth and well tanned, yet there was something about him that held her back and she couldn't for the life of her say what it was.

'I'd rather you gave me time to go home and get changed first, if that's all right by you. By the way, where are you staying?' Dee's voice was little more than a croak, and she coughed to clear her throat while she waited for his answer.

'With my mother in Camber Sands. If you're going home, I'll just be next door and I can call for you later.'

Dee gave that some thought. It made sense, though. She hadn't intended to go home; she'd half promised to stay with Jodie while she was working in Eastbourne, but it wasn't much further to travel from Camber Sands than it was from Rye, and it would please her mum and dad.

Sensing what Dee was working out, Derrick spoke up. 'I have several things to do today, visit the bank and suchlike, but I do have a car. First thing I bought when I came ashore. Makes sense for me to pick you up when you finish here.'

'It would please my mother no end, and Dad would be chuffed as well. I don't seem to be at home very often these days,' Dee said, not daring to meet his look eye to eye.

'That's settled then. Pick you up what time?' His smile was so broad it spread from ear to ear.

'Time we clear up, about a quarter to six.'

'OK, see you then.' Two strides and he was gone.

For a moment Dee did not move. She couldn't believe that had really happened. When Derrick had gone away she had cried for days, longed to see him, told herself she couldn't live without him. But since then her life had changed so much.

113

She never had any spare time, but she did have a nice little nest egg of her own tucked away in the building society, money she had earned for herself. As time had passed she hadn't exactly lived the life of a nun. There was one American guy who was responsible for the photographers' apparatus at Shepperton; she'd liked him a lot, he was generous and fun to be with, and when it came to being her dancing partner he'd been sensational. She had been out with him a few times before his mate informed her that he had a wife and two children. That interlude hadn't upset her too much, but it had made her more cautious.

Now Derrick was home. Why hadn't she thrown herself at him? Let him know how pleased she was to see him? Come to that, why hadn't he taken her in his arms? He must have felt as awkward as she did.

Brenda put her head around the door and said quietly, 'Dee, I hate to interrupt, but you have a lady ready to come out of the dryer, and Mrs Holmes has arrived for her perm.'

Dee virtually shook herself, had a quick glance in the mirror that hung on the wall, patted her hair and followed Brenda out into the salon. 'I'm sorry,' she whispered. 'It was a shock him turning up like that so unexpectedly. I didn't mean to take such a long break.'

'Not to worry, Dee. I only got a quick glimpse of him, but he could turn up on my doorstep any day of the week without warning.'

Both girls laughed, then straightened up and got on with the task of making their ladies feel that a visit to the hairdresser's was a better tonic than anything one could buy at the chemist's.

It was five forty-five on the dot when Dee stood on the pavement beside Brenda and watched her lock up the salon for the night. Derrick had managed to park his car right outside the premises and was now standing next to it waiting for her.

'He certainly is tall, dark and handsome,' Brenda laughed as she began to walk slowly away from Dee. 'See you in the morning, if you can tear yourself away.'

'Oh, I'll be here, never fear. I wouldn't dream of letting Mitch down.'

Derrick had the passenger door open and was waiting to hand her into the seat. 'Sorry for springing myself on you like that this morning, and thanks for letting me come to meet you.' His words sounded stilted, unnatural, almost as if he were apologising to a stranger.

Within seconds he was seated in the driver's seat, but he made no move to start the car, just sat there staring ahead. Then suddenly, out of the blue, he took her hand and very seriously said, 'I wish we could turn the clock back to how we were before I left.'

Dee knew instantly what he meant. They'd had that kind of easy rapport that was clearly defined. 'It's OK.' She squeezed his hand, and as he turned the key in the ignition, she was amazed at how relaxed she suddenly felt as she snuggled back in her seat. The journey home would take about fifty minutes, and from time to time he took his eyes off the road to turn and smile at her. He didn't push her to start a conversation, didn't question her as to what work she had been doing or ask about the qualifications she had acquired. He just seemed really happy that she was sitting next to him in his car. She was grateful for that. By the time they were passing through Hastings, Dee was thinking back to when she'd been sixteen. Recalling the fun she had had with him, the way he could make her laugh, the dances on the end of Eastbourne pier. How he'd whirled her around the floor so expertly and she had thought him to be so dashing and worldly. How old had she been when he had left England? Almost eighteen. It seemed a lifetime away, and yet it was less than two years.

The window on Dee's side of the car was open, and a few tendrils of her red hair were fluttering around her face. She was doing her best to keep looking ahead, but every now and again her eyes swivelled sideways to study Derrick. Was he really here? It felt good, too good to be true really, and oh, he was such a big, handsome man. Suddenly she had a yearning to do what she should have done the minute he had walked into that staff room, throw her arms around him and kiss him. It was a bit late to think of it now, though, so she controlled herself and kept her eyes on the road ahead. All the same, she now felt excited and optimistic about the evening that lay ahead.

It seemed no time at all before Derrick was pulling up outside her parents' house. 'How long do you need to change?'

Dee understood from the tone of his voice that he didn't want to come indoors with her and have to face a barrage of questions from her mother. She felt she had to laugh as she said, 'Will you give me half an hour?'

'Of course,' he grinned, 'but don't linger, and don't eat anything. I've booked a table at a pub down in Rye.'

Mary Hartfield hadn't put the light on in her front room, but the street lighting had just come on and it was enough illumination for her to see Derrick's car pull up. She watched as he and her daughter got out. Her heart felt light, and she was pleased to see them together but she still had so many misgivings. All the Underwood men were too fond of roaming for her liking; they seemed to spend more time at sea than they did on land.

Dee went straight through the hallway and into the kitchen to where her dad was sitting in his big armchair reading the evening paper. He immediately folded it up and put it down by the side of his chair, then stood with his arms spread wide, ready to hug his daughter. 'Derrick found you then,' he smiled. 'I told him Jodie would know where you were working this week.'

Having kissed her father Dee said, 'Yes, he found me. Gave me a bit of a shock, though, turning up like that.'

'But you were pleased to see him, weren't you?' her father asked sharply.

'What a daft question.' His wife had just come into the kitchen and was bristling with curiosity as to what had taken place at this first meeting after such a long absence.

Dee sensed the questions coming, and she sidestepped them by saying, 'Of course I was over the moon to see him, Dad, but I only have a few minutes to get washed and changed, because he's taking me out to dinner.' With that she gathered up her bags and headed for the stairs.

Mary sighed heavily. 'We hardly ever get to see our Delia these days. God alone knows where she sleeps half the time, and when she does put in an appearance it's like a ruddy whirlwind has passed through the house and then she's gone again.'

'Come and sit down, Mary love, and let's try and be happy for our girl. It doesn't matter what we say or do; you must know by now that she is going to make her own decisions and go her own sweet way.' He ended his speech almost triumphantly. But Mary was still going to have the last word.

'Yes, and if it all goes wrong, it will be us that's left to pick up the pieces.'

Half an hour later Dee opened her front door and was not surprised to see that Derrick was waiting by the side of the car. One look at him and she found herself taking a sharp intake of breath. He was wearing dark brown cord trousers, a fawn cashmere jumper and a camel-coloured jacket, and she couldn't help but notice the leather slip-on shoes. Casual but expensive, it said to her. As always, though, it was his striking good looks that set her heart racing.

She too had made an effort, albeit very rushed; she hoped the result was good. Derrick had said they were going to a pub, and because she knew that the pubs in Rye were in the main very olde worlde, she hadn't wanted to wear anything too outrageous. Having taken pains over her make-up, she decided to leave her long hair hanging free, only tying it back with the aid of a black velvet bow. After much deliberation she finally settled on a classic black dress that she had bought in one rash moment when on a visit to London with Jodie. They had just received their first month's pay cheque from Shepperton Studios and had agreed that splashing out on themselves for once was well in order.

The material of the dress was soft to the touch, a very lightweight velvet, with long sleeves and a scooped neckline trimmed with dark green satin and tiny silver beads that highlighted her green eyes. She hadn't bothered with a jacket, but had wound a soft silk scarf around her neck, allowing the long end to trail in front of the dress. The scarf was silver, with fine threads of emerald green woven into it, an amazing match with the decoration on the neck of the dress. Black silk stockings and three-inch-heeled black court shoes gave the finishing touch. 'You'll do,' she'd murmured to her reflection in the long cheval mirror. A quick spray of the expensive perfume that had been a birthday present from Jodie, and she'd picked up her silver clutch bag and went downstairs.

The minute Derrick saw her he burst into life, covering the few yards between them in seconds. 'My God, you look fantastic,' he said, drawing her into his arms for a long, lingering kiss which had Dee reeling. Too taken aback to say anything, she allowed him to lead her to the car and see her safely settled in the passenger seat.

The Royal Oak had its own parking area at the back of the premises and it was much easier to come into the dining room through the back entrance. Derrick had left nothing to chance: a small vase of red roses was set in the middle of their table and a bottle of champagne stood in an ice bucket to one side.

'Tell me about everything you've achieved in all these months that I've been away,' Derrick suggested as their starter dishes were cleared away and they were waiting for their main course to be served.

'I've kept you informed by writing letters, rather more than you've ever sent to me. So I think it only fair that you go first and bring me up to date about what you've been doing and where you intend to go from here.'

Derrick laughed heartily. 'Passing the buck, are you? Well, my contract with British India Shipping Lines was all right but a bit boring, so for the time being I have taken a shore job.' He paused, noticing that his last remark had put a smile on Dee's face. 'Does that please you, Dee?'

'Of course it does, it means that we'll have more time to get to know each other,' she ventured timidly.

Derrick didn't like the sound of that. Was she trying to stall him? He felt he knew all he needed to know about her and he wanted to make her his wife sooner rather than later. Already from talking to Jodie he had learnt how successful Delia had been in more ways than one, and the last thing he wanted was for her to decide that she didn't want to get married because she was going to be her own boss with a flourishing business. He decided it was time for the champagne to be opened and he signalled a waiter to do just that.

'I have already obtained details of a house on the

120

outskirts of Pompey which is up for a year's rental. The job involves working for the Royal Navy but on the army side at Portsmouth, clearing rifle ranges.'

'How long have you been home, Derrick?' Dee asked, sounding wary. 'From what you're telling me, it sounds as if you've been back a while and more than likely that you've left the Merchant Navy.'

It was Derrick's turn to tread cautiously. He knew he was going to have to own up. 'I have been back in England for about ten days, but there were so many arrangements to make that I decided to clear everything up before I made any attempt to meet up with you. No way have I broken contact with the Merchant Navy, but for the next few weeks at least I am as free as a bird, can see you every day, take you out and about to different places.'

'Oh no you can't,' Dee retorted sharply. 'I have commitments and business arrangements that I can't just drop because you want to be with me every day.'

They were each saved from saying something they might have regretted by two waiters arriving with their main course. Throughout the rest of the meal the conversation was unnatural, as they carefully skirted round any subject that might cause offence. Both of them refused sweet, but Derrick asked for Stilton cheese and water biscuits, while Dee drained her wine glass and ordered a black coffee.

Things weren't going as they should. Dee felt that so many thoughts were roaming around in her head, and more than half of them didn't make sense. First off, why would Derrick have been in the country for ten days and never bothered to get in touch with her? Couldn't he have picked up a telephone, even if he had been too busy to meet up with her?

'I'm going to the ladies',' she said, wrapping her long scarf around her shoulders and picking up her clutch bag.

'OK, I'll settle the bill and I'll be waiting in the hallway.'

Somehow tension had set in between them, and it wasn't nice, not on their first night together. Could Derrick be keeping more secrets from her? Dee washed her hands and looked in the mirror. She decided that her hair was all right but her lipstick needed repairing. As she touched up her make-up, she told herself they might just as well go straight home. It was too cold to walk about, and the edginess that had sprung up between them was not going to go away unless they could be absolutely honest with each other. Far better to leave more questions and answers until another day.

In the hallway, Derrick put his arm around her shoulders and drew her close to his side. 'It's very cold out there, but I can put the heaters on in the car and we should be warm enough. Is there anywhere in particular you would like to go?'

'I thought maybe you should take me home. I have been at work all day and I have an early start tomorrow, which reminds me, I must ask my dad the time of the first bus into Eastbourne now that the winter service has started.'

Derrick didn't loosen his hold on her as he held the exit door open with his foot and almost marched her to the car. He had to take his arm from around her to unlock the door, and he left her to get in on her own while he walked around to the other side and got into the driver's seat.

'Why do you need to know about buses? I'm right next door. I have to be out and about early; I'll take you in by car.'

'Thank you,' she murmured.

Not a single word passed between them as he drove away down the main street of Rye. He had only been driving for about fifteen minutes when he saw a vacant parking space along the side of Rye Harbour. He carefully manoeuvred the car into the space and switched the engine off.

The night sky was clear and studded with stars and the water in the harbour was flecked with white froth. This had been Dee's playground when she had been a child. It held such happy memories, and without thinking she let out a sad sigh.

'Dee, I am so sorry we seem to have got off on the wrong foot,' Derrick said, sounding full of remorse. 'If we sit here a while, will you let me explain why I didn't contact you the minute I was home?'

Dee raised her head to look at him, not allowing herself to speak for fear of saying the wrong thing.

Derrick plunged in. 'First off, I have taken the final exams that will allow me to be named as a master mariner and enable me to take charge of any cargo ship. My father always said that oil was the future, and he was right; fortunes will be made when more oil rigs are up and in operation. Sorry,

Dee, I'm getting carried away. What I am trying to tell you is that if I pass all my exams, I won't need to take the job on shore because I've made sure there is another string to my bow. A fantastic job I've lined up with a Dutch firm who have no objection to wives travelling with the masters of their ships. We'll not only start out with good pay but we shall see the world together. Will you trust me, darling? Leave all future arrangements until I get my results? I don't want to count my chickens before they're hatched.' The smile he gave her as he finished speaking, and the pleading look that went with it, was enough to melt her heart. 'I do have just one question for you,' he said softly. 'Dee, do you feel anything for me?'

'Of course I do,' she said indignantly. 'But please be patient with me, give me time. I still can't quite believe you really are back home,' she said, reaching out to touch his face gently.

Suddenly his arms were around her and he was kissing her. Dee was startled at first, but not unpleasantly so. Derrick's lips were soft and warm, and between kisses she liked the way one of his hands was caressing the side of her face. The tingle she felt down her spine was a warm, good feeling. It was awkward to get really close to each other because they were still seated in the car, so without even being really aware of what she was doing, she climbed over to sit in his lap and nestled deep into his arms.

His kisses grew intense and he was holding her so tight; then his hand moved and he was fondling her breast, and Dee felt she was on cloud nine. So many times she had imagined an even-

124

ing such as this. True, after Derrick had been gone a while, the longing for him had lessened. But now, the very nearness of him, the manly smell and the way he was kissing her with such tenderness made her feel just as she had when she first met him as an innocent sixteen-year-old.

How long they sat there huddled together she didn't know, but she knew she didn't want it to stop. Every part of her body was tingling, wanting more than kissing but afraid to pull away in case the wonder of it all came to an end.

It was Derrick who drew away first. He placed his hands one each side of her face and looked deep into her eyes. 'I know I should give you more time,' he whispered, 'but please, Dee, will you be my wife? I don't ever want to let you go again. I want us to spend the rest of our lives together.'

Gently she took hold of his hand. 'Derrick, please let me get used to having you back before we start making decisions.'

'You aren't saying you don't want to be my wife, are you?' he said, catching her fiercely by her shoulders. 'I love you so much, Dee, you do believe that, don't you?'

'Please, Derrick, will you just listen to me.' Her tone of voice was now quite forceful and she pulled herself to sit up straight before saying, 'I am not saying I won't marry you. I am just asking that you show some patience, stop trying to rush me. Just let me enjoy the fact that I have you back here with me again.'

'Don't have much choice, do I?' he said sadly. 'OK, I'll wait. But if I come to thinking you're stringing me along, I will take the first command

I can get and take myself off to the other side of the world. I will, I mean it,' he said, looking at her sternly. 'I really do love you, Dee, and I will never, ever get enough of you. Please, darling, don't keep me waiting too long for your answer.'

They stayed in the car talking, touching and caressing each other. Now and again he kissed her, but the fiery passion was no longer evident and his kisses were very gentle, almost as if he were afraid to let his real feelings show.

Much later that night, when she was in bed, Dee closed her eyes and relived the events of the evening. Derrick's kisses had been wonderful, and she savoured again the delightful sensation of being in his arms. Then without warning a thought came into her head, and she shuddered. They had come very close to having a row! And on the very first occasion she'd seen him for almost two years. What did that say to her? That they hardly knew one another?

Derrick knew exactly what he wanted and was determined to get his own way. Oh yes, his plans certainly included her, but only if she went along with his itinerary, which meant that no adjustment would be made if her own plans didn't quite fit in with his.

Did she really want to get married? Abandon everything she had worked to achieve? One thought led to another. It had not been easy; on several of the courses she had enrolled herself on she had felt incredibly lonely, isolated in a strange town and wondering why on earth she was pushing herself so hard. There had been days when she hadn't even found the time to brush her teeth, let alone write a lengthy letter to Derrick, but she had never left it longer than a week. For her it had all been about gaining certificates and credentials, without which she never would have got anywhere in the powerful world of beauty technology. Mainly because of television, this line of work had grown at a fast pace, and she felt proud to be part of it. She had, with a lot of help from Jodie, earned that privilege.

Did she want to give it all up?

Did she want to become a married woman?

Most important of all, did she really love Derrick?

As she turned her bedside light off and snuggled down to sleep, she felt guilty about her mixed-up emotions.

11

Dee was exhausted. She had tossed and turned all night, closing her eyes yet hardly sleeping a wink. She had to make it plain to Derrick that she herself had business commitments that had to be honoured. In a way she was dreading the drive to Eastbourne; it was kind of Derrick to offer to take her, but what the atmosphere in the car would be like this morning she dreaded to think.

There was a knocking on the front door. Derrick was early, but she was ready. She had dressed carefully in the very palest blue pleated tunic, cut like a tennis dress, with a white silk open-necked blouse underneath, and her new flesh-coloured nylons worn today with soft flat-heeled shoes. No one with any sense would dream of attempting to do a day's work in a hairdressing salon wearing high heels; backache was a bad enough problem as it was. She had a woolly cardigan in her bag if it should be cold in the salon, but she wasn't going to let Derrick see her wearing that. She had railed and complained when he had said he wanted to see her every day, but feeling she had been unkind, she was ready to at least meet him halfway.

Derrick sped round the car as she came out from the house.

'You are even more beautiful than I remembered, Dee. In fact you have grown into a really lovely young woman, you know.'

He spoke very softly, yet Dee felt that his words were sincere.

'Well thank you, Derrick,' she said, blushing a little.

So, they had got off on the right foot this morning, but how long would it last? It was as Derrick was driving down the steep hill into Hastings that he said, 'Dee, do you think you can have a husband and a career?'

'Is there something in your book of rules that says I can't?' she asked, sounding sarcastic without meaning to.

'Well,' he sighed, 'not if your husband is a master mariner who is set to sail the high seas.' He turned his head slightly and she could see he was grinning.

'You've had your results?'

'Yup, telephone call late last night and firm

confirmation early this morning.'

'Congratulations, Derrick, I bet your mother is bursting with pride.'

'Yes, I think she is. That's two of us that have made it to the top. Pity about our John. He should be due home any day now.' He almost added, in time for our wedding, but decided not to push his luck.

'Dee, what I mostly want is for you to share the life this success will bring me. Great ships, good living accommodation wherever we end up, servants to wait on us, private education for our children.'

'Whoa, Master Mariner, don't go getting ahead of yourself, though to be honest you sound just a bit like the letters that Jodie and I have been receiving from Laraine. She and Richard certainly seem to be enjoying a high old life.'

'Look, we're coming into Eastbourne. Before I leave you, there is something I want to ask you.'

Not another proposal of marriage, was Dee's first thought.

She was wrong.

'Could you try and get Saturday off work? I would very much like you to come with me to London for the weekend. We would be staying with some old friends of mine and you would have a bedroom of your own.'

The stylists in Michael's salons only worked one Saturday in three, and they often switched the weeks around to suit each other, so there was no problem there, but Dee wasn't going to reply in haste.

'Please try, Dee, I am going to stay out of your

way for the rest of this week, but I could pick you up early on Saturday morning. We'd have two whole days up in the smoke and I'll get you back in time for work on Monday. What do you think?'

'Can you give me today to sort something out?' Dee asked, frowning a little.

'Of course. By this evening I will have more information myself. There are only two small things I have to attend to whilst in London, and the rest of the time I shall devote myself to you. By the way, where will you be staying this week? I need a telephone number to be able to contact you.'

'Try Jodie's number tonight, it's more than likely I shall be staying there, but if not, she'll know where I am.'

'Do you keep clothes and suchlike at Jodie's house all the time?' Derrick asked, curiosity getting the better of him.

Dee laughed. 'Of course I do, Jodie's cottage is my second home.'

'What about when John is home?'

'What about John, you may well ask. It's ages since Jodie heard a word from him. Richard thinks more of Lenny and Reggie than their own father does; he has sent them mail and presents from everywhere he's been, which is more than John has ever done.'

'Hmm,' Derrick said thoughtfully, feeling a trifle guilty, although he had sent Jodie money orders for his nephews' birthdays.

As he drew the car to a halt outside the salon, he turned to Dee and said, 'We'll speak on the phone tonight, wherever you are.' He got out of the car and came around to stand in front of her. 'I'll carry these cases to the door for you,' he offered.

Once he had put the cases down, he drew her into the shelter of the salon doorway. 'I shall miss you, Dee. Please try and be free to come with me at the weekend.'

'I'll do my best,' she whispered, knowing full well that come hell or high water, nothing was going to prevent her spending this weekend with him.

Slowly he wrapped his arms around her and pulled her close. His lips felt different in the light of day; they were warm and soft but at the same time satisfying and full of promise. Inside the salon the three young ladies sighed as one as they gazed through the shop's side window, but it was the young apprentice who summed it up for all of them.

'Cor, what a fella! He could put his shoes under my bed any night.'

During the course of the day, Dee's thoughts were all over the place. It didn't take much for her to realise that life with Derrick would never be dull. Being married to him would offer her safety and yet also excitement and entirely new wonderful experiences. Was she ready for all of that? As things stood at the moment, she had little chance of being able to answer her own question.

She had to put up with a lot of teasing from her workmates during the day, and as the time to close the shop drew nearer, she began to feel a tinge of regret. She'd decided she was going straight to Jodie's, where she knew a warm welcome would be waiting, but it meant quite a long bus ride into Rye. Shouldn't have cut off your nose to spite your face, she hastily told herself. You could have had a car and driver every morning and every evening for the rest of this week if you hadn't been so pig-headed.

Even the weather wasn't on her side. It had been a cold but dry day, yet as she got off the bus down by the harbour the rain started, and not just a drizzle but pelting it down in sheets. She hastened her steps as much as she could, but she was carrying a case and her large bag holding her work smocks that needed washing and ironing. As she struggled to get her key into the lock, the door was suddenly flung open and she was being given a rowdy welcome by both Lenny and Reggie.

'Auntie Dee, we knew you were coming 'cos Uncle Derrick has been here today and he brought us some smashing presents. He brought a parcel for Mum as well and he left one for you but we're not supposed to tell you about yours until after we've all had our dinner.'

'For goodness' sake let Auntie Dee get in the door before you mob her,' their mother was shouting up the hall. The pandemonium lasted another good ten minutes, during which Dee had to admire the biggest set of mechanical toy motors and lorries she had ever seen. 'And we've got a big garage that goes with these,' Lenny informed her, with Reggie quick to add, 'But we can't play with the garage till someone helps us put it together.'

'Here, dry yourself off. You look like a drowned rat,' Jodie laughed as she threw a large towel to Dee. 'Dinner isn't quite ready, but I've uncorked a bottle of wine and we can have a drink while we're waiting.' She was already reaching up to take two glasses out of the cupboard.

Once seated comfortably either side of a roaring coal fire, each with a drink in their hand, Jodie made the opening remark. 'Poor Derrick, I hear you sent him away wondering if he has a future with you or not.'

'So, he opened his heart to you, did he? Bit melodramatic even for him, wasn't it?'

'Well, you tell me your side of the story. I'm all ears.'

'If you must know, to start off he was telling me all the things he had already lined up, and suddenly I felt he was making a fool of me. There is no way he could have done half of what he was talking about if he had only just got back. In the end I got him to confess that his ship had docked ten days ago.'

'And on the basis of that, you told him you wouldn't be able to see him all week and you weren't sure that you wanted to marry him?'

'Well yes, to be truthful, that's it in a nutshell.'

Jodie threw back her head and roared with laughter. When she had calmed herself down she said, 'Oh Dee, you take the ship's biscuit, you really do. Only a while ago in Brighton you were crying because you were longing to hear his voice. He turns up in the flesh, larger than life I'd say, and you start playing the game of hard to get.'

'So, you heard his side of the story and you've made up your mind that I'm a silly young girl who doesn't know what's good for her.'

'That's what it sounded like to me.'

'Well you can hear my side of it now. He took it for granted that I'm going to drop everything and

133

sail away into the blue horizon with him. Never mind that I have worked my socks off, done everything you advised me to do, got all my credentials, and for what, a rushed wedding and the right to be known as Mrs Derrick Underwood.'

'That's what Laraine did, and from her letters it sounds as if she's living in a dream world.'

'You probably thought the same thing when you were sixteen years old and John got you pregnant and married you. And as you so often point out to me, Jodie, you had your two boys before your eighteenth birthday.'

'Well there you are, Delia my lovely. You've got two brothers and their wives and two completely different outcomes, so whether or not you decide you want to be the bride of the third brother is entirely up to you. You've got two canvases to look at and your own blank canvas to do with as you wish.'

'Oh Jodie, I thought you would be so willing to tell me what to do, and all you've done is left me floundering.'

'I will tell you one thing before we leave it alone for tonight. I think you've boxed very clever, keeping him at arm's length for a while. You've the rest of the week to think over what your options are, and then I think you should go to London with him for the weekend, meet some of his friends, see how he spends his leisure time.'

'Mum, we're starving, isn't dinner ready yet?'

'Sorry, Lenny.' Jodie was on her feet like a shot. 'You and Reggie go and wash your hands, and by the time you've sat up to the table, dinner will be ready for me to serve up.'

Jodie and Dee looked at each other, and it would have been hard to say who laughed first. 'We haven't exactly come up with a satisfactory conclusion,' Jodie remarked. 'You refill our glasses while I dish up the food, and later on we might see things a lot clearer.'

And we might not, Dee thought as she did as Jodie had suggested. Having filled their glasses again, she realised the bottle was almost empty. Laughing to herself, she murmured, 'If we carry on like this during the course of the evening, whatever decisions we make might not be watertight.'

While Jodie was busy dishing up the meal, her mind was going in two different directions. She felt that Dee was a far gentler soul than she was, but then she herself had been on her own for a long time. Even when John had been based in Portsmouth, he'd never had a hand in running the household or seeing to the boys. Making family decisions had not been one of his strong points. The result was that Jodie was strong and unafraid, and sure of her own ideas. She had had to be courageous about making decisions and standing up to people. It had got her into trouble sometimes, but she'd become used to it, even though at times the going had been tough.

She loved Dee, she really did, but there was only so much advice she could give her. The time had come for the girl to make her own choices.

She only hoped that she would make the right ones.

12

For the remainder of the week Dee's moods swung from high to low and back again. Even Jodie reminded her, more than once, that it was her own fault that she hadn't seen Derrick, and she breathed a hefty sigh of relief when on Thursday evening Dee came off the phone with a wide grin on her face.

'Have you at last told him you will go away with him for the weekend?' Jodie wanted to be sure, and she waited for the answer with bated breath.

'Yes I have, and oh Jodie, he sounded so pleased.'

'I expect he was. You've run rings round him and you're lucky that he's stood for it.'

'Don't be like that, Jodie. He was home for ten days without contacting me.'

'So is the silly game between you two over for now?' Jodie asked, feeling she would like to knock both of their heads together.

'Yes it is,' Dee admitted sheepishly. 'Tomorrow Derrick is going to meet me from work and take me home; that will give me the chance to sort out what clothes I'm going to take with me and we'll be able to get a really early start on Saturday morning.'

'Right, well let's make the most of your last evening of freedom. Is there anything you would like to do, perhaps go out somewhere?'

'Thanks for the offer, Jodie, but I'd like to stay

in, play a few games with the boys, if that's all right with you.'

'Of course it is. Dinner is all ready to dish up, so if we eat now and then clear the table, we can get a few games in before it's time for the boys to go to bed.'

Dee and Jodie were laughing as they dealt out the cards. It meant a lot that things between Derrick and Delia were now on a much better footing, and Jodie was pleased for both of them.

'You wait until you're married, you'll be off around the world and I will hardly ever get to see you,' she told Dee, pretending to be heartbroken.

Lenny got down from his chair and ran to Dee. 'Auntie Dee, I don't want you to go round the world. I like having you here when we come home from school, and even more so when you spend Saturday and Sunday with us.'

'Lenny, you little love, I'm not going anywhere for a very long time, except for this weekend, when I am going to London. Anyhow, did you and Reggie know that the big foreign circus is coming to Eastbourne next week?'

'There are some posters about it which were pasted up on the wall in our school,' Reggie was quick to tell her.

'I know,' Dee said, a cheeky grin spreading across her face, 'and I just happen to have four tickets in my handbag, so I think that means that we shall all be going, don't you?'

The two lads looked at their mother. When she nodded her head, they laughed out loud and Dee hugged them both to her.

Jodie watched them and sighed happily. Delia

was all right now, more relaxed than she had been for some time. For months on end she had done nothing but concentrate on work, ever eager to gain more qualifications, but now Derrick was offering her an entirely different way of life. Whether she chose to take it or not had to be her own decision.

But what if Dee did marry Derrick straight away? He'd whisk her off at the drop of a hat, he had said as much in no uncertain terms. Well, there was nothing she could do about that. Half of her would be thrilled to bits knowing that Dee was leading a full life. On the other hand she would miss her like hell and so would Lenny and Reggie, and they wouldn't be the only ones.

Oh well, we will all just have to accept it, she decided, as she heaved a heavy sigh. They had no alternative; it had to be Delia's decision.

'Make sure you have a good time,' Jack Hartfield whispered as he hugged his daughter and kissed her cheek. Dee too spoke in hushed tones as she said goodbye to her father, because it was still only half past seven on this Saturday morning and her mother was still asleep

It was still only autumn yet it felt like winter and there had been a heavy frost during the night. Dee smiled happily up at Derrick as he made sure that the new travelling rug, which had come with the car, was wrapped well and truly around her knees. He drove carefully; they were in no hurry and the local roads had not been gritted. As they left Sussex behind and were motoring through Surrey, Dee thought the countryside looked a picture. Some trees still had green foliage, others had bare branches, while many shrubs were covered in red berries. Did that mean that nature was providing food for the birds in preparation for a bad winter? She instinctively shivered.

'Are you cold, Dee?' Derrick asked with a hint of concern in his voice.

'No,' she laughed, 'just contemplating a bad winter.'

'Well, who knows, maybe before a really bad spell sets in, you and I will be up and away to a lovely warm sunny climate.'

Dee decided not to pursue this line of conversation. Instead she remarked how the scenery was changing already.

'Well, we are coming into Wimbledon, which is classed as south London.' The shops were all open, and barrow boys were lining the edge of the pavements with their fruit and vegetable stalls. The nearer to London they got, the darker the day seemed, the buildings taller, the streets more narrow and hardly any trees or green grass to be seen. She got her first view of the great wide river Thames as Derrick drove over Vauxhall Bridge.

Twenty minutes later he drove into the courtyard of what looked like a large tenement building. When Dee got out of the car and looked around, she received a shock. This particular block they were standing outside was four storeys tall, but it was thrown into the shade by three enormous high-rise blocks of flats nearby. God knows how many floors there were to each of them. She stretched her neck and threw her head back, and still she was unable to count them. Do people really have to live like this? she wondered. Although she realised that these three blocks had been built since the end of the war, already they were dirty and soot-ingrained and not in the least attractive. At that moment it didn't seem as if any sunlight could ever penetrate this area.

'Hey, Derrick, leave yer cases, Tom is coming out t'give you a hand.' Coming towards them was a small, fat woman, a colourful apron wrapped around her body and her arms bare to the elbows. Following behind her was a tall, dark-haired, swarthy-looking man stretching his arms above his head.

'Sorry, Del boy, didn't hear yer drive up, I was 'aving a bit of a kip. It's great to see yer. Dolly 'eard yer though; not much she misses, but then it's not often she moves away from the bloody window.'

During this exchange Dee stood aside and continued to look about her, but she had only had time to notice the number of young lads that were leaning against the walls of the flats, all of them smoking cigarettes, when the woman said, 'And you, m'dear, you must be the Delia Hartfield we've 'eard so much about. I'm Dorothy Grainger but my friends call me Dolly.'

'Yes, I am, but *my* friends call me Dee.' Delia brought her eyes to meet those of this homely-looking woman, and she knew straight off that she was going to like her.

'Come on, lass, we can finish the introductions inside. Kettle's on, you could do with a cup of tea, I bet, and there's a few jars in fer you, Del.'

Dee couldn't look at Derrick for fear that she would laugh. Oh, not in an unkind way, but it did

140

sound queer to hear him referred to as Del boy! She followed Dolly up six stone steps to the front entrance. 'We're on the first floor and count ourselves lucky that we are,' Dolly was explaining as she pushed her front door open wide.

Dee followed her through a little square hall and into a front room where a fire was burning brightly and everything was warm, shining and comfortable. She couldn't believe it; the interior was so very different to what the outside of the building had led her to believe.

'Dee, it's time I introduced you to a very old mate of mine,' Derrick said as he entered this lovely comfortable room. 'Tom Grainger was a stoker with the Merchant Navy during the years of the war. He managed to survive what the Jerries threw at him, though he had some frightful near misses, but unfortunately the furnaces got to his chest, and he is now a man of leisure.'

'That's enough of your sarcasm, me old mate. Jealous of the large pension I get, are you?' Without waiting for a reply, he turned to Dee, gave her a playful wink and said, 'I'm more than pleased to meet you, Delia, an' I hope you'll enjoy this couple of days with Dolly and me.'

'I'm sure I shall, and will you please call me Dee.'

'Course I will, luv, as long as you call me Tom.' They both laughed, and Dee could see why Derrick had made a friend of this older man. As for his wife, Dee had no qualms; already Dolly was placing a large brown teapot on a table set for four people.

As Dolly poured the tea she talked. 'We'll have a

bite to eat now, and tonight Tom has booked us into the British Legion Hall. It's a special night, be a good dinner and a great show to follow, all in aid of charity.' She handed a cup and saucer to Dee and told her to help herself to food, then almost without drawing breath she went on. 'You're a lovely-looking lass but I don't know that you're cut out to be a mariner's wife. You're thin. You could do with a bit of this.' She patted her own stomach.

This quick change in the conversation made Dee smile. 'What exactly does a mariner's wife have to do?' she asked.

'Well, you'd need to get used to foreigners and foreign food and God knows what weather you'll come up against. Ask my Tom, he'll tell yer. He once spent weeks on end up in the Arctic towing away icebergs that were blocking the shipping lanes.'

It was on the tip of Dee's tongue to ask if he had done all that on his own, but she checked herself. This woman was friendly enough and Dee was sure she was well-meaning, but she wouldn't be used to the kind of teasing that went on between Jodie, Laraine and herself and many more of their friends. The last thing she wanted to do was upset Dolly after the wonderful reception they had received. So she contented herself by asking another question. 'Do many wives accompany their husbands?'

'Not a great many, I'd imagine, but that is something I don't really know much about. Tom was only ever a merchant seaman. I would think it's only a privilege granted to a captain or a first mate. Now come on, Dee, help yerself t'some food, or isn't there anything on the table that you like?'

'Thank you,' Dee said. 'I've been too busy draining my teacup, I was that parched, but I will have something to eat now.' Dolly passed her a large dinner plate and Dee took a slice of ham and a piece of bacon and egg pie which Dolly assured her she had made herself. She insisted that Dee take some salad and a bread roll too. 'Is that all you're going to eat?' she asked as she passed her the dish of butter.

Dee was saved from answering as a young lad came panting into the room. 'Grandad, there's ever such a posh car parked outside your steps and all me mates want to know if the owner wants them to guard it.'

Tom was on his feet like a shot. 'I'll come outside with you, Kenny. That car is going to be here for two days, and if there is so much as a single scratch on it when the owner comes to leave, then it will be Gawd 'elp the bloody lot of you young hooligans.'

Dee looked at Derrick and they both looked at Dolly, then all three of them burst out laughing. 'Still thinks he's the king of the walk, does my Tom,' Dolly spluttered.

'And rightly so.' Derrick nodded quickly. 'Pity there aren't a few more like him about.'

It was some time later when Dolly stood up and asked, 'Are you sure there is nothing more I can get for any of you?'

They all replied that they had eaten their fill, and it was left to Dee to say that she had enjoyed every morsel.

'Well I expect you'd like to have a wash an'

brush-up. Would you like to come through an' I'll show you where you'll be sleeping.' She picked up Dee's coat and put it over her arm, and Dee followed her along the long hall to the end. There Dolly opened a door, saying over her shoulder, 'I hope you'll be comfortable.'

Dee walked into the room. Then, turning quickly, she looked at this jolly woman and murmured, 'What a beautiful bedroom.'

There was a gas fire standing in the tiled grate, and the furniture was old-fashioned but solid and shining. The bed was a single one covered with a patchwork quilt, with large brass knobs at the foot and head posts. A thick eiderdown was folded in half at the bottom of the bed, and three big plump pillows were piled at the head. The floor was covered with linoleum, and each side of the bed there was a colourful rug.

'I'll show you where the bathroom is, and the other rooms if you'd like to see them.' Without waiting for an answer, Dolly went on, 'I expect you're wondering how come the council gave us this big flat when there's only the two of us. When we first moved in here, we'd three kids under the age of five and we'd all been living in two rooms since they were born. I 'ad to pinch meself every morning to make sure it was all real, 'cos it seemed like Buckingham Palace to me at the time.'

'And are the children all married now?' Dee felt she had to ask.

'Our daughter Connie is. Her husband Bert is a good bloke and that was their boy Kenny you just saw. They live in those newish high-rise flats. Our two sons were both killed in the war.'

Dee felt her heart miss a beat. How sad to lose two sons! She felt she wanted to take Dolly into her arms, but she hadn't that much courage. She felt tears pricking at the back of her eyelids.

The other two bedrooms were both larger than the one she was to occupy, both furnished along similar lines, one with a double bed and the other with twin beds. She guessed that one must have been the boys' bedroom.

'You have a lovely home here,' she murmured, wishing she could find words to express her sympathy for the loss of the Graingers' two sons.

'Yeah, well like my Tom is fond of saying, a home is what you make it, and that is always mainly down to the woman. But one thing is for sure, there are worse places than this to live. Anyhow, I'll leave yer to freshen yerself up. Come through when you're ready. Oh, there is one thing, Tom might want to persuade Derrick to go to football with him this afternoon. Would you mind if he went?'

'No, of course I wouldn't.'

'Well, we'll see. It's just that West Ham are playing at Upton Park and Arsenal at Highbury. When the boys were here, there would always be an argument. Each lad followed a different club and their father always tried to keep the peace and go to whichever... Ah well, if they do go to see a match, would you like me to take you down to Chapel Street Market?'

'That would be nice, if you're sure you want to go out,' Dee answered cheerfully.

It was one o'clock when the two women set out,

the men having left a good hour earlier. 'We've only to walk t'the Elephant and Castle and Chapel Street is just a few minutes away.' Dee's face must have shown her puzzlement, because Dolly laughed, saying, 'Elephant and Castle is a tube station. Ain't yer never travelled on the tube?'

'The tube? Is that the underground railway?' Dee queried. 'I've never travelled on them in London, but I have when we've been to Wimbledon. The train comes out into the daylight when it reaches Morden station.'

Without being told, Dee was aware that they had arrived at Chapel Street. She didn't know where to look first. She didn't think she had ever before seen such a busy street, so many people and so much noise. On both sides of this very long road there were proper shops. Some had glass fronts and posh doorways; others were open-fronted, secured at night by shutters. In the gutters opposite each other and touching almost end to end were stalls and barrows, with men and women shouting their wares. Dee was thinking how no market she had ever been to before bore any resemblance to this street. The noise was deafening.

Dolly caught the look on Dee's face, and she felt awful. 'I'm sorry, luv, maybe I shouldn't 'ave brought you here. There's a pub about halfway up. We can go in there an' 'ave a drink, and see how yer feel then.'

'No, you do your shopping. I'll just follow you around, and when you're finished, then we'll have that drink.'

'I have t'tell yer, luv, my Tom was up here at six o'clock this morning. He came on his bike and got me enough vegetables to last half the week and enough meat to feed a ruddy army. I just thought you might like to see the place. If we get through these crowds to the other end of the street, there's stalls there selling dresses, jumpers and cardigans an' all that sort of thing. There's also jewellery, an' some of it is pretty good. One man who has a stall down there is a proper silversmith and makes a lot of the stuff himself. Would you like to have a look?'

'OK, if it's all right by you.' Dee thought it would be more interesting than all these barrows loaded with food.

Forty minutes later, Dee was well pleased. She'd bought some silver earrings for Jodie and identity bracelets for Reggie and Lenny, hoping that they wouldn't think them too sissy. She had thought about a wristwatch for each of them, but decided she'd wait and give them those as a Christmas present. Satisfied, she looked at Dolly and said, 'Lead the way, I'm buying you that drink.'

Once inside the pub, Dee insisted on going to the bar and told Dolly to find two seats and sit herself down. Hearing the note of authority in the young woman's voice brought a smile to Dolly's chubby face. 'I ain't gonna argue with you, 'cos me feet are killing me,' she said cheerfully.

Like the market outside, the inside of the pub was packed, but Dee hadn't long to wait before a smart young barman spoke very pleasantly to her. 'And what can I be getting a beautiful lass like yourself?' he asked, pulling himself up to his full height.

'Two brandies and one bottle of ginger ale, if

you please.' Dee smiled in return and delved into her handbag to find her purse.

Dolly's eyes widened as she watched Dee pour half of the ginger ale into each glass. 'Blimey, living it up today, ain't we? I wondered why yer didn't ask me what I wanted to drink. Usually I 'ave 'alf a pint of draught Guinness. Is this your normal bevvy?'

'Only when my friend Jodie and I are feeling a bit flush or if it is a special occasion like today. Come on, Dolly, drink up,' Dee said, raising her brandy goblet and clinking it against Dolly's.

By the time they got home, the men still hadn't returned from the football match. As Dolly filled the kettle and put it on the gas burner to boil, she said to Dee, 'We'll have a cup of tea, and then if you like you can have a nice hot bath. Better if you have the bathroom now rather than later when the men will be wanting to shave. You bring a dressing gown, did you? If not, I've got one yer can borrow. Not worth getting dressed again until yer put yer glad rags on to go out this evening.'

Dee was taken aback and said quickly, 'I didn't know we would be going out for dinner.'

Dolly laughed. 'Don't let it bother yer, I was only joking. We're only going down to the Legion, but as it is for charity tonight they will have a late-night extension for the bar and probably a bit of dancing. Do you like dancing? It won't be rock an' roll or any of that kind of stuff, 'cos it's mainly older people that come to the Legion.'

'Yes, I do like ballroom dancing, and I did bring a black dress and some strappy sandals just in case we went out at all.'

'Well there yer go then. Sit down, you're making the place look untidy. You can pour yer own tea out, that way you'll 'ave it as yer like it.'

Dee loved the bone-china cups and saucers that Dolly was using. She guessed they had been brought out in her honour. She poured milk into her cup and then half filled it with tea from the pot before going out into the scullery and topping it up with boiling water from the big black kettle.

'Too strong straight from the pot, was it?' Dolly laughed. 'I was glad t'see you went out to the scullery and helped yerself. That tells me you feel at home 'ere. When Derrick asked if he could bring his young lady t'meet us, I did wonder how we'd get on, but you 'aven't stood on ceremony one bit. You've taken us for what we are and that's a weight off me mind. So drink yer tea up, have a bath to wash the London dirt off yerself and then we'll get ourselves ready for a good night out. How does that sound to you?'

'Perfect. By the way, did Derrick tell you I make my living as a hairdresser?'

'Yeah, I think he did.'

'Would you like me to wash and set your hair ready for our night out?'

'Cor, that would be smashing. Are yer sure?'

Dee drained her teacup, then got up and went around to the other side of the table. Standing close to Dolly, she slowly ran her hands through her thick dark brown hair. 'You have lovely naturally wavy hair,' she said. 'Most ladies would give their eye teeth for a head of hair like this.'

'Well, I 'ave been tempted once or twice to get it permed, but then I see the results that some of

149

them walk about with. Big ball of frizz half the time.'

Dee smiled. 'Having your hair permed isn't always enough. It needs taking care of every day. As I said, you are lucky. I'll be able to do a lot with your beautiful hair.'

The two men came in full of their afternoon at the football. Derrick was flabbergasted when Dolly told him Dee was having a bath. 'Christ! She's really made herself at home.'

'Now then, Derrick Underwood, we'll 'ave less of the blasphemy. As you say, your young lady has made herself at home, and nobody is more pleased about that than I am. When she's got herself ready, she's gonna do my hair for me.'

Derrick smiled. He was pleased with the way their weekend was panning out.

Dead on seven o'clock, Derrick had them all piled into the taxi he had ordered from the phone box on the corner of the road. They drove through Aldgate before pulling up in front of a very re-spectable-looking building in Whitechapel. 'Have a great night,' the cabbie called. 'I'll see yer at midnight.'

The hall was done out to look very festive but what surprised Dee the most was the fact that the majority of the people were very well dressed indeed. Especially the men!

Having said as much to Derrick, she was surprised when he laughed and even more so when he began to explain.

'This might be a poor part of London, but many

wealthy people live within its boundaries and they don't dress down, so the man in the street thinks he should be allowed to dress up once in a while, especially for an event such as tonight. That is where luck comes into it. This whole district is full of tailors' workrooms, many of them producing garments for the West End market. Frequently a tailor will have a length of suiting left over from a bulk order and will make a suit or a jacket for a reasonable price. Most working-class men have one really good suit tucked away in a cupboard to be brought out to wear to a funeral, or on high days and holidays, or even for a visit to the pawn shop when work in the dockyards is scarce.' The remark about the pawn shop really had Dee smiling.

Suddenly the band struck up and Dolly was beckoning them to a table around which there were already two other couples seated. Tom was waiting to do the honours. 'This is Barbara and Len Kingston and Joyce and Dennis Collier.' Everyone shook hands. The friends were all roughly the same age, with Derrick and Dee being the youngest.

'Dennis was in the Merchant Navy during the war, Atlantic convoys mostly,' Tom quietly explained to Derrick.

'Am I allowed to go to the bar for drinks, or is it members only?' Derrick felt compelled to ask.

'Sorry,' Tom apologised, 'they aren't allowed to serve non-members, but we thought we'd have a kitty if that's all right with you, Del. You can come with me to the bar, though, seeing as how I've only the one pair of hands.'

All four men got to their feet and without any more chat they went to the bar together. Dolly threw back her head and laughed. 'If you're wondering why they've all gone off to fetch the drinks, it's because they'll be 'aving a crafty one while they're up at the bar, but they won't have long to linger. The doors to the dining room will be thrown open at eight sharp.'

Within minutes Dennis came back to the table bringing a tray which held four glasses of sparkling wine. 'First drink of the night is on the house,' he said, setting the tray down on the table and beating a hasty retreat.

'Dolly, I've got t'ask,' Joyce Collier said, poking Dolly in the ribs. 'Where the hell did you go today to get your hair done?'

'I've been dying to ask the same question,' Barbara Kingston chuckled. 'It looks smashing, the best I've ever seen your hair look.'

'Are yer saying you don't like it, Joyce?' Dolly asked, giving Dee a sly wink.

'Quite the reverse,' Joyce was quick to assure her. 'I think it's a really smart style. Makes me wonder if you went up West to get it done.'

'Exactly what I was thinking,' Barbara admitted. 'It's different to how you usually wear your hair, very professional, and it really does suit you.'

Dolly straightened her shoulders. She looked like the cat that had got the cream as she told them, 'My personal hairdresser came to my flat to wash and set it. I left it up to her as to what style she gave me.'

'Come off it, you're having us on!' the two women said in unison.

'No she isn't.' Dee thought it was about time she owned up. 'I did Dolly's hair. It was the least I could do seeing as how she fed me and made me feel so welcome in her lovely home.'

'Cor, wish you had a shop up here, we'd be yer first customers.'

That set the mood for a really happy evening. The four-course dinner was excellent. The entertainment was great, and even if the comedians were a trifle bawdy, they were never obscene. When it came to the ballroom dancing, they had all had their fair share of drink, but nevertheless Dee was thrilled to be in Derrick's arms and floating around the floor to a slow waltz. Of course she danced with Tom, Len and Dennis, but when Derrick claimed her for a quickstep, it took her back to when she had first danced with him on the end of the pier at Eastbourne. Sixteen years old she'd been then. God! She'd come a long way since then. And Derrick too had travelled far, but he had come back to her.

It was well past midnight before all the good nights had been said and they had bundled into the taxi. In the courtyard outside Tom and Dolly's flat, Derrick was talking to the cab driver, giving a large tip and telling him how much they appreciated him coming back for them.

Dolly and Dee decided to leave the men to find their own way indoors.

'Would you like a hot drink to take into your bedroom?' Dolly asked.

'Thank you for the offer, Dolly, but no thanks. All I want to do is lay my head on a pillow and sleep for a whole week.'

Dolly accompanied Dee down the long hallway then said, 'Good night, then, pet, see yer in the morning.'

Dee kicked off her shoes and with great difficulty managed to get out of her dress. She did wonder for a moment whether she should have waited to see if Derrick was safely in the flat, but it didn't matter, because when she woke up in the morning he would still be here and that was fine by her. Absolutely fine.

When all her underwear was lying on the chair next to the bed, she slipped her silk nightdress over her head and flicked the light off. Derrick should be here to kiss me good night, she thought. She smiled in the darkness, remembering all the kisses they'd shared in the taxi on the way home. His lips had been warm and his voice had been soft as velvet as he'd whispered over and over again that he loved her.

She finally fell asleep with the smile still on her face.

The next day being Sunday, they spent a leisurely morning. Dolly said she was keeping the roast dinner back until six o'clock that evening. Derrick confirmed that he had a couple of business appointments but that Tom was more than welcome to accompany him.

'Don't know about any business appointments,' whispered Dolly. 'Like as not they'll be meeting a bloke in a pub.' Dee fell about laughing. 'D'you wanna go for a drink?' Dolly added although from the tone of her voice it was the last thing she herself wanted.

'No fear,' Dee said quickly. 'I had more than enough drink last night to last me a while. I'm quite happy to laze about today if you're sure I'm not in your way.'

'Bless yer heart, we can put our feet up, though I might let you help me do the vegetables.'

Later that night Delia was to say that it was one of the nicest Sundays she had spent in a long while. And she meant it.

The parting next morning was very affectionate. Dolly was a bit tearful as she insisted that Dee must promise to keep in contact and know at all times that there was a bedroom and a hearty welcome waiting for her. Tom and Derrick shook hands and patted each other on the back until finally Tom told Dee to get into the car. Derrick lingered, calling to Kenny, who had been watching from the sidelines.

'You did a great job taking care of my car, Kenny lad. Here, buy yerself something.'

Kenny took a quick look at the folded five-pound note Derrick had pushed into his hand. 'Cor, thanks! Hope you come to see me grandad again soon.'

With that parting shot, everybody laughed and Derrick sounded the horn as he drove out on to the main road.

They hadn't travelled very far when Derrick pulled off the road. Turning to Dee he said, 'I want you to walk around Westminster Abbey with me for a few minutes.'

'What on earth for?' a startled Dee asked.

'Just be quiet and come with me.' Gently he took

hold of her hand, and as they walked he said, 'The coronation of every English monarch since William the Conqueror has taken place here at this abbey, and I thought it would be the perfect place to ask you to be my wife. Delia, I want us to spend the rest of our lives together. Wherever I get sent, whenever possible, I want you to come with me, because I really love you, with all my heart I do.'

Even the London traffic seemed to become silent as Delia silently repeated these loving words to herself.

'Delia, please will you marry me?' A long moment passed, and Derrick said, 'I will get down on one knee if you insist, but I might get locked up for causing an obstruction.'

Dee found she had to swallow hard to rid herself of the hard lump in her throat before she could answer, and even then she only managed to whisper, 'Yes,' but she looked up at him and her green eyes were glistening with unshed tears.

He lifted her up and said, 'Say it again, please, louder, so that everyone can hear you.'

'Derrick, people are looking at us!'

'Good, I want them to see how happy you have just made me. Tell me again, Dee, you have just agreed to be my wife, haven't you?'

'Yes, yes, put me down you fool,' she shouted, but he ignored her protest and swung her round and round and round, his arms wrapped tightly about her. When he finally came to a standstill and put her down, she would have fallen but for the fact that he kept her close within his arms and with his lips softly covering hers gave her a lingering, satisfying kiss. It was a kiss the like of which she had never received before, and she knew she would remember it for the rest of her life, no matter how long she should live.

13

The whole of Camber Sands was agog with the news that Derrick Underwood had taken his young lady away for the weekend and had proposed to her.

Marian wasn't the least bit put out by all the gossip; this outcome was exactly what she had wanted. She liked Delia Hartfield very much, knew that she would get along with her no matter what, and it was certainly a relief that her remaining son would be getting a wife. Who knows, she might yet live to see more grandchildren. It also seemed that the gods were looking favourably on this marriage. When Richard had married Laraine Lawrence, it had been a hastily put-together affair and neither of her other two sons had been at the wedding. Now, if she had been told right, her John was due home, and the news from Richard was sounding good. Thank the Lord for small mercies, she murmured to herself. This wedding really should be the event of the coming year.

John Underwood was already back on England's shores. He just hadn't had the decency yet to go and visit his elderly mother. Jodie had been ready to set off to meet her two boys from school. She did her best to keep her Wednesday afternoons free for that particular purpose. She liked to give the boys a bit of a treat on the only day she was able to wait outside the school.

The front door had slammed open and John's kitbag had been dumped with a thud along the narrow hallway. He burst into the kitchen grinning like a Cheshire cat, calling, 'And where is my beautiful wife? You should have been waiting on the doorstep to welcome me home from the sea.'

Jodie came in from the scullery, wiping her hands on a tea towel. The nerve of this husband of hers never ceased to amaze her. She was so stunned by his sudden appearance, she was lost for words. She made no move to go to him, just stood as if rooted to the floor, looking him over from top to toe. He was looking remarkably well. His skin was tanned, his hair still thick and dark and those amazing big blue eyes made him a true Underwood, too handsome for his own good.

He made the first move, bounding across the room, cheerfully throwing his arms about her and planting a swift and impulsive kiss on her cheek before she had even got over the shock of him being there.

'I was just about to go out,' she murmured, trying hard to convince herself that she was pleased to see him.

'I guessed I'd timed it right. Off to meet me boys, are you? Then of course I insist that I accompany you. I'm sure they'll be dead chuffed to see me.' The cockiness in his voice showed that he was still very full of himself.

Jodie couldn't stand it one moment longer. She

slammed her hand down on the kitchen table and in a voice that was trembling with rage asked, 'Have you ever given a thought to the fact that they might not even remember you? Not a post-card, a Christmas present, nothing for their birth-days, and you've got the cheek to walk in here and call them *your* boys. You haven't a clue as to whether they are fit and well; they could have been at death's door and you wouldn't have known, would you? No, because you don't give a monkey's about either of them, only when it bloody well suits you.'

When Jodie paused for breath, there was an odd look on her husband's face. 'I know what is eating you, Jodie, you always did bear grudges, but I thought you'd have had time to come to terms with it by now.'

'And what particular grudge is it that you think I am still bearing against you? Come on, spit it out, although if you went through the whole list we'd be here for hours.'

'Well then, we'd better get it out in the open here and now, clear the slate, 'cos I'm on twenty-one days' leave and I don't intend to have you throwing it in my face every minute of every day. Yes, I took yer damn football winnings, so what the hell do you want to do about it?'

Jodie was lost for words. His arriving out of the blue was shock enough and it had turned her in-tentions upside down. Long ago she had resolved to put the matter of her football winnings to the back of her mind, certainly not accuse him of making off with the cheque the minute he walked into the house. It was the last thing she would have

159

wanted to happen. But he himself had brought the matter out into the open and was turning the tables on her. Sighing softly, she made herself sit down before she formed an answer. When she spoke, her voice was soft and steady.

'John, I long ago came to the conclusion that bearing a grudge against you is a total waste of time. When you first went off and I found out about the money, I will admit I was very angry and filled with bitterness. I really did have to give myself a good talking-to, and I decided there were two things I could do with all that anger and bitterness. I could allow it to keep eating away at me like acid. Or I could tell myself I had my health and strength and could provide a good life for my sons. That's exactly what I have done, and I have nothing at all to thank you for.'

'Is that it?' he asked cockily, and when he received no reply he added, 'We'd better be off if we're going to meet the boys.'

Jodie couldn't believe it! She took a deep breath, telling herself that talking to him was like talking to a brick wall. Honesty? John didn't even know the meaning of the word.

The ten-minute walk passed without so much as a single word between them. She hadn't been prepared for the enthusiastic show of feeling that John showed the minute the boys came into view. It was so utterly false it not only left Jodie feeling bewildered, it really hurt her that he could treat his sons in such a way. All the time John had been away, she had done her best to keep his image alive in their minds, making up stories of where he might be and what he would be doing.

160

She knew the boys' reaction to seeing their father standing there was totally natural, but it didn't lessen her pain. John called to them the minute they came in sight, yelling loudly, 'Come on, lads, come an' give yer dad a big hug.' And they responded with glee.

'Two-faced bastard,' Jodie muttered to herself, but she was determined not to spoil the reunion for the boys. 'Your father is going to take us down into the village for some tea, you can choose whatever you fancy to eat.'

This announcement delighted both Lenny and Reggie, just as their mother had known it would. Later, seated in Rye's famous bakery, the boys were munching on beefburgers and chips with strawberry milkshakes on the side and already discussing what kind of ice cream they fancied for their pudding. It was Reggie who brought the future into the conversation. 'Dad, how long will you be home for this time?' he enquired.

The question must have caught his father by surprise, and he hesitated before saying, 'Son, you might give me time to get me kitbag unpacked before you talk about me going away again.'

Jodie was rather pleased at his reaction. Reggie's question certainly seemed to have ruffled his feathers.

Having pulled himself together, John tousled Reggie's hair and said, 'Is there a special reason for you asking, son?'

'Well, when Uncle Rick and Auntie Laraine got married you weren't here to come to the wedding. Now Uncle Derrick's getting married and only yesterday Grandma Underwood said she

161

hoped all her boys would be home this time.'

John's eyebrows shot up as he turned to stare at his wife. 'Is it true? Is Derrick getting married?' He looked both concerned and intrigued.

'Up until now I've only heard what the boys told me when they came back from seeing your mother yesterday, so you know as much as I do.' Suddenly she found herself smiling at him, at that serious look which didn't seem in keeping with his Jack-the-lad attitude to life. There were such a lot of contrasts about her husband and she found herself wishing that things could be different between them. But she knew she couldn't turn the clock back. The days when he had loved her and yes, made love to her, making her feel that she was the one and only love of his life, were long gone.

The boys were having a great time. They were relaxed as John told them about some of the places he had been to, and the time flew by. By the time they got home, Jodie was surprised at how well things were going. John lit the fire in the front room for her, and she produced a couple of cans of beer. They chatted for a while about the repairs she'd had done to the cottage, and John told her how well she had decorated the front room.

'And have you been happy here?' he asked. 'Haven't you ever felt lonely?'

It was then that she realised that the boys knew a lot more about what was going on than they ever let on. It was Reggie who spoke up.

'When Mum is lonely, Auntie Dee doesn't go home to her mum and dad, she stays here with us instead.'

'Yes, and she takes us out to the zoo and lots of

other places,' Lenny piped up, not wanting to be outdone.

John looked around the room again and then back at Jodie. He smiled. 'We are still a married couple, you know.'

That remark had taken the wind out of Jodie's sails, and it was a while before she formed an answer. 'You know, John, there are times when you scare the hell out of me. Marriage to you has never been a permanent arrangement. It was a mighty delicate operation right from the start. When it worked between us – and it did for the first year or so – it was wonderful. I still have good memories of those times. Then our lives went from bad to worse. We've only limped along because of you being in the navy. You've been halfway round the world and your wife and two young sons have become a memory. No contact whatsoever for nearly two years, at least not with me.'

'And you, Jodie? Don't tell me there hasn't been anyone else. Who has become the love of your life?' It was a straight question, but he wasn't sure if he wanted a straight answer or not. He found it impossible to believe that a young, beautiful woman like his Jodie should have gone all this time without being tempted. There had to have been some goings-on and he wanted the full story. At that point he had to stop himself from grinning; he himself certainly hadn't been starved of women's company.

Jodie was able to read his thoughts, and she answered sharply, 'I have a very different set of values to you, John. I've paid a price to get where I am today. True, it has been a very lonely life at times, but having our two boys has more than made up for it.'

'We could still make a go of it; there's no reason why we shouldn't, is there?' And when Jodie made no answer, he added, 'I haven't lost all your money. I could use some of what is left to buy myself out of the navy.'

'Are you serious?'

'Never more so in my life.' His eyes met hers and held. 'Can't we at least talk about it?'

She looked up at him and there were tears in her eyes. For the life of her she wasn't able to define her feelings. He hadn't even kissed her yet, and already he was twisting her around his little finger. 'John, take your things upstairs. You can have the spare room for now, and maybe tomorrow we'll be able to start talking.'

'Oh Christ.' He stood up, looking furious. 'Spare room, that's a great start.'

'It's that or get yourself a room down at one of the pubs. You said you want to talk and I am willing to listen, but I'm making no decisions, not straight off the cuff I'm not.'

John was on his feet straight away, and Jodie felt her heart sink when she heard him tell the boys he was going out to meet some friends and have a drink and that he would see them in the morning.

'I presume my key does still fit the lock?' was his parting shot. Moments later they heard the front door slam.

The boys were delighted when Jodie told them to get the board games out. An evening playing games with their mother was always great fun. For once Jodie didn't keep an eye on the clock, and it

164

was nine o'clock when she said, 'I think you've both won enough pennies off me for one evening. Go and get your nightclothes and bring them downstairs. You can get undressed in front of the fire and I'll make us all some hot chocolate.'

When she finally came downstairs having tucked the boys into bed and kissed them both good night, she felt utterly drained. Thoughts were whirling round in her head. John turning up out of the blue, the news that Dee and Derrick were to set a date for their wedding. In a couple of months it would be Christmas. Would John be home for that? Would she want him to be?

She had been staring into the embers of the fire for long enough. She'd things to get ready for work in the morning and clean clothes to lay out for the boys. A sudden thought struck her. John had said he had twenty-one days' leave. She couldn't help but wonder what he was going to do to fill his time. Oh well, she'd just have to face things as they came, she decided as she put the chairs back in place, plumped up the cushions on the settee, and tidied the books and pencils that were lying on the side tables. Then she got down on her knees and swept the fallen ash from around the hearth before replacing the fireguard in front of the fire. When she had finished, she stood with her back to the fireplace and looked about the room.

She loved this cottage and she was more than pleased with this front room. It was small yet comfortable, and every bit of the soft furnishings she could boast she had made herself. She had worked hard and her life was good, but it could be better. If only John could think and act like a married man and the father of two growing lads. Every responsibility in the home and all matters that were relevant to the well-being of Lenny and Reggie should be discussed between both parents. That was how things should be. But it wasn't how married life had turned out to be for her, and it was probably far too late to change things now.

As she switched the light off, she sighed heavily to herself.

14

No matter how hard Jodie tried, she felt her house was a sad place. She looked down at the pile of dirty washing that John had dumped on the floor in the corner of the front room. He treated her like dirt and their home like a doss house. She felt tears run hot down her face but swiped them away. Since when did crying do any good?

If only she could manage her home life as well as she managed her staff at the salons. Her expectations were high, but in return she endeavoured to make sure they were all happy and working in a relaxed and friendly atmosphere. God knows she had tried to straighten out her life with John. She had felt that if she could concentrate her efforts on repairing their emotional wounds, they might be able to start afresh. She had soon come to realise that for any of her ideas to work, a huge effort was needed from John as well as her. Today she forced herself to admit it was never going to happen. John would go his own way, live his life as he wanted and without any regard for the feelings of others.

He had been home now for two weeks, and during that short time he had twice disappeared, staying away for two days and two nights on both occasions. She hadn't asked any questions, telling herself that she didn't care where he went and with whom he spent his time. Trouble was, she did care, though a lot of good that did her.

Apart from worrying herself about John, Jodie felt that life in general was looking up. Richard and a heavily pregnant Laraine were home and had rented a very nice house in a village called Little Common, which was only a few miles from Hastings. They were all set to stay at least until the babies were born. Yes, that had been another surprise: Laraine was carrying twins, a fact that had Marian beaming from ear to ear.

Arrangements for a family gathering over Christmas were entered into only half-heartedly. The main topic of conversation between everyone seemed to be the coming wedding, which was set for Easter weekend.

Jack Hartfield was thrilled to learn that his only daughter was to be married to Derrick Underwood. In his opinion it was a match made in heaven. His wife Mary had a few doubts. To be honest, she was more than a little put out, because she felt she hadn't been included in any of the discussions so far. She was, however, absolutely determined on one thing: her Scottish relations were to be invited to the wedding. She herself had been born in Scotland and had lived there until she had met Jack Hartfield when he had been stationed in Dundee as a pilot in the RAF during the war. Now she had a dream that one of her brothers might wear his kilt and play the bagpipes at her daughter's wedding. For the moment, though, she was keeping those thoughts to herself.

Derrick had had enough. He was sick of hearing so many different versions of how this wedding should be arranged. It had been the main topic of conversation over the entire Christmas holiday. Tonight he had brought Delia into Hastings and they were having dinner in a very old-fashioned pub where the food was excellent. It was after all Valentine's Day.

Dee felt she had grown up a lot since Derrick had come home, but sometimes when he talked about the life they would lead and the places he would take her, it almost seemed as if he were offering her a challenge, and it terrified her. But her mind was made up. She wanted this life, knew that she had to banish all her doubts and concentrate on the fact that she wanted to be with him. She looked into Derrick's eyes and smiled at him as he toasted her.

'To us, my darling, and a great life together.' He looked so handsome in a sports jacket and turtle-neck jersey. She drank, and a moment later almost choked when he spoke again. Surely she must've misheard. 'Would you mind repeating what you just said?' she asked quietly.

He was smiling mysteriously. 'I asked you if you have a passport, because tonight I am whisking you off on a plane.' He laughed outright; he had never seen her so tongue-tied before.

'You want me to go away with you before we're married?'

'Yes I do, more than anything. Get away on our own, make our own decisions. I do love you so much, Dee,' he reassured her, and his eyes were sparkling at her.

'This is ridiculous, so sudden. Maybe we should talk about it for a little while.' Dee was suddenly very nervous at the thought of flying off into the unknown with him.

'Time enough for talking when we get there. It doesn't really matter whether you have a passport or not. I'm taking you on a tour of the Channel Islands; the only need for a passport would be if we wanted to go over to France. We'll see about getting you one later on.'

Dee took a good drink from her glass before saying, 'Derrick, we can't just disappear when there is so much arranging to be done. And what about my job? I can't let Michael down.'

'That's my point. Everyone is going around in circles. Time to call a halt. Also, I have a confession to make.' He looked very sheepish as he hesitated. 'I let Jodie into my plans and she was all for it, called it breathing space and thought it was a good idea. She also promised to square things with Michael, lend him some of her staff while you're away.'

'Good God! You have been busy. I just don't know what to say.'

'You don't have to say anything. You're coming with me. We'll have time on our own, get to really know each other. We can talk about the wedding if you want to, but personally I'd like to leave that

169

subject for everyone else to argue over. I know I must sound crazy, but that's because I am crazy about you. Just say you trust me enough to come with me. All you have to do is shove a few things into a bag; we'll buy whatever else we need. When I take you home, I don't want you to go to bed. Go indoors, get whatever you need and creep out again. We'll drive straight to Gatwick tonight. If there are no flights, we'll put up at a hotel and catch the first plane out in the morning.'

Suddenly they were laughing like a couple of kids. 'I'll have to leave a note for my parents, and what about your mother? Everyone is going to be so mad at us.'

'Do we really care? They'll get over it, and by the time we're back, they will have everything settled to their satisfaction right down to the last buttonhole.'

'Derrick, I really do think you're crazy.' And she was crazy about him.

They caught a plane to Jersey that night, and thirty minutes after midnight they were sitting side by side on the edge of a double bed in a comfortable bedroom in the Royal Hotel.

Delia was laughing and crying at the same time as Derrick said, 'At last I have you all to myself. Oh sweetheart... I've waited and dreamed about this moment for the past two years.'

They spent the night in the same bed, with Dee nestled tightly within his arms, yet he never once attempted to make love to her and Delia wasn't sure if she was sorry about that or not.

Over breakfast he casually said, 'We have a lot of

shopping to do.' They walked along the seafront and through leafy lanes until they reached St Helier, the island's largest town. At one o'clock Derrick called a cab to take them back to their hotel, because they had so many parcels they couldn't carry them all. He had bought her an engagement ring and an eternity ring, both of which he immediately placed on the third finger of her left hand, to the delight of the staff in the jewellery shop. Two gold wedding bands, one for each of them, lay side by side in a velvet-lined box. Each of them had bought clothes and shoes, and Dee had made sure she chose two beautiful silk nightgowns.

They spent the afternoon in the gardens of the hotel, soaking up the winter sunshine, and as the darkness drew in, Dee said she was leaving him to have her hair and fingernails done. 'A busman's holiday,' he joked. 'Or are you just sounding out the competition?'

'It always pays to find out how the other half operates,' she laughed. 'Besides, having one's hair done always makes a lady feel so much younger.'

'God forbid,' he cried. 'If you come out of that salon looking any younger, I'll be had up for cradle-snatching.'

'Get on, you old flatterer, and take yourself off to the barber's shop. You never know, one of the assistants might be able to work wonders on you.' Dee didn't wait to hear his answer, but she was chuckling as she made her way back into the hotel.

As they walked into dinner that evening, they certainly made a striking pair, but it was Dee's

171

hair, gleaming like polished horse chestnuts, that was the envy of all the ladies present.

Much later that night, Dee felt she was floating as she once more twisted the diamond ring on her finger. She had drunk several glasses of champagne, and was now lolling on the bed dressed only in a peach-coloured silk and lace nightdress while Derrick was having a blissful time slowly running his hands over her body and drinking in the sight of her.

Finally he lifted her nightgown up and over her head and Dee was naked. She was trembling, but Derrick kissed her in a way that felt deep and rich and full, and she was no longer fearful. When he lifted his head, she sighed deeply and he laughed and kissed the tip of her nose.

Then, at last, they were making love.

Derrick had waited until he felt it was the right time and the right place, and he knew he had made the right decision. Delia was a virgin. He had to treat her carefully.

He was a big man in every sense of the word, and Dee drew a deep breath, part misgiving, part apprehension, as he entered her.

It was some time later when he dropped his head to her shoulder, his heart thundering as if it would burst. Delia was now limp beneath him, and there was nothing but the sound of their rasping breathing.

'Derrick?'

'Hmm?'

'Was I all right for you?'

'Oh sweetheart ... I've waited so long for this.' Derrick raised himself up on his elbows to look down at her. He could only gaze into those big green eyes and watch them gaze back. 'Now I know you belong to me. You are mine for the rest of our lives, and I will always love you.' He traced the outline of her lips with his fingertips and kissed the end of her nose once again.

'I love you too, Derrick,' Dee told him softly, brushing away her tears.

'Then why are you crying? Did I hurt you that much?'

'It hurt more than I expected, but the tears are because I can't believe how happy I am.'

'Women,' he muttered, as he bent to kiss her tenderly. Then, raising his head, he said, 'Delia Hartfield, you do realise that in six weeks' time you are to become a married woman. There will be no more of these elicit holidays.'

Delia was still in a state of disbelief. It had finally happened and her heart was soaring with joy. She no longer had any misgivings. She and Derrick loved each other and please God would spend the rest of their lives together.

She raised her head and said with a mischievous smile, 'Well in that case I had better make the most of this one then.'

'You little minx,' he murmured as he gathered her back into his arms and pressed a kiss to her forehead. 'For now I think we should both think about getting some sleep.'

15

During the days that followed, Dee began to think she was living on cloud nine. They had moved on to stay on the island of Guernsey, which she thought she preferred to Jersey. It was not so busy, and time almost stood still as Derrick used the car he had hired to drive her around the beautiful leafy countryside. Not once had Delia dithered. No matter what Derrick suggested they do or where he wanted to take her, she gladly went along with his suggestions.

Today was their third day. The sun was high in the sky but there was quite a cool breeze coming off the sea as they sat outside a café in St Peter Port. Their lunch consisted of fresh crab and king prawns and an enormous bowl of fresh salad. To the side were crisp French bread rolls and a large dish of Guernsey butter.

Suddenly one of the ships that had docked alongside the harbour wall sounded its siren, making Dee jump. Derrick laughed. 'That ship does the run to Alderney; we'll do that trip tomorrow. You'll like St Anne Dee, it's the main town, not large, but different, and a few of their shops are quite exclusive. They get their stock from France, so maybe you'll find yourself a couple of little dresses that were made in Paris.'

Dee still couldn't take it all in. Derrick was so generous, and he seemed to have an endless supply of money.

The balloon burst the very next night. They had taken the ship across to Alderney at seven o'clock in the morning, and it was ten thirty in the evening by the time they were back in their Jersey hotel. Derrick had gone to reception to collect their room key, and came back towards her waving what looked like a telegram. 'Who the hell knows where we are?' Delia muttered.

'Sorry, Dee, I had to inform head office of my whereabouts. I'll see you up to our room, then I must come down and use the hotel telephone.'

Dee was whispering silent prayers. Everything had been so good; *too* good! Telegrams always meant bad news.

'Don't look so worried, my love, it will only be about my next posting.' Derrick looked at her in a way that had her heart pounding. 'I'll be back up here by the time you've got yourself ready for bed.'

As he left the room, Dee sighed. It seemed impossible that she could have been lucky enough to find a man like him, and she had never dreamed of anything like what she had been sharing with him these past few days.

Derrick was back in the room within five minutes. One look at his face and Dee knew she no longer had cause to worry. His smile was wide and his eyes were twinkling merrily. Without saying a word, he put his arms around her waist and lifted her up until her feet were off the floor and her face was on a level with his. 'Darling, I have got the very job I've been craving. I am going to work for that Dutch firm and yes, once you are my legal wife you will be able to travel on board ship with

175

me. The only thing is, I shall have to cut this holiday a bit shorter than I would have liked. I have to be in London the day after tomorrow, several ends to tie up, which means I shall have to take you home tomorrow. Just one question: are you sorry you came away with me for these few days?'

'Haven't you been able to tell how happy you have made me?'

'Well, I kinda hoped that was the case, but I needed you to tell me.'

'Well now I have, and if we are going home in the morning, don't you think we had better make the most of what is left of tonight?'

'Why you cheeky wench,' he cried, making to grab her, but Dee was too quick. She made it into the bathroom and didn't come out until she was wearing nothing but the second nightdress she had bought. This one was blue, even more transparent than the peach one, and it was obvious that Derrick had got the message. He came slowly towards her, then gently lifted her off her feet and carried her to the bed.

The news spread quickly that Derrick and Delia were home, and it seemed as if in no time at all family and friends from both sides had turned up in Mary Hartfield's kitchen. All were anxious to give Delia reports on what progress they had made towards the wedding arrangements.

Derrick signalled for Dee to come outside. 'I'm not going to say that I'm sorry to be going off to London,' he said with a wide grin. 'You'll be much better able to deal with everything and everybody than I ever could. I'll phone you tonight.'

Before Dee had the chance to form an answer, he had wrapped her in his arms and his lingering kisses had her wishing that they were still in the Channel Isles. She stood at the side of the road and watched until his car was out of sight. Oh dear, now she had to go back into the house and listen to what everyone had to say. One thing was for certain: she'd never be able to please everyone. Even the Queen herself couldn't manage that.

Her mother-in-law-to-be seemed to be in charge of Mary Hartfield's scullery, dispensing cups of tea and coffee but always with an ear cocked so that she didn't miss anything, and if there was a point raised that she didn't agree with, she wasn't backwards in saying so.

It was the pregnant Laraine who was doing the talking when Dee came back into the house. 'Come and listen, Dee. I'll start again at the beginning so that you'll know what I'm talking about.'

Dee didn't answer but shot an enquiring glance at her mother, who merely raised her eyebrows and flapped her hands in a helpless gesture.

'Actually it has all worked out better than any of us could have hoped for.' Laraine was smiling. 'Your mum asked me to find out who in the family could put up some of your relatives that are coming from Scotland for the wedding. When I saw the length of the list your mother had made out, I thought it was a hopeless task. Then my Rick had a brainwave. He took me up the road to the Golden Sands holiday camp; Michael Woodward is the manager there, great friend of the boys, they all went to school together.' Laraine paused in the telling and took a few sips from her cup of coffee.

'For goodness' sake get to the point, Laraine,' her mother-in-law ordered. 'We'll be here till midnight the way things are going. Better still, if you've all got a drink, for God's sake let's move out of this scullery and sit in comfort in Mary's front room.'

Everyone saw the sense of that. Now with two cushions tucked at her back Laraine looked a whole lot more comfortable, and once she had finished drinking her coffee she went on, 'At first Mike said he wasn't able to offer any accommodation, because with the wedding being over the Easter weekend, and that being the first week of the season, he hadn't got any vacancies. Rick and I thanked him and were almost off the premises when he shouted for us to come back. The long and short of it is, Mike took us to the far end of the camp grounds to where there is a whole line of chalets. Apparently these are no longer used for paying guests, not posh enough but they are good enough to house staff during the very busy parts of the season when they take on students and suchlike. He offered to let us use them if we thought they were suitable.'

Dee looked around the room. Jodie, Marian, Ethel and her own mum were all smiling broadly and giving her the thumbs-up sign.

'Are you happy to go along with that, Mum?' Dee asked cautiously.

'Indeed I am, lass, a blessing in disguise. I'm gonna be allowed over there to give the chalets a good cleaning. They each have their own kitchenette and a toilet, and Mike said he can provide all the bed linen. I've said we'll pay for the laundering of it all when they go home.'

'Oh Mum, I'll help you. Have you had replies from everyone?'

'Yes we have, and yer dad has been moaning 'cos every night as soon as it's six o'clock and the cheap rate starts, our phone never stops ringing.'

Dee wrapped her arms around her mother and held her close, saying, 'You sound happier than I've heard you for a long time, Mum. Everything is going to go off all right, isn't it?'

'Delia my girl, you can lay money on it. Even your father's got himself embroiled in the arrangements, so all you have to do is start thinking about yourself and what you need for the great day.'

By now Delia was almost on the verge of tears. So much had happened in the last few days, not the least being that she had come to realise that having a great family and good friends was worth far more than anything that money could buy.

As Dee was saying goodbye to everyone, Jodie hung back. 'Dee, I'm not pushing you, but if you decide you don't want to tour the shops looking for a ready-made wedding dress plus a decent going-away outfit, you are leaving it a bit late to contact Chloe Goldsmith.'

'I know, I know. If Derrick hadn't whisked me away on the sly, I was going to ask you to come up to town with me and pay Chloe a visit. I did find one decent dress and a tailored suit in the Channel Islands, either of which may be suitable for going away in. It would help a lot if only I knew where we're supposed to be going on our honeymoon.'

'What about the actual wedding dress?' Jodie asked.

'Nothing as yet,' Dee admitted. 'Can you spare the time to come and visit Chloe with me?'

'Try stopping me. It's a case of all hands to the wheel to get this wedding up and running. The third bride for the third brother. It has got to go off perfectly, and it will. Everybody is rooting for you, and everyone seems so happy. Your mother because all her relatives are going to be here. Derrick's mum because she will have lived to see all three of her sons safely married and because all three of them will be there on the day. All you've got to do is turn up looking utterly beautiful from your head right down to your toes.'

'If only it were as easy as that,' Dee almost screamed. 'You've all been scurrying around getting things organised, and I haven't even got my head round what I am going to wear yet.'

'All the more reason for you to phone Chloe tonight and ask her which is the best day for us to come up to town. By the way, I'm glad I was here when you got back. I missed you.' Jodie was thinking how young and vulnerable Dee looked, which didn't make sense. She was grown up now. Had been away with a man for a few days and the date for her wedding was all set. These past few days should have taught her something, at least made her a little more mature, less sensitive.

She couldn't help herself; her mind had flown back to the time when she had married John. She had only been seventeen years old and full of hope for the future, and look how things had turned out.

Smothering a sigh she said, 'Let me know what Chloe has to say...' Her voice trailed off and she looked at Dee with a tender smile.

'I love you, babe.'

'I love you too, Jodie,' Dee told her in a voice that was filled with emotion.

16

The weeks had flown by, and Mary Hartfleld was exhausted. She had that row of chalets at the holiday camp shining like a dollar. To be honest, she'd had a great deal of help, but she had done far more than was ever expected of her. Every single and double bed was made up ready; all furniture had been closely inspected, and polished and repaired where necessary. Her husband had been roped in as a handyman, fixing drawer handles, repairing window latches and making sure that all toilets were in working order.

'I thought I was the father of the bride,' he had been heard to mutter, 'not the odd-job man!'

Today, with three days to go to the actual wedding, Jack was to drive a car in a convoy of seven to meet his wife's Scottish relations from Eastbourne railway station. The other cars were being driven by the three Underwood brothers, Bob Collier, who was to act as Derrick's best man, Michael Connelly and his partner Danny Spencer. Derrick had chosen Bob to be his best man for two reasons. Not only had he done a wonderful job on the day of Richard's wedding, but it also saved Derrick from having to choose between his two brothers.

That night the whole of Camber Sands was well aware of the arrival of twenty-six of Mary Hartfield's relatives. As for Mary herself, she went to bed that night with a beaming smile on her face. She was guaranteed a good night's sleep, for she had drunk deep and often during the evening from the malt whisky that had travelled all the way down from Dundee.

Come the day, everything went off perfectly. The sun shone and the wedding was absolutely beautiful.

The bells were ringing and the organ was playing as Delia came slowly down the aisle on the arm of her father, wearing a truly fabulous dress. High-necked and with long sleeves, it looked as if the soft white crêpe de Chine had been moulded to her body. She wore her chestnut hair long with just a few curls on top, and a hint of a veil, kept in place by a richly jewelled tiara courtesy of Chloe. Her bouquet was small but exquisite, cream roses and green fern.

Her dad squeezed her arm as he whispered, 'Be happy, my darling,' and stood aside for her to take her place beside her husband-to-be. Derrick looked at her in such a loving way that her heart missed a beat. The church was packed, with folk standing around the walls and even at the back. Dee found it hard to believe that so many folk had come to see her get married.

Once the ceremony was over, endless photographs were taken both by professionals and by their many friends. There was a wedding breakfast for sixty people at the Grand Hotel in Eastbourne, where numerous toasts were drunk and several speeches were made. Later in the evening there was a welcome for everyone. A hall at the holiday camp had been given over to the family, a licensed bar set up and staff provided; best of all, a six-piece band was to play for the dancing, which would continue until the early hours of the morning. The mother of the bride and the mother of the bridegroom both voiced their concern as to whether there would be enough food to feed the hundred and fifty people who had already arrived.

'Please, ladies, stop worrying. This is as much your day as it is Delia's and Derrick's, and I assure you, there has been enough delicious food provided to feed an army.' At Michael's request, Danny Spencer had come across to try and pacify the two mothers. 'Come along, darlings, I am going to show you something.' Taking hold of their arms, he led them to the back of the hall and through swing doors.

Mike Woodward, having been given the wink, was waiting for them. 'Mrs Underwood, Mrs Hartfield, I have to congratulate you and everyone else who has had a hand in planning today's event. Everything had gone off so well; this wedding will go down as a feather in the cap of the management and staff of the holiday camp. The success will rub off on our reputation, and that can't be a bad thing. Now...' With a flourish, he swung open two heavy doors to reveal the inside of an exceptionally large refrigerator, the shelves of which were lined with trays of succulent food. 'Happy now, ladies? Besides all the food laid out in the main hall, this is your back-up. You can in the main thank the Underwood men and their friends, who over the past week have taken their boats out to sea and caught some of the finest seafood your guests will ever have tasted.'

The two women were dumbstruck.

Mike looked at Danny, and they winked at each other. 'Shall I escort you back to the ball, ladies?' Danny asked. As they walked away, he turned his head slightly to look over his shoulder, and was rewarded by Mike giving him a thumbs-up sign.

It was a wonderful evening, but at midnight Derrick suggested to his wife that they call it a day. 'Let's leave everybody to continue to enjoy themselves,' he pleaded. 'I have a car waiting, and everything you need is already in our bedroom.'

'And which bedroom would that be?' Dee asked, suddenly aware that she didn't know what was to happen from here on in.

'I wondered when curiosity would get the better of you,' he laughed. 'We'll be off in two days' time, but in the meantime, I have booked us a room at the Grand. I need to have you to myself for a while. You, young lady, are my wife, and together we're going to enjoy all the benefits that come with married life. That is, if you have no objections.'

Dee looked up at him, smiling shyly, and he gently took her in his arms and kissed her. Slow and lingering was that kiss, and it seemed better even than all the kisses that had preceded it.

It was a wonderful two days. They slept late, had a leisurely breakfast, walked along the promenade and the length of the pier, and Dee loved it when the staff addressed her as Mrs Underwood. On the late afternoon of their second day, as they were standing at the far end of the pier staring out to sea, Derrick pulled his wife closer. He was holding her back to his front, his arms around her waist, and he rested his chin on the top of her head and watched as the waves broke beneath the very spot where they were standing.

'Dee,' he whispered her name, 'you do realise that tomorrow will be the beginning of an entirely new life for you.'

Dee twisted her body to enable herself to look up at him, a smile lighting her eyes. 'Derrick, as long as it is with you, then I shall be the happiest woman alive.'

'I hope you will still feel the same way when we are at sea and the weather turns rough,' he said, only half in jest. He still couldn't bring himself to believe that this adorable young woman was going to be by his side for the rest of his life.

Dee's thoughts were mixed, and she deliberately glanced down at the three rings that were now on her finger. 'For better or worse,' she told him as she resettled herself against him, burrowing closer, and as always the feeling of him tight against her told her so many things.

'I think the quicker I get you back to the hotel the better,' Derrick said, grinning as he nudged her in the ribs.

'I love you, Derrick Underwood,' she told him, her face one big grin.

'I love you too, Delia Underwood, but the sooner I get you back to the hotel, the safer we'll both be. There ought to be a law forbidding young wives to tempt their husbands while out in public places. Come on, let's get going before somebody spots me behaving indecently in public and calls the police.'

Laughing loudly, Dee broke away from him. When she was a few feet away, she called back, 'I've never been accused of being a temptress before.' Then she turned and ran swiftly back along the pier.

'I should bloody well hope not,' he roared, as he set out after her.

They were both up early next morning, and having eaten a hearty breakfast were in the car being driven to Gatwick airport by ten o'clock.

From Gatwick they flew to Rotterdam, where they were met by two well-dressed gentlemen who introduced themselves as representatives of the Tercol Shipping Line. They handed two thick packages to Derrick. 'All the information you need and a full itinerary is enclosed,' one of them said.

The second man stepped forward and held out his hand to Delia. 'We understand congratulations are in order for your very recent wedding, Mrs Underwood. Unfortunately the ship your husband will be taking command of has been held up in dry dock. It will be at least six days before it will dock here in Rotterdam, but in the meantime we have made reservations for you both in the Astoria Hotel, which is one of the finest hotels in Holland. We hope you will be very comfortable.'

Delia could only smile her thanks, it was all so unbelievable. Looking round, she saw that Derrick had been drawn aside by the other gentleman, but she was still able to hear most of their conversation. The gist of it was that the currency and documents that he was being given would act as his credentials when presented at the bank. All this business was carried out in such a cordial way that Delia was left feeling that she was more than welcome to the hospitality not only of this new company for whom Derrick would be working but also from the country as a whole.

To her utter surprise, one of the gentlemen put two fingers to his mouth and blew a loud shrill whistle. Almost immediately a cab drew up at the kerbside and the door was being held open for her. Dee settled herself back in the well-worn leather interior and watched as Derrick supervised the placing of their luggage into the boot. As they drove along, she got a glimpse of some very fine buildings, and approaching the dockyards she needed no telling that Rotterdam was certainly an important seaport. The docks were extensive and very large vessels were berthed there.

As the taxi drew to a halt, Dee couldn't help but exclaim, 'It's started to snow!' Easter had been early this year, but when they had left Gatwick there hadn't been any signs to show that the weather would change this much. Derrick took her arm as she stepped out of the taxi, and as they walked, their footsteps made a crunching sound over the frosted ground. Dee shivered. She hadn't expected it to be this cold.

As they turned a bend in the drive, they both looked up. Later they agreed that *splendid* was the only word to describe this hotel. A sweeping terrace with a range of columns, walls of warm-coloured stone and what seemed liked dozens of windows, and although it overlooked the harbour, it appeared to have trees in abundance, almost as if there were woods stretching behind the building up and over the hills in the distance. It looked like a winter wonderland, because the snow had begun to leave a thin coating on everything.

The welcome they received from every member of the staff they came into contact with left them feeling that they couldn't have been better treated if they had been royalty. As the door to their bedroom was flung open, Dee was amazed and thrilled all within one minute. It was to her like entering the drawing room of a wealthy family, and her grin spread even wider as she turned to see a real fire burning in the grate, stacked high with logs. The crackle of the burning wood sounded great, and as she sniffed, she knew she would remember being greeted by the gorgeous smell of burning logs for a long time to come.

Derrick and Dee had been married for six weeks before the Dutch tanker *Bobodi* finally berthed in Rotterdam. For Dee, the time spent with Derrick had been something the like of which she could never have dreamed of. Waited on hand and foot in their hotel, she often wondered if one morning she might wake up and find herself back in Camber Sands and it had all been one long dream.

Together they visited fine museums and wonderful buildings. It was sad to see that even after all this time the city centre still bore scars from when the Germans had bombed it in May 1940. By the time a month had slipped by, Delia felt she knew more about the Netherlands than

188

she did about Sussex where she had been born. She had learnt that the country was primarily agricultural, producing cereals, potatoes, sugar beet, butter, cheese, eggs, fruit and vegetables, and had been introduced to folk who earned their living by growing bulbs on a large scale for export. Derrick had been particularly interested in the country's important fisheries. They were invited to so many important gatherings, and the hospitality was overwhelming. Her life had suddenly become an amazing experience, and time and time again Dee had to pinch herself to make sure it was reality and not a delusion.

Once a week Derrick had to report in person either to the main offices of the Dutch shipping line, or on board one of the largest vessels berthed in the dockyard. When the *Bobodi* finally arrived in Rotterdam, Delia was in for another surprise: she was to be the only female on board. Of the ten crew members, only one spoke English: Ian Paterson, Derrick's second mate. Everyone treated Dee with the utmost courtesy.

Derrick told her that the route they'd be taking was first to Las Palmas and then down to Brazil. She was surprised to learn that their cargo was a certain type of oil used in the manufacturing of margarine. She didn't consider that to be very exciting, but when she voiced her opinion to Derrick, he sternly told her she had a lot to learn. 'Most cargos are far from glamorous; most times it is the everyday commodities we carry and which earn the money.' He added, 'My father was right: oil is paramount in the world today and it will dominate so much in the future. Every walk of life will be ruled by oil, from the man in the street who wants to run a car to the industrialists who rule vast commercial enterprises.' Dee decided that in future she would listen and learn but keep her opinions to herself.

The food served on board was excellent, but Dee suffered severely from seasickness. She would lie in bed with her hands clasped together on top of her tummy, trying, as she said, to stop her stomach from rising up and bursting out of her body. However, she bravely declared her suffering worthwhile, because never in her wildest dreams had she thought she would ever see such wonderful sights and such interesting places.

From Brazil, Derrick was taking the *Bobodi* partway up the Amazon. Three days into this journey and Dee's screams had the whole crew thinking she had fallen and sustained life-threatening injuries. Taking the steps two at a time, Derrick was beside her within minutes. Appraising the situation at a glance, he didn't know whether to take her in his arms or throw her overboard.

On leaving the cabin that morning, Dee had not slid the double bed back into its slot in the wall of the cabin. She had also failed to close and lock the portholes. Now, on opening the cabin door, she had been met by the sight of flying fish flapping and floundering on the bed and slithering like snakes on the floor.

By the time the *Bobodi* made its second port of call, Dee had almost found her sea legs and was ready to go ashore with Derrick. As she used a strange currency to pay for postcards and stood listening to the smiling shopkeepers speaking to her in an unfamiliar language, she looked around her in wonder. So much of ordinary day-to-day life here was entirely different to what she was used to.

Derrick had promised that he would take her to visit Rio de Janeiro, and for this journey they would use river transport. Two days later, here she was, wearing open-toed sandals, a flimsy chiffon sleeveless dress and a wide-brimmed floppy hat, being transported up the Paraguay-Paraná river system. She was a long way from home in more ways than one, and in every respect was living an altogether different life. She certainly wasn't complaining, yet at times she still had her doubts as to whether this radical change could really be all true.

Smiling to herself, she gazed up at her brawny, suntanned husband. If all this was a dreamy delusion, she hoped against hope that she wouldn't suddenly wake up!

17

With Dee and Derrick out on the high seas and according to their postcards enjoying life to the full, Jodie was once again left to ponder on where she had gone wrong in her marriage.

Any day now Laraine was going to be delivered of her twin babies, and Jodie couldn't help but wonder whether Richard would go back to sea or remain at home to play happy families. Truth was, she missed Dee more than words could say. That girl had become her young sister and the daughter she'd never had all rolled into one.

John had stayed at home, coming and going as it suited him, for at least a month after his brother's wedding. Since then, however, she hadn't set eyes on him. She was still receiving her naval allowance, but whether or not John was still a serving member of the Royal Navy she had no idea. Had he been true to his word and bought himself out of the service? And if he had, what on earth was he going to do for a living?

Jodie herself hadn't allowed the grass to grow under her feet. It had been one dull Monday morning when she had taken it into her head that Sussex was too restricting for her. No sooner the thought than the deed! She had sold both of her salons and had immediately started negotiations for two new premises, one in the Royal Borough of Kensington and the other one in Epsom in Surrey. With help and advice from Michael Connelly, she had diversified when it came to employing staff. Two male and two female stylists in Kensington, and just one male and two females in the Epsom salon.

She was still doing quite a bit of regular work at Shepperton Studios. More and more chat shows were being shown regularly on TV, and presenters and celebrities had to have their hair and make-up done before appearing on screen. It was during this time at the studio that Jodie met Philip Conti, one of the directors of light entertainment. Philip was a gentleman, well-mannered, kind, attentive and caring. He was also extremely good-looking.

Tall, with dark hair and tanned skin, he was always well dressed, his body toned. When working alongside Philip, Jodie was more than happy; in fact she found that even being near him awoke in her feelings that she had thought were long forgotten.

As Jodie's income increased, her dissatisfaction at having to keep travelling backwards and forwards from Rye grew. She received an offer for her small cottage and decided to accept it. After taking advice from her bank manager, she took out a mortgage and also laid down a decent sum of money from her own savings to buy a four-bedroom house within walking distance of Epsom racecourse.

With the upheaval of sorting out all the legalities, finding the right school for her two boys and getting them settled in, there wasn't a day that she didn't miss Dee and Laraine. Quite unexpectedly, though, it was from Shepperton Studios that the biggest offer of help came. To be told that on the day that she made the move to Epsom she could have the use of two big vans and two drivers was not only a pleasant surprise but a sheer godsend. And by golly, she would breathe a sigh of relief once the date to exchange contracts had been decided upon. It would be a day of hustle and bustle the day she finally made the move, but on the other hand she would be so thankful when she was eventually settled in her new home. She couldn't wait.

Before the date of completion had been settled on, however, Jodie received a panicky phone call from Laraine begging her to come and be with her, and for Christ's sake to send someone, anyone, to find Richard and have him come to Hastings Maternity Hospital. The telephone became a hotline. Jodie phoned their mother-in-law first; best to do things right and keep the peace. Then she phoned Michael and asked him to make sure that her staff locked up her salons safely later in the day. 'I can't be in two places at the same time,' he'd laughed, but he quickly added that he'd get Danny to check on the Epsom salon. He also instructed Jodie not to panic; babies were born every hour of every day, he reminded her, and to that remark she just had to reply, 'Well you'd know all about that, wouldn't you, darling!'

Within the hour Jodie was sitting beside the bed on which Laraine was writhing in pain while Jodie herself was fighting to stop her own panic from rising. She began pleading with her sister-in-law to calm down and urged her to just keep on taking deep breaths. As she wiped the perspiration from Laraine's forehead, she did her best to reassure her that Richard would be there any minute now, but meanwhile she had to be a brave girl and concentrate on delivering her babies. But Laraine still lay there panting, her lovely hair damp, her eyes pleading with Jodie to do something to help her. And all Jodie could do was breathe with her and hold her hand and tell her how proud she was of her.

She heaved a great sigh of relief as the midwife came back into the side ward followed by two white-coated doctors. Jodie didn't need any telling; she was on her feet in a second. 'I'll wait outside,' she mumbled as she made a hasty retreat.

What seemed like endless minutes passed before

the two doctors came out. The older of the two approached Jodie with hand outstretched. 'I am Dr Craig. Are you a relative of Mrs Underwood?'

'Yes, I am. She's my sister-in-law. We are both Mrs Underwood.'

'Has her husband been informed that she has been admitted to hospital?'

Jodie sighed. 'I can't answer that because I don't know. I have made several phone calls and left messages. I thought he might have been here by now.'

'The thing is, Mrs Underwood,' the doctor paused, 'we might have to operate in order to deliver your sister-in-law's babies. I am not saying we will have to, but if it did come to that, we will need Mr Underwood's signature on the consent form.'

At that moment there were sounds of a commotion further down the corridor, but even before the offenders came into view, Jodie had recognised Richard's voice. Saved by the bell, she muttered under her breath. She turned to the doctor and said, 'I think Mr Underwood has just arrived.'

With long strides Richard came towards her. His hair had been tossed about by the wind, but apart from that he was immaculately dressed, and looked larger than life and taller than any other man present. As he reached Jodie, he placed his hands on her shoulders and drew her close before kissing her on both cheeks. 'How is she?' he asked quickly, his voice little more than a croak.

'Richard, calm yourself down. Now you're here she'll be fine.'

Once the doctors had finished speaking to Richard, Jodie explained to him that she had to leave right now. 'There are so many things I have to take care of, but I will ring the hospital later. If there isn't any news, I will meet my boys from school and take them over to stay with either your mum or Dee's mum and dad. Once they are settled I'll come back here to be with you.' She was hoping and praying that by the time she telephoned later this afternoon, Laraine would have safely delivered her babies and would be sitting up in bed.

'Promise you will be in touch later?' The colour was fading from Richard's cheeks. 'And Jodie, if it is all over when you ring, would you do me a favour and collect my mum and bring her with you.'

'Richard, you know I will. I have just told you, I can always leave my boys next door with Dee's mum and dad.' Jodie had sensed Richard's meaning straight off. Marian Underwood would want to be the first to see her new grandchildren. Jodie herself would see that Laraine's father was informed once there was some good news to tell him.

Having kissed and hugged her brother-in-law and told him to make sure that his wife knew she was thinking about her, Jodie gathered up her handbag and gloves and practically ran towards the car park.

At precisely seven o'clock that evening, a very tired Laraine gave another great shudder and lay back thankfully against the pile of pillows that had been placed behind her head. 'Your second daughter is just as perfect as her sister, even if she has taken an extra five minutes to be delivered.' A staff nurse was leaning over Laraine. 'Both babies will be washed and weighed, and then we'll bring them to you.'

At last Richard was allowed to get near his wife. 'You have done so well, sweetheart.' His voice was hoarse and his face grey as he kissed her very tenderly.

Laraine's eyes filled with tears as she reached out to him, and it wasn't long before two nurses came to the bed and gently put a baby in each of their arms. 'Your daughters,' one nurse murmured.

Now it was Richard who was smiling through tears. 'Oh Laraine. Ever since I met you I've thought you were the most beautiful woman in the world, and now you've given me two gorgeous daughters. Just look at them. Was ever a man more blessed?'

It was quite dark before they took Laraine back to her room that night. Richard stayed with her until she drifted off to sleep, the babies asleep in separate cots. As he stood up, he accidentally scraped his chair and Laraine opened her eyes. Pulling her arm out from beneath the bedclothes, she reached out for him. 'I love you, Richard, you'll never know how much.'

He leaned over her and lightly kissed her forehead. 'I love you too, my darling, but you must sleep now.'

'Rick...'

'Ssh ... go to sleep. I'll love you for ever.'

He placed her arm back beneath the sheet and turned to stand and gaze at the two sleeping babies in their cots. Everything about today had been wonderful. Unbelievable! Just looking at these two tiny creatures – his daughters! – had him longing to pick them up and hold them oh so tightly. By God, they were truly beautiful.

As he walked down the long corridor, he vowed to himself that as they grew up, he would kill anyone who attempted to harm even a hair on their heads. He was their father and he would take care of them. He would see that they wanted for nothing.

Jodie had been given the news from the hospital over the telephone, along with the advice that no visitors would be allowed tonight. She had called in to see Dee's mum and dad and had found Lenny and Reggie happily playing card games with Jack, whom they had grown up thinking of as an extra grandfather. Mary and Jack were over-joyed to hear that everything had gone so well and that Laraine and Richard were now the proud parents of twin girls.

'Have you been in next door to tell Marian the good news?' Mary hastily asked.

'No, that's my next port of call, but I'm dying for a cuppa. I feel ready to drop, I am so tired, and I have to get my boys home and make sure everything is ready for school in the morning.'

'Judith!' Mary exclaimed loudly. 'Will you please sit down and draw a few deep breaths. Jack, leave those cards for a moment and go and make a strong cup of tea for our Judith. She's all but done in.' Then, looking up at Jodie, Mary Hartfield smiled the sweetest smile before saying, 'You may not always have realised it, lass, but Jack and I look upon you and your two lads as if you were our own. With our Delia on the other side of the world, we feel right privileged to have you dropping in every so often, and it's no burden for us to mind Reggie and Lenny whenever you feel you'd like to leave them with us. Our Delia's bedroom has always had twin beds and it's been standing empty for too long. Look, here's Jack with your tea. Take yer time drinking it, and then you can pop in next door and give your mother-in-law the good news.'

Jack carefully pulled a small table nearer to Jodie, and as he placed her cup of tea on it he lowered his head and gave her a sly wink. 'Why not leave the boys here for tonight? Our Brian will see they get to school on time in the morning, and if it's raining I'll take them in the car. That way when you do finally get yourself home tonight you'll be able to flop out and have a good night's sleep. How does that sound to you?'

She hesitated, looked across to where her boys were sitting and saw they were smiling broadly. She silently mouthed, 'All right with you two?'

'Yes, Mum,' Reggie declared, and quick to follow Lenny called, 'We can go on playing our games then, can't we?'

'You can indeed, Lenny, and I will make sure that you and Reggie have a mug of nice hot chocolate before it's time for bed,' Jack told them as he glanced at his wife and saw that she thoroughly approved.

Jodie looked from one to the other. 'You talk about being grateful that I pop in and visit you, but really it's me who should be saying thanks to both of you. My boys look upon you as their grandparents, and as for myself, I don't know how I would manage my busy life sometimes without you two to fall back on.'

'Well, that's enough thanks from all of us,' Mary said, doing her best to wipe away a tear without being seen. 'We miss our Delia more than we can say, and having your boys around is good as a tonic; they help to keep us young. So come along, Judith, you'd best get in next door, give Marian the good news and then do as my Jack said – get yerself home and have a good night's rest.'

Having gratefully drunk her tea, Jodie got to her feet and went to give each of her boys a hug and a good night kiss. Jack wrapped her in his arms, kissed the top of her head and told her to take care of herself.

Mary walked to the front door with her, and they hugged each other tightly before Jodie went next door. Marian's front door opened as she walked up the path.

'Come along in, Jodie. Tell me, is there any news?'

'Good news, Marian. You now have two grand-daughters to go with your grandsons.'

Marian's face lit up. 'And Laraine, is she all right?'

'Very sleepy, they told me over the phone. But otherwise absolutely fine. Rick was still with her when I phoned and they said no visitors tonight, but I will come and take you into the hospital sometime tomorrow. I'll ring you when I'm on my way, give you time to get yourself ready.'

'Why are we standing talking by the front door?

Aren't you coming in?'

'Yes, of course I am, but only for a few minutes. I've had one hell of a day. The boys are staying the night with Mary and Jack, so they will come in and see you before they go to school in the morning.'

'You sound tired out, Jodie, can I get you anything?'

'I've just had a cup of tea, thanks all the same.'

'Well I know you can't drink because you're driving, but how about a hot milky coffee with just a dribble of brandy in it?'

'Sounds wonderful,' Jodie said, sighing softly, not wanting to offend her mother-in-law but longing to be home.

It had certainly been a day with a difference!

The Underwood family were well known for their parties. They didn't need an excuse; if there wasn't a reason, they would think one up. Marian Underwood was hosting this one. The twins, Adele and Annabel, were six months old and Richard simply adored them. They were absolutely gorgeous and he loved spending time with them. It was a leisurely way of life and he wasn't short of money, but the call of the sea was always there.

This party was supposed to be a belated christening celebration; the twins had been christened three months ago. The house at Camber Sands was overflowing and the sun was shining. Marian had invited the world and his wife, and it seemed everybody had children to bring with them. Every person present was remarking on the various games Marian had organised and the numerous prizes she had ready for the children.

There were no tears; every child was allowed to choose a prize as they played pass the parcel, musical statues and bobbing for apples. The twins were being so good, laughing and gurgling as they sat on the floor amongst all the feet, never grizzling when picked up and passed from one adoring adult to another. The only time the din lessened was when Marian declared that the buffet in her front room was open.

How the kiddies laughed. Standing behind a table in the bay window was a chef, rigged out right down to his tall white hat.

'No adults allowed,' Chef called loudly as he speared sizzling sausages on the end of a very long toasting fork and asked each child what they would like in their hot dog. 'We have onions, we have pickles and sauces and we have salad,' he almost sang to them. Lenny took the wind out of the chef's sails by asking for 'Two sausages in a long roll, not a round one, with loads of butter, please.'

The adults weren't doing too badly either. The work-tops in the kitchen were loaded with food, and Jack Hartfield was making himself useful by carving a ham that had been oven-roasted then glazed with honey and brown sugar. Marian Underwood was a great cook when the fancy took her.

As for the generous array of cakes and gateaux, these, as always when family parties were being organised, had been left up to Judith Underwood. Nobody could match Jodie's standards when it came to pastry- and cake-making.

'All right, my love?' Richard was watching his wife with a saucy grin on his face as she ate a slice of coffee gateau. 'You've almost got your figure back in shape; you look great in that dress.'

'Now don't push yer luck, Rick, you know what a job I had to get into this dress today. I have lost five pounds this week and I am determined to get back to my original weight. I've got the evening off tonight; I'll diet again tomorrow.'

'Ha!' he laughed at her. 'I love you as you are now. Just a little more flesh to get hold of.'

'And you didn't love me when I was slim?'

'Can't remember that far back! We are an old married couple now with a growing family.' He was still laughing as he teased her.

'Oh! So that's the reason you've let yourself go round the middle. Preparing to be a stay-at-home layabout, are you?'

'God forbid! In fact I was only thinking this morning it's about time I went back to sea. How do you feel about travelling with the twins, or would you rather I took a post without you until they are a little older?' He reached out and took her in his arms. 'Don't suppose now is the time to talk about the future. Mother has just ordered me to blow up another load of balloons.'

Laraine stayed within his arms and they laughed together. Both of them were well aware that important decisions would have to be made, but as Rick had said, the timing wasn't right.

It was between eight thirty and nine o'clock when most of the children began to show signs of being tired. As it was a Saturday night and no one had to get up for work on Sunday morning, Richard suggested that Jodie and the boys might like to come back to Little Common and stay the night with him and Laraine. 'Please come,' Laraine added to her husband's invitation. 'I'll do a Sunday roast and Rick can take the boys and the twins down to Bexhill seafront in the morning.'

Both Reggie and Lenny were loudly expressing their approval at the invitation when their father walked into the room. For a moment the silence that fell over the room was unbearable.

Marian Underwood broke it. 'Son, do you ever keep a promise? Three days ago you called in here and swore you wouldn't let me down.'

'Take that injured look off your face. I said I'd be here and I am here. What's eating you now?'

'We had our meal ages ago and the children have played all the games, but as usual there hasn't been a sight of you. Everyone is getting ready to go home now.'

'Well, that's all to the good,' John told her, grinning. 'I'll stay a couple of hours and we can have a few drinks. That way I get you all to myself.'

'I give up,' his mother murmured, and the rest of the people in the room didn't know where most of their sympathy lay, with John's mother, or with his two young sons.

Reggie told himself that he was the eldest and therefore he should speak first. He stole a glance at his mother, took a deep breath and said, 'Dad, we're just going to get our things together because Auntie Laraine and Uncle Richard have asked us to go home and stay with them for the weekend.'

'I'm not stopping yer, lad,' his father said, with a lot more bravado than he was feeling, 'but the pair of you might spare a hug for your old dad before you tear off.'

No words were necessary. Both lads went to their dad, even if they were a little hesitant. Within seconds he had them wrapped in his arms and was tickling the life out of them.

When it was time to leave, John stood on the doorstep with his arm across his mother's shoulders and waved as his brother's car drove off, followed by Jodie with his two sons in the back.

Marian's cheeks were streaked with tears as she broke free from her son's arms and turned to go back inside. 'If I live to be a hundred years old I will never understand you, John,' she muttered.

Jack and Mary Hartfield were in no hurry to go home and leave Marian on her own after the last guests had departed. Instead they had gathered up the dirty glasses, plates and cups and saucers and were now standing at the sink, Jack doing the washing-up while Mary dried the dishes.

John went straight to the sideboard, where he poured himself a generous shot of whisky, calling to Jack to ask if he wanted a beer or a short.

'Nothing at the moment, lad, thanks all the same,' Jack called in reply.

Mary shook the tea cloth she had been using and hung it over the rack fixed beneath the sink, then tossed her head to her husband, indicating that he should go into the other room with John and leave her and Marian alone. Then, turning to face Marian, she asked, 'Shall I make a pot of tea, just for you and me?'

'Yes please, luv. You know, Mary, you're a true friend.'

'Well if we're not good friends by now we never will be. Been next-door neighbours now for more

205

years than we've got fingers to count them on.'

'Tell me then, Mary, what do you make of my son John?'

'Can't really answer that,' Mary told her, not wanting to throw caution to the wind. 'One thing I will say, though, he never ceases to surprise me. Doesn't seem to know when he's well off.'

'Mary, you've hit the nail right on the head there. Lovely wife like Jodie! Works herself to the bone for those two boys she does, and he waltzes in and out of their lives just as the mood takes him. God knows how or where he's going to end up. Frightens me to even think about it.'

'Then try not to, Marian. I know it's easier said than done. We still worry over our children even though they are grown up, but perhaps that is what we mothers are supposed to do. Now wipe away those tears and get the biscuit tin out, that's if there's any left after the way your kitchen has been raided today.'

They grinned at each other. 'Was a good party, though, wasn't it, Mary?'

'Aye, it was. But then tell me when any party thrown by you or yours wasn't a great success.'

That answer pleased Marian and she stirred a spoonful of sugar into the cup of tea that Mary had poured for her, all the while thinking about John. Just where did he think his way of life was going to lead him? Was it too late for him to mend his ways and settle down to a proper married life? Become a good husband and a good father to those two lovely sons of his?

If she were honest, she thought it was probably far too late.

18

It was six o'clock on Monday morning when Jodie crept downstairs to find Richard and Laraine seated at the kitchen table each nursing one of their daughters, who were busy guzzling their first bottle of the day. Adele and Annabel both looked and smelt so good as Jodie bent and kissed the top of their silky blonde heads.

'Oh, you've bathed and dressed them already. I was hoping I would have been in time to join in.'

'You're up early enough as it is,' Laraine remarked. 'I thought you delegated your staff to open up the salons these days.'

'Mostly I do, but today I have to take the boys home to get them into their school uniforms and have them at school by a quarter to nine. Before I go, though, I want to thank both of you. Yesterday was a smashing day, especially good for Lenny and Reggie. Thanks for taking them to the beach, Richard, and playing football with them. There's times when I worry that they don't have enough male influence in their lives. I don't want them growing up mollycoddled, looked upon as mummy's boys.'

'You've no need to worry on that score,' Richard was quick to assure her. 'If you'd seen them playing football yesterday you'd be well aware that both of them can handle themselves. I do feel that their father has let them down badly. I know John is my brother, but there are times when I could cheerfully disown him. One thing you must always remember, Jodie, if you ever need anything, even someone just to talk to, both Derrick and I will always be here for you. Even if we are at sea and you don't know how to contact us, all you have to do is get in touch with whatever shipping line we're with. There is always ship-to-shore telephone communication.'

Jodie had to swallow the lump that was stuck in her throat before she could form an answer, and when she did it was a very emotional one. 'Thanks, Richard, I've always known that if the worst came to the worst, both you and Derrick would be there for Reggie and Lenny, and for that I am so grateful. As for John, I'm sorry, but I've given up on him.'

Adele and Annabel lightened the moment. Bottles now empty, they were restless, demanding attention, and Laraine quickly grabbed the chance to put a smile back on Jodie's face. 'Here, you can hold Adele, Jodie, and Rick, you take Annabel upstairs with you and make sure the boys are up and are using the bathroom.'

'My wife is good at issuing orders,' Rick said as he winked at his sister-in-law. To his wife he said, 'And what are you going to be doing?'

'Me? I'm going to see about getting a hearty breakfast on the table for all of us. Best way to start the day is to eat well; one never knows what the day is going to bring.'

Jodie was in seventh heaven. She had Adele nestled in her arms, her little head resting on her shoulder as she walked back and forth and quietly crooned to her and rubbed her back. Laraine was busy at the cooker when she turned her head and said, 'Are you anywhere near being straight in your lovely Epsom house yet?'

'Funny you should ask that. It has been four and a half months since I moved in, and I have scarcely started to unpack. In fact some of the boxes and crates are still standing unopened in the garage, but I never seem to have any time to spare. The thing I am most pleased about is that both Lenny and Reggie are doing fine. They really like their new school, have made quite a few friends and are enrolled in a great number of activities. They even go swimming, and Reggie tells me his class teacher thinks he is almost good enough to join the water polo team. While we're on the subject, a couple of days ago I had a letter from the Walkers, the couple who bought my cottage in Rye. When all the negotiations were going on, they seemed a very nice, decent couple, though I only met them a couple of times.'

Laraine stopped buttering toast and moved the frying pan full of rashers of bacon further away from the heat of the gas. 'And what has happened to change your mind about them? Have you met up with them since they moved in?'

'No, but that's the point. They haven't yet moved in. I knew at the time they weren't going to live there permanently. They have a business in France, or so I was told at the time, but wanted to keep a base here in England, and when the purchase was going through they seemed delighted to have found my cottage.'

'And now? What did they write to you about,

some fault they've found in the property?'

Jodie stopped pacing and shifted Adele more securely in her arms. 'No, nothing like that. What they are asking, in a very roundabout way, is whether I still have relatives or friends using the cottage. Apparently they have received a letter from a relative of theirs who is keeping an eye on the place for them, informing them that it seems to be occupied, mainly at weekends. And they asked if I have given a key to anyone.'

At that moment Richard came down the stairs bringing Annabel and the two boys with him. 'Cor, smells good. What d'you say, boys?'

'Yeah!' replied Reggie and Lenny in unison, sniffing loudly and laughing.

'Well all of you sit up to the table,' Laraine ordered as Rick and Jodie started seating Adele and Annabel in their high chairs. With a good English breakfast in front of everyone and a Farley's Rusk in the hand of each baby, Laraine said, 'Tuck in.' No one needed a second telling.

It was when the plates were almost clean and toast and marmalade was being eaten that Laraine began to tell Rick of the letter that Jodie had received.

'Have you been over there to check for yourself?' was Rick's first question.

'No, I haven't had the time. Besides, I didn't think it was anything to do with me. Surely if they have relatives taking care of the property it should be down to them to either go and confront whoever is in there or call the police. You never know, it might be squatters.'

'You might well be right,' Rick answered

thoughtfully. 'Tell you what, it's no great distance. When we take the twins out today, I'll drive over there and see if anyone is about. Two questions: do you still have a key? And are there still any curtains at the windows?'

'No, I don't have a key. I handed mine and a spare one to the solicitor on the day of completion. As far as I know, every window should still have curtains hanging. Mrs Walker said she had fallen in love with the soft furnishings and would I allow her to purchase them. She was a very determined lady. We came to an agreement and she paid me in cash.'

Richard looked very thoughtful. 'It sounds as if it might be someone who knows the law, has seen the place empty and seized the chance to live without paying any rent or rates. Be rotten for the new owners if that is what has happened. It will take some time for them to obtain an eviction order from a court. Anyway, we'll have a look round, but stop worrying yourself, Jodie, it isn't your problem.'

For the next ten minutes it was sheer pandemonium. At last the boys were ready, the twins had been kissed and cuddled and Jodie had managed to cram all of her equipment into one case and finally got the zip to close. Then she and the boys were in the car, more thanks, a final wave, and they were off.

Jodie settled back in her seat and concentrated on her driving. A new day. A new week. It had been an absolutely amazing weekend, one that everyone had really enjoyed. Apart from John, but that was his own fault. She smiled and hoped that the day that lay ahead would be as good. She allowed herself a rare moment of pride in her own achievements. The boys had settled in well to their new school. She herself was always busy and was successful in more ways than one. Yes, she decided, for someone with no one to rely on for help, she was doing remarkably well. She suddenly sighed. Yes, she did have a prosperous life with great prospects, but there was no getting away from it. At times it was a lonely one.

It was just after seven that evening when Jodie glanced at the clock, then turned her eyes on her boys and laughed out loud. 'I thought you were supposed to be doing your homework.' Reggie was grinning, but it was Lenny that spoke up. 'Reg helped me to do mine because he did his own during a maths test. He's such a clever clogs, he finished before everyone else, and as the teacher wasn't looking he got his English books out and did his homework. So is it all right if we watch telly?'

Before Jodie had time to think of an answer, the telephone rang. 'Yes, all right, but turn the volume down a bit. I'll go in the other room and take this call,' she called over her shoulder.

'Hi, Jodie.' Laraine's voice was loud and clear as Jodie picked up the receiver.

'Hi, Laraine, was your trip worthwhile?'

'Yes, luv, it was, in more ways than one. We went to your cottage first and it was quite obvious that someone has been occupying the place. There were empty milk bottles on the doorstep and whoever put them out hadn't bothered to even rinse them. Rick could see over the back wall and he said the dustbin standing outside the kitchen door was overflowing with tins and beer bottles. Couldn't see into the house because the curtains at the windows were tightly drawn, all the way round on the ground floor.'

'Never mind, you did your best.'

'Hang on a minute, Jodie, you haven't heard the half of it yet. Rick suggested that we have lunch at the Malt House. We none of us have been regular customers there, but on the other hand all the family are known in Rye and we did use their restaurant on high days and holidays. It turned out that Tim Gardiner, the eldest son, was on duty today, and he and Rick know each other well. He gave us a good table where there was plenty of room and provided two high chairs for Adele and Annabel, and we had a smashing lunch. Tim came and sat with us when we were having coffee, and that was when Rick broached the subject of the cottage. Tim knew you had moved, told us his own boys missed Lenny and Reggie, and Rick began to tell him about the letter you'd received from the new owners. Tim looked so amused, and then he started to really laugh. We both felt really embarrassed until he explained.'

When Laraine stopped talking, Jodie got the feeling that she was being hesitant, and she quickly asked what was wrong.

'I'm a bit worried as to how you will react if I tell you what Tim told us.'

'Oh please, Laraine, don't be daft. I'll be worried sick all night if you don't tell me what it is.'

'OK then, here goes. Your John has been coming into the Malt House at weekends, not to the restaurant but to the public house side where the licensed bars are, and he always has the same tarted-up dolly bird with him. Tim's description of the lady, not ours. Apparently John told one of the barmen that he owned half of the cottage and that you'd sold it over his head. He also made it quite clear that until you send him a cheque for half of what you sold it for, he has every right to use the place whenever he feels like it.'

'Good God above!' Jodie was astounded, and it took a while for her to bounce back from the shock. 'That husband of mine has the cheek of the devil. What he's claiming is ridiculous. Apart from my navy allowance, he has never contributed a single penny towards the upkeep of our boys. And since he is being such a rotter, I'll tell you now, he robbed me blind before he went off to Hong Kong.'

'I'm not with you,' Laraine interrupted. 'What has Hong Kong got to do with it?'

'It's something I've never meant to bring out into the open and until now I have kept it to myself.' She paused and sighed. 'I'll go into the full details next time we meet, but for now it will be sufficient to tell you that I won seventy-five thousand pounds on the football forecast. I never bother to check the results and I was out when the men came to bring me the cheque, which was made out to J. Underwood. John saw his chance, took the cheque and never said a word. A couple of days later he was on his way to Hong Kong with my cheque in his pocket. It wasn't until Sadie Johnson came round to collect my monthly dues that I became aware of what he had done. God above! I felt terrible that evening. There was Sadie expecting me to give her a nice little backhander and I didn't know what the hell she was talking about.'

'Oh Jodie, what can I say? What is there to say? Is it all right if I tell Rick about this?'

'I don't care who gets to know now. I've kept quiet for a good many reasons, the main one being I just didn't want our boys to know that their father had walked off with that vast amount of money, which rightly was mine, without a thought as to what good it could have done them. Not one penny, no birthday or Christmas presents; he kept the lot. And now he wants half of the money from the sale of the cottage that I worked and saved for. No, he's gone too far this time. I'll see him in hell before I'll give him a penny.'

'Jodie, I'm so sorry, what else is there to say? Are you covered as regards the sale of your cottage?'

'Don't worry, Laraine, I'm sure I am. Everything was done through a reputable law firm. I don't think John can touch me. For Christ's sake, he wasn't even in the country when I bought that cottage.'

'That's what Rick said, but hold on, he wants to have a word with you. I'll say good night now, catch up with you soon.'

'Good night, Laraine, kiss Adele and Annabel for me.'

'Hi, Jodie.'

'Hi, Rick. You found out more than we bargained for, eh?'

'Doesn't really come as a surprise. John thinks

up more scams than we've had hot dinners, and the trouble is he is his own worse enemy. More often than not it's him that comes off worst in the end.'

'Huh!' Jodie huffed. 'Not always. I've just been telling Laraine about how John made off with my football winnings. To this day I've never seen a penny of that cash, and neither have the boys.'

'What? When did this happen?'

'I've told Laraine the bare details; the rest can wait until we meet up again, which I hope will be soon.'

'Of course, it won't be long. We'll talk before the weekend.'

'Rick,' she began, and then, almost unwillingly, she said, 'I've just had a thought. Of course I should have remembered, but John had a key. When I knew the sale was finalised I should have asked him to return it, but with all that was going on I didn't give it a single thought.'

'Jodie, don't start blaming yourself. Would you like me to take over and deal with this?'

'Oh Rick, yes please, as long as it is no trouble to you.'

'None whatsoever. Tomorrow we'll arrange to meet up somewhere, even if it is only for a few minutes. I want you to bring with you the letter you received from Mr and Mrs Walker. I'll contact them – they must be on the telephone in France – and explain as much as possible, and also tell them that we will have the main lock on the front door of the cottage changed immediately and pay all expenses. How does that sound to you?'

'Rick, you are a saint.'

'Hardly that, Jodie. Anyway, ring me in the morning and let me know what your movements are going to be. Night, luv, tell the boys we'll see them soon.'

'Night, Rick, God bless you.'

The phone line went dead and Jodie replaced the receiver. She allowed herself a few minutes to reflect on her husband's latest trick, but quickly abandoned those thoughts. 'He's not worth the hassle,' she said loudly.

Count your blessings, name them one by one, and it will surprise you what the Lord hath done. She was humming the hymn she had learnt as a child as she pushed open the door to the lounge.

'I have Mars bars and Kit Kats for whoever can give me the biggest hug,' she called out, but to her surprise there was no immediate reaction.

Lenny and Reggie were laid out flat on their stomachs, elbows supporting their hands on which their chins were resting, watching the TV.

'My boys are refusing the offer of a Mars bar?' said Jodie, feigning amazement.

Reggie sighed, and without turning to face his mother said, 'Mum, we're watching *Ivanhoe* and we don't want to miss the end. We'll hug you later.'

'Well that's me told,' she said, smiling to herself as she snuggled down in a deep armchair, but all the same as she sat watching her boys she was still counting her many blessings. As for John, if he didn't want her or the boys, why did he keep popping up? What he didn't realise was how much he was missing by ignoring his sons. The truth would hit him one day, but by then it would be too late.

Far too late.

19

Jodie replaced the telephone receiver and picked up her cup of coffee, which by now was lukewarm. Why does it always have to be me? she moaned to herself. She had come into her Epsom salon this morning determined to spend most of the day in the office bringing her accounts up to date and at the same time taking note of how well the staff here were managing. Time had flown by so quickly. Already it was the beginning of July, and the boys would soon be breaking up for their long summer holiday. She was going to have to make some arrangements as to where they could go.

The early post had arrived before she left the house this morning and she had brought it with her. So far the contents hadn't done much to boost her morale. Two postcards from Dee and Derrick saying that they were having a wonderful time and the weather was glorious. It was the postscript that rankled a bit: please would she make sure that Derrick's mother wasn't left on her own too much.

Nice letter from Laraine, who was living in Great Yarmouth, where Rick had taken a shore job in connection with the oil rigs. Another postscript. Would Jodie please go to their house in Little Common and pick up the post, put it all in one large envelope and redirect it on to them.

Hardly had she finished reading her mail than

the phone rang. It was Marian. Apparently she had a hospital appointment tomorrow afternoon and would Jodie be able to take her because her back was playing her up and she couldn't walk properly without somebody to lean on.

'I wish to God that *I* had someone to lean on,' Jodie said aloud as she stared at her reflection in the mirror on the wall in front of her desk. There were times lately when she thought she was head postmistress and chauffeur for the family, as well as nurse, carer and chef all rolled into one when it came to the boys. Marian's demands on her time were steadily getting more and more frequent. Tomorrow Jodie had a whole day's work mapped out at Shepperton Studios, for which she would receive an amount it would take her two full weeks to earn working in one of her own salons. It would be a long day, between twelve and fourteen hours, and she'd already arranged for Mary and Jack to stay at her house and see to the boys. Why is it I manage to sort my own life out and stand on my own two feet, and yet all my troubles stem from having to sort out the rest of the family? she wondered.

'Hello. It must be a great feeling to be able to scarper away into the back room while your staff see to the clients.'

The sound of that familiar voice caught her unawares. Normally the very sight of Michael Connelly, impeccably dressed and looking as if he had just stepped out of a bandbox, would have gladdened Jodie's heart. Today his smiling face and easy-going attitude were like a red rag to a bull. Jodie got to her feet and practically fell into his arms while playfully punching away at his chest.

'Hey, calm down, this isn't a bit like you. Tell me what's wrong and we'll see if I can help to put it right.' Michael as always had the patience of Job.

'Unless you can put more hours into the day and cut me into about four different pieces, I can't see that you can be of any use whatsoever.'

'I'll go then, shall I?'

'No, of course not. Sorry, Michael,' Jodie said, standing on her toes to reach up and kiss his cheek. 'It just seems as if everyone wants a piece of me. Dee and Derrick have asked me to make sure that my mother-in-law isn't left on her own too often, and now Marian herself has rung to tell me she needs me to take her to the hospital tomorrow. I hadn't the heart to tell her I couldn't, but I have a full day's work booked at Shepperton. If I were to phone at such short notice and say that I was unable to turn up, I doubt very much that any more work would be coming my way in the near future.'

Michael pretended to look terrified. 'It goes without saying that Shepperton is a must. There are plenty of us that can do the hospital trip; just leave that to me, and if the worst comes to the worst I will take Marian myself. Has nobody ever told you that a trouble shared is a trouble halved?'

'Thanks, Michael.' There were tears in her eyes.

'What for? Your friends are there for you, always will be, only you're too pig-headed to ask most of the time. Do you feel any better now?'

'I'll be all right, thanks to you.'

'Are you sure?' Michael knew Jodie wasn't herself these days. She seemed so quiet, so subdued.

It was a dramatic change in such a short time. 'Look, darling, if things are getting on top of you, let me take you out one evening. We'll have a slap-up meal and you can tell me everything. There must be ways in which I can help.'

Jodie gave a sigh of relief. Suddenly the weight on her had been lifted, and as she stared at Michael she began to feel human again. 'I'll take a rain check on the dinner, but a really good hot cup of coffee would go down well, and the café up the road will supply that if you can spare the time.'

'Jodie my love, I wouldn't be here if I couldn't spare the time, and coffee sounds great, so repair your make-up while I explain to your staff that I am going to steal you away for half an hour.'

'Stop licking your fingers,' Jodie said, but she was laughing fit to bust. Michael had insisted that the speciality of this café was their doughnuts, and they went so well with a cup of coffee they had to have one. He was right. They were still warm, covered in sugar and absolutely oozing with raspberry jam. He was acting like a child, but he was such a dear, a really good friend.

Time to go back to work. Michael took her hand and linked it through his arm, drawing her close to his side as they walked the short distance back to the salon.

'I'll go and see Marian as soon as I leave you,' he assured her. 'You are not to worry, I will take good care of her. Are you going to be all right now?' He looked at her hopefully, and she nodded with a smile. 'Remember, whenever you have the free time I am taking you to dinner, yes?'

'Sure, I'd like that, and about this morning, sorry I was such a grump.'

'Don't let it bother you. Have a good time at Shepperton tomorrow. Who knows, you might meet the man of your dreams.'

'Oh yeah, and pigs might fly.'

'Now you're being coy. What about this Philip you told me about?'

'He's all right. A nice man.'

'Darling Jodie, after what you've been through with that pest of a husband of yours, anybody has got to be a vast improvement, so doll yourself up, waggle those hips of yours and let him know you're ready for a fling.'

Jodie stared at him in disbelief. 'Michael Connelly, you should be ashamed of yourself,' but she was smiling as she walked away from him.

Where did the time go? Jodie had given herself the day off because it was the last day of term for the boys and she had promised to meet them with the car as they'd have so many books and papers to bring home. So far so good, as regarded arrangements. Mary and Jack were going to come and live at Epsom and take care of Reg and Lenny during the whole of their six-week holiday. It was a life-saving arrangement for Jodie, but it hadn't gone down too well with her mother-in-law, who was used to having the Hartfields living next door and always there at her beck and call.

It hadn't been so bad when Ethel, John's twin sister, had been living with her mother, but out of the blue Ethel had got herself a job with the Cunard shipping line, cruising with the transatlantic

222

service. Seemed it wasn't only the Underwood men that had salt in their veins. Jodie didn't blame Ethel; in fact there was many a day when she envied her. However, luck was on Jodie's side for once. She'd come to a financial arrangement with Florrie Stevens, who worked at the Golden Sands Holiday Park and lived only a short distance from Marian. Florrie would check on Marian every morning, would take her shopping once a week and also to the holiday park to have her lunch in the restaurant three times a week. This lunch idea was with the full approval of Mike Woodward.

Two weeks into the boys' school holiday everything was going according to plan. In fact with Mary and Jack living in Jodie's house things couldn't have turned out better. Jack was happy to do odd jobs around the house and also attend to the garden, while Mary had set to and unpacked all the boxes and crates that had stayed in the garage for so long. She had washed every piece of china and polished the furniture until it sparkled. To the boys' delight, several outings had been arranged; a visit to the Zoological Gardens in Regent's Park in London had been pronounced fantastic. Jack had also taken them to Whipsnade, where the animals lived in wide spaces in the open air. The weather was unbelievable, continuous sunshine for days on end, and it was on one such Sunday afternoon, when the adults, including Marian, were snoozing in deckchairs and the boys had two friends over and were down in the wooded area at the bottom of the garden, that the shrill of the telephone shattered the silence.

Reluctantly Jodie got to her feet and hurried towards the house. Placing the earpiece comfortably, she heard the polite clipped voice of a telephonist say, 'Caller, will you hold the line please. I have a Mrs Delia Underwood on the line.'

'Jodie, can you hear me?'

'Yes, Dee, loud and clear, but hang on a moment, your parents are in the garden and I must shout to them... It's all right, Dee, they're coming. How are you, is everything all right?'

'Never better. I've got some great news, but as Mum and Dad are there, I'd better tell them first.'

Jodie felt disinclined to hand the phone over to Jack, but she quickly did so as he arrived first and a breathless Mary came running behind him.

Jack spoke briefly to Dee and then handed the receiver over to his wife and took a few steps backwards. He looked as if the wind had been knocked out of his sails, but then without warning he began to laugh, really laugh. Jodie was feeling at a loss as to why when Mary turned and handed the phone to her. 'Delia wants another word with you,' she said. Her eyes were brimming with tears and yet she looked so happy.

'Hi, Dee, it's me again. Your dad can't stop laughing and your mother is on the verge of tears. Is someone going to tell me what's going on?'

'Derrick is here, I'm going to let him tell you. Bye for now, will get a letter in the post to you, tomorrow at the latest.'

'Hello, Jodie, I'm gonna be a dad, and it seems that whatever Rick could do I can also manage. I've taken Dee to the hospital this morning and she is carrying twins! Lots to sort out yet, might send her home to have the babies, but we'll have to wait and see. Would you mind breaking the news to my mother? We have tried to phone her twice today but there is no answer.'

'It's Sunday, Derrick, your mother is here with me. Just a minute...' Jack had already gone to fetch Marian from the garden, and Jodie handed her the receiver. By the time Marian came off the phone, she was beaming all over her face.

Jodie didn't follow Jack and Mary straight back out into the garden; instead she decided it was time for afternoon tea. Cutting and buttering bread gave her something to do while she sorted out all the thoughts that were whizzing around in her head. She laid two trays, one for the adults and the other with food to suit the appetite of four growing lads. To ham and cheese sandwiches she added salty biscuits and pots of cheesy dips with chives. For the boys she had done beans on toast and bangers, even though it was only four hours since all four of them had sat at her table and eaten a three-course dinner. On the dresser she had placed a raspberry meringue and a rich fruit cake, both of which she had made yesterday.

Jack put his head around the door and gasped as he saw the trays of food. 'Here, let me give you a hand with all of that. Mary said this was what you'd be doing, and Marian will be thrilled to hear she's going to get a cup of tea.'

The conversation over tea was all about the exciting news. Would Delia come home? Would that be for the best? What would Derrick do left on his own in a foreign country? No one had the answers, yet the delight everyone had experienced on hearing the news had not diminished. There was so much to look forward to. A leisurely Sunday afternoon had suddenly brought contact with loved ones on the other side of the world, and each person present was grateful for the telephone.

For the rest of the afternoon Jodie dithered between the house and the garden. She was in a really happy mood, and why wouldn't she be? Dee would be coming home, and that surely had to be a blessing.

20

Changes were not coming singly. Not in the Underwood family they weren't.

A healthy-looking but unmistakably pregnant Dee had arrived at Heathrow airport to be met by a host of friends and family. There had been a great deal of discussion as to where she was going to live for the foreseeable future. 'Your mother-in-law has expressed a wish that you should stay with her,' Mary had quietly informed her.

Dee had shaken her head and her eyes had made contact with Jodie's. 'I'd rather stay with you, Jodie, if that is all right with you. If I stay with Marian it would upset you and Dad, wouldn't it, Mum? I know you will say differently but it would be your right to be upset, and the same thing would apply if I came home to stay with you. Marian would feel left out.'

Everyone had been surprised at Dee's honesty.

The situation had been a challenge to all concerned but Jodie was thrilled at the outcome. Dee would be coming to stay with her.

Then Richard had been given further promotion, which meant that he was frequently out of the country. Uncertain of exactly what the future held for him and his wife, he had decided against hanging on to any property for the time being. However, with the twins coming up to their first birthday, rented accommodation was proving unsuitable. The final straw broke when out of the blue Richard was ordered to Tunisia for a six-month stretch. To travel with the twins would be difficult enough, but for a stint of only six months it hardly made sense. The solution was inevitable. Much to Jodie's delight, Laraine and the twins would also temporarily be moving in with her.

So for the last three months there had been three Mrs Underwoods living in Jodie's house in Epsom, together with Reggie and Lenny, Adele and Annabel, who would be a year old in four weeks' time, and another set of twins who were waiting to be born to Delia Underwood. This was proving to be an eventful year!

It was also a happy year. The absence of the men in their lives was to a certain degree made up for by having Jack Hartfield around a lot of the time. Michael and his partner Danny were always popping in too. Brian, Dee's younger brother, had recently signed on with the Merchant Navy and was stationed in dry dock at Portsmouth. Whilst in training he had most weekends free and he too liked nothing better than to dump himself on Jodie. 'After all,' he would argue, 'there's no point me going home. Mum and Dad are much more likely to be here with you, seeing as how you're housing my pregnant sister.' Jodie had no objections. She loved keeping an open house and she often thought how lucky she was to have been able to buy this beautiful house.

The time was edging on for Dee. She looked enormous and was obviously getting more tired as the days passed. One Sunday morning, when she had not put in an appearance by nine thirty, Jodie took a tray of breakfast and a pot of tea up to her bedroom. She tapped lightly on the door and edged it open with her foot. Dee was sitting on the side of the bed, her ankles badly swollen, and when she attempted to get up, she could barely stand. According to the doctor's calculations the baby wasn't due for another three weeks.

'Not doing so good today?' Concern sounded in Jodie's voice as she endeavoured to smile. 'Are you in any pain?' she added.

'Not pain, I just seem to ache from head to foot and somehow I just cannot get comfortable.'

'Well I'm going to call our doctor out to have a look at you. I know you are booked to go to Epsom Hospital, but you don't have to sit around feeling so uncomfortable. Have a cup of tea and a piece of toast even if you don't fancy anything else, and then I'll help you to have a nice warm bath before I make that telephone call.'

Dee looked up at Jodie and a tear slowly trickled down her cheek as she managed a weak smile. 'I wish Derrick were here,' she murmured sadly.

Jodie shrugged and smiled in sympathy. 'Part of the price we've to pay for having chosen to marry seafaring men,' she said, thinking back to when she herself had been in this situation. She poured milk into a cup and then filled it with tea from the pot, setting it down next to Dee. 'Sit where you are while I go and run the water for your bath.'

When Jodie came back into the room she was pleased to see that Dee had eaten one of the rashers of bacon and a slice of toast and was now sipping her cup of tea. 'Right, I think I'll get Laraine to come upstairs and walk the other side of you while we get you to the bathroom.'

It was a difficult task getting Dee along the hallway, but she never even got one leg over the side of the bath. Her waters broke as she stood there, and she suddenly clutched at her sisters-in-law, terrified. She had been told what to expect, had known this would happen eventually, but suddenly it was starting now, and she had the overwhelming urge to scream, though common sense told her that wouldn't do any good. Laraine and Jodie knew how frightened Dee must be, and they did their best to comfort her.

'Everything's going to be fine. I'll leave you here with Laraine and pop downstairs to phone the hospital,' Jodie said when they had managed to get Dee sitting down on the bathroom stool.

'Thank you, Jodie. I am so sorry, I have made a mess on your floor.'

Jodie and Laraine stared at each other, then burst out laughing. 'At a time like this you're worried about my bathroom floor? Silly girl, it's only water.'

Jodie came back bringing with her a clean nightdress, a dressing gown and a pair of fluffy slippers. 'Would you like to lie down on your bed for a while, or shall we get you downstairs? The ambulance shouldn't be too long. The operator was insistent that you should come to the hospital straight away; she said first baby and the fact that you are expecting twins makes it imperative that you be brought in without delay.'

Laraine went to fetch Dee's bags from her bedroom, and by the time Jodie had got Dee dressed in the nightdress and dressing gown they could hear the sirens of the ambulance sounding as it turned into Jodie's drive.

There wasn't time for Laraine to phone and ask Dee's parents to come over to look after Adele and Annabel, so it was only Jodie who went in the ambulance with Dee. Once again Jodie found herself pacing the corridor and sitting for what seemed like endless hours waiting for Underwood twins to be born. There was no escaping this time; there was no one else. Derrick was thousands of miles away.

She was startled as a doctor lightly tapped her shoulder; she had actually fallen asleep. 'What time is it?' she asked wearily, stretching her aching arms out in front of her.

The doctor grinned. 'Six o'clock in the evening, and Mrs Underwood has been delivered of two healthy sons.'

'Thank God for that!' Jodie said, breathing a heavy sigh of relief

The doctor smiled down at her; she looked worn out. 'I'll get one of the nurses to make you a cup of coffee, get you feeling a little more awake before you go in to visit your sister-in-law and your two new nephews.'

'Thank you,' Jodie managed to murmur, thinking how welcome a cup of hot coffee would be.

Jodie couldn't help it: she took one look at Dee, who looked little more than a child herself, sitting propped up in bed with her reddish hair spread out over the pillows and a baby cradled in each arm, and she wanted to weep. She had to take a deep breath before she was able to speak.

'Oh well done, Dee, and all on your own. Just look at them, aren't they both so beautiful...'

'Yes, they are, aren't they?' Dee murmured as she smiled, even though her own eyes were brimming with tears. 'If only Derrick could have been here.'

Jodie had no answer to that, but she stayed there stroking the back of Dee's hand until she drifted off to sleep and the nurse came to put the babies into their cots.

Ten days Dee was kept in the hospital, and the family had drawn up a rota as to whose turn it would be to visit each day. Beautiful flowers from Derrick had arrived, and Richard wasn't going to be outdone. 'More exotic blooms from the other side of the world,' the ward sister said, beaming as she came to Dee's bedside, her arms filled with brilliant-coloured flowers.

The baby boys were doing well, thriving according to the doctors. Dee was breast-feeding them both and she found this very tiring, but all the while she'd enough milk she knew it was the best thing to do. No names had yet been decided on.

There had been lots of suggestions, but what Dee wanted most of all was to be able to discuss them with Derrick. He was the father and it seemed only right that he should have a say in the matter. Oh why the hell couldn't he have been here? she ranted to herself as she thumped at each of her pillows in turn. I almost feel as if I am an unmarried mother.

Once Dee and the new twins were allowed home, the problems seemed to mount. First off, names for the baby boys *had* to be decided, and Dee was of the opinion that the christening should not be delayed. God knows how long it would be if they waited for Derrick to come home.

Then there was a need for a great deal of organising to be set in motion, in order that the occupants of the house could continue to lead their different lives. Thank God money was not a problem. Laraine in particular was tugging at the reins. Adele and Annabel were both so sweet, and she loved spending time with them. She took them on long walks, and when she got down on the floor and played with them, their mischief and frolics made her laugh. At least once a week she took them to Camber Sands to spend the day with their Grandma Underwood. It was an easy, laid-back way of life and she didn't feel at all unsettled.

That was until the day Mary came to Epsom with Jack to look after Adele and Annabel in order to give Laraine a break. It had been Jodie's suggestion that Laraine should accompany her to Shepperton Studios. What an experience that had been! It had opened her eyes to an entirely new world, and she found herself longing to be part of it, more so since Jodie had told her that after her visit she had been the main topic of conversation among the administrative executives. It had been good to hear the flattering remarks they'd made about her, and the suggestion that there might be a place for her in their fashion programmes had certainly given her food for thought.

It was also Jodie who had put forward a proposal that a nursemaid should be taken on to give Dee a hand with her two baby boys, and someone similar to give Laraine a break, if only for a couple of days each week. Both Dee and Laraine were receiving a good regular income from their husbands, so money was not a problem. It would make things a whole lot easier and certainly add a little spice to their lives until they were able to each take their set of twins and rejoin their husbands in roaming around the world.

That day would come, no doubt about it. Jodie was well aware that both Derrick and Richard would want their wives and children to join them, and where would that leave her and her two sons? And how about her own husband?

She was not going to think about opening up that can of worms, at least not for the moment.

It was surprising how well things worked out when everybody made an effort and put their minds to it. A chat with a local employment agency soon produced three applicants for the position of nursemaid. It was a unanimous decision between the Underwood mothers that the second candidate should be offered the job of helping Dee. In her late twenties, Lillian Craig had good references and was quite willing to accept the fact that the position would be for a temporary period only. It didn't take Dee long to really believe that Lillian was heaven-sent. She had such a knack with the babies. And even names for the boys had now been sorted, thanks to a ship-to-shore telephone call to Derrick: Martin, the eldest by four minutes, and Michael for his younger brother.

Finding someone to help with looking after Adele and Annabel proved to be a much harder task. It was Dee's mum who came up with the idea of asking Margaret Finch if she would be interested. Margaret lived in Camber Sands and was a state-registered nurse who had given up her job when she was forty years old to care for her aged mother. Her mother had only lived for a further nine months and Margaret had yet to go back to work. 'Three days a week helping to care for the twins might be just what would suit her,' explained Mary. 'It would get her back into the swing of things, because she was very down after she lost her mother.'

'Thanks for the suggestion, Mary, sounds just the kind of person we're looking for, but how is she going to get to Epsom from Camber Sands each morning?' asked Laraine.

'I had that worked out before I put forward the suggestion,' Mary quickly assured her. 'Jack comes over to you most days; what's to stop her coming with him in his car?'

'Well if you wouldn't mind speaking to this lady, find out what she thinks of the idea, I would be grateful.'

'Of course I will, I'll do it tonight. She only lives a few minutes' walk from me,' Mary said, smiling to herself. If Margaret were to agree to take on the task of minding the two little girls two or three days a week, it could turn out to be of great benefit to everyone.

Mary reported back that Margaret was more than happy to accept the job. Problem solved to everyone's satisfaction, and the routine began to work smoothly, allowing a certain amount of freedom to the mothers of the young children.

Laraine in particular had openly declared that she was going to make the most of this temporary bout of independence. She was well aware that her liberty could be cut short at any point in the near future. Once she had agreed that she would like to work with the advertising department at Shepperton Studios, the ball had started to roll. Her first real interview was with Mr Donaldson, one of the directors of the Rank Organisation. His office was very posh: mahogany desk, leather armchairs, a wonderful thick-pile rug in the centre of a parquet floor which had been polished till it gleamed. Just the setting for Mr Donaldson, who wore tweeds and brogues, a fine-check shirt and a plain brown tie. He was of medium height, clean-shaven and ruddy-cheeked, with silver-grey hair, and looked like a wealthy country gentleman.

'Sherry, Mrs Underwood?' he asked.

'Please.'

He gestured to one of the armchairs, and poured them both a glass of amontillado, then sat down opposite her. 'Tell me about yourself,' he said, smiling.

'I am married to Richard, who is a master mariner and with whom I had intended to travel as much as possible. Things haven't worked out quite as we'd planned. I have twin daughters just one year old, and travelling is not in their best interests at the moment. However, as they get older, and if the opportunity should present itself, then we will possibly be shore-based abroad and able to live as a family.'

'Meanwhile you thought you'd like to get involved with television work,' he said, his voice suddenly sounding grim.

'The offer was made to me by these studios,' Laraine quickly retorted.

'Quite right.' The voice that had rapped out these two words had come from behind Laraine, and she turned her head to see a tall, broad-shouldered young man dressed in a black suit, white shirt and discreet tie, with shoes polished until you could see your face in them. He had a thick head of fair hair and was sporting a lovely suntan.

'My son, Andrew, Mrs Underwood.' Mr Donaldson had got to his feet to make the introduction.

'Pleased to meet you,' Laraine and Andrew said in unison as they shook hands.

Turning to his father, Andrew said, 'Dad, if you got out of this office more often, you would know that Laraine has been the talk of the studios since she made her first visit here with her sister-in-law, Judith Underwood. Everyone from the advertising department right through to the modelling agencies is clamouring to put her to work.' Andrew chuckled. 'She looks very sedate sitting drinking sherry here with you, but if she were to stand up and let down her beautiful hair, I think even you would give a gasp of surprise. She really does have a sensational figure, and our clients who have bought time on TV to advertise their hair products are queuing up to have her work with them. Big names are also clamouring for her to model their garments.'

Mr Donaldson was on his feet again, and his cheeks were flushed red as he said, 'All right, I think you have laid out Mrs Underwood's potential quite clearly enough. All I'm asking now is that you take her to wherever she is supposed to be.' Then suddenly his features lit up and he was smiling broadly as he said, 'Looking at you two young creatures has made me wish I could have some of my youth back again. Now then, the pair of you, off you go, and Mrs Underwood, I do apologise if my early behaviour was less than congenial.'

Laraine was so bewildered by all that had been said that she was unable to form an answer. Instead she smiled and held out her hand, which Mr Donaldson clasped between both of his, holding on to it for several seconds longer than was necessary.

'I'll show you around,' said Andrew, and the offer had Laraine feeling a whole lot more relaxed. 'Have you been scheduled for any advertising today?' he asked pleasantly.

'I'm not sure. I think it is a Miss Whitcomb I have to report to first.'

'You're a freelance?' He sounded as if that fact surprised him.

'Why, yes,' said Laraine. 'I suppose I am.' For

237

some reason the thought was pleasing. 'I haven't ever done any modelling and I certainly don't have an agent.'

'Do you think you will enjoy it?'

'Enormously, I hope, but that remains to be seen. Would you please direct me to Miss Whitcomb's office,' she added, feeling a lot more confident now.

'Are you sure you don't want to go somewhere first and talk about your forthcoming layout?'

'Quite sure,' said Laraine.

'Very well, I'll lead the way. I shall also point out to you where my office is, and if at any time you feel the need to talk or ask questions, please don't hesitate to come and see me.'

Miss Whitcomb's office too was furnished in a lavish, luxurious style. Laraine was by now totally convinced that she was stepping into an entirely different world to that which she herself was used to. Was she doing the right thing? Maybe by the end of the day she would be more capable of answering that question.

21

For the first two days of Margaret Finch being in charge of Adele and Annabel, Laraine didn't leave the house. She did not intrude on what Margaret was doing, but neither did she stray far. By lunchtime the twins had made it quite clear that they approved of all the attention they were receiving, and they even ate their meal without any fuss.

Delia was walking about with a permanent smile on her face. Trying to bath both babies without shouting to Jodie for help had been impossible, and at feeding time she had been at her wits' end. It had been a complete nightmare. Never in her wildest dreams had she ever imagined that caring for two small babies could be such an arduous task. Now, with Lillian Craig in charge of the nursery, every single chore seemed to run smoothly. Time and time again Dee had hugged Jodie and thanked her profoundly for having put forward the suggestion of hiring help.

With both sets of twins under safe supervision, it hadn't taken much persuasion to get Laraine to set off with Jodie to hear first hand the outcome of her interview, which had been followed by several screen tests at the studios. The results had been amazing. Laraine had overnight become a great topic of conversation amongst the programme managers and fashion designers. Everyone was of the opinion that she had a style of her own. Slim, such long legs and that fabulous long silky hair. Advertising outlets and big companies, together with the fashion houses, were queuing up to work with her.

On arrival at the studios Jodie had to go straight to make-up, but she suggested that as Laraine was early for her own appointment she should go to the canteen and have a coffee. Laraine was doing just that when a smart-looking young man appeared at her side. 'You must be Laraine Underwood,' he said loudly as he thrust out his hand.

Laraine made to stand up. 'No, stay where you

are,' he said, pressing her to sit back down. 'I'll get myself a coffee and join you. Can I get you a refill?'

'No thank you, I've only just got mine,' she said, wondering who the hell he was.

Once they were both seated at the table, each now with a cup of coffee in front of them, the young man leaned towards Laraine. 'Steve Cooper, in overall charge of advertising,' he said, and then without any warning he suddenly began to question her.

Steve was a good-looking guy, but Laraine had already formed her own opinion of him. He obviously thought a great deal of himself and probably believed he was God's gift to women. Even at such a short acquaintance, he was very full of himself.

'Are you really going back to travelling on the high seas the minute your husband sends for you?' he asked, rather too loudly.

'Yes, of course I am. I made sure the studios were made aware of that fact before I took a single test. Besides, as I have previously pointed out, it was the studio representatives who approached me,' she told him in no uncertain terms.

'Take it easy.' He grinned. 'Of course I was put in the picture, but it seems such a waste. I've been told you have twin girls aged one year and a half? Are you truly going to be happy being a full-time mum when you leave these shores?'

'How come you know so much about me?' asked Laraine, doing her best to control her temper.

'Television studios are shocking places for gossip – quicker than the bush telegraph, I always think.'

'I would have thought you had better things to

do with your time, but about my future, you are completely wrong. You have no idea what a wonderful life lies in front of me. Maybe the girls did come along more quickly than we expected, but it is good for them to have a young mother. When I am able to travel with them, we shall start to live wherever my husband's employment takes him. The world will be my oyster.'

'Why don't I believe you? If you are so convinced of that, why are you here now?'

This Steve Cooper was getting far too big for his boots!

'To be honest, when I first came here with Jodie I was flattered. Everyone was so free with their praise and their compliments. Perhaps it went to my head, or perhaps I fancied seeing how the other half live.'

'Rubbish! Utter rubbish. I think the truth is you were bored stiff, and to while away the time before you're summoned back to being a loving wife you decided you would try another string to your bow.'

'Maybe you are right, but so what?' When Steve didn't say anything, she continued. 'It's not like you go into a marriage being able to look into a crystal ball, or as if you're diving into a clear pool.'

'No,' Steve said thoughtfully. Then, laughing, 'More like wading through murky waters.'

'Exactly. You soon find out once the honeymoon is over that life is what you make of it, as folk are so quick to remark. It is all about making the best of any situation you find yourself in, at any given time.'

She wasn't going to own up to the fact that her life had fallen into a rut and this was a chance to

241

find out if the grass was greener in somebody else's backyard.

'Well said, young lady. You have a wise head on those young shoulders and perhaps it is as well that you have taken up a different profession, even if it is only to be a temporary one. Who knows, you might be very glad that you do have a second string to your bow at some future date in your life. Meanwhile, we at Shepperton must count ourselves lucky that we have discovered you. Maybe this time it will only be short-term, but who's to say what the future holds?' He got to his feet, saying, 'Duty calls, see you around.'

Laraine sat on, staring after Steve Cooper. 'Cocky sod,' she murmured. He was taking all the credit for having discovered her, acting as if he owned the whole works. Jodie had warned her that in the world of television there were a lot of men around like that, but she had also stated that the bigger the head, the harder the fall when it came.

Laraine was counting herself really lucky. She was having a great time. Now and again she fingered some of the lovely material of the dresses she was being asked to wear for photographic sessions, and the accessories that went with the clothes were items to die for. Strings of pearls, diamond necklaces, ruby brooches and gold bangles. Whether they were real or fake she had no way of knowing, and to be honest she didn't care. They were all a joy to wear and they always looked expensive in the glossy magazines where most of the photographic work done here in the studios ended up. When it came to modelling for advertisements for

242

shampoo and tints, the make-up artists did such wonderful things with her hair. Oh yes! Laraine was getting a lot of enjoyment out of these working days, for which she was also being well paid.

She had been working part-time at Shepperton Studios for five weeks, fourteen full working days in all. It had been a period in her life that she wouldn't have missed. A real eye-opener and a wonderful experience. But she had told herself repeatedly that it wouldn't last. And she was right.

Nevertheless, she was thrilled to learn that at last she was going to join Richard. She was going to Tunisia, and Adele and Annabel were travelling with her. The very thought of what was to come had her flesh tingling.

22

The last seven days before Laraine was due to fly out with her twins to be with Richard were fraught with tension. Jodie knew it was only a matter of time before Dee and her two little boys would be following the same path.

Laraine was worried about Jodie. It seemed as if both she and Delia had used her and were now going to fly off into the great blue yonder and leave her entirely on her own. All three of them were gathered together in a newly opened wine bar; Epsom was certainly moving with the times.

'You know, Jodie, both Dee and I have been so full of our own plans that neither of us have thought to ask you about your Philip. From what you've told us, it sounds as if you've found yourself a good man at last.'

Jodie made a face at Laraine and they all laughed.

'I mean it,' Laraine said, nodding her head to emphasise her meaning. 'You should hold on to this one. After the strokes that your John has pulled over the years, you deserve some happiness. Marry the guy and give us all some peace of mind.'

'You must think I'm barmy. I am still married to John, for all the good it does me. I would never think of getting married again, not ever.' She laughed, but she had spoken too quickly, and both Dee and Laraine, looking at her, saw something they had never seen before. Her big dark eyes had a vulnerable expression, so unlike the capable, efficient Jodie they knew and loved so dearly.

'Anyway, stop worrying about me, the pair of you.' She patted Laraine's arm. 'I haven't got a chance in hell of getting a divorce from John. I even sought advice from a lawyer.'

'And?' they both asked in unison.

'I had to admit that I had no idea as to where he was living, though the fact that the navy haven't stopped my allowance makes me think that he could be anywhere in the world and I wouldn't know.'

'You could write to the Admiralty Board,' Laraine suggested.

'And open up a whole new can of worms? No thanks, I am going to let sleeping dogs lie. John will turn up again eventually, like he always does

244

when he has nowhere to go and has run out of money.'

Both Laraine and Delia looked momentarily concerned, but they had to admit that in Jodie's shoes they would probably do the same thing.

It so happened that Reggie and Lenny were going away for the weekend on a school trip and Jodie told the girls that she was working at Shepperton Studios. The way they looked at her she knew they didn't believe her, but she didn't mind. She just wasn't ready to spell it out for them.

Philip had booked them into a hotel set at the foot of Box Hill in the heart of beautiful Surrey. It had all the modern conveniences but still clung to some of the rustic features of the original hotel.

Having enjoyed a superb dinner and quite a few drinks, the two of them lay on the rug in front of the fire that had been thoughtfully lit in their bedroom. They were talking, thinking aloud, each remembering things that had happened to them long ago. Philip came from a typical large Italian family. He was a kind, thoughtful, caring man who had never married, and Jodie was telling herself how easy it would be to let herself fall completely in love with him.

'Would you ever consider getting married again, Jodie?' He looked thoughtfully at her and she smiled. She looked delightful in the soft glimmer of the firelight, her perfect delicate features and deep brown eyes glowing as she looked up at him.

'I have always vowed I never would.' She traced his lips with her fingertips. He really was a handsome man, not in the least like the well-built

Underwood brothers. Philip was tall and broad-shouldered but lean, and his permanent tan was so attractive. He also wore expensive clothes that looked immaculate on him no matter what the occasion.

'Wouldn't you make an exception for me?'

'Is that a proposal, Philip? You don't have to go that far, you know. I am perfectly happy the way my life is at the moment.'

'I know you are, but I can tell that you're feeling apprehensive about being on your own when your sisters-in-law fly off to join their husbands.'

'Well, isn't that natural? Obviously I shall miss them like hell, but I shall still have my two lovely sons.'

'I haven't ever been allowed to meet either of your boys.' He looked at her strangely. 'Is there a reason for that?'

She shook her head. 'No, I suppose I have been overprotective of them, maybe because their father has treated them almost as if they don't exist. I do my best to make up for that and so do their uncles. I wouldn't want them to form a bond with you if it wasn't going to last.'

'You sound as if you don't trust me, yet you haven't given me a chance. I want more than what we have now, Jodie. I have never felt the need to get married to anyone before, but I want you with me all the time.'

'But I am still married to John, and he won't willingly release me, I'm pretty sure of that. If he thought you wanted to marry me and that we'd be happy together, then he would be as awkward as he could be. He might not want me, but he'll make damn sure nobody else can have me.'

'Will you marry me not if, but *when* you are free?'

'Yes, if only,' she whispered.

And that had to be good enough for now.

He took her in his arms and made love to her ever so gently in front of the fire, and afterwards he lay for a long, long time and looked at her, and then finally he spoke, his hands still stroking her body. 'I shall never let you forget you've promised to marry me the minute you are free. Is that right?'

'Yes.' She said the word eagerly, and she meant it now. It would be a second attempt, but she was older and wiser now and Philip loved her with all of her faults. He had to learn to love her two sons as well, and she prayed that he would. She wanted them to accept each other, for them all to become one happy family.

Was she hoping for too much? she asked herself, knowing what it would take to find out.

When they parted early on Monday morning, she was still a little overwhelmed by what they had promised each other. 'Did you really mean everything you said, Philip?'

'How can you even ask?' He looked horrified, and instantly crushed her tight within his arms as they stood by his car. 'Every single word. And next time, no matter where we go, we shall take your boys with us. In the meantime, I'll work on being a father figure,' he said, grinning at her now.

She grinned back at him, looking far less worried than she had lately and a whole lot younger too.

There was one long, lingering kiss before they parted.

He called her two or three times a day for the next few days. On the fourth day he made a suggestion that had her rocking on her heels.

'I mean it, Jodie, I want you to see about getting passports for yourself and for your two boys. What better way could there be to get to really know each other than for me to take you all to my home in Italy?' He didn't even pause for Jodie to catch her breath. 'Poppa died some years ago, but Mamma lives with my sister and her family, and I have four married brothers all living within a short distance.'

'Hey, Philip, you just hold your horses. Your mother and the rest of your family are not going to be thrilled to learn that you are thinking about getting married to a woman who still has a husband and two growing boys.'

'Jodie, you are enough to exasperate the saints themselves. Of course Mamma would have preferred me to marry when I was much younger; over the years she and my sister have picked out half a dozen young women for me, but they never got me up the aisle. She might not welcome you with open arms at first, but once she gets to know you and your sons, all her prejudices will be laid aside and soon she will be telling you that she can now die a happy woman because her beloved Philip has at last found a lady who'll care for him.'

I wish! Jodie was saying to herself.

When at last she put the telephone down, she wasn't sure whether she was coming or going. God above! He didn't waste any time. All the same, she just couldn't see his plans coming to fruition, not now, not ever. There were just too many complications in the way.

But she chuckled loudly anyway. Maybe he would just prove her wrong!

The day for Laraine's departure had finally arrived, and in Jodie's house nothing seemed to be going right. The strain was telling on everyone and the babies appeared to be aware that something out of the ordinary was happening. Martin and Michael were irritable, while Adele and Annabel were being downright crabby.

'Mum, come quick, you've got to see this.' Reggie's loud command had all three women staring at each other, Lenny had already raced up the hall to see what was the cause of his brother's excitement.

'Well if that doesn't beat everything,' Dee muttered, her voice showing her surprise. 'Zapata Shipping Line certainly look after their master mariners.'

'And their families by the look of it,' added Jodie.

'I was notified that I was being escorted for every part of the journey, but even so, I didn't dream the company would go this far.' Laraine was just as astonished as her sisters-in-law.

'It's the biggest car we've ever seen,' Lenny remarked in awe to his brother.

The girls looked at each other and burst out laughing. The car really was enormous, and standing beside it was a chauffeur wearing full uniform, every button gleaming, his shoes highly polished and on his head a cap with a shiny peak. To his right stood a young woman wearing a

249

nurse's uniform.

Laraine stepped forward and introduced herself. The chauffeur snapped to attention and saluted, which had both Reggie and Lenny covering their mouths with their hands in order to smother their giggles.

It took a while for Laraine's one trunk, several cases and multiple bags to be loaded into the enormous boot of the car. Meanwhile the nurse had been invited into the house and was gratefully sipping a cup of coffee. Her name was Christine Bristow and she would be travelling with Laraine and the twins until they reached their final destination.

What a job they had just getting the twins into the car. The little girls knew something strange was happening, but they were too young to have the facts spelled out to them. Adele clung to Jodie while Annable had her arms tightly around Dee. 'Why aren't you coming with us?' was their heart-rending cry.

By the time the twins and everything that was going with them were safely in the car, it only remained for the three sisters-in-law to say their goodbyes.

'Dear God,' Jodie murmured. 'Anyone would think you're all going off to be executed.'

'It feels a bit like that,' Laraine admitted. 'Certainly we're off into the unknown. Don't be surprised if the twins and I land on your doorstep in a month's time because we can't stand the natives.'

'Get on with you, Laraine, you know you'll be living the life of Riley before you've been there a few days,' Jodie told her, still trying to smile, though there was an ache in her heart and the backs of her eyes were stinging with unshed tears.

'Goodbye, Dee, you'll be the next one off.' Laraine hugged her tightly and kissed her gently.

The final goodbye, to Reggie and Lenny, *was* heartbreaking. The boys cuddled Adele and Annabel in turn and even they had tears glistening in their eyes. They had become like brothers and sisters instead of cousins during Laraine's long stay. But at last the doors were closed and the driver put his cap back on and took his seat behind the wheel. Soon the car was out of sight, yet Jodie and Dee still stood on the pavement, staring into the distance that now separated them from Laraine.

Jodie suddenly felt Dee's eyes on her. 'Where are the boys?' she quickly asked.

'I've just looked in on them.' Dee smiled. 'Your two are acting the big men, stacking all the wooden blocks up high on the carpet and pretending to be cross when Martin and Michael knock them flying. The twins are loving it.'

Jodie sighed, but she managed a smile at the same time, 'We'll leave them for the time being, but as soon as we've got ourselves ready, we'll take them out, have a meal somewhere, my treat. Work can go to pot today; we'll spend the whole day with our boys.'

23

Correspondence from Laraine was unpredictable, and even when a letter did arrive, it was short and to the point. Richard was not at all happy with his posting and had already requested that Zapata carry out an inquiry into how business in Tunisia was being run. Too many masters issuing too many orders and no one to see that they were being carried out. Also the fact that any money earned in Tunisia couldn't be taken out of the country at the moment was a worrying factor. There were no nice newsy bits, such as where and how they were living.

When Jodie left for work each morning, she felt relieved that Lillian Craig was there with Dee. It was not so much the help with Martin and Michael as the fact that Dee had no other company; she was missing Laraine a whole lot more than she was willing to admit. When Shepperton Studios announced that there was to be a celebration day, Jodie had a sudden brainwave. She was going to ask permission to bring Delia and her twin boys along with her for the day.

She made sure that they arrived at the studios nice and early, because her hair-styling talent was in great demand, but she didn't have to worry about Dee and the boys. They were being swarmed with loving attention.

Philip came to stand beside Jodie, and as she

worked, he reeled off a list of eminent guests who would be arriving during the day. Actors, actresses, aristocrats and musicians – even a couple of Members of Parliament.

Jodie listened, enthralled, but then said, 'Please excuse me for a moment, Philip.' Turning back to the blonde news-reader whose hair she had just styled, she stood behind the chair and held up a mirror so that her new hairdo could be viewed from the back. 'Well, what do you think? Have I achieved the exact shape and design you were hoping for?' she asked.

'Perfect,' Jane Osbourne declared warmly. 'Thanks, Jodie. I often think how hard you must have studied to be able to work the wonders you do on so many different types of hair. Don't you think so, Philip? She's done a marvellous job, and as always she achieves whatever the client asks for with apparently no effort at all.'

'Do I indeed?' Jodie said, laughing.

'You do, you do. Believe me you do.'

'It's easy to perform for you, Jane; you have a good head of thick hair,' Jodie told her.

'Don't put yourself down, Jodie. There is no one who can match you when it comes to styling. Whether they have long or short hair, you always finish up with a very satisfied customer. Do you do some of the styling when the actors are wearing period costumes?'

'Not really. The hairpieces come back from the wig-makers in baskets and all we have to do is brush them out, or maybe put the hot tongs on a stray curl or two. Of course we do have to powder the wigs that the gentlemen wear. It's the ladies who make the wigs that are the virtuosos. I must admit that as today is special, I have added a few false pieces at the back of your head.'

'Whatever,' Jane grinned. 'I do appreciate what you do for me.'

'I'm going to take a short break now,' Jodie said to Philip. 'I think I'd better see what Dee is up to and where she has put the twins.'

'OK, I'll catch up with you later,' he told her.

Jodie walked the length of the vast salon and went on into make-up. She was aware that many important people would be in front of the cameras today, and that meant that both males and females would have to be given facial or hair treatment. What she wasn't prepared for was to see Delia, wearing an expensive white coat bearing the Shepperton lettering on the collar, working in the middle of a busy line of stylists.

'Good heavens,' said Jodie. 'Who set my sister-in-law to work, and what on earth has she done with her two baby boys?'

Jodie was unaware that Steve Cooper was standing behind her, and the sound of his voice had her jerking her head round.

Steve was grinning. 'Calm down, Jodie,' he said. 'The staff here are working flat out today and were thrilled to accept Delia's offer of help. You've been working here long enough to know that we have a first-class sick bay with two registered nurses always on hand, and today it would seem it is being put to good use. Come along and see for yourself.'

The sick bay was only a few yards away down the hall. Two mattresses covered in blankets had been set out on the floor, and Martin and Michael looked as if they were enjoying being the centre of attention. It was unbelievable! Women *and* men were talking playfully to them, and it was no wonder. Martin and Michael did look absolutely adorable in their blue and white romper suits, and the sunshine coming in through the window shone on their golden hair. As alike as two peas in a pod, Jodie thought. From this distance even she would have trouble distinguishing one from the other.

'Did you arrange all of this?' she asked Steve.

He threw his hands up in mock horror. 'Certainly not. We all of us have our work cut out today with so many dignitaries on parade. You don't really mind that your sister-in-law has offered her services, do you?'

Jodie hesitated. 'Not really. It was a surprise, that's all, but as long as the babies are being well cared for, I'm sure our Delia will be loving every minute of it.'

It was much later that day before Jodie and Dee sat down together to have a glass of wine. There had been food and drink flowing freely all day but neither of them had been able to take a break. An exciting, unusual day in so many ways, they both agreed as they slumped back in their chairs and sipped at their wine. It wasn't long before Phillip appeared, bringing them each a plate of food fit for the gods.

This great day was drawing to an end. They went together to fetch Martin and Michael from the sick bay, where it took ages for the nurses to hand them over. So many people were eager to say their goodbyes and to tell their mother how delightful her babies were.

At last the twins were safely harnessed into Jodie's car. 'I really have had a most interesting day,' Dee said as she settled herself into the front passenger seat.

'Me too. I'm so glad it turned out well for you, Dee,' Jodie told her as she put the key in the ignition and started the car.

On arrival Dee opened the back door of the car and the two women looked at each other and smiled. Both baby boys were fast asleep.

'I suppose you could say that must be the perfect ending to a perfect day,' Dee said. 'But how the hell are we going to get them out without disturbing them?'

'With great difficulty,' Jodie laughed. 'I'll go round to the other side, and remember, easy does it.'

As Dee wriggled her hands beneath Michael's bottom in order to lift him out of the harness, she was wondering how on earth she was going to manage without Jodie when it was time for her to leave England and join Derrick. Without Jodie's help and worldly wisdom she was going to be at a loss for a long time to come, she thought dismally as she carried Michael into the house.

Later that night, with the twins finally settled in their cots, Jodie and Dee settled down with a cup of hot chocolate. Emotions were running high. Each had agreed they would long look back on this day and smile. It had been a great day. But where would they be as they recalled not only this memory, but countless others?

Not together. That unfortunately was the truth.

And the truth had to be faced.

Jodie had been up since a quarter to five, had seen that Reggie and Lenny ate a good breakfast and then at six o'clock had driven them to catch the coach. They were going with their school on a day trip to France.

Back home she looked around at her tidy living room and she felt she wanted to scream. The only thing that was stopping her was the knowledge that if she started she didn't think she would be able to stop. God almighty, what was she supposed to do? The silence in this big house was driving her mad.

For three weeks following the open day at Shepperton, she and Dee had made the most of every minute. The boys had cuddled and played with the twins, Reggie had discovered that Martin had cut his first tooth and it was always Lenny that Michael crawled to when he wanted help to try to walk properly. Amidst all the happiness had come a phone call from Derrick.

Really big promotion this time. They were off to Singapore. Seven days' notice for Dee to be ready. Mad panic!

The exact same procedure that had been set in motion for Laraine had been followed for Dee. Same big car complete with chauffeur, same sad parting, although Jodie thought it was even worse because over the years she had come to count Dee as her own. She had invited Dee's parents to come and spend those last seven days here in Epsom. It seemed only fair. Jack and Mary had every right to be with their grandchildren. Who knew how long it would be before they saw them again? So for a week there had been eight people in the house, and now for the last three weeks there had only been Jodie and the two boys. No wonder the silence was deafening. Would she ever get used to it?

'I think I shall sell my salons and give up work altogether, get rid of this house, buy something a whole lot smaller, stay at home and be a proper mum, have some time to myself.' She was talking aloud and suddenly her voice got louder.

'Oh no you don't. Not yet. Perhaps not ever, but certainly not yet. What on earth would you do with all that spare time? And you are not having today off either. Get yourself ready and get off to work. You carry on like this and the men in white coats will be coming to cart you off to some loony bin.'

She felt better for having given herself a good talking-to.

Within half an hour Jodie was out in the drive just about ready to unlock the door of her car when she saw the postman rest his bike against the wall and start to walk towards her.

'Good morning, Mrs Underwood. Plenty of mail for you this morning, and I guess this fat letter is the one you've been waiting for,' the postman said merrily.

'Oh thank you so much,' Jodie said, glancing at the Singapore postage stamps.

She was tempted to go back into the house to sit quietly and read Dee's letter, but having glanced through the pile the postman had given her, she saw there was also a letter from Laraine. 'Get yerself going,' she muttered sternly, 'there'll be plenty of time to read them later.' The letters would keep, and she would get all the more enjoyment from them if she could read them slowly and without any interruptions.

As she was driving to work, Jodie started to smile. Then she began to laugh, and soon she was really chuckling. Just who do you think you're kidding? she asked herself. Can you really see yourself selling up and living a quiet life? Won't be too long now before the boys will be thinking about going to university or out into the big world of business. Whatever! It's ten to one they won't want to be hanging on to your shirt-tails for much longer, and when they do go, if you've no other interests left, where would that leave you?

She wasn't going to even try to answer her own questions.

She was actually very pleased when she got to the salon and was informed that one of the stylists had phoned in sick. 'That's all right,' she said, taking a clean overall out of the linen cupboard and putting it on. 'A change of scene is exactly what I need today. If you will bring me the appointment book, I will check on what I have to do and then I'll get started.'

That evening, Jodie met her boys off the coach at eight o'clock. She cooked steak, fried onions, peas and chips for their dinner, and was rewarded by two empty plates and remarks about how it had been smashing and that it really was their favourite meal. 'Well in that case you may do the washing-up,' she told them with a smile. The only answer she got from her two sons as they pushed back their chairs and flew up the stairs to their bedrooms was, 'Sorry, Mum, we have a load of homework to do.'

'Come back down here,' she called. 'You can't have any homework because you haven't been to school.' She could hear them both giggling, and so she called again. 'All right, it has been a long day for both of you, so I'll let you off for tonight, but you do the washing-up every night for the rest of the week.'

'Thanks, Mum. Are you coming up to say good night?'

'Not just yet. Don't forget to clean your teeth, then when you're in bed you can read for a while and I'll be up later.'

She set about washing the few dirty dinner plates before settling down in her favourite armchair to read her two letters. She had been patient since this morning, dealing with all the harassment of a normal working day, but now she couldn't wait to get started.

24

Two days since her longed-for letters had arrived and Jodie had read them both over and over again until she almost knew the content of them by heart.

Laraine's letter was not a lengthy one. Short and to the point, and Jodie felt for her. It was so obvious that she was not at all happy, and Richard had added a postscript to the bottom which basically said that he was waiting for a transfer.

Another postscript written by Laraine sent loads of love and big hugs from Adele and Annabel. It was enough to tug at her heart strings.

Oh, if she could only go to them! Pick those delightful little girls up in her arms and comfort their mother. Poor Laraine, she was such a loving, friendly person and yet there wasn't a word about her having made friends or being invited to any social activities. That was one of the things that Jodie had always been envious of: the social life that came with their husbands' job of travelling the world.

But what could she do about it? Nothing!

And it was that short, sharp answer that had her in tears.

I shall have to think long and hard before I sit down and write to Laraine, she thought mournfully.

How different Dee's letter was! Seven pages in all, and each and every line bursting with news and most of all how wonderful and loving Derrick was.

He really is an absolute darling. He can't take his eyes off Martin and Michael and is forever picking them up. And I can say this to you, Jodie, because we've never had secrets, Derrick is so wonderful when he makes love to me I feel if we don't start being more careful I shall be sent home again to await another birth.

Dee's parents and Marian had also received letters from Dee. Mary and Jack phoned to say how pleased they were that she seemed to have

261

settled in so well.

Marian also phoned, said she hadn't seen anyone for weeks, and could Jodie bring her a pair of reading glasses when next she came over because she wasn't able to read Dee's handwriting properly.

I must find time to take Marian to the optician's, Jodie rebuked herself. In the meantime she would take the boys over and would read her letter to her. She certainly wouldn't read her own; she didn't want to give her any shocks.

Ten o'clock on Sunday morning found Jodie, Reggie and Lenny on Marian's doorstep. Marian was thrilled to bits to see them, and the welcome she gave them made that very obvious, more so as Jodie unpacked her shopping basket and said, 'No arguments, I have brought everything with me and I am going to cook a roast dinner for all of us.'

'Grandma, do you know if Grandad next door is going to be in today?' Reg had been waiting patiently to get his question in.

Marian glanced up at her clock. 'I know he's going to watch a football match this morning, but whether he has left yet or not, I couldn't say. Though Mary did say she'd come in and have a cup of tea with me when he went, so if you want to see him, you'd better pop in there now.'

Neither lad needed any urging; they were off like a shot. Within ten minutes they were back again. 'Mum, Grandad Jack said we can go with him to the football match if that's OK by you.' Reggie's words came tumbling out and were quickly followed by Lenny saying, 'It is all right for us to go, isn't it? And Grandma Mary said to tell you she'll be coming in here as soon as she's seen us off.'

Jodie looked at her mother-in-law and they both grinned. 'Of course it is,' their mother assured them.

'Reggie, if you pull open the top drawer of my dresser you'll find two bags you might like to take with you, but don't eat everything that's in there, because we shall wait until you're all back before we have our dinner.'

That was a long speech for their grandma. Reg did as he had been told, and the gleeful look on the boys' faces as they gazed at the contents of their paper bags really pleased her.

'I still know how to treat young boys, it seems,' she said smiling as they each put an arm around her shoulders and planted a kiss on her cheek.

Jodie, Mary and Marian stood outside in the street and watched as the boys piled into the back of Jack's car.

'Couldn't have worked out better if we'd planned it,' said Jodie, sounding really happy. 'I was wondering what we could do to keep the boys amused all day. Now thanks to Jack they'll be happy as Larry.'

As soon as they were back indoors, Jodie turned to Mary and said, 'I'll make us a nice pot of tea, we'll have a good old chat and then you can decide: would you rather do the vegetables – there'll be six of us for dinner – or make the pastry for an apple pie? The choice is yours.'

'You're counting Jack and me in for dinner – you don't have to do that, Jodie.'

'I know I don't have to, but I want to. I have bought a whole leg of lamb so there will be plenty, and it will give us a chance to have a good natter.'

Mary still tried to protest that she did not want to impose.

'Oh for God's sake, Mary, you and Jack do enough through the week for me, and you're always there for my boys when I can't get home. Besides, do you honestly think it makes sense for me to drive all the way over here to cook dinner for Marian and you to cook a separate dinner in the house right next door?'

'When you put it that way, it's an offer I'd be a fool to refuse. Thanks, Jodie.'

Jodie was busy laying out cups when Mary turned to Marian and said, 'You haven't lit the fire in your front room for ages. Don't you think it'd be nice to have that room all nice and warm when the boys get back?' Without waiting for an answer she went on, 'I'll see to it if it's all right by you.'

'Thank you for offering, Mary, I should have thought of it myself. Please carry on.'

As long as you are not offended. After all, you weren't to know you were going to have six of us for Sunday dinner.'

'No, it was a complete surprise but nevertheless a really nice one.'

Mary slipped out to her own house and came back with a cardboard box full of sticks of wood that Jack had chopped. The coal scuttle that stood in Marian's hearth was filled to the brim and it wasn't long before she had a fire burning brightly. Task finished, she closed the door to keep the warmth in and went back out to sit in the kitchen, where by now Jodie had the tea made and waiting to be poured out.

Mary winked at Jodie as she sat down at the table, and Jodie gave her a thumbs-up sign behind Marian's back.

'Seeing as how we shan't be having our dinner until late this afternoon, I think we can cut into this fruit cake I brought with me,' said Jodie as she took a large plate down from the dresser and set it in the middle of the table.

'My God, Jodie, why on earth did you buy such a large cake?'

'I would have thought you knew me much better than that, Marian. When have I ever bought a cake?' Jodie asked as she picked up a knife and cut the first slice. There were oohs and aahs from both Marian and Mary as they saw the inside of it; rarely would a shop-bought cake be so rich and dark and packed with such an abundant amount of fruit.

The three women lingered over their tea and cake, and Jodie told Marian that she had booked an appointment for her to have her eyes tested the following Thursday at ten forty-five at Boots in Hastings. Before the old lady had time to protest, Jodie quickly said, 'I shall drop the boys at school earlier than usual that day and come straight on here to take you myself. I'll write it up in big letters on your wall calendar just to remind you.'

'Thank you, Jodie, I don't know what I would do without you.'

Mary got up and began to clear the table of their empty cups and plates. 'I'm going to make a start on some of those lovely vegetables. Marian, why don't you take the Sunday paper and settle yourself down on the settee in the front room? It should be nice and warm in there by now.'

'Good idea,' Jodie agreed. 'Come along, Marian. I'll see you settled, then I'll bring the paper in to you.'

Jodie and Mary grinned at each other. With the door to the front room closed tightly, they could leave all their chores for the moment and get down to discussing Delia's letters.

'I was astounded by the first two pages of our Dee's letter. Shall I read them to you?' Mary asked.

'Yes, OK, you go first,' Jodie said eagerly.

'I'll skip the family bits. *The first thing that struck me was the cleanliness of Singapore. The streets are so neat and orderly. No gangs are allowed, only three people walking abreast is permissible and no chewing gum anywhere! A hefty fine for anyone who chooses to disregard the regulations.*

'*There isn't a house ready for us yet, but who cares. Derrick, I and the twins are staying at the Hyatt Regency Hotel and we shall be here for at least a month. We have been given an executive suite and all expenses are down to Tercol Shipping Line. Derrick is shore-based, so he is able to get home quite frequently. The good news is that he has made many friends and they all think Martin and Michael are adorable. This will please you even more: Tercol have agreed that wives and children may fly home to England once every six months, all expenses paid. Whether Derrick will be able to accompany us will largely depend on what his schedule entails at that point in time.*

'What do you think of all that?' Mary asked,

266

grinning broadly. 'The fact that we shall see our Delia and the twins every six months is like a God-given gift. It certainly put a smile on my Jack's face. Did Dee tell you anything else?'

'Not a great deal. I'll read you the parts of mine that do differ. *The Hyatt Regency Hotel is marvellous. From the very first meal of fillets of sole followed by lamb cutlets, which we both chose from an enormous menu, I knew we were extremely lucky. The dining room itself is elegant, the smartly dressed waiters are so skilful and the diners all dress formally. When I remarked on this, Derrick said he would take me shopping for clothes as soon as he had a free day. I had to wait for three days, but when I first set eyes on the various shopping arcades, most of which are on two or three floors, well let's say my mind was boggled. The clothes are brilliant and so much cheaper than back home, and as for the electrical goods, Derrick describes the choice as awesome.'*

Jodie decided she had disclosed enough of her letter to please Mary, and so she folded the pages and slipped them back into the envelope. Then, reaching across the table, she took hold of Mary's hand and held it between both of hers. 'Doesn't it make you feel great, knowing that your daughter is wonderfully, deliriously happy?'

Mary sniffed and brushed away a tear before saying, 'Oh Jodie, you know it does, and thank you for sharing your letter with me.'

'That's fine, Mary, we shared each other's. Actually, I've just remembered there was a piece at the end of my letter that concerns your Brian. Apparently Derrick is going to ask whether he can go to Singapore for a holiday.'

Mary looked thoughtful. After a minute had ticked by she said, 'Brian's in the Merchant Navy now. I suppose he'll be the next one flitting off to faraway places.'

'Well in that case, perhaps you and Jack may be able to visit one of those places together. You'll have two choices now.'

'That's a daft suggestion. Do you really think a young lad, say out in India or wherever, would want his parents flying out to see him?'

'Yes, I do. Nothing daft about it. Family ties matter, well at least if you're lucky they do. Let's not go into it further now; just be grateful that Dee will be able to come back and see us in six months' time. I know I am! For now I think we had better make a start on the dinner. I'll just baste the leg of lamb, and later on we can put a pan of potatoes in to roast.'

'Right, but before I make a start on the parsnips and cabbage, I'd better just check up on Marian.'

Two minutes later, Mary was beckoning for Jodie to come and take a look. In the front room, Jodie's mother-in-law was stretched out full length on the settee, fast asleep.

The return of Jack and the boys meant that someone had to wake Marian. The job fell to Mary, and she wisely decided to take a cup of tea with her when she tiptoed into the front room.

Four adults and two young lads soon made short work of everything that had been served up for their Sunday dinner, and not one amongst them refused a dish of apple pie and creamy custard.

It was almost dark when Jodie saw the boys

settled into the back of her car, ready for the journey home. Mary and Jack stood with Marian out on the pavement to see them off. All six of them had enjoyed this day. It hadn't been a typical Sunday, but they had all shared time with loved ones, and Reg and Lenny had had some male company and a football match thrown in, where they would have been allowed to let off steam.

Now it really was time to go. As Jodie started the engine, she thought she knew precisely where she stood as regarded friendship. She counted her blessings and told herself that really good friends were something that money could never buy.

Everyone was calling goodbye. Jodie felt easier about leaving her mother-in-law because Mary and Jack had said they would see her safely up the stairs and into bed before they went next door to their own home.

Much later that night, with her boys safely tucked up in bed, Jodie had a lovely hot bath and was more than ready for bed herself. She quietly closed her bedroom door, took off her dressing gown and laid it over a chair. Once in bed, she laid her head against the pillows and closed her eyes. She had had such a happy day. Try as she would, though, she couldn't stop herself from thinking of where her own marriage had gone wrong. A sob broke from her as she turned in the bed and lay on her stomach, her face buried in the pillow. She lay there quietly for what seemed like hours until at last she fell asleep.

Something strange was happening. She was dreaming of John. He was so tall, so good-looking, and an expert at making love to her, always insisting that she was the one and only love of his life. He was *never* going to leave her.

She woke suddenly, wishing heartily that her life with John could have turned out better and asking herself bitterly why everything had gone so wrong. She was getting so tired of always facing the world with a smile on her face which more often than not was covering another heartache.

John and his promises! It made her so mad to think of all the times he had said 'Give me another chance and I promise things will be different.'

His promises were just like piecrust. Made to be broken.

25

It was five weeks before Jodie received her second letter from Dee. Meanwhile Reg and Lenny were happily taunting her that they had twice received picture postcards from their Uncle Derrick and Auntie Dee, and on the bottom of each Martin and Michael had, with help, scrawled with a colouring pencil. Dee had written that they talked to the twins about their cousins each and every day, and there was no way they would let Martin and Michael forget them.

Jodie generally picked her early-morning post up from the doormat on her way out, and today was no different. To her immediate delight there was a fat letter bearing air-mail stamps from Singapore.

She laid the rest of the post on a small table, and hugged Dee's letter close to her chest, feeling that this flimsy envelope with its pages of news brought Dee and the twins closer to her. All the same, a feeling of sheer frustration flooded through her. 'So near and yet so far!' she murmured as she placed the letter with her other mail. It would have to wait until this evening; she had a really busy day ahead of her.

Having spent part of the morning at the accountant's, Jodie was resigned to the fact that she had quite a bit of income tax to pay. Come lunchtime she was at Shepperton Studios making herself a coffee when to her utter surprise she thought she saw Michael Connelly walk past the open door. Swiftly she put down the spoon she was holding and ran to look up the corridor. She was right, it was Michael, and she called out loudly, aiming her voice at his retreating back. He stopped, turned around and walked back to where she was standing. 'And how did you find your way here?' she asked.

'I do have a car.' He smiled sweetly at her. 'Actually, I have an appointment with Steve Cooper.'

There was something different about Michael today. He was as well dressed as always, but at the same time there was a mood of irreverence about him which showed through and added spice to his flippant words.

'Do you know Cooper, then?' Jodie asked.

'We were at college together for three years.'

'And?'

'He played a great game of rugby, always handled himself well, flunked at least half of his

271

subjects and thinks all women should fall at his feet, but in reality he has no magnetism whatsoever.'

Jodie laughed. 'I've never had much to do with him, but in the short time that Laraine was here, she didn't take to him.' She laughed again before saying, 'Your characterisation is almost exactly the same as the description she gave.'

'Good on Laraine, she soon sussed him out.'

'So you've nothing nice to say about our Steve?'

'They're not going to pay me to be nice.' He looked mischievous as Jodie made him a coffee.

'Well, do you know what they are going to pay you for?'

'Not yet, actually.' The cheeky smile appeared again, and with raised eyebrows he said, 'it's some new commercial advertising campaign for hair products. Apparently the clients complained that the feedback was terrible, so Steve has asked me to sit in on today's assignation.'

Jodie stared at him. 'Oh, so there's been more to him and you in the past than you're letting on.'

'Jodie, dear, don't go putting the cart before the horse.' He was quick to turn the tables on her. 'He's just an old college friend, for Christ's sake.'

'So he's calling on you because you have friends in high places, is that it? Doesn't that upset you, Michael? I mean, you're certainly well known in the trade.'

Michael shrugged and downed the rest of his coffee. 'I have to get going. Are you doing anything tonight?'

'Actually I have a letter from Dee, came this morning but I hadn't time to read it. If you're at a loose end, come to dinner. It is ages since the boys have seen you, and you know they'll be thrilled if you turn up. Bring Danny too if he'd like to come.'

'Danny is in Jersey on business for his firm, so yes please, I would love to come to dinner. I'll bring the wine.'

'If you don't want black looks from Reg and Lenny, you'd better bring some Coca-Cola too.'

His impish smile was back. 'Will do. See you six thirty to seven.' He took Jodie in his arms and kissed each cheek. 'Never forget I love you dearly,' he whispered. He was halfway out of the door when she called after him, 'Love you too.'

Then, like so many previous times, she sighed heavily. Michael was such a darling. What a pity he had never fancied getting married and having children of his own. On the other hand, he and Danny had been together for more years than she cared to remember and they were certainly doing fine. And better friends would be hard to find, she told herself with a smile.

Promptly at six thirty, Michael rang the bell, and before he'd hardly put a foot inside the door, the boys were on him. Reg and Lenny adored both Michael and Danny. They asked no questions as to why the two men lived together; rather they had great admiration for both of them. There was no form of sport these two men didn't understand. They would always make time to explain the rules of any game, and given half a chance they were in there participating with Reg and Lenny. It was the kind of encouragement the boys should have been getting from their father, but as that had never been on the cards, Jodie was more than grateful for the time that Michael and Danny shared with her boys.

Dinner was a jovial affair. As usual, the wine that Michael had brought was extremely good, and after two glasses Jodie was feeling quite merry. He had not forgotten the boys' drinks either, and he had also bought them one of the latest board games. Main course over, the boys were tucking into bowls of ice cream and Jodie and Michael were attacking the cheese board when Jodie's inquisitive nature got the better of her. 'So how did the secret meeting go today?' she asked, with what she hoped was an innocent look on her face.

Michael threw back his head and laughed. 'I was wondering how much longer you would be able to contain your curiosity.'

Jodie almost choked on her cream cracker, and both the boys were grinning.

'I shall let that spiteful remark pass,' Jodie said, doing her best to eat humble pie.

Michael playfully slapped her arm. 'I am quite prepared to tell you everything. I was just waiting for the right opportunity.'

'Well for God's sake get on with it. What with all the jobs there were to do when I got home, including cooking the dinner, I haven't had a chance to even glance at Dee's letter.'

'Well, Steve is looking for a young model who is sylph-like but not spindly with a glorious head of hair, preferably blonde. They want to bring out a new set of advertisements very quickly to promote this brand-new merchandise that a very valued patron has come up with. The model does not necessarily have to be well known, but it would help. First thing that sprang to my mind was, it's such a pity that Laraine isn't still here. Her slim figure is an absolute sell-out, and add to that her long fair hair ... well, imagine filming her with her hair up, topknot, French pleat, whatever, and then close in with the cameras, take out the pins and let her hair flow. There has never been an advert like that, it could be a first, but who else could we find who has hair reaching down to her backside? I'm telling you, Jodie, with the right girl and the right photographer's apparatus, this product would fly off the shelves not only in chemist's but in hair-dressing salons and boutiques all over the world.'

'Heavens, you do paint a good picture when you put your mind to it. Did you agree anything with Steve?'

'If only I could have had Laraine as the model, I would have bitten his hand off and the contract would have been written on my terms.'

'But you haven't got Laraine, so what now?'

'We'll have to wait and see. I do have a few young ladies in mind, but I cannot think of one single blonde. Strangely enough, most professional models on the agencies' books are dark-haired. Anyhow, keep your eyes and ears open, and in the meantime we'll clear this table and get down to reading Dee's letter – well, at least the parts you're going to allow me to see,' he added with a wicked smile which greatly endeared him to Jodie.

The first three pages of Dee's letter were taken up by the news that the family had moved out of the Hyatt Regency and were now very comfort-ably installed in a three-storey town house. Jodie shared this information with Michael before passing him a couple of pages, and he began to read aloud.

'*I have never before been inside such a large property, let alone lived in one. Each and every room is vast, and my mouth fell open when I got my first glimpse of the landings. On each one there is furniture laid out really nicely with a television set on a nearby table. I can't understand why you need a settee and armchairs on the landing when there is so much space in the dining room, the lounge, the office and the play room, not to mention the four bedrooms and we must not forget the kitchens, yes there are two! Also a laundry room with all the latest equipment. Oh, and I haven't mentioned that the property comes with an army of staff. There are two amahs, nursemaids to you, and a chauffeur whenever needed. All the staff have their own live-in quarters in the grounds. Both Derrick and I have decided that Emmy is our favourite. She is twenty-seven years old, with short dark hair and smooth skin that is nicely tanned. She was born in the Philippines, and has a very large family there to whom she sends part of her wages every month. While with us her sole job is to take care of the twins. Thank God both Martin and Michael appear to have taken to her, and beyond any doubt she is enchanted with them. Life at the moment is almost too good to be true!*'

Jodie took the pages back and they looked at each other in amazement. 'You and I are in the wrong profession,' Michael remarked.

'You can say that again. Listen to this next bit. *The social life here is very good and everybody is so friendly. Last week got a bit hectic, and can you believe that come the weekend I actually asked Derrick if we*

276

might stay at home one evening for a change.' Jodie laid down the page and looked at Michael, and soon the pair of them were laughing fit to bust.

'Our young Delia pleading to be allowed to stay at home rather than go out on the town with a crowd of friends? Takes some believing, doesn't it?' Michael declared.

'Michael, have you ever been to Singapore?'

'Yes, Jodie, I have, twice. What made you suddenly ask that?'

'I was wondering what the weather would be like over there now.'

'Right now will be the beginning of what they class as the cooler season, but it never actually gets cold. I have friends who live there two thirds of the year and only possess lightweight suits. If they come home, say at this time of the year, and stay for Christmas, they always have to buy warm clothing.'

'Another thing, what the hell are we going to do about Christmas presents for Martin and Michael, and of course we mustn't forget Adele and Annabel. Derrick tells us that everything there is so cheap to buy, but it hardly seems right to send the children money.'

'Well, I wouldn't advise you to send many parcels. The postage would be costly and ten to one whatever you buy will cost considerably less in the shops over there. How about you discuss all of this in your letters? You could suggest that we kill the fatted calf and have great celebrations when they are here on leave.'

'Michael, you are an absolute genius. Let's hope that Richard and Laraine manage to get leave at the same time.'

'You don't hear so often from Laraine, do you?'

'Unfortunately, no. She doesn't seem to have settled down at all well this time. She was over the moon when Richard took her on that first trip after they were married.'

Michael smiled knowingly. 'Darling, there was only the two of them then. Now they have two little girls wanting their attention. Honeymoons are often short-lived.'

'Oh Michael, please don't say that. You make it sound as if they are unhappy.'

'Maybe Laraine is. She saw there was another side to life from the first day you took her to Shepperton Studios.'

'Michael, stop it, you are going from bad to worse and you're making me feel guilty. What do you suggest I do?'

He laughed, reached for the bottle and shared what was left of the wine between their two glasses. Pushing Jodie's glass back towards her, he said, 'Drink up, there's nothing you can do except sit down and write her a nice long letter. Let her know that you are missing her.'

'I keep meaning to do that anyway, though I did answer her last letter within days of receiving it. Perhaps when Richard's transfer comes through he will be as lucky as Derrick has been. Meanwhile we just have to wait and see.'

'Uncle Michael, we haven't got along very well with this new game. Would you come over here and explain the instructions, please.' Reggie's voice held a note of pleading. Before Michael had moved a muscle, however, their mother was up on her feet.

'Not tonight he won't. It is well past your bed-time but I will make one exception: if you both go upstairs, wash and clean your teeth and put your pyjamas and dressing gowns on, you may come back down and have a nightcap with us before your Uncle Michael has to leave.'

Both lads ran out into the hall and made a dash for the stairs, but it was Lenny's voice that came back clearly to Jodie and Michael.

'Mum said a nightcap, but I bet she won't put a drop of whisky or brandy in our hot chocolate.'

Before Jodie could think of an answer, the boys were out of earshot and Michael and Jodie could hear the clomp-clomp as they kicked their shoes off in their bedrooms above.

'A right pair those two are growing into,' Jodie remarked, but she had a smile on her face as she said it.

Michael was grinning widely. 'Both your boys are a credit to you, Jodie, they really are. When you think about how you've made a success of your career, bought this beautiful house and at the same time fed, clothed and brought up two de-lightful boys, I'd say you've made the grade and then some. You really should be very proud of yourself.'

'Thank you, Michael. I don't often get such praise, but I can't claim that I own this house, not yet. The bank allowed me a hefty mortgage.'

'Well that only goes to show that they saw you as a woman of prestige, and they were not wrong. In my opinion you have always come through with flying colours, so stop trying to put yourself down.'

'Thank you, Michael,' she murmured and he could hear the sadness in her voice which made him wish that she had been a lot wiser when she had married John Underwood. She had certainly been very young, but she had done remarkably well and he felt very privileged not only to have her as a friend but for him and Danny to be allowed to be part of her family.

Jodie was thrilled to hear what Michael thought about her; it gave her a sense of pride. Besides keeping her head above water financially, she was saving a little each month as well. She was not certain why she scraped and saved; she just felt it was the right thing to do, and it was a great feeling to know that she had money behind her to fall back on if at any time she should need it.

The boys came back downstairs, washed faces shining and their hair brushed back, looking as if butter wouldn't melt in their mouths. All four of them were sitting around the kitchen table drinking their hot chocolate when suddenly Lenny said aggressively, 'Uncle Michael, we didn't quite get the hang of that new game because my rotten brother is a know-all and he's a bloody pain in the neck.'

His mother was on her feet in a second, leaning across the table, her face only inches from that of her younger son. 'You, my lad, will have a pain in your backside if I take you upstairs and give you a good walloping.'

As quickly as her temper had flared, it receded. Her nerves were a bit frayed this evening and it had only taken a spark to set her off. Did she let her boys have too much freedom? Without a father to shoulder some of the discipline, had she gone too far the other way?

In the meantime, Michael had gently touched Lenny's arm. When Lenny turned to him, Michael stayed silent, but his look said more than any words could have done.

Immediately Lenny apologised to his brother, and to his mother he said, 'I'm sorry, Mum but he will keep on that I'm not as clever as he is 'cos I'm younger.'

Both Michael and Jodie had to hide their smiles before Jodie was able to form an answer. 'Lenny, it is up to you to study and learn, but I promise you, the day will come when Reg will wish that he was as young as you.'

Neither of the boys believed what their mother had just stated, but peace was restored as Lenny passed the plate of chocolate biscuits to his elder brother.

When it was time for Michael to leave, the boys came with their mother to the front door to say good night and wave him off. They listened for a minute until the sound of his car could no longer be heard, then Jodie closed the door and shot the bolts, turned the porch light off and walked behind her sons as they climbed the stairs.

'Good night, Mum, it was great having Uncle Michael here tonight.' Lenny smiled contentedly as Jodie tucked the blankets around him and he snuggled down in the bed.

'Good night, Lenny, God bless, don't forget to say your prayers.'

In Reggie's room she hesitated. His dark curly hair made a splash of colour on the white pillowcase, but his eyes were closed and his breathing was already soft and regular. She bent low and gently kissed his forehead before she turned away. In the doorway, she glanced back and heaved a sigh. It was unbelievable how much her elder son resembled his father. As alike as two peas from the same pod. Sadness almost overwhelmed her as she pulled the bedroom door to, and slowly made her way downstairs. The quietness of the house now was devastating. With a heavy heart, Jodie leaned her head on her hands and stared into the slowly dying fire.

Why, she asked herself, do I always feel that I am the odd one out?

26

The dark days of November and early December leading up to Christmas passed quickly. The wind was bitter, and most mornings there was a heavy frost. Scarves and gloves were fished out from the bottom of cupboards and out of drawers. Jodie took the boys to buy new footwear, and while in the shop she treated herself to a gorgeous pair of knee-high boots. She also bought two new hats. Not the fancy type, of which she already had several, only brought out for weddings and suchlike; no, today's purchases were sensible cloches designed to be close-fitting and to keep one's ears warm. Snow had been forecast, and she was making sure that she and the boys would be prepared.

Every child in the land was disappointed. Instead of snow, there were gale-force winds and endless torrential rain. Reggie and Lenny began their school holidays by decorating the house with fancy chains, paper lanterns and sprigs of holly. Jack and Mary Hartfield arrived three days before Christmas, bringing Marian with them. Jodie had issued an open invitation to come and share Christmas with her and the boys in Epsom. If there had only been herself to consider, she would gladly have spent the entire holiday curled up in the warmth of her own home. She wasn't that selfish, though. The boys needed company, and she was rather hoping that Michael and Danny might decide to join them. If she knew where her bloody husband was, she felt she'd have been half inclined to invite him, if only for the sake of their two sons.

Jack had straight away taken the two boys off to find what he said had to be a gigantic Christmas tree, and Mary had arrived with considerate and very welcome gifts: the beautiful cakes and puddings that she had known Jodie hadn't had the time to make. Marian had made mince pies and filled three airtight tins with them. Jodie hugged and kissed Jack, Mary and Marian warmly. 'How many more times are you going to step into the breach when I most need you?' she asked.

'Don't be so daft,' Marian protested. 'We are so pleased that you decided to have all of us together for Christmas.'

The house was warm and festive-looking, full of happy people, and Jodie was grateful that there was indeed a good sprinkling of men. Neither Reggie nor Lenny would have been pleased if they had been swamped with female company. On Boxing Day morning, six car loads of friends and neighbours, together with a few children, set off to see the hounds ride out over the North Downs, and Reg and Lenny were full of it when they returned home. The women left behind hadn't felt in the least bit hard done by; they had retreated en masse to the local pub, and when the landlord called time had wandered home slowly and put their feet up for a very welcome rest.

On New Year's Day, as Jodie tried to organise her desk diary for the coming months, the telephone rang. 'Hello?'

'Happy New Year, Jodie.'

She recognised the voice and shuddered. 'Why now, John? What is it you want, and how did you get this number?'

'Jodie, please, give me a chance. My mother gave me your number. I don't want anything from you. I just want to see the boys.'

'How long have you been home?'

'Only a week or so. I wanted to see them for Christmas. I came to the house but I hadn't the heart to ring the bell. I could see through the window that you had a houseful.'

'I wouldn't have stopped you seeing the boys.'

'No, but I doubt you would have invited me into your big new house.'

Jodie didn't answer, and the line crackled. 'Jodie?'

'Yes, I'm still here.'

'The boys are still on holiday, aren't they? Could I come this afternoon?'

All Jodie's determination and resolve collapsed, crumpling like tissue paper. 'Yes.'

Very slowly she replaced the receiver. Was she going to let him back into her life again? She smiled wryly and said out loud, 'I've done it again, felt sorry for him, told myself he has the right to see them and they have the right to see their father. But what about my rights, and come to that, what about my heartache?'

Over a light lunch, Jodie told the boys of their father's proposed visit. They didn't show much emotion, but neither did they object. And so at two o'clock, when the doorbell rang, it was Reg and Lenny who opened the front door, while Jodie went upstairs and made herself scarce.

At four o'clock, there was a soft tap on her bedroom door and Jodie put down the book she was reading. 'Come in,' she called, and was relieved to see Reggie's head appear round the door. 'Dad is just going, but Mum, he said to ask if he can have a word with you.'

Jodie felt she had no choice. She would have liked to question Reggie as to how the meeting with their father had gone, but on second thoughts she decided it wouldn't be fair. 'OK, I'll come down, just give me a few minutes,' she said, hoping she wasn't going to live to regret this decision.

John was standing staring into the glowing fire, his arms outstretched, his hands resting on the mantelshelf. The very sight of him took her unawares. Gosh, he was still a very good-looking man, and he was well dressed too. He'd no right to come here looking so prosperous when he hadn't sent a single thing to his sons for Christmas. She pulled herself up sharply; maybe he had brought them gifts today, she'd better wait and see.

He looked up as she entered the room. 'You're looking very well, Jodie, and you have a really lovely home here. I must admit you have done very well for yourself.'

'*By* myself,' she snapped.

There was a long silence. Jodie was giving nothing away and it was John that broke it. 'The problem with us is that we look at things from different angles. We both see something totally different. And we're both as stubborn as mules.'

Jodie was watching him, waiting for him to go on.

'Oh Jodie, I'm sorry, really I am.'

She gave a sarcastic grunt. 'Just what are you apologising for?'

He shook his head. 'Everything.'

'I notice you've no wish to give me itemised details. Just as well, we'd be here until doomsday.'

'Why didn't you tell me you were selling up in Rye and moving here?'

'It was impossible, I didn't know where you were, and anyway, I knew you'd try to stop me.'

To her surprise, he laughed, throwing his head back in real amusement.

'Jodie, you really take the cake! Stop you? Me? When have I ever actually managed to stop you from doing something that your heart was set on? When has anyone? I'd as soon try to stop the sea coming in at high tide.' He made to reach for her, but she moved back quickly. They stayed as they were, in silence, for a very long moment.

Again it was John that broke it. 'I suppose you

286

could say I've been a fool. We Underwoods have always needed to be top dog. Stiff-necked lot where our women are concerned. It's just that...' He ran out of words.

'Your brothers wouldn't agree with you,' Jodie said very quietly. 'More likely you should have married a woman who would be content to stay at home, have a baby every year, do the washing, ironing, cleaning, never willing to argue with you, nor make a decision on her own, but still think that the sun shone from out of your backside.'

Again he took a step nearer to her, but his big eyes were screwed up with anger now. 'And look what I got landed with, a self-willed baggage who argued with me every time I opened my mouth, who thinks running a home and taking care of her kids is only a part-time job, something to do in her spare time. You add insult to injury by buying property and putting only your name on the title deeds. And another thing, you send my sons to a private school just because you think it will be another smack in the eye for me.'

'If I had been a stay-at-home wife who devoted her time to the children, where was our income supposed to come from? Naval pay for the rank and file of the service wouldn't keep body and soul together. And of course any money that came your way was badly needed by public house managers and bookmakers. You never gave a single thought to our boys, not even when you stole my winnings from the football pools.'

'Oh for Christ's sake, Jodie, do you need to drag all that up again? I never stole that money. The cheque was made out to J. Underwood and it was handed to me all square and above board.'

Jodie wasn't the least bit surprised that he could still turn the tables to suit himself, but what she did find hard to believe was the fact that he believed every word he was saying. How could he pretend concern for his sons, accuse her of only being a part-time mother, when he never gave so much as one penny to their boys from that seventy-five thousand pounds he had walked off with? Now she was upset. She had promised herself that she would never again refer to that incident. It was over and done with. She hadn't the slightest idea where the money was. Probably every penny was gone, but it was nothing to do with her and she wanted to make that point very clear. The businesses she owned, this lovely house and the fact that the boys were being given a good education was all down to her and her own hard work. How dare John be so offensive?

'I've listened to enough. I want you to go now, and I don't give a damn what you think about me.' Jodie was having a frightful job holding her temper in check. She moved swiftly, thankful that she had sent the boys into the kitchen and made sure that the door was closed. As she turned the handle, she was already calling, 'Boys, come out and say good-bye to your father. Go to the door with him and I'll see about getting our dinner cooked.'

She turned to see that John had followed her out into the hall. With a great effort she composed herself enough to say to him, 'If you let me or your mother know where you are, we can start to make arrangements for you to see the boys on a regular basis, if that is what you want.'

'Of course it is what I want,' he said, struggling into his overcoat and flinging a huge scarf around his neck. 'What about us, can we meet up?'

'I think you have said all you needed to say to me. There is no *us*.'

Even John could find no answer to that. He put an arm around each of his sons, and Jodie watched them walk to the front door.

Back in the kitchen, she took down saucepans and laid out vegetables. Suddenly it all seemed too much. She sighed wearily and was on the verge of tears when Reggie came quietly up behind her.

'Sit down, Mum, we're not starving for our dinner just yet. I'll put the kettle on, and Lenny, you get the cake tin out, and the three of us will have a nice cuppa.'

Jodie smiled, even though her eyes were brimming with tears. 'Thanks, boys,' she said. She had so much to be grateful for.

At the end of January, the snow did come. Jodie stood outside the house, well wrapped up, watching six boys and two girls having fun in the field opposite. Several of the men had made three long, narrow sledges for the children, and their laughter was good to hear as they tobogganed down the far slopes. Not everything about the winter was bad.

Two days later, Jodie was not so sure about that. She had had a terrible night, hardly any sleep. She coughed as she put a foot to the floor, and her chest hurt really badly. She felt awful. Every joint in her body was stiff, her lips were dry and sore, her forehead was burning hot. With a great effort she put on her dressing gown and slowly made her way downstairs. Having made a pan of porridge, she laid out four slices of bread ready for toasting. All this was done in a haze of discomfort and pain. Her throat felt worse, it was painful to swallow and she knew it would be impossible to eat, but she had to see to her boys, make sure they had some breakfast, and really she felt she ought to get the car out and run them to school.

It was at that point that the boys came into the kitchen washed and smartly dressed ready for school.

'Mum, whatever is the matter with you? You look awful.' Reg looked concerned.

'I've just caught a nasty cold from somewhere. Maybe I'll make a few phone calls and stay at home today. Reg, will you ladle out the porridge into those two bowls while I fetch the milk in.'

Having crossed the wide hall, she undid the bolts on the door and turned the latch to open the big front door. The bitter air hit her like a physical blow. It took a great effort to bend down and pick up the two bottles of milk, and a mighty gust of wind almost knocked her off her feet. She leaned against the wall of the porch for a moment, gasping for breath. Her chest felt as if a constricting band of iron had been clamped around it. For a frightening moment flashes of colour seemed to light up the dark morning. Although the air was bitterly cold, her body was hot, her forehead was burning and she felt a sweat break out over her as her body flushed with fever. She slid to the ground and never noticed that one bottle of milk had rolled away, while the other one had hit the wall and splintered. Suddenly, not caring any more, she felt herself falling into pitch darkness.

It was the sound of breaking glass that had Reg and Lenny rushing to her aid. In the darkness, Reg almost fell over his mother, but quickly regained his balance. 'Lenny, you take Mum's feet. I've got her by the shoulders. All we need to do is move her inside the hall, just enough so that we can close the door, keep that ruddy cold out.' Neither of them needed telling; they ran and grabbed blankets and pillows and soon had their mother safe, lying on the floor still, but warm, comfortable and dry.

It was four days later, after two visits from the doctor, that Jodie came back to the land of the living. She opened her eyes to the light of a glowing fire, safe and sound in her own bedroom. She felt incredibly frail, almost as if her body had wasted away. The bitter taste of medicine was still in her mouth, and it was then that she knew she'd never been left alone. She had been aware of a reassuring presence. On several occasions warm, strong hands had held her, preventing her from slipping back into the peaceful darkness. There had been two faces, and all at once she knew: Dee's parents, oh she owed them such a debt of gratitude. Jack would have cared for her boys as she now knew Mary must have looked after her, night and day.

'Well thank God for that! Our Sleeping Beauty is back with us,' Mary whispered, then, raising her voice, she called out, 'Jack, put the kettle on and lay a tray with a pot of tea. She may only be able to sip at a cup, but I bet that will be the first thing our Jodie will ask for.'

Later that day, her boys sat one each side of the

bed, each holding their mother's hand. Jack Hartfield stood at the end, leaning forward, his face solemn.

'Welcome back, lazy bones.' His eyes glistened with unshed tears. 'Perhaps now you've had a warning you'll slow down a bit and stop trying to be wonder woman of the year. Must say, though, you have trained those two boys of yours well. They've been not a bit of trouble, good as gold the pair of them, though I fancy you frightened the life out of them that morning. Talk about sensible, though. The doctor had nothing but praise for them and the way in which they handled you.

'Come on now,' he ordered the boys. 'Downstairs. It's sleep yer mum needs now. And when the phone calls start, as they have every evening, we shall tell everyone the good news but we will stipulate no visitors, not for a day or two. We must get her eating properly and some flesh back on those bones; maybe even get her downstairs into the lounge before she can cope with callers.'

Everybody had to leave the room because the doctor had arrived. He stayed twenty minutes and his parting words were, 'Don't start overdoing things just because you feel better. Make sure you drink plenty and rest up still; you're not out of the woods yet, you know.'

Later, Mary came blustering in, a big smile on her face. 'I spoke to the doctor. He said that you were feeling better.'

Jodie struggled to sit up. She felt as weak as a kitten. 'I am,' she murmured, sniffing. 'Yes, I am.'

Mary's eyes were glowing. 'God, am I relieved. Please, Jodie, don't ever do that to me again.

There's been a few times over these past days when I thought you were going to give up. You had me thinking we were going to lose you, you know.'

Jodie managed a weak smile. 'I must get up. There are things I have to do. I have to check on my salons.'

'There'll be time enough for you to check on everything later. Meanwhile, anything that needs doing, Michael will do for you.'

'Thanks, Mary, for everything. What me and the boys would have done without you and Jack, I dread to think.'

'Stop it, Jodie. It makes a change for us to be taking care of you. Usually it seems to be the other way round.'

'All the same, I don't want to put you to more trouble.'

'It is no trouble. Besides, look at it from our point of view. We both absolutely love being here with you and the boys in this lovely house.'

Jodie let her head drop back on to the pillows. How lucky she was to have such special friends.

27

Jodie had had a bath and for the first time in ages she was fully dressed. It had taken a great effort and left her feeling as weak as a kitten. Now she was in the lounge, seated in one of the big armchairs, which Jack had turned around so that she was able to see what was going on in her lovely garden. The birds were a great source of amusement as they fed from the nuts in the numerous feeders she had hung from the trees. The smaller birds such as the blue tits seemed to prefer the food from the bird table that Mary had set out, though they didn't have it all their own way. The greedy grey squirrels seemed to think the table was their territory and were willing to fight for it. Same in all walks of life, Jodie was thinking, survival of the fittest.

The door was thrown open and a smiling Mary said, 'This should brighten your day.' She crossed the room, coming to stand beside Jodie's chair, and held out a pile of post. Jodie took hold of it and they looked at each other, smiling, for a moment or two. Jodie made the first move by flicking through the letters she was now holding, taking note of the various postage stamps.

'I hope Jack and I have got a letter from our Delia and that she has bothered to tell us a lot more news than her last letter did. There was hardly any mention of our grandsons, would you believe.' Mary had spoken sharply, and Jodie picked up on her tone of voice.

'Well from the look of these I have a letter from Dee and also one from Laraine, so I'm sure you too will have letters waiting for you at home.'

'Maybe,' Mary said huffily as she turned to go. Thinking better of it, she looked back and her words were softer as she said, 'Ring your little bell when you're ready for coffee. I'll bring the tray in here and Jack and I will have ours with you.' And with that she left, closing the door firmly behind her.

Jack was at the kitchen sink holding the kettle under the cold tap. He didn't turn round to face his wife but hearing her enter he said, 'All good news I hope. How is our Delia and Martin and Michael? Suppose Derrick is happy enough as long as he's within yards of the sea.'

'How the hell would I know how any of them are faring?' Mary's sharp words were like a shot from a cannon. Jack carefully put the now full kettle on the ring and lit the gas beneath it before turning round.

One look at his wife's face and he smiled ruefully. 'Hasn't Jodie shared the news with you?'

'She didn't even open the letters, not while I was in the room,' said Mary, sounding unusually vicious.

'Well there you are then,' Jack said amiably. 'She'll get round to it all in good time.'

Mary tilted her chin in a severe gesture. 'Jodie is our daughter's sister-in-law, a relative only by marriage. We are Delia's parents and her two sons are our grandsons. And what about poor Marian? She's the mother of all three men who are married to those girls. Has she had a letter from any one of them?'

'You don't know that she hasn't,' he snapped tartly, then, thinking better of it, he softened his voice and almost pleaded, 'Ease up will you, please, Mary. As soon as we've had a cup of coffee I will go back home and collect our mail, and I will also pop in and see Marian. In the meantime I suggest you think on. I know we're here now because Jodie needed our help, but what about Christmas and all the other times when Jodie never leaves us out. And she also remembers to invite our Brian each and every time.'

Mary had been about to ask how he knew there would be any mail at home for him to collect, but she sensed his sudden anger and knew she had better not push him too far.

Jodie's intuition had told her that Mary was annoyed because she had not immediately opened her letters and shared them with her. It wasn't that she didn't want to; she just had to be sure there was nothing of a confidential nature for her eyes only. She was very aware that she was only related to Dee by marriage, but unofficially it went so much deeper than that. They were friends, good friends. She didn't blame Mary for being upset. Naturally she missed her daughter and felt she was being robbed of seeing her grandsons grow up. But it was Dee's life, and she had chosen to marry Derrick. Slowly she reached over and picked up the small handbell and rang it. A cup of coffee together might ease the situation a little. She certainly hoped so; she was still too weak to deal with ill humour, especially from a grown woman.

Jack had poured the coffee into three cups and Jodie had taken several sips before she placed the cup back down on the saucer and picked up one of her letters. Every one of the half-dozen had now been opened and scanned, if not read fully.

'Mary and Jack, you did receive a letter from your Delia telling you that she and Derrick had moved out of the Hyatt Regency, didn't you?'

'Yes we did,' Mary said sharply, 'but that was ages ago.'

'So was my last letter. I've heard nothing since until this one arrived today, and now I am going to read the first page of it out loud for both of you to hear.'

An awkward moment passed as Jodie withdrew a flimsy sheet of notepaper from the envelope and began to read.

'Dear Jodie, This is going to be a short letter because my fingers are aching from just having written a very long one to my parents. I told you all about Emmy in my last letters. She is still a godsend but this afternoon is her time off and I have promised to take Martin and Michael to the park. I'm sure you won't mind if I cut you short for I'm aware that you all share your letters from us around the family and that is good, especially for our mother-in-law. Please don't ever let her feel that I am writing to one more than another. I feel bad enough as it is, Jodie, that she has all three of her sons so far away, but I promise, and you must remind her, that when we come home, probably in May, we will take her out with us wherever we go.'

The silence felt dreadful as Jodie stopped reading and folded the sheet of notepaper in half.

'Would you like another cup of coffee? There's plenty in the pot. I just need to heat up some more milk. I won't be two minutes,' Jack said, picking up the milk jug and making for the door.

The tension still hung heavily, until Jodie said, 'Mary, why don't you go with Jack to pick up your post? You'll be able to pop in and see Marian, perhaps read her letter to her, or if she hasn't received one, maybe read yours to her. I'm sure Derrick will have scribbled something to his mother, even if it is only a short note. It would be a nice ride and a chance for you to get some fresh air.'

'But what about you? We can't leave you here all on your own,' Mary said, sounding sheepish.

'Oh yes you can, no arguments. I shall be fine, probably sleep until the boys get home.'

It was Jack who helped Jodie to the downstairs loo. He also placed a jug of drinking water and one of home-made lemonade on a table beside her chair. 'Three hours, four at most, Jodie, and we'll be back. Here's today's paper and a couple of magazines, and thank you, you're a gem.'

'It should be me thanking you and Mary for having taken such good care of me,' said Jodie.

'It's got nothing to do with that and you know it,' he said staunchly. 'Lass, I don't know how you acquired the habit, but you are certainly great at pouring oil on troubled waters.'

Jodie gave him a sweet smile, but when she heard his car draw away from the house she sighed in relief. Perhaps now she could read her letters and take as long as she liked over it.

It didn't work out like that.

When Reggie and Lenny came home, they crept into the lounge and what they saw had them smothering their laughter. Their mother was fast asleep, a sheet of airmail paper lying over her face, her regular breathing fluttering the flimsy paper steadily up and down.

It was another two weeks before the doctor declared Jodie fit to go out, but with an added warning that she needed to take things easy, not rush straight in to work as if it were a matter of life or death.

As usual her friends and staff rallied around her. Those really close to her felt relieved that she had come through that nasty bout of influenza as well as she had. Michael made sure she didn't drive her car yet. He promised to pick her up each morning but not before ten o'clock, and had left strict instructions with her staff as to what she could do and could not do. Not that they needed telling. There wasn't a single employee who wouldn't agree that Judith Underwood was a fair-minded employer, and to most she was a friend as well as their boss.

This morning Michael had dropped her off at her Epsom salon. She stood looking about her for some minutes, collecting her wits and her thoughts, before she carefully set down her case and handbag and advanced into the shop, stopping at each working station. Every leather armchair was clean, the rungs beneath free of dust. The huge mirrors were bright and shiny, no nasty smears. Life had gone on while she'd been ill, and she counted herself lucky as she watched two of her favourite operators in action. She really did have good, reliable staff.

'My goodness,' said a male voice, husky and distinctive. 'What have we here?'

Jodie turned and opened her arms wide. 'Danny,' was all she was able to stammer before she felt him pull her close. For a second she couldn't think what she was supposed to be doing here. It felt so good to be held in Danny's embrace and she suddenly realised she was clutching his arm so tightly that it seemed to have become welded to her fingers.

'Why the hell didn't Michael tell us you were coming here today?' Danny half turned his head and waved a hand to the three young women who were each working on a customer's head of hair. 'We're absolutely thrilled to see you, Judith, aren't we, girls?'

A chorus of voices which included every client declared that she had been missed and that they all thanked God that she was up and about again.

'Thank you, all of you, it is great to be here. I didn't realise that I had missed the salons so much,' she sniffed loudly, 'and indeed, the smell of shampoo, conditioner and hairspray. Nothing to beat it, not anywhere.'

'Well, well,' Danny said softly. 'Is it too much to ask you to come through and let me make you a cup of coffee?'

'I'd like that, please.'

'OK. And,' he added, 'that's the first time you've smiled since you walked through the door. I was just beginning to wonder if you could, thought maybe your illness had left you bereft.'

'Please, Danny, don't make fun of me. I need some TLC.'

'Then, my darling Jodie, you have come to exactly the right place. I was surprised when Michael asked if I would mind being here today. He didn't say you were coming in; wanted to give me a nice surprise, I suppose. He knew that I would be the right person to take care of you, seeing as how you're insisting on coming back to work so soon after having been so poorly.'

'I've been dying to come back. It feels as if I have been out of my normal routine for ages.'

'Well, I think you should stay in the background for today, go through the accounts, whatever, but don't think you can immediately do a shift. Hours on your feet won't do you much good.' He patted her hand affectionately.

Jodie put her other hand on top of his, telling him in a low voice, 'I am so pleased Michael asked you to be here today, though I shall have a go at him later on for not telling me. I really am grateful for your company. The staff are all busy and I wouldn't want to intrude on their routine ... but,' she swallowed deeply before adding, 'I still miss Dee and Laraine so much. We all need something, don't we?'

'You're just feeling low. That nasty bout of illness has taken it out of you, but yes, Jodie, you're right, we do all need something, or rather somebody.'

As Danny made the coffee, he thought about the fact that there was another side to Mrs Judith Underwood. How come he had never realised it before? She was prosperous and successful, making sure that every minute of every hour she was occupied, but in other ways life had dealt her a lousy deal, and it all stemmed back to that husband of hers. True, she had two very nice young sons, but when they were in bed at night, who was there to comfort Jodie? No one was the short answer, she was on her own. Poor Jodie! She had got over the ailments that had attacked her body, but no one had given a thought to the worst sickness of all: loneliness.

Tonight, without fail, Danny was going to broach the subject with Michael. It was time that those who cared for her did something about it.

28

Jodie loved it when letters from Dee and Laraine arrived on the same day, but she couldn't help feeling a little envious. As ever Dee was full of how wonderful life in Singapore with Derrick had turned out to be, and even Laraine had been more optimistic since Richard had been transferred to Dubai.

Now the time had slipped by. It was the second week in May, and both families were coming home on six weeks' leave. Jodie couldn't wait, and she wasn't the only one. Marian could hardly contain herself, and Mary and Jack Hartfield were acting as if ten Christmases were being rolled into one.

Two weeks before the families were due to fly into Heathrow, Shepperton Studios announced that their new extensions were to be officially opened, and Jodie received an engraved invitation card.

'We are making quite a splash of it. I'm sure you will enjoy the day,' Philip Conti said, smiling.

Jodie hadn't seen much of Philip recently. She had heard he had gone home to Italy during the period when she had been ill, but he hadn't written or picked up the phone. She had tried to adopt an air of indifference, but one look at him and the physical attraction was almost palpable. She stepped back, putting space between them.

'Oh no, I don't really think that... A day? Oh no, I certainly couldn't manage a whole day.'

'Of course you'll come.' Philip was not going to take a refusal. 'After all the hard work you've put in behind the scenes, you deserve to be there.'

Jodie smiled, and was more than a little surprised to realise that she was not entirely immune to Philip's distinctive charm.

'There'll be people there you should meet,' he continued. 'Nothing like personal contact, nothing at all. You of all people should realise that. You won't regret it, I assure you.'

'Must it be a whole day?'

'But of course.' His voice was friendly, even gracious. 'You can hardly walk out halfway through. You need not bother with your own car; I shall be using the company's courtesy car so I might as well pick you up. About ten o'clock, and I'll see you get taken home at six. All right? Good. That's settled, then.'

Come the day and Jodie was up at the crack of dawn. She spent ages deciding what to wear and even longer arranging her thick dark hair. A long look into her full-length mirror and she was well pleased. The grey suit had cost her a bomb but was still a darn sight cheaper than if she had bought it from a shop. Isaac, the little Jewish tailor who had a workshop just off the Strand, was indeed a useful gentleman to know. A white silk blouse with a pussy bow added a little frippery to the severity of the suit, and she had swept her hair up high in an effort to add to her height. High-heeled court shoes, black seamed stockings and she was ready to go.

They arrived in good time, but after a few pleasant, politely applauded speeches, a glass or two of champagne and trays of smoked salmon and nibbles, the guests gathered up their briefcases and made ready to depart, while the employees wandered down the corridors, some to their old offices, others to settle into their new departments.

'I have come to realise, Philip, that you do most things exceptionally well,' Jodie said reproachfully, 'but you don't always tell the truth. Is it too much to ask what you have planned for the rest of my day?'

'I thought a mystery trip into the unknown. Just you and me. Lunch at some quiet little place we are sure to come across. A few hours together. A chance to really talk to each other.'

'Business?' she asked, her eyebrows raised.

'No. Definitely not.'

'And if I say I am going straight home?'

Philip watched her with steady eyes that were not smiling. After several seconds had passed he said quietly, 'Then I promise you I will not bother you again.'

Jodie pushed a hairpin more securely into place. 'Well, we can't have that, can we?' she said sharply. 'Think of all the contracts we've both of us signed.'

Philip had his own car parked at the studios, and they drove through weak spring sunshine along the lanes and byways of glorious Surrey. Box Hill and the Devil's Punch Bowl had a canopy of new green grass, and the rich dark mould of the earth was warming up enough to allow bulbs and shrubs to show signs of new life. Jodie was quietly admitting to herself how much she was enjoying the ride.

'You're very quiet,' Philip said.

Jodie nodded and smiled. She was thinking back to her courting days, when John had first brought her to Box Hill. He had rented a caravan for the weekend, but having paid for it he had hardly any money left, and although they had spent a few hours in the famous pub there, could afford only one beer each and a sandwich between them. For once she was nursing a good memory of John: his handsome laughing face and his warm hand in hers, the attention he'd paid her in those days. She stifled a sigh. It had all been a very long time ago.

She found herself relaxing. She was no longer cross with Philip. It was a beautiful day and it would be stupid not to enjoy it.

Philip had turned the car off the main road and was driving down a long, narrow lane. Finally he turned into the car park of what appeared to be an ancient and rambling inn. Must be a popular place, Jodie decided, for there was hardly a vacant space in which to park.

The innkeeper treated Philip with that mixture of deference and familiarity which normally was reserved for only a very few special customers.

'Good day, Mr Conti. Just the weather to have brought you out for a spin in the country. Would you like to eat straight away, or would you and the young lady prefer to have a sherry first?'

'Sherry first, please, Mr Sturdy. May we have them in the small bar, and we'd like to eat in say half an hour.'

'Certainly, Mr Conti, certainly.'

No sooner were they seated in the tiny snug bar than Jodie turned on Philip.

'He was expecting us,' she said.

'Yes, he was.'

Jodie made no further comment. She was coming to know Philip better and better as time passed. An elderly waiter wearing a bibbed white apron brought their sherry, two large glasses, not the small ones that sherry was normally served in.

Philip had settled himself into a deep, rather shabby leather armchair.

'Is the sherry to your liking?' He was watching her intently.

'It is perfect, thank you.' Jodie drank the sherry rather too fast. On top of the champagne and hardly any breakfast, the effect was a little alarming, though not at all unpleasant.

He leaned forward. 'I am full of admiration for you, Jodie. You seem to have made a success of everything you touch. I really believe you're going to go places in your life.'

'So do I,' she came back at him promptly.

His voice was low. 'Be careful, Jodie. Too much success can be like a drug, habit-forming. If you've never had it, then you can manage very well without it, but the first taste and that is where the danger begins. Do you think you are in danger of addiction?'

She didn't answer. A slight recklessness seemed to have overtaken her. And why not? she asked herself silently. Was it such a crime that just for a few hours she should feel free? Not have to worry about whether the boys had enough clean shirts, had she banked enough money this month to pay the mortgage, ought she to get someone to look at the tiles on the roof of the house. What the hell did any of it matter! She felt someone very near to her. She looked up. Mr Sturdy was at her shoulder.

'Lunch is ready when you are, madam.'

'Thank you.' She smiled sweetly and got to her feet, albeit a little unsteadily. Mr Sturdy showed them to their table, which was set in an alcove, and a very young waiter poured white wine into tall glasses. When he left them alone, Philip lifted his glass and said, 'Cheers.'

They ate king prawns on skewers served with a variety of dips and a side salad, which Jodie thoroughly enjoyed. It wasn't until a chef, still wearing his tall white hat, appeared at the table to carve the meat for their main course that she realised that nobody had asked either of them what they would like to eat. They had not even been shown a menu.

'Scottish venison,' the chef announced as he lifted the domed cover off with a flourish. 'How would you like it, madam? Well done, rare, or maybe somewhere in between?'

Jodie's face was already flushed with wine, yet still she felt it turn red, but she was saved from answering as Philip gently said, 'Medium for the lady and I'll take mine very rare, please.'

There was not a single fault to be found. Even the vegetables which were served with this delicious tender meat were entirely different from the usual run-of-the-mill. Best of all, in Jodie's opinion, was the large silver gravy boat which had been placed in the centre of the table, brimming to the top with rich gravy, so that they might help themselves.

In spite of the fact that she had not wanted to come to the opening of Shepperton's new building, and had been really annoyed to find that Philip had lied to her, she would now willingly agree that she was thoroughly enjoying herself. Philip made her laugh; he also flattered her. Now he was talking nonsense, but that too was funny. Then something he said jolted her to reality.

'Malta?' she repeated, aware that she sounded dismayed. 'You're going to Malta?'

'Yes, that's right. I shall also be visiting Sicily. I have one more week before I leave. Have you ever been to either of those islands?'

Jodie shook her head, and without thinking complained crossly, 'My two sisters-in-law, who are my best friends, both live abroad, and now you. Me? Eastbourne is about as far as I shall ever get.'

He threw back his head and laughed, a great roar, and it took a minute before he was able to reply. 'Good lord, you think I am going for good? Well I am not. Nothing would induce me to leave England. Many's the time I've thought of returning to Italy, but I have left it too late, I fear. No, I shall be away five, maybe six months at the most.'

'I see,' was all that Jodie could manage.

There was amusement sparkling in his eyes and he swallowed deeply before saying, 'You don't seem too happy at the idea of me going away. I thought you might have been glad to see the back of me.'

In that moment it came to Jodie that perhaps there was more to this day's outing than he was letting on. All was not as casual as he would like her to believe.

'What difference will you not being here make to me?'

'That's no answer. It's just clever, answering a question with a question.'

'Well, it would sound silly to say that I shall miss you. There was a time when that would have been true, but we've drifted apart, wouldn't you say?'

'No, I wouldn't. You have been made aware that I've been to Italy, but has anyone told you the reason why?' He took her silence as a no. 'My journey was essential. My father had died. The funeral arrangements were pretty straightforward and the respect paid to my father by so many was of great benefit to my mother. However, my responsibilities did not end there. Mamma and my sister both decided to sell their properties and to live together. It made sense, but there were so many legalities for me to sort out. I didn't know until I returned that you had been seriously ill.'

He reached across the table and took her hand. It seemed the most natural thing in the world for him to do.

'Some people you can know for years but you never get close. Sometimes – very rarely, but it does happen – one outing and you know. A bond is formed, no matter how much you might try to deny it. I think I loved you from the first moment we met, but I suppose that is asking too much for you to believe. Try this, then. How about our weekend? Does the memory stay with you?'

Jodie opened her mouth to answer, but he stopped her by reaching a hand across the table again, and this time he traced the line of her mouth with one finger.

'I made promises to take you and your boys with me to Italy. Family duty prevails very strongly in my homeland, but I did come back as soon as it was safe to leave my mother and my sister. They are still grieving and so am I, but I have the advantage of being able to lose myself in my work. My father was a lovely, lovely man. Perhaps that word is too demonstrative for you; you English are not good at describing your feelings.'

Jodie shivered, unable to find the right words to say.

'So far we haven't done any harm to anyone.' He smiled. 'When I come back from Malta, we'll be well into autumn. Then we'll see. Meantime shall we both make an unbreakable promise? Once a week we shall telephone each other, and more often if the mood takes us.'

She nodded, and he leant towards her as she lifted her face. His kiss was just as she remembered, only infinitely more so. Jodie was instantly aware that she was caught again in that web of fascination that Philip wove so effortlessly around her. She sat back but was unable to take her eyes from his face.

'Now, we've done justice to two wonderful courses, but Mr Sturdy will be most displeased if we don't partake of his Italian dessert, made especially for us, and we'll have coffee and brandies to round off what I think has been a very successful business meeting. And then, my darling – I am allowed endearments again now, am I not? – then I shall take you home.'

'Wow, hold up, Mr Conti, you are in no state to be driving your car now, and yet you are suggesting that we have brandy with our coffee. No way. You are not fit to drive.'

'How very perceptive of you, Jodie, but I foresaw this situation and have made arrangements for my car to be picked up from here tomorrow morning and delivered to the studio. Meanwhile by the time we have finished our sweet and our coffee, the hired car complete with driver will be waiting for us outside.'

Philip was grinning broadly as the waiter removed their dinner plates and set out fresh spoons, forks and serviettes. The minute they were alone again, he leant towards Jodie once more and whispered conspiratorially, 'I shall be travelling in the back seat of the car with you on the journey home.'

Somehow they both got through a very large portion of the delicious sweet, drank proper coffee and drained their brandy goblets.

'Time to go,' Philip said softly as he helped Jodie on with her jacket. Almost as an afterthought he added, 'Remember about the weekly phone calls; we both made the promise.'

Jodie looked into his tanned face. It would be so easy to fall deeply in love with this tall, handsome man. Today had been a wonderful experience, even if it had been a surprise at the outset.

'Time to go,' he repeated, holding her in his arms.

Suddenly she could not, for the life of her, have said if she was relieved or disappointed. It was probably all to the good that they were still in a public restaurant.

29

Jodie was to look back on the home leave of her sisters-in-law and their families as a period of great happiness. Many mornings she thanked God that she was in a position to take time off whenever it suited her. To be able to spend time with her extended family meant such a lot.

It was the middle of June and it had been decided unanimously that there would be no travelling today. It was Saturday, and everybody was to come together in Camber Sands. With Marian's house right next door to Mary and Jack's, there was ample shelter and amenities on hand when needed. The sky was blue and the sun would be very hot come midday, but at the moment there was a slight breeze coming in off the sea. Everyone was getting ready to go to the beach.

My goodness, thought Jodie, the whole crowd of them were a picture to print on one's mind, to be brought out and remembered in lonelier times. Adele and Annabel were quite the grown-up little ladies and Martin and Michael real tomboys. Jodie never tired of looking at them, and she wasn't the only one. When a tiff arose or one child took a tumble, there was a rush from all sides with offers of cuddles and hugs. Just to feel the baby skin, so soft, so smooth, so gently tanned; each child felt good enough to eat.

Within half an hour of arriving on the beach,

Richard and Derrick had set up a tent. Adele, Annabel, Martin and Michael were having the time of their lives paddling in the shallow waves that lapped the sands, and there were more than enough females to make sure they were never left unattended. At ten o'clock the men called out that they were going to Hastings to fetch the boat that Derrick had moored there. 'Lenny, are you and Reg coming?' Richard was calling from further up the beach.

'Yes please,' they both answered, running like the wind along the sand.

Jodie looked at Laraine. 'This holiday of yours has been so good for my two lads. I do appreciate that they and myself have been included in almost everything you've done.'

'Don't be daft. When it comes down to it, we are one big family, don't you agree?' Without waiting for an answer, Laraine added, 'If only your old man could see sense. He must know what he's missing. All the years your boys have been growing up, John will never be able to recall those times.'

That was one subject that Jodie wanted to avoid; it would be like raking over cold coals, and nobody ever got far doing that. Quickly she changed tack. 'Would you like to know which parts of this break I have enjoyed the most?' she asked.

'You're going to tell me anyway,' Laraine said, laughing.

'It's when we all go down to the pub; lucky really there are so many child-minders available. The men enjoy a game of darts – they still seem to have a great many friends wherever we go – and we get to hear all that's been going on far from these English shores.'

'Our men meet so many old pals because they were born and brought up in this neighbourhood,' said Dee. 'Most of their mates here are seafaring men with their own boats. That's how Derrick has been able to call in a few favours; that boat was put at his disposal before the request had left his mouth.'

Jodie smiled. Young Dee had certainly grown up, and by golly she had altered; no longer was she backward in coming forward.

'Another thing,' Laraine began. 'In Dubai there are no such things as public houses. Plenty of clubs where drinks are to be had if you know the right people, but the atmosphere is nothing like it is in England.'

Jodie sat up from the sunlounger and began to rub lotion on her shoulders, although she was the least likely one to get sunburnt, with her dark complexion that already sported a good tan. 'Tell me more about Dubai so that I can imagine what you are all doing in the long months when we are separated.'

'Well, Richard is of the opinion that Dubai is an up-and-coming country. It is certainly a place in the sun, and life is led at a more leisurely pace than it is here at home. No matter where Richard has taken me, I have been struck by the cleanliness. I suppose they must have poor areas, maybe even slums like we have in the East End of London, but if that is so, I haven't been shown them yet. Demand for property is significant but there is a long way to go yet before the focus will be on the country as a holiday venue. There is a lot of talk about building new runways to enable the airport to be enlarged. Richard is convinced that good investors will be sought but the trend will be towards the higher end of the market. Dubai is already rich, but to expand, it needs good businessmen, men who not only have their own company's interests at heart but who will also look forward to the good of Dubai. What the country does not need is folk dropping in just looking to make a quick turnover. I think it is a wonderful place and I feel privileged to be allowed to live there.'

'And how about you, Dee, is life in Singapore still to your liking?'

Dee laughed. 'Very much so. I have even got used to being waited on hand, foot and finger. You only have to decide to change an article of clothing and you'll find it has been whipped away, washed and ironed. As for the children, I almost have to insist that I spend some time with Martin and Michael. Their every whim is catered for, from the time they wake up in the morning until they have their bath and are put to bed. Derrick is shore-based at the moment so is home most nights, and the social life we lead you wouldn't believe. There is a health club quite near our house; it is owned by one of the bigger airlines, so a lot of pilots and cabin crew frequently stay overnight there. The sporting facilities, not to mention the huge swimming baths, are superb, and have all been made available to us any time we wish to use them. Emmy and I take the boys there at lunchtime. We all have a lovely meal and the boys are made a fuss of by everyone; they are thoroughly spoilt but always in a very nice way. After

315

lunch Emmy takes them back to the house and I have a round of golf.'

'You play golf?' Jodie was flabbergasted.

'All the wives play.' Dee grinned. 'It was one of the first things I cottoned on to. Mind you, the instructor was great. I never thought I would be any good at it. When Derrick first took me for a round I think he thought he was doing me a favour, humouring me kind of thing, but in the end he told me that if I practised enough I might make the grade. Next time I went to the clubhouse I was presented with a set of clubs, leather golf bag and proper shoes, the complete works. Bought and paid for by my dear husband. What does that tell you?'

'You really are living the life of Riley by the sound of it,' Jodie murmured softly.

'I'll agree with you there. Never in a million years did I ever think my life would have changed so dramatically, and Derrick, he is a gem, he really is a joy to be with.'

And this is the little girl who started out working for Michael on Saturdays, Jodie was thinking, but she had to admit she was intrigued by it all. 'Any more pastimes or adventures?' she asked.

'Well, this might interest you. There is only one man with a higher rank than Derrick, Curtis Colwell; he deals more with the administration side rather than the actual shipping. He's very nice and so is his wife, Veronica. Curtis and Derrick were going to Hong Kong on business and suggested that we wives join them. I was worried about leaving the twins but nobody listened, and Emmy was delighted to have them to herself for a while. The four of us had only been in Hong

Kong for a few hours when a message came through for Derrick to fly on to China. Apparently he was to be involved in setting up new shipping lines. He was away for five days, during which time I stayed in Hong Kong with Curtis and Veronica and we had a whale of a time.'

'All right for some,' Jodie said, smiling, yet she couldn't quite manage to keep the envy from her voice.

Dee quickly changed the subject. 'Jodie, isn't it about time you had a real holiday? Why not think about coming out to us for a month or so?'

'Oh yeah, and who do I leave my boys with? Come to that, who the hell is going to run my businesses while I'm away?'

Dee didn't need any telling that she had said the wrong thing, but she was saved by a voice yelling, 'Ahoy there,' and relief flooded through her as the women got to their feet, each of them taking the hand of a child and walking down to the water's edge. Richard had lowered a rowing boat over the side of the large fishing vessel and was making for the shore, calling loudly, 'We're taking a small cargo down to the Newhaven docks; there's plenty of room on board if any of you'd like to come.'

Reg and Lenny had cupped their hands around their mouths and were yelling for their mum to come aboard. Jodie was a little reluctant; the boat wasn't exactly a luxurious-looking yacht.

Marian, holding tightly to Mary's arm, was making her way down the smooth sand. 'Would you like to go for a trip with the boys? They're going to Newhaven,' Jodie explained, pointing to where the boat was anchored.

'No thanks, my love, but I would like to sit down and take off my shoes and stockings. I thought it would be grand to have a paddle, do my old feet the world of good to have them in salt water. You might not believe it, but although we live so near the beach, I think it must be years since I've been down here.'

'No problem, Marian, hang on there just a moment and I'll run back up and bring one of the folding chairs for you to sit on.'

In no time at all Jodie was back. She and Mary peeled off Marian's stockings, and then each put an arm under her armpits, lifted her up and they were off.

'Oh, that feels so, so good.' Marian's face was wreathed in smiles as she waggled her feet about in the gentle waves. Jodie turned to Mary and asked, 'Why the hell don't we do this more often?'

By this time Laraine had joined her husband, who in turn had lifted Martin and Michael into the small boat and was now rowing the three extra passengers out to the fishing vessel. Dee was promising Adele and Annabel that their mummy and daddy wouldn't be away for too long, but the two little girls didn't seem in the least concerned as they waved at their parents; they were more interested in watching their grandmother splash about in the shallow water.

When the boat was out of sight, Jodie became aware of the silence, and she looked up to see Mary standing hands on lips glaring at her daughter.

'You and your big ideas, Delia,' Mary burst out. 'You've got all this lovely coastline, but it isn't

318

enough for you, is it? You had to get married before you were scarcely grown up, and then what do you do, you have two delightful little boys that yer father and I never get to see. How can we when you live halfway round the other side of the world? You always did hanker for something different. I remember saying to your father the day you got that job with Michael, she thinks she's going places. And I wasn't wrong, was I? But we aren't all on our way to being rich, you know, love. Some of us have to be content with what we've got, even if it means our only son ups and joins the Merchant Navy and we only get to see our daughter and our grandsons when it suits you to come home for a holiday.'

Jodie had listened to every hurtful word, but she couldn't interfere. This was between Dee and her mother. And yet the criticism had startled her. And what about Marian? Her three sons weren't exactly regular visitors. Oh dear, Mary, why did you have to upset the apple cart today of all days?

There was a long, tense silence. It was Marian who came to the rescue.

'I've dried my feet as well as I can, but I shan't put my stockings back on, just my shoes. Didn't I hear my Derrick say he'd brought that paraffin stove down and put it in the tent?'

'Yes, you did, Mum, and I know what comes next,' Jodie said, grinning.

Marian smiled and gave her a knowing look. 'Well get going then, put the kettle on an' for God's sake make a pot of tea. All that walking up and down in salt water has practically parched my throat.'

Peace was restored.

While Jodie made the tea, Dee sat on the floor just inside the tent playing with Annabel and Adele. Suddenly she looked up at Jodie and very quietly asked, 'How come you managed to keep your life so much simpler than the rest of us?' Without giving her a chance to reply, she laughed softly then said, 'I guess it is because you cut ties with your own parents; no one to question your motives or to interfere with any decisions you care to make.'

Jodie had to swallow deeply before she could form an answer, and when she did, her voice was far from being firm. 'Believe you me, Dee, it was not from choice. I think my two boys have missed out on a lot, not having contact with my parents. In the short time that my mother and father knew John, he managed to do a fair amount of damage with his lies and what he called his business propositions. I was young and in love and was absolutely sure that I knew best. Even after all these years, I'm sorry that I haven't found a way to heal the rift. I suppose there are some things that aren't meant to be. Probably we all feel that at some point in our lives.'

'Are you two ever going to stop talking? That ruddy kettle must have boiled dry by now.' Marian was impatient for her cup of tea.

'Just coming, Mum,' Jodie called.

As she stood up, Dee said, 'No one is worth looking that sad for, Jodie.'

Jodie smiled. 'You revived old memories.'

'Forget them, then they won't hurt any more.'

Jodie couldn't bring herself to answer, but as

she poured boiling water into the teapot to warm it, she thought how that was a whole lot easier said than done. John Underwood still had much to answer for.

30

Why couldn't both families have flown out on the same day? Was nothing in life ever simple? They had come en masse yesterday to Heathrow in order to see Laraine, Richard, Adele and Annabel off back to Dubai. There had been tears and hugs, promises to write, and even the twins had become tense and agitated, so many adults had wanted to pick them up, snuggle them close, because it would be a long time before they got to see them again. The whole period of waiting for their flight to be called had been traumatic.

Now, only a day later, it was happening all over again, only this time they were seeing Derrick, Delia, Martin and Michael off, and Mary was in a sorry state, bemoaning the fact that although she had two children, half the time she didn't know exactly where either of them was or when she was likely to see them or her grandsons again. Jodie was very tempted to remind Mary that she had Jack, a true gentleman, the kind of man one could refer to as salt of the earth. However, she wisely kept her thoughts to herself, though as they watched the four of them go through the depar-ture gate, she made sure she had her arm across

Mary's shoulders and a large dry handkerchief ready in her hand.

'Ah well,' Jack muttered as soon as they could no longer see the boys waving goodbye, 'let's go find the car and get ourselves off home.'

These two days at the airport were to set the pattern for the Underwood families' comings and goings for the next few years. Whenever home leave was granted, which was nowhere near as often as had been promised, Dee returned home tanned, happy and contented. Wherever Derrick went, she and the boys followed. Postcards arrived frequently, and Jodie's boys were popular with their geography master because they shared the cards around. The various places where their uncles were working were often made a subject for a geography lesson.

Cards from South America were always a great favourite, even with the girls. One in particular was a picture of a Dutch-style house which Dee and Derrick were living in. No glass in the windows, only shutters, and beautiful weather day in, day out, Delia wrote. She also told a sorry tale of how one evening she and Derrick had seen their two boys safely to bed and then sat on the veranda having a glass of wine. During the night Dee had been taken ill. Both her legs were swollen and bitten to pieces by various insects. Another favourite postcard was one of monkeys swinging from the trees.

During this period, Derrick was still shore-based. One of his best friends was captain of a supply ship, and he often took Martin and Michael with him to the rigs. On one such trip the crew caught a small white shark, and photographs were taken of the twins standing one each side of it. When Jack Hartfield received a copy of this special picture, his pride knew no bounds. The photo also showed how very fast the twins were growing. From the tender age of two, both boys had attended school daily. The shipping line provided an English-speaking teacher, educational procedures were flown out from England and the twins were taught on a one-to-one basis.

After a few years, home leave was suspended, with no reason given. This was sad for the relatives at home, but to be honest, not only did Delia appear to be quite contented with her life, but Laraine too sounded happy enough, though she was nowhere near as proficient as Dee when it came to writing letters.

There came a lull even in Dee's correspondence, however, and when Jodie heard the reason she had a good laugh. Derrick had been given another promotion, but it came with seven days' notice of a transfer. The family had been in South America for five years; they must have accumulated so much in the way of possessions, and they only had a week in which to prepare for the move from South America to West Africa. Derrick personally wrote to his mother as soon as they were settled in. Which resulted in a hasty telephone call from Marian to Jodie.

'Please, Jodie, I am so glad that my son has taken the trouble to write to me, but I can't see to read his writing, well not all of it.'

'All right, Marian. I can't make it today, but as it's Saturday tomorrow, why don't I come and fetch you in the morning. Pack yourself an overnight bag and stay the night with us. The boys will be pleased to see you and I'll run you home Sunday evening. How does that sound to you?'

'Lovely, if you don't mind having me, but will you read the letter when you get here?'

Jodie sighed softly, reminding herself to be patient. 'Why don't you bring it with you and we'll go through it slowly together. I shall be there to pick you up about eleven tomorrow morning. All right?'

When Jodie drew up outside the house next morning, it was Mary and Jack who came out to greet her from their house next door. 'Morning, Jodie,' said Jack, kissing her cheek. Mary added, 'Marian is sitting in my front room with her hat and coat on and Derrick's letter in her hand. She won't let me read it to her, says she's waiting for you. You go in to her. I've laid a tray. By the time you've read her letter, you'll be ready for a cuppa, won't you?'

'I certainly shall. Thanks, Mary.'

'Oh, by the way, we've received a whole lot of photos in with our letter this time. Haven't said a word to Marian yet. We don't want no upsets, do we?'

Jodie had to hold back on what she was thinking, but aloud she said, 'Oh isn't that great! I shall enjoy looking at them.' As an afterthought she suggested, 'Why don't you both come back with me too? Spend the night. I can bring you back with Marian tomorrow evening.'

The offer had been made half-heartedly, but when she saw the way Mary's face lit up, she was very pleased that she had thought of it.

'If you're sure, Jodie. I've got some nice fresh vegetables that Jack has dug up. I'll bring them. Oh it will be nice to have Sunday dinner together again.'

After much gentle persuasion, Marian had agreed to leave the reading of Derrick's letter until after lunch. The meal passed off very well. Mary had shared the chores with Jodie, and was being cheerful, pleasant and helpful. In fact she was in such a good mood she made Jodie nervous, particularly as the boys had boasted that they too had received photographs of the twins and of their aunt and uncle.

It was with great excitement that the boys accepted Jack's offer to take them to watch a football match. Jodie cornered them in the hall all rigged out in their woolly hats and colourful scarves. 'I want to ask you two a big favour before you go out.' For answer Lenny swung his wooden football rattle and the clatter vibrated around the hall. 'Stop that and listen to me for a minute,' Jodie said firmly. 'Would you mind if I show Grandma the letters and photos you received from your Uncle Derrick?'

'Course not,' they said in agreement, while Lenny added, 'They're in the drawer of my bedside table.'

'Thanks, boys, an' here, make sure you pay for the refreshments at half-time.' She pressed a ten-pound note into Reggie's hand.

'Cor, gee, thanks Mum, see you later.'

Jodie was actually enjoying the afternoon. The house did seem deadly quiet, but she was thinking how truly comfortable the three of them were. Lovely fire burning halfway up the chimney, comfortable deep armchairs in which to sit, and on a side table a huge bowl of chrysanthemums, their wintry fragrance filling the air. Jodie had set up a card table, and the photos and letters were laid out, enabling everything to be viewed with ease.

Priority had of course been given to the reading of Derrick's letter to his mother. Jodie cleared her throat and began. *'Hi, Mum, hope this note finds you as it leaves me, fit and well. Port-Gentil is where I am, the second-largest town in Gabon, quite a large area with a South African population and a good sprinkling of French inhabitants. I am now in charge of all ports in the south Atlantic Ocean. We don't have a house this time but a bungalow. You would love it though, it is very large. We have two live-in staff and two daily maids.*

'At the far end of our property there is a huge garage-type building, equipped with radio ship-to-shore. Two desks and every bit of office equipment you could imagine. This is where my secretary and myself work.

'Living within the grounds I have a huge black man. His name is Amos but he's known as the Gaffer. He seems able to produce anything and everything that is needed. He also takes charge of the Africans who surge around my office every morning. Each and every one of them is longing to be picked to be allowed out on to the huge oil rigs, where they know food is plentiful and the wages are good. We ourselves have so much to be grateful for.

'All for now, Mother, but am sending loads of photos. By the way, both your grandsons very often

speak French. Tons of love from all of us, your ever loving son, Derrick.'

Marian wiped a tear from her eye as Jodie finished reading. 'Done all right for themselves, my Derrick and Richard. Only wish I could say the same about my John.'

Jodie wasn't going to let that subject go, and she immediately took the bait. 'Do you know something I don't?'

Marian looked up quickly. Jodie's tone of voice had been fierce. 'I don't know what you're asking.'

'Well in that case, I'll tell you. Are you trying to let me know that my John is not doing so well for himself? Because if you are, then it's news to me. But then again, if you're only making an assumption, we might as well believe that he is living in the lap of luxury. Don't you think we both know him well enough to know that if he is on his uppers he would either be crawling back home to you or he might just as easily come to my door with some far-fetched story about how sorry he is.'

Marian laughed nervously. The last thing she wanted was to upset Jodie, so she quickly changed the subject. 'Shall we look at the photos now?' she asked timidly.

'Yes, and you can pass them around because there is a message on the back of each one so we'll know who they belong to.'

The photos were grand, so colourful, no expense had been spared. From the look of them, endless parties and social events were ongoing. Delia as always looked reassuringly healthy and brown, her long reddish hair flying free. One photo showed her wearing well-ironed white shorts and a white

327

sleeveless top; on the back of that one she had written, *Off to play squash.* Underneath she had added, *I also attend yoga and keep-fit classes. The companionship is great, mainly consisting of women about my own age, but we are all of mixed nationalities whose husbands are employed by the large oil companies which are very prominent in this area.*

However, it was the photos of Martin and Michael that evoked so many memories for their grandmothers. Jodie did feel compassion for both women. When they had last seen them, the twins had been at the delightful age when they didn't mind being picked up, cuddled and spoilt. Now they were sturdy, healthy young boys who by the look of the various-shaped balls they were holding in the photos were into every kind of sport you could imagine. They had left behind their babyhood and were well on the road to being young men. Both women would be feeling gratified and proud as they sat staring at the pictures, but at the same time who could blame them if their feelings ran to gut-wrenching torment because they were not in any real way part of the boys' lives.

When every photograph had been passed around and examined, and all the pros and cons debated, Marian said, 'Don't you supply tea in this house any more?'

A conspiratorial look was exchanged between Mary and Jodie before Jodie said, 'I was about to tell you, my plan is to take you in the car to the Fox and Hounds, which overlooks the racecourse, and order afternoon tea for all of us. We won't have to boil a kettle and we won't have to wash up. Another bonus being that you will be offered freshly baked scones and you may have both jam *and* cream, but only after you have eaten all the dainty sandwiches from which the crusts will have been cut off. Now, how does that sound to you?'

'Lovely. But what about dinner? Jack and the boys will come home starving.'

'Not if I know anything about my Jack,' said Mary. 'He'll have bought them hot dogs at half-time.'

'And I have everything prepared for dinner, which I aim to be serving about half past seven this evening, if that's all right by you,' Jodie said, smiling sweetly. 'Now, are we going out, or are we going to sit here until it gets dark?'

'I'll have to spend a penny before we go any-where,' Marian mumbled, but as she got up and walked across the room she too was smiling.

'It was your offer of jam *and* cream that she couldn't resist,' Mary laughed.

'Yeah well, be a nice change for all of us. We'll sit and be waited on and imagine that we've got servants.'

As they entered the dining room of the hotel, Jodie knew she had made a wise choice in bring-ing her mother-in-law and Dee's mother here for tea. Several tables were occupied, the whole room looked delightful and as usual Jodie felt the place reeked of opulence. A real fire was burning brightly in the huge open fireplace, every table was covered by a heavy white damask cloth with a smaller cloth of palest green overlaid in the centre and on this stood a tiny pot of white cyclamen from the hotel's own greenhouses. As nice a welcome as any words would have been.

After the sandwiches and scones had been demolished, a pretty young waitress appeared bringing a three-tier cake stand to the table. 'We shall be here for ages if we're supposed to eat that lot!' gasped Marian.

Jodie couldn't resist it. She got to her feet, placed her arms around her mother-in-law's shoulders and kissed her on each cheek.

'What did you do that for?' Marian didn't sound indignant, merely surprised.

'Because, Mum, you always come up trumps and we all love yer to bits. And just to reassure you, it is not obligatory that we eat every cake on the stand; a wide choice is offered so that each of us may make our own choice.'

'Well if I'm going to have one of those pastries I shall need another cup of tea, and that pot will be cold by now.'

The waitress was hovering nearby and she looked at Jodie. It took a full minute for each of them to suppress their amusement, and it was the waitress that spoke first. 'Shall I take that pot away, madam? Bring you a nice fresh brew?'

'Well, lass, you've got yer head screwed on all right. Yes please, we would like a fresh pot of tea.' Marian Underwood had shown she could be assertive when the occasion arose.

With a fresh cup of tea in front of each of them, it was surprising just how many cakes were missing from that stand when they made ready to leave the hotel.

It had been a long day but a very good one, Jodie decided as she looked in at her two sleeping boys before making her way to her own bedroom. Undressed, washed and now wearing her nightdress, dressing gown and slippers, she climbed into her bed and placed three pillows one behind the other. Well propped up, warm and comfortable, she opened the drawer of her bedside table and withdrew her own letter from Delia. She had willed herself to wait until she was on her own and able to read it in peace. One never knew what spicy titbits Dee might include that she wouldn't want read out to her mother.

She skipped most of the first page. It was Dee raving as usual. About how beautiful this place was. White sand and blue sea, an absolute paradise, just about summed it up.

Second page the news heated up.

One evening at the town's one and only casino, Derrick had won a large amount of money and decided to use it to purchase a catamaran. One lunchtime Dee accompanied by three friends had ventured out to sea. Amid much laughter and frivolity they were having a grand time but failed to realise the wind had died down. *Marooned out at sea we had no choice,* she wrote, *we all jumped overboard and it was purely a matter of swim, push and pull until we eventually reached the shore.'*

'Silly buggers,' Jodie chuckled to herself, half wishing she could have been there.

On the third page Dee had written in capital letters: *THERE IS A DOWNSIDE TO THIS IDYLLIC LIFE-STYLE.*

Libreville was the nearest large town to where Derrick and Dee were living. Apparently one evening Dee had taken Derrick's Suzuki Jeep

331

four-wheel drive and with the same three female friends had set off to celebrate a birthday at a restaurant on the other side of the town. The meal and the company had been excellent, but just as they were making ready to leave, Derrick had telephoned the manager and asked to speak to his wife. When Dee came to the phone, he warned her that the police were setting up roadblocks to stop vehicles not showing a licence or carrying stolen goods. If Dee should see any roadblocks, she should put her foot down and get the hell out of there.

Jodie was trembling and for a moment she released her hold on the letter. God, she was frightened just reading about it. What must Dee have been going through? She must have been terrified. She had told Jodie before that in cases like this it was women most of all who had cause to fear the police.

Jodie picked up the letter and began to read again.

No prizes for guessing what I did. Foot flat down, heading straight for home. On the way, there were a few bullets flying. Two at least hit the side of the car and my three friends were crouching on the floor, their heads tucked between their knees. I kept driving like a bat out of hell, and one thing was for certain, all four of us were praying like we never had before.

The girls' husbands were waiting with Derrick and we women were literally dragged out of that car. Jodie, I'm sure you can guess what Derrick said as we all trooped into our house: 'Brandy is in order for everyone.'

Jodie blew her cheeks out in a great rush of relief. Thank God she never read this letter out to Mary or Marian. But there again, in this life one had to take the rough with the smooth. And when you counted the happy hours they had spent today looking at all the wonderful photographs and listening to the lovely letter that Dee had written to her parents and Derrick's to Marian... Well, Jodie decided, the odds weren't stacked too badly against Derrick and Delia. If asked, she would certainly say that the good times for them were beyond any doubt outweighing the bad.

And long may it remain so, she prayed as she switched off her bedside light.

31

It was New Year's Day and Jodie was supposed to have gone out to lunch with Michael and Danny to celebrate, but when she had told them the ghastly news, they had agreed to come to her house instead. She had got together a reasonable lunch and passed a bottle of wine to Michael to open. They really were trying their hardest to make her feel wanted and cared for, but her thoughts were elsewhere.

How the hell could they look forward to a happy new year when Richard Underwood, the youngest of the three brothers, was dead at forty-four. Poor Laraine, no warning, no nothing.

Jodie knew that Michael was watching her, and she was trying hard to appear normal. She turned away from him now, muttering, 'Why? How?'

Even Michael's voice was little more than a croak as he struggled to find an answer to give her. 'We have to be patient, the details will come through eventually. What time was it when Jack phoned you, Jodie?'

'About half past four this morning. I'd been with Philip till the new year was rung in, and Reg and Lenny arrived to take me home soon after one.'

'Didn't you feel you should go over and stay with your mother-in-law?'

It was a question she'd been asking herself. 'Lenny offered to take me this morning if I didn't feel up to driving, but I have to keep reminding myself that he is twenty-three years old and Reg is twenty-four and they both have young ladies. I didn't want to spoil any arrangements they might have made for New Year's Day. I probably would have asked one of them to go with me if it wasn't for the fact that Jack and Mary live right next door.'

Michael was sitting beside Danny on one side of the table, with Jodie opposite, facing them both. 'I wouldn't know what to say to her.' The words were spoken in barely a whisper, then, her voice still low, she said, 'It's John's place to be there. Surely the police will find him. I may be wrong, but I feel sure Marian knows where John is. She sees him or at least hears from him a whole lot more than she lets on.'

Danny leant forward and took hold of Jodie's hand, clasping it gently between both of his.

'Derrick will have been notified straight away. I would imagine he'll be on his way home as soon as possible. Try not to worry, Jodie, he'll take charge of everything.'

'How can I not worry? Poor Marian, she didn't expect one of her sons to die before her. She will be heartbroken. I know I should go to her, and I will, but I cannot be in the house with her if John is going to be there. I just can't face him.'

'Why ever not?' Michael sounded appalled. 'What on earth have you got to reproach yourself for?'

'My views on that subject would be entirely different to those of my husband, and now would not be the time to let him air all his grievances. Though knowing John as I do, he will think it is an appropriate opportunity and one that he will not hesitate to grasp. No, I am sorry, but I can't face another argument, especially not under these sad circumstances.'

Jodie was at a loss to describe her feelings. A death at any time was disturbing, but this was so totally unexpected. Rick hadn't been ill, and he was so young. Her thoughts flew to Adele and Annabel. Rick adored those two girls; they meant the world to him. How in God's name did you explain to them that their father had gone for ever? Jodie was trying to work out exactly how old the twins were, but her thoughts were in total confusion. It must be all of three years since they had last come home on leave with their parents, and even then they'd seemed so grown-up. Adele and Annabel were one year older than Martin and Michael, and she had a feeling that the boys were about sixteen years old. Hard job to keep tabs on the children when she didn't see them from one year's end to the next.

Danny broke into Jodie's thoughts by asking a question that over the years her friends had fought shy of.

'Jodie, are you frightened of John?'

'No, I wouldn't say so, though it is years since I've had any contact with him whatsoever. At one time I did encourage the boys to meet up with him. Their grandmother tried hard to bring them closer, but as they got older I decided the choice was theirs to make.'

'And there's been no communications between them since then?'

'Not as far as I know. Not that I have ever asked.'

'Jodie, don't answer if you think I'm intruding, but darling, why in heaven's name have you never considered divorcing John?'

Jodie sighed softly. 'What makes you think I haven't? Too many complications, and John only knows one way to fight and that is dirty. The crux of the matter has always been the same: John doesn't want me but he's going to make damn sure nobody else can have me.'

'Well, Michael and I – and I think we are speaking for every one of your friends – long to see you and Philip get married. You are two of the nicest and kindest people that we know and every one of us wishes for you both to be happy.'

Jodie had always known that Danny was a sentimentalist, but today of all days he had touched her heart. 'Oh Danny, and you Michael, thank you both. You always seem to be there when I need you most. Philip and I not getting married isn't for the want of asking on his part. Although in these latter years I think he has become resigned to the fact that it is never going to happen. But I am happy to say that our feelings have stood the test of time and we truly are content knowing that we love each other.'

It was Michael who spoke up. 'We're not going to pry any further, but I should like to see the day when John Underwood gets his comeuppance. Now, Jodie, I have a suggestion. Why don't we persuade Danny to make us a nice fresh pot of coffee, and while he's doing that you go and get changed and put on a little paint and powder. Then I think it would be appropriate for us three to get in the car and drive to Camber Sands. Danny and I will stay in the car while you go to Mary and Jack's house and find out from them just what has happened and if there is anything to be done that would help in any way. When you think about it, it wouldn't come as a surprise to find out that your mother-in-law is being comforted in Jack's house. Not much else any of us can do until we receive further news. And...' He stopped short.

'Michael, you had better finish what you were going to say.' Jodie's voice was very low.

Heaving a sigh, Michael added, 'Should John be there, we'll play it by ear.'

'Well, if you're sure that's the best thing to do.'

'Jodie, none of us really knows what's best, but sitting here talking isn't going to solve anything. Come on, be a good girl and get yourself ready.'

The weather didn't help. It poured with rain for the whole of the journey. Danny was driving, while

Michael sat in the back of the car with Jodie. Both men had been to Marian's house on numerous occasions and Danny knew exactly the location he was making for. He drew his car into the kerb outside and the three of them sat in silence for a minute, each feeling loath to make the first move.

The front door of the Hartfields' house opened and Jack stood in the porch attempting to unravel a large black umbrella. Having got it open, he came down the front path and stood beside the car. Poking his head through the window he exclaimed, 'Thanks for coming, never more pleased to see anyone in my life. Perhaps you can help me cope with two hysterical women.' Then moving to the side where Jodie was sitting, he opened the passenger door and held the umbrella over her head and shoulders as she stepped from the car, giving her protection against the rain until she was inside the house.

For a full minute no one spoke and then Marian's voice rose in an anguished wail.

'Oh Jodie, what are we going to do? My boy has died, not here where we can see him but on the other side of the world.'

Jodie had no choice; the sobs that were racking her mother-in-law's body were enough to break anyone's heart. She wrapped her arms around her and over her head she looked into Mary's eyes. Dear God, Mary looked as if she was at breaking point herself. Despite the fact that her husband was holding her hand, her every limb was shaking. Jack lowered her back down into the chair she had been sitting in and turned to shake hands in turn with Michael and Danny. 'Thanks, both of you. I really cannot thank you enough.'

Danny had remained standing just inside the doorway. Now he spoke. 'I shan't be a moment. I've got a bottle in the car, I'll just go and fetch it.'

Danny wouldn't have bothered with making tea; he would have administered the brandy to the women straight from the bottle. Jodie had more sense. 'Hold your horses,' she ordered. 'I'll be as quick as I can.' And she was quick! One tray, two cups of very strong tea but the cups only two thirds filled. 'Now you can top them up,' she told him, managing a weak smile. Turning to Michael, she instructed him to see that Mary drank from one of the cups, while she herself took charge of her mother-in-law. Protests from each woman, but eventually both of them began to sip the hot liquid, pushing the cups away when they had drunk about half. Jodie made to place the cups back down on the tray, then she hesitated and instead held one out to Michael. The other one she raised to her own lips, draining it until there were no dregs left. Which seemed only fair seeing as how Danny had poured brandy into two glasses and given one to Jack and drunk the other one himself.

There was a knocking at the front door. Jodie looked up and was thankful that both Mary and Marian were showing signs that the brandy had calmed them down. Jack went to answer the door and returned a few moments later with a burly-looking man wearing a heavy dark overcoat and a trilby hat. He removed his trilby and produced an identity card from an inner pocket of his coat before saying, 'I am Detective Inspector Rawlings. I am sorry to have to call on you when you have received such sad news. Normally this is not a matter the police would be involved in, but apparently there have been problems with ship-to-shore telephone lines today. May I ask who has contacted you so far, and exactly what news you have been given?'

It was Jack who took charge and made the introductions. The detective nodded in acknowledgement and Jack carried on. 'Our phone rang, I suppose it must have been about three o'clock and it was Laraine on the line, Richard's wife. She said that Richard had been at sea and that he'd died suddenly, totally unexpectedly, of a heart attack. That was about all I heard before the line broke up, and we've no way of getting in touch.'

Poor Marian! Her sobs were heart-rending. How did one go about consoling a mother who had just lost a son? wondered Jodie. Made even worse by the fact that his body was thousands of miles away.

This was the part of the job that the detective and most of his colleagues detested. The desolation in this room was wretched, and it was New Year's Day! He cleared his throat before saying, 'I do have a little more information to offer you.' He crouched down in front of Marian, took hold of her hand between both of his and said gently, 'I understand you have another son, Derrick, who is also a master mariner.'

Jack felt he should shed light on their relationship with Derrick. 'Our daughter Delia is married to that son,' he said simply, not feeling that he could at this moment go into further details.

The detective looked confused, but having

340

received a nod from Marian he carried on. 'The authorities have located him and I have been informed that arrangements are being made to take him off his ship and bring him ashore. He will be in contact with you before the day is out and no doubt will be boarding a plane home tomorrow. I am only sorry I cannot do more to help, but I do sincerely commiserate with your sad loss. If there is any way in which I or my fellow officers may be of assistance to you, please don't hesitate to ring the station.'

'Thank God,' Jodie murmured as Jack came back into the room having seen the detective off the premises. At least Derrick had now been made aware that his brother had died and that Laraine, Adele and Annabel were on their own in Dubai.

'So what now?' Jack asked. Jodie felt strange as she heard his question, and an odd feeling crept over her. Until everything had been put into order of some kind, it would seem that a great many lives would have to be put on hold. She supposed Jack's question had been directed at her mother-in-law, but Marian was unable to make any response. She was shaking from head to foot.

'I'll make up the fire.' Jack nodded to where the embers had burnt low in the grate. No one had noticed that the room had grown cold. Still, that wasn't anything to worry about. It was the next few hours, even the coming night and probably quite a few days to follow, that would give everyone enough worry and sorrow to cope with.

Michael had helped Jack to make some sandwiches and a fresh pot of tea. Danny was worried about Marian. 'We should call a doctor,' he whispered to Jack. 'At her age we shouldn't take any chances.'

'We've got our doctor's number by the phone, Dr Morrison,' replied Jack. Danny nodded and went to make the call.

It was Jodie who opened the front door. 'Hello, Dr Morrison, you got here quickly.'

'You were right to call me,' he replied. 'Better to be safe than sorry.' By now they were in the front room of the house and the doctor greeted Marian. 'Good afternoon, Mrs Underwood, let's see what I can do to make you feel more comfortable.'

Marian was protesting loudly that nothing ever again was going to make her feel any better. The doctor got down on his knees and looked at her closely, then he glanced across at Mary, and his eyes remained on her for a time before he looked again at his patient. Standing up, he placed his bag on the table and opened it. 'I am going to give Mrs Underwood an injection,' he said to Jack. 'And with your permission I will administer the same to your wife.' Jack nodded.

Mary was sweating and her face was flushed, and she made no objection when the doctor rolled up the sleeve of her dress and dabbed the skin above a vein with cotton wool that he had soaked in a solution of antiseptic. 'Sorry, that was cold, but it isn't stinging too badly, is it?' he said before tying a thin rubber tube around her arm. He massaged the vein for a few seconds before inserting the needle. 'In a short while you may feel sleepy. Go with the flow and have a nice little sleep.

'Now let's have a look at you, Mrs Underwood.' He smiled down at his patient. He really did feel

342

for this elderly lady. No matter what he said or did, he was never going to make her feel the slightest bit better. What could be worse than losing a son?

As the doctor put his coat on and prepared to leave, he turned to face Jodie. He looked at her for a long moment before he said, 'You're going to have your hands full over the next few days.'

He could see her eyes were bright with unshed tears as she answered. 'It won't be me you'll have to worry about, Doctor, it will be poor Laraine. Maybe you will be able to find a few wise words of comfort for her when she arrives home, because I sure as hell won't be able to.' Her tone was bitter, and didn't alter as she added, 'Hard sometimes to really believe that there is a God of love who is watching over us. Thank you for coming, Doctor.'

Jodie just made it to Mary's bathroom, where she sat down on the toilet and cried as if her heart was breaking.

32

Jodie had taken it upon herself to visit Laraine's father. The poor man had been devastated, and his concern for his daughter and two granddaughters was understandable. Jodie didn't hesitate. 'Come on, Mr Lawrence, pack a few overnight things and come home with me.'

'Oh Jodie, you are so kind, but I couldn't impose on you, really I couldn't.'

'Who said anything about imposing? I shall be

glad of your company, believe me, and besides, whoever meets Laraine and the girls at the airport is going to bring them straight to me. It might help Laraine to see you there the minute she walks into the house. She'll feel so pleased to have her dad's shoulder to cry on, don't you agree?'

'Well, yes, if you're sure, I will gratefully take up your offer, but please will you drop the Mr Lawrence. My name is Edward, and yes, I do answer to Ted.' At that they both managed a weak smile.

No member of the family had to go to the airport. At this sad time quite a few associates had used their influence to make the journey home for Laraine and her daughters as easy as possible.

Curtis Colwell had moved quickly to help Derrick, and he was back at his mother's house before Laraine had left Dubai. Unfortunately Delia together with Martin and Michael had not been so lucky; without Derrick to vouch for them and to settle the legalities for travelling at such short notice, they'd not been able to make the journey.

Everything possible had been done for Laraine. Zapata Shipping Line had taken charge and smoothed her passage home. One of the directors and his wife had accompanied her and the girls on the flight, and a hired car and chauffeur had met them at Heathrow and brought them to Jodie's house in Epsom.

Laraine looked absolutely exhausted. The very sight of her alarmed Jodie. Where was the beautiful young woman who had always sparkled with life? She sighed as she took Laraine into her arms. Her sister-in-law wasn't crying; she was just staring into space as if she wasn't sure where she was, but as her father stepped into her view it was as if a dam had broken. Ted gathered her into his outstretched arms, holding her close and gently massaging her back, all the while murmuring, 'You're home now, pet, we'll help to make things better, you'll see.'

Later she was to relate to Jodie the harrowing ordeal at both the beginning and the end of their flight. Officials had been kind in both cases, but they were not allowed to board the plane in Dubai until the coffin had been opened and Laraine had identified Richard's body. The same had taken place at Heathrow. They were required to remain on the plane until all passengers had disembarked, and then Laraine was taken to the holding sheds to await the unloading of the coffin. Once more the lid was prised open, and in front of authorised officials she again had to establish that the body was that of her husband, Richard James Underwood, as stated on the death certificate. Only then were the firm of undertakers that Marian had selected allowed to take possession of the coffin and begin the journey to Camber Sands which would bring the body of Richard Underwood back to the village where he had been born.

Was it any wonder that Laraine was halfway to becoming demented? She wouldn't eat, all she drank was water and she had refused all tablets offered to her by Dr Morrison.

Marian was not quite so bad since the arrival of Derrick, but Mary was ten times worse. Her daughter and grandsons were now stranded in a strange country without kith or kin nearby.

345

How to fill the days until the funeral? God, what a prospect! To even start a conversation was like treading on eggshells. The twins were now coming up to seventeen years old. What did the future hold for them here? What was there to discuss? Finances, housing, employment: all these things would have to be considered, but one glance at Laraine was enough to tear at Jodie's heart strings. Never in her whole life had she felt so incapable of dealing with a situation. She yearned to do something, but what? No one seemed to have the answer. Not even Derrick, and he had bent over backwards to help.

There was a dilemma facing him and it was one that he didn't feel able to discuss with anyone. When he had been given the news of his brother's death he had been in charge of a ship in Russian waters. It had been some while since he had seen his own wife and sons and the future for them was murky to say the least. Oil was the golden commodity and pipelines were being laid at a tremendous rate, but the deals that were being made had become a curious state of affairs, with the right hand not knowing what the left was doing. Precarious contracts written in sand was how he saw the situation, and he did not want his family involved. It was time they went home to the UK. The boys both had exam results that would gain them entry into a prestigious school back home. If one or both should hanker after a life at sea, there was no better training in the world than that which was available at either Portsmouth or Plymouth.

The death of his brother had been a shock. Also a warning, never to put off until tomorrow what one should do today. He couldn't in any case extend his leave beyond the day that they were to bury Richard. Once back on board ship he would put into motion plans for Delia, Martin and Michael to return home.

For Laraine, each day was a blur. She knew full well that people were doing their best to be kind, trying to get her to eat something, but she wasn't hungry, and even if she were, the lump in her throat would stop her being able to swallow anything. She did drink the hot sweet tea that they pressed on her, because it was easier than arguing with them. Jodie's neighbours came in with offers of help, but they left feeling helpless at the sight of such heartbreaking grief.

Other people came, the undertaker to talk about arrangements, the vicar from the local church where as young children the Underwood boys had attended Sunday school. Father Jonathan, his own eyes filled with sorrow, offered to pray with Laraine because he thought it might ease her grief a little. Laraine was feeling too bitter to listen. She couldn't bring herself to talk to a God who allowed a man to drop down dead at such an early age. He'd worked so hard to become a master mariner, was so proud of his title and of what he did for a living, and now what? Had it all been worth it?

Come the day of the funeral, Laraine sat quietly watching as Jodie laid out the black clothes Laraine was supposed to wear. Despite all the love and kindness that surrounded her, she knew that nothing'd ease the despair she was filled with. All she could think of was, how am I ever going to be

347

able to get through this day? Dr Morrison came, and once more offered her two tablets. 'They may help, Laraine. I'll fetch you a glass of water.'

Laraine just stared at him, for she was fully aware that nothing on earth would help, but the throbbing inside her head was unbearable and so she said, 'Thank you, Doctor.' He fetched the glass of water and she did swallow the two tablets he held out to her, hoping they would dull the pain. Within a very short while she felt as if she was disconnected from all that was going on around her.

The whole family were astounded at the numbers who attended the funeral. Right to the back of the church the pews were packed with neighbours and friends, many of whom had come from Hastings and Eastbourne, Richard's old fishing haunts. Also present were several dignitaries from shipping lines around the world.

When it was all over and Richard's body had been committed to the ground, Laraine stood perfectly still, her father on one side of her, Derrick on the other. Her two beautiful daughters were right behind her. Endless people filed by, expressing their deepest condolences, that much Laraine knew only by the looks on their faces. She didn't remember making any reply and was thankful when Adele said, 'Mummy, we're going to get you into the car now. Come along, we're going home.'

That remark did have her head jerking upwards.

She sank back into the soft leather of the huge funeral car, Adele and Annabel sitting one either side of her and holding her hands. 'Tell me, my darlings,' she murmured, 'exactly where is home?'

That remark really wasn't fair. Adele and Annabel were at a loss to find an answer. They were both confused, heartbroken and frightened about what was going to happen to them from now on. Whatever solution was put to them, nothing would be able to compensate for the loss of their beloved father. He had been the light of their lives. Young, handsome, fit, energetic, with loads of friends, he lit up every room he walked into and they had lived for the times when he had shore leave. They were old enough to know that they had led a life that had given them many privileges and taken them halfway around the world. What now? Where would they live? More to the point, *how* would they live?

Back in Jodie's house somebody put into Laraine's hand a glass of brandy, which she finished off in just two gulps.

And that was her last memory of that dreadful, terrible day.

The chalet bungalow Laraine had rented was at Little Common, and she was fully aware that it was only half a mile away from the house that Richard had rented for them when she had been pregnant. Jodie had implored her to stay at Epsom a bit longer, but Laraine had been adamant that she had to stand on her own two feet sooner or later. The bungalow was sufficient for their needs but nothing like the accommodation they were used to. There were three bedrooms, one of which was very small, a lounge with a dining area at one end and a kitchen with a glass door that looked out into the fair-sized pretty garden. It would do until Laraine could finally wind up all of Richard's estate and learn exactly where she stood financially. She knew the girls felt uncomfortable living there and she felt badly for them. This was an entirely different world and she was aware of how hard it was for them to adapt. They had never done their own washing or cooked a meal in their whole lives. Every single thing was foreign to them. In the world of shipping, men were the masters and their women and children were well housed and provided with servants to take care of them and every amenity possible to see that their lives were pleasant and enjoyable. Both Adele and Annabel were beginning to realise that all of that was far behind them now.

Their reaction to their present circumstances had not been very good. Their tempers were short, and they were offensive when the question arose as to what kind of jobs they were going to consider. Most days they hadn't left their beds before twelve o'clock. Laraine felt for them, she really did; she wanted to cradle them in her arms, tell them everything would soon be back to normal. But how could she? She knew damn well it was never going to happen. She had no quick solution to offer, and so she took the easy way out and just let things slide.

The final blow came when two huge lorries arrived bringing every stick of their furniture plus crates containing not only their personal belongings but Richard's too.

'What a rotten thing to do,' a very bad-tempered Annabel cried, as she watched her mother pleading over the telephone for the firm to keep it in store for her until she had a place of her own in which to house it. When Laraine came off the phone, she was relieved that the firm had agreed to her request. There were tears in her eyes, yet she cleared her throat, explained the situation to the drivers and invited them both in to the bungalow for a drink.

Laraine, who had been pampered and spoilt, had lived the life of the idle rich, was now learning day by day that this sudden alteration could in no way be described as a temporary situation. They were not in England paying a fleeting visit. This was life as it was now. She would have to pull herself together and realise that from now on she herself would have to be the family's breadwinner. Over the past few weeks several ideas had come into her head, but they never lasted long. She ignored them, prepared to let the time slip by as she idled the days away. 'I'll do something about it soon,' she said to Jodie.

Then came the telephone call that would at least lift some of the burden from Laraine's shoulders. A London-based firm of solicitors had been given the task of dealing with Richard's estate, and a Mr Tisdale was asking if she would prefer to come to their London office or to have them bring the necessary papers and attend to her affairs in her own home.

'I don't know. I...' This wasn't her own home, it was a rented bungalow and not a very impressive property whichever way you looked at it. 'I really should make the effort...'

'No, really, Mrs Underwood, I quite understand, it is not obligatory for you to make the journey.

351

Myself and my colleague will gladly come to you. Will tomorrow morning be convenient for you, if we arrive at about eleven thirty?'

'Yes, that'll be fine, Mr Tisdale, and thank you.'

'Then we shall be there. No need for you to feel apprehensive. The estate of your late husband is very straightforward, and in the main all we shall need from you is identification and a signature on a few documents. If that sounds all right to you, I promise we won't take up too much of your time.'

'Thank you,' Laraine managed to mutter again before replacing the receiver.

For the first time in a long time she smiled to herself. At least Richard had left a will and everything sounded as if it was in good order. Maybe after the visit from the solicitors she would be able to see the future more clearly. Knowing exactly where she stood as regarded security would, she hoped, make a difference.

'Adele, Annabel, I want you to listen to what I have just been told on the telephone.' Their mother walked into the kitchen and found they were making fresh coffee. 'As this seems to be the first piece of good news we've had in a long time, I thought we might go out to lunch. Would you like that?'

'Mum, you don't know that it is going to be entirely good news, do you?' Adele sounded hesitant.

Laraine looked at her sharply and shook her head. 'No, I don't. But neither am I going to worry myself about the outcome until I hear what these lawyers have to say tomorrow.'

'Mum, I am sorry, I didn't mean to be a wet blanket.' Adele looked at her twin and asked, 'Is

352

that coffee nearly ready? Because if it is, I suggest we all sit down, have a cup and decide where you are going to take us for lunch.'

Laraine let out a soft breath. Thank God for that, she was thinking. It was the first ray of sunshine that had entered her life for some time now. Suddenly all three of them were laughing.

Later, they were seated in the main dining room of the Cooden Beach Hotel, which was only a fifteen-minute drive from the bungalow. The glass doors were flung wide open on to the few yards of green lawn separating the hotel from the beach. The early spring sunshine hadn't much warmth in it, but its rays glistened on the sea, the sky above was a cloudless bright blue and several people were walking along the beach.

They were studying the menu when Annabel looked at her wristwatch and said, 'It's one o'clock, but a lot of English people call this dinner time.'

'Dinner?' Adele queried. 'We've got used to having lunch.' And for the second time this morning all three of them laughed.

Laraine was still feeling vulnerable, which didn't make sense. She should by now have come to terms with the fact that Richard had died. The twins noticed that their mother had drifted off in thought again and looked so sad when only min-utes ago she had been laughing. 'Mum,' Annabel whispered, 'please try and be happy. We know nothing and nobody'll ever replace Dad. It's been hard for you, but for us as well. So shall we try to put on a brave face and smile a bit more often?'

Her voice drifted off and Laraine looked at each of her daughters and thought how selfish she had been.

She forced herself to smile at them.

'Let's all promise that we will try.'

33

As the first anniversary of Richard's death approached, Laraine felt her spirits drop. She remembered every minute of that terrible day and of the traumatic time leading up to the funeral. Yet she was doing her best to count her blessings, for her life had turned out far better than she had imagined possible at the time.

Both Mr Tisdale and Mr Blenheim had gone to great lengths to ease her through all the legalities involved with Richard's estate. Richard had certainly made his will with a great deal of forethought. Besides the very large insurance policy that the shipping company had taken out, as was normal practice with all master mariners, Richard had himself bought cover in the event of his death, which provided not only for his wife but for his two daughters when they reached the age of twenty-one. Laraine'd also been relieved to learn that the company were paying her a pension which would continue for the duration of her life or until such time as she should remarry. Mr Tisdale had also ensured that she understood that her living accommodation would be the responsibility of the company, and under the same contract terms.

Laraine had quickly asked for clarification on that statement. 'Does that mean that Zapata Shipping Line is going to pay the rent on any property in which I and my daughters decide to live?' Doubt was obvious in the tone of her voice.

'Not at all, Mrs Underwood. If you find a suitable property, subject to the details being approved by the company and their surveyor passing it as sound, they will purchase the property for you outright, and that will be a separate issue not subject to the remarriage clause.' Mr Blenheim had this time fully explained the situation, leaving nothing to chance.

With the help of Jodie and other friends, Laraine had, within three months, found a suitable three-bedroom house in Banstead, Surrey, not far from Epsom.

What she eventually decided to do with her everyday life had come as no surprise. With Jodie's prompting and a whole lot of encouragement, she had paid a return visit to Shepperton Studios. Her welcome had been sad but generous and she had resumed what had previously been a very short stab at a career in the advertising business.

She had half dreaded the first meeting with Steve Cooper. It hadn't been hard to recall that he had mocked her during the first few days she had been working at Shepperton. However, their meeting had been cordial, and nothing untoward had been said. Quite the reverse, in fact. Steve had been kindness itself. His concern had rung true and his condolences she'd felt were sincere. Indeed she had the impression that he and all the other members of the advertising department were happy to have her back with them.

She had taken up the threads of a whole new life, but there were still times when she was unable to prevent the memories of her darling Richard and their wonderful life together seeping into her consciousness, so vividly at times that she would ache with the pain of it.

As the anniversary drew near, Jodie asked her if she wanted to talk about it. She replied that talking wouldn't help; this wouldn't be the only bad time and she had to learn to live through it and count her blessings. On the actual day, she worked without stopping, hardly saying a word to anyone, and late that night when they were all in bed, her daughters heard her crying as if her heart was still broken.

Delia too was having to adjust to her new circumstances. After Richard's funeral, Derrick had taken several weeks' leave, which he'd used to pack everything up and bring Delia and their two sons home to the UK.

It hadn't come as a complete surprise to Dee, and she had welcomed the chance to come home and see the family and all her friends. What she hadn't reckoned on was the fact that since Derrick had gone again, leaving her and the boys behind, she had had scarcely any communication with him or from him. Certainly she had no cause to complain: a generous amount of money was paid into her bank account regularly on the first of every month, and she and the boys were thrilled to bits with the house they were now living in.

When they had first arrived back in the UK, they had divided their time between Marian's house and Jodie's, because although they had viewed several properties, none seemed to suit their requirements. With only ten days to go before Derrick was due to fly out again, he got a phone call from a long-standing friend who had heard of a man who had recently died and whose widow was anxious to sell their large seafront house in Newhaven. From then on it had been all systems go.

Martin and Michael had been reluctant to go with their parents to view yet another property, yet within ten minutes of getting out of the car they and their father were punching the air and saying 'YES!'

It was a very large double-fronted old house that over the years had been kept in good repair. The interior consisted of five bedrooms, two bathrooms, two lounges and a large dining room. Some modernisation had been carried out but nothing to alter the character of this beautiful family home; that was until they came to view the kitchen, which had only recently been refurbished. 'Amazing' was the only comment that Delia managed to come up with.

Outside in the large garden was a huge shed, a summer house and a powerful winch, very useful for hauling and hoisting boats. The title deed also stated that the owner of the house and surrounding land owned the rights to the seashore up to the level of high water. Mrs Bingham, the lady who was selling the property, had asked Derrick if he would be interested in buying the boat which was berthed in front of the house. It was safe enough, she assured him, adding that it came with two life jackets and ample flares. The looks on his sons' faces had begged him to agree.

It was another three weeks before the day of completion arrived, but it turned out to be a day that the Underwood family would never forget. Each and every one of their many friends, together with some local people and neighbours they had never previously met, all gathered on the seashore to celebrate. 'Let's hope this is the beginning of happy times to come,' Dee had said as she thanked everyone who'd helped with so many various jobs.

Laraine, with Adele and Annabel, Jodie, Reg and Lenny had all stayed that first night in Marine House with Dee, Martin and Michael. That one day and night was to set the pattern for a long time to come. Marine House and the generosity of its chestnut-haired owner, Mrs Delia Underwood, had in a very short time become quite well known. No matter what the occasion, be it a birthday, bank holiday or merely because the sun was shining and Marine House was a great place to be, friends and family would turn up knowing there would always be a welcome. The women would bring food with them and the men would supply the drink. Jodie loved to cook and she never came empty-handed. Philip too was in his element when Dee allowed him the run of her fabulous kitchen, and everybody thoroughly enjoyed his meals, which naturally always had the Italian touch.

Delia made a great effort to forget the easy life she had so enjoyed, telling herself that in this world nothing lasted for ever and nothing and no one should ever be taken for granted. Both

Martin and Michael had decided to answer the call to the sea which was so strong in their blood, and the pair had enrolled at Portsmouth Historic Educational College. Dee had no money worries, but neither did she feel she could fill the hours of her day just doing housework. The remedy was staring her in the face. For the time being she was going to be a hairstylist again. Working with Jodie, or for her, in either one of her salons. Talk about turning the clock back.

One particular day she went with Jodie to an old folk's home in Hastings where Jodie had four regular clients who were too old and frail to come into the town and visit a hairdressing salon.

'Jesus, I must have been about sixteen years old when you first took me out to visit clients. Do you remember, Jodie?' Dee asked, her voice full of laughter.

'Quite vividly, actually,' Jodie answered thoughtfully. 'They say that what goes round comes around, so perhaps we had better look out for ourselves.'

'I think it's wonderful that all three of us are back in good old England,' Dee told her, still smiling. 'It wasn't what Laraine wanted, or me, come to that, but it has happened and here we are. If you count up the right-hand side of the ledger, it'll tell you that each one of us owns our own house, we each have two beautiful, healthy, strong children, we are all fit and well, and in addition to all that we have each other. Can't ask for much more, can we?'

Jodie could have added to Dee's list the fact that she herself also owned two successful businesses, and that they had been acquired entirely with the profits from her own labour. There had been no years of pampered living abroad for her. Her grown-up sons had also sought a life on the ocean wave as a means of making a good living catching fish and selling it to large hotels or at Hastings Sheds, where the fishing industry still thrived. They were buying their own houses now and had their young ladies, though all the hinting in the world from her hadn't brought a mention of a wedding yet. She had to keep reminding herself that these days two young people living together was no longer regarded as sinful.

She and her boys were lucky. Very lucky indeed. Dee had given permission for her two nephews to anchor and moor their huge boat on her foreshore, and that meant that often when she visited Dee she got to see Reg and Lenny too. The arrangement worked out well in many other ways. Whenever Martin and Michael were home from college, they were thrilled to be able to go out fishing with Reg and Lenny and it was good to see how well all the cousins got on. That companionable togetherness also went for Adele and Annabel. It didn't seem so long ago that the three mothers had themselves been going to various dances; now it was the six cousins, and it was a relief to Laraine that the boys were mostly on hand to see that her girls returned home safely and at a reasonable hour. The only fly in the ointment seemed to be the lack of men in the lives of their mothers. Both Laraine and Dee were forever teasing Jodie about Philip. He was such a dear, nice man, loved by the whole family, yet the two of them never seemed to make any progress.

Jodie's trip to Italy had never materialised.

One weekend there had been a party at Epsom and for some reason Philip had had to leave early in the afternoon. Jodie had spent a long time out in front of the house saying goodbye to him and had seemed rather down when she had come back into the lounge.

It was Dee who plunged straight in. 'Why the hell have you two never tied the knot? It might be down to your John, cantankerous sod that he is, but that doesn't alter the fact that in this day and age there cannot be any reason why the two of you can't make your lives so much better by living together. Now that Reg and Lenny are away and settled, you must rattle around in this four-bedroomed house like a single pea in a colander.'

When no answer was forthcoming from Jodie, Laraine took up the challenge. 'Everyone who sees the two of you together can tell straight off that Philip adores you. He positively devours you with his eyes. And you're always going on about how wonderful he is.'

'Will the pair of you please leave the question of Philip and myself alone.'

'Give us one good reason why we should,' Dee was quick to say.

'If you must know, I'm afraid. Once I allow Philip to move into this house, how do I know that things won't change?'

'That's not a very nice thing to say about the poor chap.'

'I know it's not. But that is truly what I fear. Things are great between us, but then they have never been on a permanent basis.'

'Jodie! How can you say that? If you don't trust him, why have you spent so much time with him and over such a long period of time?'

Jodie smiled. 'That's easy to answer. Because he's charming, handsome, fascinating and always so well dressed.'

'But do you love him?'

'Yes.' Her voice was little more than a whisper. 'But there was a time when I dearly loved John and he became the father of my two sons. You would have thought that would have counted for something, wouldn't you?'

'Have you heard anything about John recently?' Dee asked, and there was a tremor in her voice.

'No, but it sounds like you have. Are you going to tell me?'

'Well, it's always been a bit difficult with my parents living next door to our mother-in-law, and mostly I do try to ignore their gossip. John does pay visits to his mother, of that I have no doubt, and recently, since his last visit ... well, between them I've had to listen to two versions.'

'Since you've got so far, Dee, you can't stop now. I'm all ears.'

'Fine, if you're sure. First account: John is living with a wealthy woman who is much older than himself. Second version: he is playing happy families with a young girl who has two young children by two different fathers. You take your choice and hope for the best, I suppose.'

'To have a choice of any kind would be nice, but to be honest I all but gave up on John a very long time ago. He seems to come and go just as he likes, but the fact that he never comes near any of his own family must speak for itself, so why should I bother?'

Jodie's voice sounded sad, and her sisters-in-law could see no way in which they could help.

'At least you made something of your life,' Laraine ventured.

'Yeah, I got married and had two kids by the time I was eighteen.'

'Oh come on, Jodie, you know full well that isn't what I meant. Businesswise you've carried on and succeeded well beyond your own expectations. You don't need me to remind you how you've triumphed against all the odds.' Laraine got up and came to stand beside Jodie, gently brushing her lips against her cheek, and for an instant she held her close.

'Thanks, Laraine, and you too, Dee.' There were tears in Jodie's eyes.

'What for?' they asked together, and both were having to fight back their own tears.

'For everything. Understanding, just being there, over a great many years.'

The moment lingered. They might only be related because they had each married an Underwood brother, but their feelings went far, far deeper than that. They had all lived totally different lives, with thousands of miles between them, but none of it had made any difference. Everything had come full circle, and the three women knew that they would always be able to count on each other.

Come what may, their lives would always be interwoven.

34

It was the last Monday in May and was therefore a bank holiday. The sky was a clear blue, showing no sign of clouds, and at ten thirty in the morning the sun was already feeling very warm. As usual there was no need for a debate; it was taken for granted that anyone and everyone would meet up at Dee's house, with strict instructions that swimming trunks and costumes were obligatory.

Michael and Danny had been among the first to arrive and had taken charge of the outdoor arrangements. 'Don't any of you go down to the shore empty-handed.' Michael was using his most persuasive voice. 'That pile of blankets and rugs needs to go out, and there are cushions, deckchairs and loungers all ready and waiting in the summer house. Everything needs to be set out firmly and safely; a disaster such as Mrs Underwood senior's deckchair collapsing is one we can well do without.'

'Understood.' 'Yes, sir,' came with laughter from several voices, accompanied by mock salutes from all sides.

Laraine was watching Dee as she mingled with everyone on the beach. Even wearing beach clothes she still looked elegant and self-assured, but Laraine realised with a sudden flash of perception that Derrick's absence was worrying her far more than she cared to admit. It was quite a time now since his last brief visit, when he had settled his wife and two sons back in the UK. According to Dee, his allowance was still being paid regularly into her bank account, yet not a word had she heard from him since he had left.

'Dee is far more worried over Derrick than she is letting on,' Laraine murmured to Jodie, who had just come alongside her.

'I do know that, but for the life of me I can't think of any way in which we can help, and today is not the ideal time to broach the subject, is it? Let's leave it until another day.'

'Yes, of course,' Laraine agreed quickly enough. 'Dee will be fine all the time she is surrounded by friends and family.'

Nets had been set up on the sand, ball games of every description had been played and now the most hardy of Dee's relatives and friends were splashing about in the sea.

'I think we'll leave the food in the house, don't you?' Dee asked her sisters-in-law as they walked back inside. 'It is all laid out in buffet style; everyone can help themselves. I have left the desserts in the big fridge until we're ready for them. With so much cream on the various gateaux, we don't want them spoiling.'

'What was that noise?' Laraine was on her feet looking out from the side window of the kitchen. She turned to face Dee. 'It's your Michael, he seems to be saying that someone is knocking on the door.'

'Well he knows I keep that gate bolted and barred; sometimes people like to use that side path and go through our garden as a quick route to and from the beach.'

'Shall I open the front door?' Jodie offered.

'No, you two stay here, pour yourselves a glass of wine. I'll go and see who it is.'

Two women were standing on her doorstep, both total strangers. In age they could have been mother and daughter; in their choice of clothing they differed thoroughly. The younger woman's attire was smart and expensive. The older one had a motherly look, and even on this lovely summer's day she was wearing a long dark coat and a felt hat.

'Good morning,' Dee smiled, 'how can I help?'

'Good morning,' the elder of the two answered. 'Would you mind telling me if a Mr Underwood lives here?'

'Well that would largely depend on which Mr Underwood you are seeking. At present there is more than one man here that can lay claim to that name. Perhaps you would like to identify yourself and tell me the nature of your visit.'

'Of course, I am sorry. I am Ethel Davison, a social worker in the Hammersmith district of west London; this is my niece, Joyce Marsden, who is employed by the same council but mainly works in the office. I do realise that today is not really an appropriate time for me to be calling on you, but we are going on to Brighton to visit friends and as we were passing through we thought it might be a good idea to check out this address.'

Dee felt bewildered, completely at a loss. 'Would you care to come to the point?' she asked sharply. 'I have a house full of guests and I would like to get back to them.'

Ethel Davison did her best to smile as she held out a folded sheet of notepaper and said, 'So far this is all we have to go on.'

Dee, lacking enthusiasm, took hold of the slip of paper. She wanted to tell these women to be gone, they were spoiling her lovely day, but what was written on the paper had her gasping.

MR UNDERWOOD, MARINE HOUSE, NEWHAVEN, ENGLAND.

'Are you Mrs Underwood?' The young woman had found her voice and had spoken for the first time.

Dee had had enough. To be honest, she was badly shaken. Her imagination was running riot. Had Derrick been hurt or maybe killed, and if so, why hadn't the proper authorities contacted her? This was either a sick joke on someone's part or ... or what? For the life of her she couldn't fathom what it meant. She had to get to the bottom of this, but the two women were not being at all co-operative. She was going to have to bring in Jodie and Laraine, but she didn't want everyone in the house to start asking questions. As she turned her head to call to her sisters-in-law, they appeared behind her. 'What's keeping you, Dee?' said Jodie. 'Your guests want to know if it's OK to start eating.'

Dee thrust the slip of notepaper at Jodie, saying, 'This lady tells me she is a social worker, but she's not been very forthcoming as to why she's here, nor has she thought fit to tell me how she comes to have this in her possession. They want to know if I am Mrs Underwood and whether Mr Underwood lives at this address.'

367

Jodie read the name and address on the paper, then took a deep breath before addressing the two visitors. 'This is neither the time nor the place to discuss any matter whatsoever,' she said firmly. 'Today is a public holiday, so I suggest you go back to your supervisors and point out to them that it would be a good idea to make an appointment to speak to Mrs Underwood. Now I think it is time you both continued on your journey and left us to enjoy the rest of our day.'

As Dee slowly closed her front door, it was a toss-up as to whether the three of them would laugh or burst into tears. Laughter won the day. But in Dee's case, only just. She knew that in some shape or form that scrap of paper had to be something to do with Derrick. Where the hell was he?

'Oh there you are, girls.' Michael sounded relieved to have found all three of them together. 'I think that between you you're hatching something up, a surprise for this afternoon? If that is so, please may we eat first? We've most of us been in the sea, had a good swim and now we really are a hungry lot.'

It took a great effort on Dee's part, but she sternly told herself she was the hostess today and lunch was down to her. Pulling herself together, she ran her fingers through her hair before grasping hold of Michael's arm. 'Come on, Michael, you can take the big brass gong outside and bang it good and hard, let everybody know that there is plenty of food waiting to be eaten, and when you've done that, ask Danny if he will kindly preside over the drinks. There are plenty of ice cubes in the top of the big fridge.'

'Will do.' He grinned at her.

'Thanks.'

'Any time. And by the way, don't think you've fooled me. I can be free any time tomorrow if you need to discuss anything with me.'

Dee's eyes softened and she smiled at him. 'I might be very glad to take you up on that offer tomorrow. Meanwhile, don't let's spoil today.' She had partly recovered from what had been a nasty shock, and now she was telling herself not to let her imagination run away with itself. Even so, she needed no reminding that come tomorrow she was going to have to find a few answers.

'Do either of you want a nightcap or a hot drink?' Laraine asked. The guests and most relatives had long since departed, Adele and Annabel had gone to bed, and only Jodie and Laraine were with Dee in the lounge.

'No thanks,' Dee and Jodie both murmured. 'I think we've all had sufficient, at least I hope so,' Dee added.

'Everybody was singing your praises and saying how lucky you are to live in such a wonderful place.'

'Yeah, aren't I just,' said Dee, smiling faintly. 'I might be more wholehearted about my luck if I'd the least idea of where Derrick is. If you only knew how worried I am. How could he do this to me?'

For the first time, both Laraine and Jodie heard the raw bitterness in Delia's voice, and it shocked them both to the very core.

'Almost a year and not a single word,' Dee went on. 'No letters, no telephone calls, no nothing. It

369

isn't as if he has abandoned me and the boys; ample funds are still going into my bank account each month. I have tried every way I can think of to make contact with him, and nothing. A blank wall is all I come up against. The shipping agency no longer answer my letters.'

'Darling.' Jodie was up on her feet, had crossed the room and her arms were now holding Dee close.

Absolute silence reigned for a full minute, then Jodie said, 'Why on earth haven't you let on about all this heartache long before now?'

Laraine needed no telling about raw pain, but she loved Delia enough to put her own feelings aside. 'That visit from those two women today has set you off, hasn't it?' When Dee made no response, she carried on. 'At least it's out in the open now. Trust me, nothing fatal could have happened to him or you'd have been notified quick enough. Remember, I've been there. Derrick can take care of himself, he can't have come to any real harm.'

She couldn't think of anything more to say that would be at all helpful, and so she too came to stand beside Dee and squeezed her arm in what she hoped was a reassuring way.

'Come on, let's all go to bed and hope that tomorrow will bring some helpful answers.'

Upstairs in her room, Dee undressed and brushed her teeth. Before getting into bed she smoothed out the offending slip of paper and studied it. It had certainly been handled quite a lot. She could only hope that it might shed some light on where her husband was.

By seven thirty next morning, all five females had eaten toast and drunk coffee. Laraine was the first to leave the house, taking Adele and Annabel with her.

Dee had originally planned to go to Jodie's Kensington salon with her for the day. The arrival of those two women flashing that slip of paper had changed everything. As the telephone in the hall rang, Dee glanced up at the kitchen clock. It was only eight fifteen, and her every instinct told her that whoever was on the phone to her so early in the morning had to be, in some way or another, connected with that incident.

'Good morning,' she said as she placed the instrument to her ear.

'Good morning, my name is Jeffrey Brent, may I please speak with Mrs Underwood.'

'I am Mrs Underwood.'

Jeffrey Brent cleared his throat. 'It would appear that I owe you a deluge of apologies, Mrs Underwood. I've made this an early call in the hope that I would reach you before you set out on your day.'

Silence hung heavily, but Delia didn't think it was up to her to break it.

'Please believe me, the visit you received yesterday from Mrs Davison and Miss Marsden was totally unauthorised, not sanctioned by any official in my department. However, I would like for us to meet. We might have a lot to say to each other, but on the other hand this incident may well turn out to be of no interest to you whatsoever.'

Still Delia made no reply, and eventually Mr Brent said, 'Is there a possibility that we might meet this morning?'

371

'Where are you now, Mr Brent?' Delia asked.

'Only in Brighton. Depending on the traffic, it shouldn't take me more than half an hour to reach you.'

'Very well then, I'll be expecting you,' Delia said, very quietly, before replacing the receiver.

Having been given the full run-down on the conversation, Jodie said, 'This guy might turn out to be a dead loss, but on the other hand he may be able to enlighten you as to how and when that slip of paper came to be in that woman's possession, and that is what counts at the moment, isn't it?'

'Yes it is. I'll phone you later on today to let you know what he has to say.'

'Oh no you won't,' Jodie was quick to declare. 'I'm going nowhere until we find out what this bloke has to say.'

'I'm in no mood to argue with you.' Dee smiled, 'In fact I'm glad you are going to be here when he arrives. This whole set-up has a fishy smell to it.'

When Dee opened her front door, she got a pleasant surprise. Mr Brent was a tall, well-dressed, good-looking man in his early forties. He was wearing very light fawn trousers with an extremely smart navy blue blazer. His white shirt was wide open at the collar and it showed how nicely tanned his skin was.

He held out his hand and Dee took it. 'I have really come to apologise for the intrusion of Mrs Davison yesterday, though in all fairness I am convinced that her motives were good. She is to my knowledge a kind person, and that does count in the welfare work that is sometimes thrust upon her.'

Jodie had come out into the hall and now held her hand out and introduced herself. 'Can I offer you tea or coffee?' she asked.

'No, nothing, thank you. First off I must ask if that all-important slip of paper is still in your custody?'

'Yes, it is,' said Dee. 'I'll fetch it. Jodie, will you take Mr Brent through to the lounge. I won't be a minute.'

Only minutes later the three of them were seated facing the sea. The tall glass doors were open and a gentle breeze was blowing in. For the moment the only sound was the lapping of the waves as they broke on the shore and the wailing of the seagulls.

When Mr Brent broke the silence by rustling a sheaf of papers he had taken out from his briefcase, both women flinched. It was as if they were terrified of what he might be going to tell them.

'I'll start at the beginning and make it as short as possible.' His serious tone of voice didn't help. 'One of my officers took a call from Hammersmith Hospital about five days ago. A cab driver had picked up a pregnant woman who insisted on being taken to the nearest maternity hospital. The lady spoke hardly any English and as yet we have been unable to establish her nationality. More to the point, on her second day in the hospital she gave birth to a baby girl and on the morning after the birth the mother disappeared and hasn't yet been found.'

Both Delia and Jodie remained silent. They knew full well that Mr Brent had not reached the crux of this story.

The slip of paper that Dee had brought down from her bedroom was lying on the coffee table in front of Mr Brent. Dee and Jodie never took their eyes from him as almost in slow motion he leant forward and picked it up. There was a horrible pause before he said, 'This was pinned to the pillow of the cot in which the baby girl was lying.'

'What the hell are you saying!' Jodie almost exploded.

Mr Brent was talking, something about different departments all working together in cases such as this. Dee just wanted rid of this man who had come into her home and dropped a bombshell. She got to her feet slowly, because if she had moved quickly she would have fallen over. 'Mr Brent, I am going to ask you to leave now, please.'

In his haste he almost overturned the coffee table. 'Please don't take on so badly, Mrs Underwood. I would like you to talk to someone, your family, your doctor or even your solicitor, and I will be in touch with you if anything else should come to light.'

Dee wanted to scream at him, tell him to get lost, go away, stay away and never come back, though already she was coming to the conclusion that this matter was not going to go away. It would have to be dealt with one way or another. In the meantime, was she any closer to establishing Derrick's whereabouts? No, of course she wasn't. And she wasn't about to blacken her husband's name on the strength of one silly little piece of paper. Somehow she'd get to the bottom of this, and then God help whoever was responsible.

When Jodie came back from seeing Mr Brent off the premises, she was immediately aware that Dee had worked herself into a raging temper. That wasn't a bad thing; much better than shedding buckets of tears. 'I don't know about you, Dee, but for once I'm dying for a cup of tea. Let's both go to the kitchen and I'll put the kettle on,' Jodie said, already on her way.

Very soon she was pouring a cup of tea for Dee, and all the time her mind was racing. The suddenness of the confrontation with Mr Brent and the significance of the look on his face when he was talking had made her stomach turn over. She couldn't put her finger on what it was exactly – wariness, or surprise, or even fear – but there had been something. As she handed the tea to Dee, she said very quietly, 'I think we should have the family here before we discuss anything further.'

This was exactly what Dee had been dreading, but she knew she had no option.

35

It was the Thursday evening before everyone had gathered at Marine House.

Dee felt it showed a great deal of love and affection, everyone being so concerned about her, but in spite of all their kindness she still felt utterly alone. This was her problem, if indeed it did turn out to be a problem, and she could not rid herself of the feeling that she alone was going to have to deal with it. She looked around the room. Her parents were here and her sons, plus Jodie and her two and Michael and Danny. Marian was sitting beside Laraine and beside their mother were Adele and Annabel.

It couldn't be much longer before the truth came to light; maybe things would get settled then. Maybe Martin and Michael, who up until now had refused to even discuss this delicate situation, would begin to talk to her. Maybe if the so-called social workers didn't stir up any more skeletons in Derrick's cupboard, she could stop being afraid.

Yeah, she muttered to herself, and maybe there are far too many maybes. Another problem was that so many different pieces of advice had been offered to her, all coming from well-meaning folk, that everything in her own mind had become muddled. In fact she didn't know what to think. One minute she loved Derrick desperately, next would come utter disbelief that he could have fathered another woman's child. Then hate, such hate as she never would have believed, followed by resentment and anger and bitterness. All of these feelings battling for precedence in her head until she felt her brain would explode.

Jodie had been watching Dee's face and she did not like what she was seeing. She crossed the room and touched Dee's arm, saying, 'Whatever you think you've found out, please, Dee, try and wait a while rather than jump to conclusions.' Her voice was very quiet but even she appeared agitated.

'Jump to conclusions?' The words were harsh and shot from Dee's mouth like a bullet from a gun, but there was no stopping her now. 'A baby is born and within hours its foreign mother has disappeared, leaving only Derrick's name and address pinned to the bedding in its cot. Do I really need any more proof than that?'

'Yes. You do.'

It was Michael who had spoken, and it brought Dee's head up sharply.

Michael came close, and bending his knees he took hold of both of her hands. 'Dee, stop and think for a moment, Derrick is not here to defend himself. Even a condemned man has the right of reply.' He looked into Dee's lovely big eyes and saw that they were brimming with tears, and he was sorry. He hadn't meant for that to happen. Lowering his voice and speaking more gently, he said, 'Don't you think you might be imagining things because you're letting your fears get the better of you?'

She nodded to let him know that she had understood what he was trying to say to her, but speech was beyond her at this moment. She did her best to mouth her thanks for his kindness, and he lifted a hand and touched her cheek before pulling her to her feet. When she was standing, he drew her close to his chest, not saying a word, not moving an inch as he held her for a long, long time.

Danny had seen that everyone had a drink, but it was Jack Hartfield, Dee's father, who stood up and called the gathering to order.

'I've given a lot of thought to this matter, but I would still like to hear some of your views on the advice I am thinking of offering to my daughter. Is that all right with everyone?'

Nods of approval gave Jack the confidence to continue.

'First off, I think Dee needs some professional advice, and I think she should at least have a word with one or other of the solicitors that Derrick used when he bought this property. They saw her through all that legal business, didn't they? So maybe they can at least offer her some advice,' Jack paused. This wasn't easy for him. He took a deep breath and let it out slowly before he continued.

'We know from the newspapers that there are hundreds of babies abandoned in Russia, and we also know that Derrick has been in Russia on several occasions. Another known fact is that being a single mother in Russia is a huge stigma. Maybe this woman met Derrick socially, sensed her chance and has jumped on the bandwagon. Then again, there is still the possibility that Derrick has never set eyes on the woman. I agree with Michael. Derrick is being damned without a trial. Having said all of that, we aren't even sure the woman is Russian. So before any of us pass judgement, or offer to help, Dee needs to start digging, and to my mind a solicitor will be the best person for her to turn to.'

When Jack sat down, everyone in the room was full of admiration for him. They were also flabbergasted. Until tonight, Jack had always been thought of as a man of few words.

Dee physically shook herself before she made to answer. 'Thanks, Dad,' she managed to say. The emotion in her voice as she continued had everyone feeling for her. 'My thanks to each and

378

every one of you too. I can't tell you what I'm going to do, because I really don't know myself. Of course I am torn this way and that. One minute I hate the very sound of Derrick's name, I want to kill him, then Michael, bless him, reminds me to hold my horses and I can only think of Derrick as he has always been: my loving husband. So tomorrow morning I shall take my dad's advice and contact Derrick's solicitor. From there ... well, it has to be a case of wait and see. Now I'm going to ask Danny if he will see to it that everyone has a nightcap, and just for my mum and my mother-in-law I am going to make a pot of tea.'

As Dee made for her kitchen, she saw Marian turn to Mary and remark loudly, 'Fine state of affairs, isn't it? But you have to give it to that girl of yours, she's coming up trumps. I'd give a whole lot to know exactly where my Derrick is, though. Anyway, when Dee brings our tea out I'll get Danny to pour a good measure of whisky into our cups; at least then we might get a decent night's sleep tonight.'

Dee smiled, but at the same time she was chiding herself for being selfish. Poor Marian, not so long ago she'd lost Richard, and John couldn't be much of a comfort to her. Now this. Oh for God's sake, Derrick, why can't you pick up a phone and let us know where you are? That single thought had her rocking on her feet. Was Derrick's disappearance all tied up with this woman practically identifying him as the father of her child? I don't know about Marian needing whisky to help her to sleep, thought Dee. If I don't get some straight answers soon, the men in white coats will be coming to take me away.

As Dee poured boiling water into the teapot, she had to fight back her tears. This was turning out to be a very sad situation for everyone even remotely involved. And the saddest thing of all was that no matter how it eventually turned out, a great many lives would undoubtedly be affected.

Early next morning, Friday, Dee made a telephone call and at her request was put through to Mr Blenheim. At two o'clock that afternoon, she was sitting on the opposite side of his desk giving him a brief run-through of the events that had led her to seek his advice. He was leaning towards her and the look on his face was very thoughtful.

'Mrs Underwood,' he began, 'first off I have to tell you that I cannot be of any help to you. While I have every sympathy for you, such a situation does not come within my jurisdiction. However, I am able to offer you some very good advice. You said Hammersmith Hospital is where this baby was born?'

'Yes,' Dee murmured, nodding her head.

'I have knowledge of a Mrs Hammond, who has been a lady almoner, a medical social worker, at that hospital for a number of years. If there is any information forthcoming regarding this abandoned infant, then she will have the details.'

'Thank you, you've been most helpful,' Dee said, standing up and preparing to leave.

'I am truly sorry for the dilemma in which you find yourself,' the solicitor continued. 'Nevertheless, I must advise you to try and be patient and to curb your instinct. Nothing will be gained if you try to take matters into your own hands. You will need to be absolutely sure that you are in possession of the true facts before you make any bitter accusations, and even more so you will need documents that will substantiate any claims you may wish to make.'

Dee stayed silent. What he'd really like to say to me, she was thinking, is calm down and don't tear into that hospital like a bear with a sore head.

'Mrs Underwood?'

'Yes? Oh, I am sorry, I was giving thought to what you've just said.'

'Would you like me to phone Mrs Hammond? She may be able to see you this afternoon, and that would save you another trip up to town. I'm sure my secretary will have her number.'

'Yes please, if you would.' Dee smiled gratefully at him and sat down again.

While Mr Blenheim was out of the room, she did her best to stay calm. It was difficult. There were still a hundred and one questions that she badly needed to gain answers to. Would she feel any better when she got to the bottom of this nightmare and had those answers in front of her?

Only in time would she be able to answer that question.

Dee stood in the middle of the crowded London pavement and wished she had accepted Mr Blenheim's offer to call her a taxi. There were many double-decker buses about but she hadn't thought to ask what number she needed. Somebody was on her side. A taxi drew in close to the pavement where she was standing and a well-dressed City

381

gentleman with a rolled-up umbrella practically jumped out and was about to slam the door when Dee politely asked the cabbie, 'Please, will you take me to Hammersmith Hospital?'

'Oh, allow me.' The City gent held the door of the taxi wide open with one hand, placing the other under Dee's elbow, allowing her to step into the cab in the most ladylike way. Dee rewarded him with a sweet smile, a toss of her chestnut hair and a softly murmured, 'Thank you.'

He tipped his hat and said, 'My dear, the pleasure is all mine.'

She felt a whole lot better already. Whether she would still feel as good after she had been to this interview with Mrs Hammond was another matter altogether.

Within a short space of time Dee was again sitting in front of a rather large desk. This time it was a woman who was seated opposite her. They had shaken hands and introduced themselves, and already Dee had a feeling that she was going to like Mrs Hammond. She was aged about fifty, and was very smartly dressed in a navy blue single-breasted suit, crisp white blouse buttoned to the neck and just above the top button a gold cameo brooch. Before she had taken her seat at the desk Dee had noticed the smart nylon stockings and soft leather navy blue court shoes with a three-inch heel. She was wearing a wedding ring and a single diamond engagement ring, but there was no coloured polish on her fingernails.

'Shall I start the ball rolling, or would you rather go first?' she asked Dee.

'I just wouldn't know where to start,' Dee said.

'All I have been told is that a baby was born in this hospital, the mother of that infant has since disappeared and all that was left behind was a slip of paper on which was written the name of my husband, the name of the house in which I live and the town. Although I should point out that there are a number of other men, of various ages, who can lay claim to being Mr Underwood.'

After a brief pause, Mrs Hammond softly asked, 'How many of them live with you at that address?'

It was a blow below the belt for Dee, and her face showed the answer.

'I am sorry,' Mrs Hammond said hastily. 'I wasn't trying to be clever. I can tell you that the powers-that-be have gained the information that your husband is a master mariner; they also have acquired the address of the head office of the shipping line for which he works. I do want to assure you, Mrs Underwood, that everything is being undertaken as discreetly as possible. But if you want my help, then I do have to ask you two very relevant questions.'

Dee hesitated. But she had come this far, and if she didn't cooperate, then she might just as well get up and leave right now. Raising her eyes to meet Mrs Hammond's open gaze, she said, 'Please, carry on.'

With a soft sigh Mrs Hammond asked, 'Do you know the current whereabouts of your husband?'

Dee couldn't form an answer; she merely shook her head.

'Will you please tell me how long it is since you had contact with him.'

'Almost a year.'

'Mrs Underwood, as much as I would like to be of help to you, I am not the person you should be talking to. I myself have been in contact with Apex Shipping, and if and when you feel ready to talk to them, you only have to make a telephone call and they will be there for you.'

Dee felt she had lost her bearings. She had come here to talk about a newborn baby and the consequences that scrap of paper might bring about. But suddenly they were on an entirely different track.

'Why do I need to be in touch with my husband's employers?' Dee asked and waited for the answer with bated breath. Then a sudden thought struck her and she bleated, 'You said Apex Shipping. I have never heard of them!'

'Please, my dear, I would like you to believe that I have only your best interests at heart. I promise you it will be to your benefit if you could bring yourself to do as I suggest. If and when you've had a meeting with the directors of the firm and you feel you need my further help, don't hesitate for one minute: just come to the hospital, give your name at reception and someone will bring you to me. Meanwhile I wish you well, but before you go I'd like to give you this, you may find it helpful.' She was holding out a large sheet of paper. 'I typed these notes out for you from the memos I made while talking to the officials at Apex Shipping. I think you may find the information useful.'

Both women were on their feet now, and Dee was about to turn and go when Mrs Hammond laid a hand on her arm and said tentatively, 'The baby in question is a little scrap of a girl weighing barely five pounds. The doctors fear that the mother might have taken something to induce an early birth. Would you like to come along with me and have a peep at the child?'

To Dee, the question felt like a slap in the face. Horrified, she flung her arm out, pushing Mrs Hammond away from her, and with gritted teeth said, 'I can't believe you just asked me that. It is the last thing I would want to do.'

Dee had reached Victoria railway station by taxi. She was still reeling from shock. Trying to make sense of all that Mrs Hammond had told her was like looking into a pond of muddy water. There was so much that she hadn't told her. The journey to Eastbourne would take something like two hours, so she might just as well pull that sheet of paper from her handbag and see if Mrs Hammond's notes made any sense.

Apex Shipping, Quay Side, Newhaven. Head Office, Great Yarmouth. She read that first line twice, then screwed her forehead into deep wrinkles, trying her hardest to think whether the name rang any bells. Many a time over the years she had stood on the wharf at Great Yarmouth and watched the loading and unloading of vessels, knowing that far out in the North Sea there were men working on the mighty oil rigs, but still she couldn't recall having heard that name before.

The typewritten notes might indeed prove useful in the future, but at the moment they were merely a list of names and occupations together with telephone numbers. She refolded the sheet of paper and placed it back in her bag. It had only added to her frustration.

On reaching Eastbourne, Dee made her way to the car park. She was dead tired, in a foul mood and still had to drive herself back to Newhaven.

Half an hour later, she locked her car and walked through the front garden. Oh, our beautiful house, she breathed. If only Derrick were here to share it with me. A sudden thought struck her. Derrick had never lived here. He hadn't slept a single night under the roof of this wonderful house which he had bought and paid for.

Something was wrong. She wasn't able to fit her key into the lock; someone was inside the house and had left their key in the door. Well, that was no surprise, not really: both Martin and Michael had keys, and also a few of her close friends. She was about to press the bell when the door was opened and Jodie and Philip were standing there.

'Oh, bless you,' Dee said gratefully as she felt Jodie's arms go round her.

'Perhaps in future you will be a little less independent,' Philip scolded her. 'We came in here at lunchtime and found your hastily scribbled note. Why didn't you let us at least take you to the railway station? Never mind, explanations can wait. Dinner is all ready; I've only to put the steaks under the grill. Ready for a glass of wine, are you?'

'Never more so, Philip.' She smiled, as always appreciating the value of good friends. They had asked no questions. All they were concerned about was her well-being.

'Just give me a few minutes to kick my shoes off and wash the dirt of London from my face and hands.'

Jodie watched Dee go into the ground-floor bathroom and quietly remarked to Philip, 'She looks done in, doesn't she?'

'Yes, she does, although I fear she has more to come before she gets to the bottom of this trouble. But never fear, Dee will make it.'

Jodie only hoped and prayed that Philip was right.

36

'So you're no nearer getting to the truth than you were before you went to the hospital?'

'No, well I didn't expect to get very far.' Dee looked across the table at Jodie and quietly added, 'I was so pleased to find you and Philip here when I got back last night, and it was good of you to stay the night with me. Pity Philip had to go.'

'It works both ways, Dee. I would only have been going home to an empty house.'

'And today? Are you sure you can spare the time to spend the day with me?'

'Of course, everything's fine; at the moment the staff in both of my salons couldn't be more helpful. Where's that list? Let's plan our operation, 'cos today I'm coming with you no matter where you go.'

'Right.' Dee got up from the table and picked up the sheet of paper that Mrs Hammond had given her. 'I'd better begin by making some of these phone calls.'

Jodie made a start on clearing away the breakfast things, but before she had finished the washing-up, Dee was back in the kitchen with a very disheartened look on her face. 'I hate these calls when you get passed from one person to another. When I did eventually speak to the person in charge, all I got was that he needed to see me in person. He offered to send a car for me, but the office is only on the docks in Newhaven, and we can get there quicker ourselves.'

'Well, that's a turn-up for the books. Newhaven, right on your own doorstep!'

'Yeah, strange, isn't it. Have you ever heard the name Apex Shipping mentioned amongst the family?'

Jodie thought for a moment. 'Can't say that I have. Does it have any connection with what Mrs Hammond told you yesterday?'

'Well I suppose it must do. She put it at the top of the list she gave me, and I got the impression that Apex are the people who will have all the information about where Derrick is and what he is involved in.'

'Well it sometimes pays to follow your intuition, and if there's any chance that this firm is holding all the answers, what are we sitting around here for?'

Jodie had offered to do the driving and it was her car they were using. The short journey was uneventful, but on their arrival at the docks they did have a job discovering where the Apex offices were situated. Finally two young lads gave them directions and it turned out that the offices were not on the quay but directly behind it. The inside of the building was far more luxurious than the outside had led them to expect.

'A Mr Rowan Doughty is expecting me,' Dee informed a smartly dressed man of about thirty who was working behind a huge desk set at the far end of the large reception area.

'And you are?' he politely asked.

'I am Mrs Delia Underwood, and this is my sister-in-law Mrs Judith Underwood.'

'Oh, yes. I'll get someone to take you up to Mr Doughty's office.'

To their surprise, a young girl with a mass of blonde hair who looked to be no more than seventeen or eighteen years old but was dressed in a very smart business-type suit said, 'Would you like to follow me, please.' There was no further conversation until they were ushered into a very large office on the fourth floor of the building, the picture windows of which gave a good view of the harbour, where several huge vessels were moored.

Introductions were made, and soon they were all seated. Mr Doughty was a very tall gentleman; even sitting down, his broad chest and wide shoulders gave him an impressive look, and the silver threads in his dark hair only served to enhance his good looks. He began, 'I understand you are relatives of a master mariner, Derrick James Underwood?' His voice was cultured and respectful.

'Yes, I am Delia Underwood, Derrick's wife, and this is my sister-in-law, Mrs Judith Underwood.'

He nodded and looked thoughtful for a moment.

'I have been given to understand that you have

had no communication with your husband for a year. Is that right?'

Dee thought this cut and thrust could well go on for ever. She still hadn't a clue as to why she was here. Sitting up straight, she spoke in a low voice. 'Mr Doughty, before we go any further, may I please ask you to explain how and why you are associated with my husband's affairs?'

'I was about to come to that,' he said, 'though to be honest, I cannot think of the best way to approach all that I must tell you. I don't suppose you have ever had the need to become familiarised with Apex Shipping?' Dee shook her head. 'I thought not,' he murmured. 'We are shipping agents, a company that manages the administrative business of a ship on behalf of its owner. We are affiliated to most of the biggest shipping lines.' He paused and gave Dee time to reflect on these facts.

When he resumed, his voice was not so self-assured. 'To put it more simply, we are an assurance company which deals with problems and claims of compensation for accidents that take place at sea.'

That statement had in a single moment brought all of Dee's worst fears together. She hung her head low as she felt the colour drain away from her face, then clasped her hands so tightly in front of her that her knuckles showed white. All the worries she had been forcing herself to keep under wraps for these last months were threatening to surface and swamp her.

Mr Doughty sighed heavily as he got to his feet. Minutes later he was standing looking down at

390

her and holding out a glass of water. 'Please, have a drink, it may help.'

'Thank you,' Dee murmured, and taking hold of the glass, she drank deeply.

Seated once more behind his desk, Mr Doughty began again. 'Mrs Underwood, I am indeed sorry that the task of informing you of your husband's accident has fallen to me. First off, please accept sincere apologies on behalf of myself and our entire company that until now you have not received any notification of the accident or indeed your husband's welfare or whereabouts. Up until three days ago, Mr Underwood had remained adamant that no such details were to be issued or forwarded on to you. His one and only stipulation has been that you were to be taken care of financially.'

'Thank you.' Dee tossed her head impatiently. 'From the little you have told me, I take it I may assume that at least my husband is alive. Am I to be given a further explanation?'

'Well, that I don't think is for me to decide. I'm pretty sure the decision will be made within a day or two.'

'A day or two! Mr Doughty, you have kindly told me in a very roundabout way that my husband has been involved in an accident at sea and has been hidden away for months, and you expect me to walk out of this office with just that awful scrap of information. Tell me this, why now? Why have you agreed to see me and disclose these few facts? All very sudden, isn't it? Even though I think it is long overdue.'

Poor Mr Doughty, thought Jodie. She had half a mind to butt in and tell him that he might just

as well start at the beginning and tell Dee everything, because now that she had the bit between
her teeth, nothing and nobody would move her
from this office until she got the full story.

Mr Doughty stood up, pushed his chair back
and said, 'Will you ladies please excuse me for a
short while. I will bring a colleague back with me
and I think we all deserve some refreshments.'

The person who came back into the room with
Mr Doughty was a neat, slim female, probably in
her early thirties. She was pushing a tea trolley
which held enough very nice china for four people
and an ample array of sandwiches, savouries and
dainty cream cakes. The serviettes she handed out
were embossed with the Apex logo. She introduced herself to Dee and Jodie as Sheila Craig,
administration officer, before pouring out cups of
tea and offering the food. Polite conversation
about the weather made Dee want to scream, but
at last Miss Craig said, 'You would like to be
brought up to date on your husband's condition?'
She would have continued, but Dee almost rudely
interrupted her.

'I've a feeling that I am only now being brought
into the picture because another matter has arisen
which may or may not have to do with my husband. So I am asking you outright, will you please
begin at the beginning and try telling me the truth,
because all these hints and evasions are just about
sending me mad. Oh, and the matter that I am
referring to is to do with Hammersmith Hospital
in London. A Mrs Hammond, a medical social
worker there, gave me a list of phone numbers that
I should ring, and this office was top of the list.'

'Very well, Mrs Underwood, but I must confirm that we are imparting all of this information against your husband's wishes.' Miss Craig sighed softly before speaking again. 'I'm sorry to have to tell you that there was an explosion on one of the oil rigs and your husband was badly injured. He lost his left arm above the elbow, and was extensively burnt on the left side of his face.'

'Oh my dear God! My poor darling Derrick.' Dee's words were scarcely heard, so low was her voice. 'How long ago?'

'Just days after his return from taking you and his sons back to the UK.'

'And all this time he's suffered on his own, no family, no visitors. Nobody thought to inform me?'

'Those have been his instructions all along, Mrs Underwood. But I can assure you, he has been receiving the very best of attention that money can buy.'

'Where is he now? Which hospital is he in? Come to that, which bloody country is he in?'

'I do realise what a tremendous shock this has been for you. All the staff involved with this case have done everything possible to ease conditions for your husband, and we will continue to do so. What you have to remember, and we have to keep reminding ourselves, is that we are basically an insurance company. Money is not, and never will be, a problem in this case; if money could have made Mr Underwood a fit man, he would have been back at sea a long time ago. Really it is not me or Mr Doughty or any member of Apex you should be talking to. We are managing your husband's financial affairs, but as to the state of his health, you need to get in touch with the medical team who are taking care of him.'

'Then please, tell me how I am supposed to do that when I don't even know where he is.' It was pitiful to listen to the sadness in Dee's voice.

Sheila Craig turned to Mr Doughty, and it was plain that she was silently asking his permission to say more.

He nodded his head, and she continued.

'I can truthfully say that I am not aware of which hospitals your husband has been treated at. As he was so very badly burned, he is going to need specific treatment probably for some time to come. This wasn't possible to begin with because of his mental state, but recently I have been informed that he is to be transferred.'

'When? And will he be brought back to the UK?'

'I cannot give you an answer to either of those questions, at least not yet. It will be a matter of transport and, of course, whether he is fit to travel. If you would like to phone me in two or three days' time, I shall likely have all the new paperwork through by then and be able to give you further information.'

It seemed that that was that. Miss Craig was on her feet, had already shaken hands with Jodie and was moving towards Dee when she turned back and, staring at Jodie, asked, 'Is your husband the only brother of Mr Derrick Underwood?'

Jodie frowned, looking puzzled. 'Well, yes, he is.'

Miss Craig took a deep breath. 'I am going to tell you something that I probably shouldn't. Derrick Underwood's brother was informed of the accident right from day one. I also happen to know that he has been a regular visitor, not frequent, but according to my records three or four times since the accident.'

Dee's mind was in complete turmoil. Her dear, good-looking husband'd been burnt, the left side of his face, Miss Craig had said. Was it so horrible? So terrifying to look at? Was that why Derrick had given orders that she was not to be allowed to visit him? Or even to know where he was?

What possible difference could it make? She was his wife! She loved him, for God's sake! His sons loved him; why couldn't they be allowed to see him?

Jodie too was upset. Burns of any kind could be horrific, but to his face! That had to be appalling. She was also shocked to hear that John had been going abroad to visit his brother. She and Dee'd have to pay a visit to their mother-in-law. Even if Marian hadn't been told about Derrick's accident – and it was feasible to assume that she hadn't, because she never would've been able to keep that to herself – she could at least be made to understand that they needed to know where John was.

It wasn't until they were back in Jodie's car that Dee broke the silence that had lain between them as they left the office.

'Jodie, didn't you think that was an abrupt ending to that meeting?'

'Funny, my mind is running along the same track. That was quite a bombshell Miss Craig dropped about my John, wasn't it? But I think I know what you're going to say.'

'Mmm, once she had told us about John having visited Derrick, she ushered us out of that office as quickly as she could. I think she saw a chance to avoid the subject of Mrs Hammond and Hammersmith Hospital.'

'Exactly. You told her outright that Apex was top of Mrs Hammond's list of telephone numbers and she didn't once query it.'

Dee smiled for the first time since they had set out on this mission. 'Jodie, I am so grateful you were there with me, and we did both pick up on things. There's more going on than that company are willing to come clean about, we both agree on that. But as to the baby lark at Hammersmith Hospital, well, I can at least push that to the back of my mind. My worrying over whether Derrick has been with another woman vastly diminishes when I think of what has happened to him.'

'Well, that has to be all to the good,' Jodie told her, giving Dee's hand a good squeeze. 'I've had thoughts on the matter too, and in the light of what we have learnt today, I can't see that it could be feasible for Derrick to have fathered that baby. Didn't you tell me that Mrs Hammond said it wasn't a full-term pregnancy?'

'She didn't say positively, only that the doctors had made that assumption.'

'Anyway, how much longer are we going to sit here in this car park?' Jodie laughed. 'I think sooner rather than later we need to pay a visit to our mother-in-law. For the first time in I don't know how long, I am dying to meet up with my husband, and I am not going to be put off by Marian swearing she doesn't know where he is. So do we go straight to Camber, or do we go home first?'

'It's getting on for five o'clock and the traffic will be building up. Let's go home to my house. It would be great if you could stay with me another night. We can sort things out in our minds, make some notes and go to Marian's early tomorrow morning.'

'That's settled then,' Jodie murmured as she turned the key in the ignition.

Dee settled back in the passenger seat for the short journey. In her head she was trying to decide when would be the best time to tell Martin and Michael about their father. Derrick had been so reluctant for her to see how badly his face had been burnt, and yet apparently he had allowed his brother to visit him, and that fact might not sit too well with his sons.

Well, she decided, there was never going to be a good time, but she would wait until she'd heard what John had to say.

If they could find him.

37

It was just after ten o'clock when Dee pulled her car to a halt outside Marian's house. She had telephoned her parents telling them that she was coming to Camber, but she had warned her mother that she had to go in to see Marian first.

It was now a quarter to eleven and Marian was

sobbing in Jodie's arms. Dee had given her a brief outline of Derrick's accident, and she was absolutely convinced that her mother-in-law had been totally unaware of this catastrophe.

'Oh no, Dee, losing an arm he could have managed, they do such wonderful artificial limbs these days, but to be badly burnt! Oh no, no, no, please God not his dear face.'

Listening to Marian was gut-wrenching for Dee, and she sighed heavily. She was so tired and sad. If only somebody would allow her to go to see Derrick, they'd be able to comfort each other. It wouldn't matter how badly his face was burnt; it couldn't possibly alter the fact that they loved each other. Suddenly she was trembling from head to foot, unable to control her limbs.

They all heard the opening of the front door and Dee's parents coming down the hall. At a single glance Jack took in the situation, and turning to his daughter he said quietly, 'Derrick?'

Dee couldn't bring herself to answer; she merely nodded her head and leant against her dad. 'There, there, come on, Dee,' he murmured as he patted her back with one hand, keeping his other arm placed tightly around her shoulders.

'Oh Dad,' she cried, clinging to him. 'Whatever am I going to do?'

They stumbled across the room and practically fell on to Marian's sofa.

'Sit with me a minute,' she begged him.

'What's happened?' he asked. 'You've been so brave up until now. Your mum and I have been amazed at just how well you've been coping. What's happened to set you off?'

'Oh Dad, too much to tell all in one go,' she said, still shaking.

He began to rock her back and forth, humming at the same time, until Dee asked, 'Why are you humming?'

''Cos today you don't seem to be a grown woman, mother of my two grandsons; more like my little girl that your mum used to go on at me for spoiling. Whatever it is that's upset you will seem better if you share the problem with me. Don't you think so?'

'Yes, all right, Dad,' she said, giving him a watery smile. She took a deep breath and blurted the information out without a pause. 'There was an explosion on an oil rig. Derrick lost his left arm, up above the elbow, but the worst part is that he's very badly burnt.'

'Heaven help him.' Her mother quietly mouthed the words.

'A shipping insurance company has been dealing with his affairs. They insist that it has been on Derrick's instructions that I have been kept in the dark all this time. They have assured me that money does not come into it. Derrick is receiving the best medical attention that money can buy.'

'I should be there with him,' Marian cried loudly as she broke away from Jodie's grasp.

'That is exactly how I feel,' Dee responded quickly, 'but not a soul will tell me where he is and why it has taken so long for any of us to be told about the wretched accident. I hope you're listening to me, Marian, because I want some answers from you. You know where John is, don't you? No, please stop shaking your head, the time

399

for you to cover for him is long gone. I want to go and see my husband, and my sons will more than likely demand to come with me. What am I going to say to them?' She had been speaking in hushed but forceful tones, and now tears were trickling unheeded down her cheeks.

It was Marian who was shaking now as she walked over to a bureau that stood in the corner of the room. Opening a small drawer, she removed a holiday brochure and held it out to Jodie.

Jodie took a quick glance and exclaimed loudly, 'This is for the Golden Sands Holiday Camp. Are you telling us that John is living there? Why, it's only yards up the road from here.'

'No, he's not living there, but he has a contract at the camp. He has a dozen or so men working for him. Oh Jodie, don't stand there looking at me like that. Come here. Come here please. He begged me not to tell you.'

It was a while before either Jodie or Dee moved, but when they did it was as one. With the three Mrs Underwoods' arms wrapped around each other, Jack and Mary Hartfield stood looking on, and it was a job for them to work out who was comforting whom.

Three days later, Rowan Doughty contacted Dee at her home. He was happy to be able to tell her that at last Derrick had given his permission for his wife to be brought up to date with his affairs. 'Once again I would like to apologise to you, Mrs Underwood. I know it was wholly his own decision, but I suppose the doctors themselves were keen to keep you and the family away for the time being, because as I have been given to understand, your husband's mental condition was causing as much concern as his physical injuries.'

'Thank you for that explanation, it helps,' Dee assured him.

'So I can now bring you up to date with the news that when the explosion happened, Derrick was hospitalised in South America for the first six weeks. For the past ten to eleven months he has been in hospital in Belgium, Brussels actually.'

'Marvellous, I'll go as soon as I can.' Already Dee's voice sounded different; for the moment her joy knew no bounds.

'Hey! Hold on,' he called down the line. 'The doctors in Brussels have done everything that is possible for your husband, at least for the time being, and now he is to be transferred to the Queen Victoria Hospital in East Grinstead, which I'm sure you have heard of. It is quite near to you. He is being brought home.'

'Oh thank you, thank you, the whole family will be so relieved.'

'No thanks are necessary. I am just sorry that you were kept waiting for so long without any news. Myself and my whole team wish Mr Underwood a very satisfactory recovery. I have been given to understand that that particular hospital has a great record with their burns unit, especially since the Second World War. He really will be in the best of hands and I shall still be kept abreast of his progress. As regards yourself, Mrs Underwood, if at any time I may be of service to you, please don't hesitate to get in touch.'

As Dee replaced the receiver, her heart felt

lighter than it had been for a long time. Derrick was coming home and that was marvellous news, but it was only the beginning, she reminded herself. Now she had no choice but to tell Martin and Michael that their father had been hurt in an explosion. What would they say when they saw that his face was badly burnt? At least they would be able to go together to see him, but she would have to be so careful about what she said to him and how she reacted to his injuries. Dear God, give me strength to be there for Derrick. I really do not know how to handle this.

Without warning, her limbs crumpled and she flopped down on to the floor. As much as she was telling herself she must not break down, not now, there was no stopping her. Anguish, misery and sorrow were swamping her, and she just couldn't cope with it all. She wanted Derrick to be able to put his arms around her, to tell her that she was still his one and only love, but that was never going to happen; he no longer had two arms. She was crying now, really crying as she had never cried in her life before. She wanted Derrick to be as he always had been, her Derrick, tall, good-looking and strong. A man who made other women look and envy her.

It was three weeks later when at last Dee was told she could visit her husband. A male nurse led the way down a long, wide, white-walled corridor. Dee followed with her sons each side of her. They passed a number of side wards. Some of the doors were closed, but through one of the open ones they glimpsed a man propped up in bed playing cards. Beside the bed was a man in a wheelchair; he had a tray across his lap and it was clear that he had lost his legs. Dee's heart ached for the poor soul; he looked so young.

At the far end of the corridor the nurse pushed open a door and ushered the three of them into a large, bright room. There was a fair-sized bed but it was neat and tidy, with no occupant. A male orderly was in the far corner of the room stacking linen into a cupboard. He turned and said, 'Good afternoon.' All three of them muttered something, Dee wasn't sure what, because their attention was on the man standing near the window with his back to them. He was wearing a long dressing gown, the left sleeve of which hung empty by his side. The nurse who had escorted them said something to the orderly, then to Dee he said, 'Mrs Underwood, I'll be back shortly.' He went out of the room and the orderly indicated a large armchair. Dee sat down, but Martin and Michael remained standing.

You could have heard a pin drop. The silence was awful.

'Derrick ... Derrick, darling, it's me.'

The tall figure turned around. The bandages round the face moved, at least where the wide slit was, and a muffled sound came forth. It wasn't words, and the sounds in no way resembled her dear Derrick's rich, deep voice. Dee nodded to her boys, both of whom had lost the colour from their cheeks.

'Hello, Dad,' Martin managed to say, but his brother simply wasn't able to force any words through his lips.

The muffled voice came again, and the tall figure took several steps, bringing him nearer to Delia. She took a deep breath, wondering why he was almost bald and why she couldn't smell Derrick's manly smell and his nice light aftershave that she remembered so well. What was filling her nostrils was the scent of disinfectant and iodine. Then she distinctly heard the word *Dee* and a long string of other words, but she was unable to understand them. She turned and looked helplessly at the orderly, who said in a low voice, 'He's telling you that he's sorry he made you stay away for so long and sorry too that he cannot write letters.'

Dee looked at her sons and they all three nodded, and the man went on. 'He can write, his right hand isn't affected, but he can't see.'

Dee said, 'He's my husband, you know, and these are his two sons.'

'Yes, I know that now, but until recently I was given the impression he hadn't anybody. I suppose the doctors have kept you away all this time because he wasn't right in his mind. He went raving when he was told we were leaving Brussels, but he has really cheered up now we're back in England.'

'You said *we;* have you been with my husband all along?'

'Yes, ma'am, wouldn't have had it any other way. He's a great guy, didn't deserve what he got. But that's life. By the way, I'm Robert Patterson, my mates call me Bob,' he said, showing her a wide smile.

Dee looked away from the orderly and stood up. Slowly she covered the distance between her and her husband. Moving to his right side, she took hold of his hand and slowly began to squeeze it. Suddenly the pressure on her own hand tightened, and it was not from her efforts; Derrick was letting her know that he knew she was there. Dee waited a moment before raising his hand to her mouth, then she placed her lips on the skin on the back of his hand. A moment passed and she heard what she took to be a sigh come from him, then turning his hand over in her own, she placed the palm gently against her cheek and held it there for what seemed a long time.

When she finally let his arm drop down to his side, his hand was wet with Dee's tears.

Martin was the first to move forward and take his father's right hand between both of his. 'Dad, oh Dad, it's so great to see you.' Poor lad, his voice was thick with emotion. Michael still couldn't bring any words out, and so he followed his mother's example and clutched at his dad's right hand, holding it up against his own cheek.

It was about a quarter of an hour later when a doctor came into the room. Introducing himself as Dr Wilkinson, he said, 'I'm sorry your stay will have to be a short one today. As your visits proceed, you will be allowed to stay longer and hopefully will begin to see a marked improvement in your husband.'

Oh, dear Father in Heaven! How could she leave him like this? She hadn't even been able to have a glimpse of his dear face. So many bandages even after all this time.

A female nurse had also now entered the room, and she gently took hold of Dee's arm and led her into the corridor with the doctor. Michael rushed past her. Once outside the main door he vomited, and Martin too looked drawn and ill.

'Your sons will be fine,' the doctor assured her, 'but I would like you to come into my office. I think we'd better have a little talk.' He held open a door. 'Here we are, just take a seat.' He pointed to a comfortable leather chair, then went over to a sideboard. 'May I offer you something to drink, I'm sure you must be feeling in need of it.'

'I won't have anything at the moment, thank you,' Dee answered softly.

'Your husband has been in a very bad way and it cannot have been nice for you seeing him as he is today.'

'What exactly is wrong with his face?'

'It might almost be easier to tell you what isn't wrong with it. He was very badly burnt. The whole side of his face and neck caught the blast. His jaw and mouth will have to be rebuilt, and now that the flesh is healing somewhat, we hope to make a start soon. The left cheek has responded to treatment and will improve further when at last we're able to begin plastic surgery. His ear, well, we hope to build him a new one. All of this has taken a long time but it is far from being over yet. He will still need a number of operations. Every doctor involved will do his utmost, but I'm sure you'll understand that even today, with all the progress that has been made, there are no miracle-workers in this field yet. As I've already said, the doctors will do a remarkable job, but his face will still be disfigured.'

It was Dee's turn to feel sick. She closed her eyes for a moment, then said, 'May I have a glass of water, please?' She had almost emptied the glass before she asked the next question. 'And the rest of him?'

'Well, you have been told he has lost two thirds of his left arm, but thankfully there has been no harm done internally, although parts of his body down the left side are badly scarred at the front. Having told you that, body scars are nothing compared with those of the mind. Fortunately, though, with time and treatment, everything will be put right. Nothing will ever be as it was, but we'll do our best to help him to look normal as soon as we possibly can.'

'Where will the plastic surgery be done?'

'Almost certainly here. And you and your sons will be able to visit him from time to time. However, it will be better if he doesn't have any other outside contacts, at least for some time to come.'

Dee had hedged long enough. The most vital question of all, and she had to ask it: 'Dr Wilkinson, will my husband regain his sight?'

He leaned forward and laid his hand on hers, and said calmly, 'We must hope and pray.'

'Then I have a second question, please. All the operations to build up his face, how long will they take?'

'That is a most awkward question to answer. Each operation will be linked to another, but I would say two to three years.'

'*What!*'

The doctor sighed. 'It might be even longer.'

'He'll have to live in that state all that time?'

'No, of course not. His doctors will see him daily and will be working on him and for him.

He'll be improving the whole time. And Mrs Underwood, I have to tell you, it may seem a long time to you, but that isn't any length of time for such cases. We have patients in this hospital who wouldn't leave to go out into the world if you paid them. We have every facility they could wish for: games rooms, large comfortable lounges, a well-stocked reading room which can supply talking books. All that besides the swimming baths and exercise and therapy quarters. Perhaps next time you come, you will allow me to show you around. I think you will be surprised, and it may help to alleviate the worry about your husband having to be with us for a long stay.'

Dr Wilkinson stood up. Dee attempted to do the same, only to find her legs were wobbly. They walked together to the front entrance to find Martin and Michael sitting on a bench. The doctor took a deep breath before speaking directly to Derrick's two sons.

'It must be a great relief to both of you to have your father so much nearer to home. Your mother will pass on everything that I have told her; meanwhile I will add that your father is very much aware of what has happened, particularly to his face. So if you will kindly phone me when you wish to visit, I shall tell you whether or not it'd be wise to come along. Also, there will be periods when he is undergoing operations when all visiting will be stopped. I hope you understand.'

Both heads were nodding and hands were shaken all round as the doctor took his leave of them.

Michael spoke first. 'I don't think you're fit to

408

drive home just yet, Mum, so I suggest we find out where the cafeteria is and order a pot of very strong coffee.'

'Yes?' Martin prompted his mother.

'Yes, that's fine by me,' she murmured.

'Good, that's settled then. Come on, Mum, tuck your arm through mine.'

In the cafeteria, they sat in silence, each alone with their thoughts. Dee couldn't begin to imagine what Derrick had gone through, and what lay in front of him. Operation after operation. She could understand now his refusal to let her see him. But oh, how she wished she could bear some of the pain for him. Poor, poor Derrick, where he was concerned she was utterly helpless.

Closing her eyes, she longed for someone just to take hold of her hand. She was no fool, though, it was now perfectly plain to her that not only now, but for a very long time to come, she was going to have to cope with what life had thrown at her. She also knew she had never before felt so sad or empty or so utterly lost.

38

Eight days since their visit to East Grinstead, and Dee knew she looked a terrible sight. She hadn't been able to eat or drink anything but water, and trying to sleep was driving her mad. All the while she was asking herself what she was going to do, and that in itself was a damn silly question.

She was sitting in the kitchen, and even after all this time she knew how fortunate she was to have this beautiful home with its spacious rooms and huge windows at the back which overlooked the sea. This was a dream kitchen: the floor was tiled, the units and surfaces were the best that money could buy and the views from the windows on all three sides were of the sea. The year was rambling on; summer was certainly over and the sea was rough this morning, the waves as they crashed against the breakwaters noisy and almost frightening. In the centre of her table was a vase of pink carnations, their heavenly smell filling the air. Yes, she had so much to be thankful for. Each and every one of her friends had stayed close, visiting as much as possible, always bringing flowers, fruit and chocolates. It made her feel a fraud. She wasn't the one that was ill, but she was certainly suffering. Tormenting herself day in, day out. Why couldn't she do more for Derrick? She wondered, if like her, he felt lonely. Even his friends weren't allowed to visit him.

The ringing of the doorbell broke into her thoughts, but she ignored it. Again it rang, and moments later there came a persistent thumping and hammering on the front door. 'What the hell is going on?' she shouted as she reluctantly got to her feet and walked through the hall. She undid the bolts, top and bottom, took the keys down from where they were hanging on a rack on the wall and struggled to open the heavy front door. 'God, I feel as weak as a kitten,' she muttered.

She was shocked to see John, Jodie's husband, standing on her doorstep, and the surprise showed as she said, 'What the hell do you want?'

John made a shrugging movement with his shoulders. 'You and I need to talk, and I am not going away until we have, so please let me come in.'

'Why do you want to talk to me all of a sudden?' she queried.

'I'm doing nothing all of a sudden. I've known for ages that you and I would have to sit down and have a chinwag.'

She couldn't believe it, John actually sounded sincere. She stepped back and opened the door wide, then turned and walked back towards her kitchen. Once inside John looked at her carefully, then said, 'Oh Dee, sit down, luv, before you fall down. I'm sorry to say this, but you look awful. I'll put the kettle on and make us a pot of tea.'

Seated again at the table, Dee lifted her eyes and looked at him. He was still handsome, and she thought sadly how he was the only one of the brothers left now who was. From his movements she gathered that he hadn't lost any of his arrogance, nor did he seem the least bit embarrassed to be here in her home. But then John Underwood had always been a law unto himself; he cared for no one and gave nothing away. He'd always been ruthless, and up to all sorts of tricks, but somehow all of that had only added to his charm. Especially where the ladies were concerned. Suddenly she thought of Jodie and immediately felt she was betraying her dear friend by having John here.

Feeling ill at ease, she told him, 'Say what you've come to say and then leave, because to be honest with you, John, I don't feel able to trust you.'

411

Bitterness flooded through her when she thought how badly he had treated his wife and sons over the years. Right now, uppermost in her mind was the fact that for a whole year since her Derrick had been hurt in that explosion, John had not only known which hospital he had been in, he had actually visited him on more than one occasion.

'Do you really want me to go, Dee? You'll never stop worrying about what it was I came to tell you, and besides, the kettle is boiling and I'm about to make the tea.'

Slowly, reluctantly, she looked up at him again. 'You're right, John, I would like to hear what you have to say, because no matter which way I look at it, you seem to have been allowed to have more to do with my husband since his accident than I ever have.'

John didn't answer; instead he busied himself setting out two cups and saucers and taking a jug of milk from the fridge. When the kettle came to the boil, he first warmed the pot before making the tea. Jodie would be astonished at all this domestic activity, thought Dee. It wasn't the John they remembered. He poured milk into the cups and then lifted the teapot and filled each one almost to the brim.

There was a long silence while he drank his tea and Dee slowly sipped at hers, and each regarded the other. Twice John felt the need to clear his throat before he managed to form the words, and then his voice was very husky.

'You're not going to like the topic I'm going to bring up, but it does need to be brought out into the open.' He waited a moment to judge Dee's reaction, and when she didn't say a word, he rushed in like a bull in a china shop. 'Decisions have to be made about that baby girl still lying in Hammersmith Hospital.'

Up until this moment Dee had been full of bravado, but now she was terrified and it showed. She sat slumped in her chair facing John, and she was finding it hard to look at him without showing her distaste. 'You bastard,' was all she could manage.

John stared at her silently. Finally he spoke. 'Derrick asked me to come here. Me? I'd rather be miles away, but I made him a promise and here I am.'

Dee closed her eyes in distress. 'Are you telling me the truth? Derrick asked you to come to me?'

John nodded sadly. 'It's bound to come out eventually. Far better that you hear the whole story from me.'

'How do I know it will be the truth? And why should you do the telling? If Derrick is in any way tied up with this baby, shouldn't the truth be coming from him?'

John balled his hands into two tight fists. 'Dee, for Christ's sake stop a minute and think what you're saying. He still has to have an operation on his mouth, and his lips will need to be built up. Until that happens his speech is always going to be hard to fathom. If Derrick were able to speak to you, this affair would never have taken place.'

'Oh, so you're here to tell me that my husband had an affair with some foreign woman and now you're going to ask me to help clean up their mess.'

'So help me, Dee, you're being an awkward bitch! There is no affair. There never was. I used the word wrongly. What I should have said was, if Derrick had not been caught up in that explosion, he would never have been put in the position that has led to that child being born.'

'So now you're saying that my Derrick sought comfort by sleeping with another woman and the result is he's the father of that baby.'

John shrugged helplessly. 'In a bloody nutshell, the answer is yes! But if you have as much love for my brother as you'd like us all to think, then you will at least listen to the whole story and not keep picking at it like a dog with fleas.'

The insinuation that she might not love Derrick was like a red rag to a bull, and Dee would have swiped at John had he not seen it coming and grabbed her wrist.

She struggled, he offered to release her, 'Providing you drink your tea and keep calm. I think it will be best if I start at the beginning. Tell it to you the way my brother told it to me.'

Dee was crying, whether from bad temper or sheer frustration John didn't know, and at that moment he didn't much care. The quicker he got this job over and done with, the better he'd like it. He had never pictured himself as a peacemaker. He could certainly understand the situation from his brother's point of view, but there again he was a bloke, and blokes were like that. Whether or not he would get the same amount of understanding from Delia remained to be seen.

He very much doubted it.

Dee didn't have the patience to wait for John to

start. She just opened her mouth and said the first words that came into her head.

'Given the state that my husband must have been in at the time, are you going to tell me how and when he slept with this woman?'

John thumped the table with his clenched fist. 'Derrick did not sleep with any woman at any time.' By now he sounded really brutal. 'He merely had sex. He was in Brussels, a country where prostitution is legal. It was a commodity. Derrick felt in need of it. His body being seriously damaged and burnt didn't alter the fact that he is still a red-blooded man, and there was nothing wrong with his tackle. The woman was able to provide a service, and he paid her for it. So there you have it.'

Dee's face had drained of all colour and she was doing her best to avoid eye contact with her brother-in-law. John was fully aware of how embarrassing all of this was for her. He wasn't enjoying his part in it, far from it, but he'd come this far and he had no choice but to press on.

'This is how his orderly, Bob Patterson, tells it. Bob has been with my brother more years than I can remember, and he would move heaven and earth to help him. It was Bob that arranged it, in the hope, I may add, that he was helping Derrick to feel a bit more human than he had been of late. The woman was not a flighty young tart. She was a clean, sensitive thirty-year-old woman who was fully licensed by the authorities to hire herself out for sexual intercourse. Derrick had taken it for granted that she practised safe sex. He has since been told that nobody was more upset than she was when she found herself to be pregnant.'

The silence was unbearable, and John put out a hand to comfort Dee. She knocked it away with all the strength she could muster.

More minutes ticked by, until John asked quietly, 'Would you like me to tell you what I think you should do next?'

'Well,' she sighed heavily, 'we've come so far, I suppose you might as well, but first off, please will you pour me another cup of tea.'

John stood up and went to switch on the kettle. 'I'll do better than that. I'll make us a fresh brew.'

While waiting for the kettle to come to the boil again, John leant forward with his elbows resting on the edge of the deep shiny sink. The garden was looking a bit untidy; the trees and shrubs had shed most of their leaves. Still, the sight of the sea right at the foot of the property was a joy to behold, and for once he was praying not for himself but for his own brother, that he might recover his sight, that his body would be repaired as much as was humanly possible, and that he would come home to enjoy not only this wonderful house but the love of his sons, and most of all the love and companionship of his wife.

He of all people could vouch for the value of all of that. He'd thrown his own chances away many years ago.

With a fresh cup of tea in front of them, John was in two minds as to where he should begin, so once more he dived straight in. 'Am I right in thinking that you've already had one visit from a Jeffrey Brent?'

'Yes. He came to make an apology after a couple of his social workers turned up here.'

'Well I've met him, only once, and then very briefly, but I think it would do you a world of good if you went to see him.'

Dee was glaring at him and John held up his hands in mock surrender. 'OK, have it your own way. I've done all that I promised Derrick I would; the rest is up to you. Decisions are going to have to be made, and they will be made with or without your cooperation. Think about it, Dee, and if you decide you don't want anything to do with the arrangements, that's fair enough, but don't start moaning when it's all over that you weren't consulted in any way.'

'I'll think about it. In the meantime, how come you're so aware of what's been going on?'

'Put it this way. I'm being Derrick's ears and his mouthpiece for the time being. You might not like it, but my brother has decided to do the honourable thing regarding that newborn baby, and as he is not in a position to act for himself, and won't be in the foreseeable future, he's turned to me. Who else was there?'

'There's me, I am his wife!'

'Yes, and nothing alters that fact. However, if asked, would you have been willing to go to the bank or the insurance company to arrange to pay for that little mite's medical expenses until such time as she is adopted?'

Dee's mouth dropped open in sheer surprise. 'How do you know she's going to be adopted?'

'The mother is a Roman Catholic – that is why she didn't have an abortion – but apparently she is unable to keep the baby herself and adoption appears to be the only solution.'

417

'Is Derrick going along with that?'

'I don't know, you'll have to ask him yourself.'

'Why is Derrick seeing to the financial side of all of this?'

'For a number of reasons, or so I gather. He feels it is partly his fault that the baby was born prematurely, and that is the reason she has been kept in the hospital for this length of time. He also reasoned that the woman had acted in a very trustworthy way by coming to London, making sure the baby was born discreetly and safely and covering the costs herself. She has never once approached him for help, though she probably bribed one of the staff in the hospital to find out where Derrick's family lived in the UK, and that's how she was able to leave that slip of paper. What she hoped to achieve from that is anybody's guess. Anyway, that's it, my part is all done and dusted, and what you do from here on in is entirely up to you.'

'Will you accept my thanks, John? I know I was downright rude to you earlier on, but having taken in all that you've told me, I can see now that you have been a good friend to Derrick.'

'He's not my friend, Dee, he's much more than that. Derrick is my brother and he would have done the same for me. Blood is always thicker than water. You might do well to think about that.'

39

Had John really been here? Had he really talked to her at great length about all the most intimate details of this startling business? Dee sat up straight on her big settee and stretched her arms above her head. Good gracious, it was almost dark outside. She must have slept for quite some time. Her head felt muzzy and it made her wonder if John had put some whisky or brandy into her tea. If he had, she was more than grateful; she had badly needed that sleep.

Oh yes, he'd been here. And he had certainly opened her eyes to what had been taking place. He'd made sure she understood and believed, even though some of the facts had horrified her. He had been almost brutal in the telling, and to be made to face the true details had been petrifying. Not to mention the embarrassment. Of one thing now she was very sure. She must stop all of this lying about, wallowing in self-pity. Poor Derrick was the one who was suffering. Dee didn't need her friends pitying her any more; she just needed to make up her mind what she was going to do.

It was too late to put all these determined notions into practice today, but come tomorrow morning she vowed she'd be up and about before the streets were aired. I shan't be bothering with any phone calls; straight to the fountainhead, that's where I'm going, she promised herself as

419

she stood with the doors of her wardrobe wide open trying to decide which would be the best outfit to wear. Not only was she going to wear something smart, she was going to wash and set her hair, and that very thought had her smiling. John had been right, she did look a mess, had really let herself go, but now she was facing facts and she was going to do her very best to solve at least a few of the problems that she'd allowed to get the better of her.

It was a little after eight a.m. when Dee drove her car into the parking lot at Lewes railway station. Her father had suggested on the phone last night that it would shorten the journey if she caught the train here rather than from Eastbourne. She put coins into the pay machine and collected her day's parking ticket, which she then propped up prominently on the front of the dashboard before locking the car and walking towards the booking office.

There was a middle-aged man behind the glass of the ticket office; no one else was about, and that fact rather surprised Dee. They must all catch the early train, she decided.

'Morning, luv,' the ticket operator called cheerily. 'Sloping off to London, are we? Nothing you ladies like better than a day going round the big shops spending hubby's money.'

Dee's only answer was a sweet smile and a polite request for a day return to Victoria, please.

Cheerful chappie passed a ticket through the open end of the glass panel, and Dee slid the money through. 'You've about seventeen minutes to wait,' he told her, adding with a broad grin, 'Take yerself off into the waiting room, luv, I put the heater on in there bright an' early this morning so the place should be warmed up by now. You can buy a paper from the book stall if you'd like something to read while you wait.'

Here was a gentleman who really was happy in his work, Dee thought. She'd bet anything that the regular travellers loved this man. They should do, if her treatment was anything to go by.

The few minutes she had sat in the warm waiting room reading the headlines on the *Daily Mail* had been a very good start to the day, she told herself as the announcement that the Victoria train was approaching platform one came clearly over the air.

On arrival in London, Dee walked outside Victoria station and flagged down a cab to take her to Hammersmith Hospital. On the journey she did her best to sort out in her head just what she was going to do when she got there. She didn't get very far; her intentions were good, but her thoughts were still muddled. In the end she decided that the only thing she could do was to play it by ear. She did give herself a stern warning not to allow herself to become emotional; she had gone through more than enough of that already.

The main entrance hall of the hospital was really busy, and Dee had to wait in turn before she asked for directions to Mr Brent's office.

'I am not sure that Mr Brent is going to be in the hospital today,' a big young man with a smiling face told her in answer to her request. He took a plain card from the pocket of the white coat he was wearing and wrote some numbers on it. 'I'm Alan Cooper,' he introduced himself. 'This is the number where you'll be able to reach Mr Brent. There are three public phones on the wall to your left,' he added, holding out the card.

Dee took it and thanked him. Foraging in her bag, she came up with a handful of coins and went to the bank of telephones.

Mr Brent answered on the first ring. 'Of course I will see you, Mrs Underwood. If you had thought to make an appointment beforehand, it would have been easier.' There was a pause before he asked, 'Are you in the hospital now?'

'Yes, the young man at the reception desk gave me this number.'

'Very well, I can be with you in about three quarters of an hour. If you go to the cafeteria, get yourself a coffee, I'll come and find you.' Without giving her time to say thank you, the line went dead.

It seemed ages before Mr Brent came striding towards where she was sitting. He had a flustered look about him, and Dee jumped to her feet muttering apologetically. 'I'm sorry to have dragged you here... I am sorry.'

Jeffrey Brent placed his hand on her shoulder, pressing her back down on to her seat. 'It's all right, there's nothing for you to be sorry about. It just meant I had to break up a meeting a little earlier. I see you've had coffee; would you like another?'

'Oh, no thank you.'

'Well in that case I suggest we go straight to my office.'

Mr Brent's office was one floor above the cafeteria, and they climbed the stairs side by side, not saying a word. As he turned the key in the lock and pushed the door open, Dee smiled at the warmth that enveloped her. It felt so good after the chilly journey. 'Thank God for central heating,' he said, guessing what she was thinking by the look on her face.

Mr Brent went behind his desk but suggested to Dee that she sit on the leather couch. When they were both settled, it was he that spoke first. 'I did have a phone call from your brother-in-law last night, so hearing from you was not a total surprise, just a little sooner than I expected.'

'Again, I must apologise. John told me a few home truths which made me realise how selfish my entire attitude had been. You might say I gave myself a good talking-to and decided to strike before I had time to change my mind. Mr Brent, it really is very kind of you to have altered your own arrangements to suit me.'

The two of them stared at each other, then exchanged a faint smile which broke the tension. 'And now,' Mr Brent said, 'before we go any further, would you agree to us using our Christian names? I have the feeling that you and I are going to have to work together for some time to come. I think it might make things a lot easier.'

Dee nodded her head, smiling.

'Fine, I know you are Delia, and I'm Jeffrey. I think perhaps it might be better if you tell me what stage you had reached when you and your brother-in-law parted.'

Dee screwed up her face. She had supposed that

here in this office everything was going to be so cut and dried, but what did it matter? Nothing she might learn today could be more embarrassing than the details that John had outlined for her.

'Delia, you obviously don't know where to begin, so would you like me to bring you up to date on what has been happening with regard to the baby girl?' He asked the question with a tremor in his voice, well aware that he was treading on thin ice.

'Very well, perhaps that'd be best. Before John came to me yesterday I'd heard no more news other than what I learnt from you on your visit.'

'No, well, you wouldn't have been expecting any, would you? You made it quite plain that you didn't believe a word I said and that the baby was of no concern to you.' He had replied sharply and immediately regretted it.

Dee felt her cheeks flare up. 'It was all such a shock,' she mumbled.

'I fully understand that, and I'm amazed that the proposed plan has progressed so well without you being involved. Your husband, I have been given to understand, has stood by his principles.'

'Please, Mr Brent...'

He put up a hand to stop her. 'Jeffrey is what we agreed.'

Dee did her best to smile as she began again. 'Jeffrey, would you mind filling me in as to this proposed plan? John didn't get that far.'

'Well, with the mother's consent the adoption is already in process and some of my team have been assigned to the case, because even if both parents are in agreement, there will still be mountains of paperwork to wade through. Also, any prospective couples will have to go through a severe vetting process.'

'Are you saying that my husband has also agreed that this baby should be put up for adoption?'

'No, Delia, that is not what I am saying. If you want an answer to that question, you will have to put the question to your husband yourself.'

'Can you give me any idea as to how long all of this will take?'

'Not really. Any couple that does apply to adopt a child has to supply the courts with proof that they are married and that they have had no criminal convictions. Their friends and relatives will also be interviewed and perhaps even asked to complete a questionnaire about their suitability as parents. And even then there would be no guarantee that at the end of it all they would be allowed to adopt.'

Dee couldn't come to terms with what she was being told. It was as if these people had got together with Derrick and were all working together behind her back. To exactly what end? She couldn't be sure.

'I think I'd better go now. Doesn't seem as if there is anything left for me to do here,' she said, standing up and reaching for her coat.

Jeffrey Brent wasn't sure if it was frustration or annoyance that he'd heard in her voice, but suddenly he felt great sympathy for her. 'No, no, you'll do no such thing, not without first making a few decisions. Please, correct me if I've got it wrong, but are you now feeling that you would like to have some participation in whatever decisions are being made regarding this child?'

Dee kept her head low; she couldn't bear to meet his gaze. 'I will admit to having a host of conflicting thoughts.'

Jeffrey looked as if he were deep in thought. 'Would it help if I took you to see the baby?' he suggested. It sounded as if it were an idea that had suddenly come into his head, when in reality he had been attempting to ask that very question from the moment they had met today.

She still didn't raise her head, but she nodded, and that was enough.

He came from behind his desk and held her coat while she slipped her arms into it. 'We'll take a lift; we're going down to what is known as the basement, though I prefer to call it the garden floor. Come along, you'll see for yourself.'

On the way down, Dee was so distressed that Jeffrey was wondering if he was doing the right thing.

After the hustle and bustle of the busy hospital, the room he eventually led her into seemed to Dee a totally different world. You couldn't call it a hospital ward, she decided. To her this was like a nursery belonging to a wealthy family. It was very large, and everything seemed to be painted either cream or yellow, so that it seemed as though the sun were shining brightly.

Dee stood on the threshold gazing in amazement, but also feeling very hesitant as to how she should proceed. The two nurses were wearing an unusual uniform, very smart but different. One nurse broke away from what she had been doing and had a quick whispered conversation with

Jeffrey Brent before coming over to where Dee was still standing.

'I have the advantage of knowing that you are Mrs Underwood.' She smiled and offered her hand. 'I am Kathleen Parkinson and my colleague is Lynn Bryant.' They shook hands, and then Kathleen said simply, 'Come and meet our only little girl; the other two babies are both boys.'

'Here she is,' Lynn Bryant said, pointing to a cot in the far corner of the room.

Dee looked down to where a very small baby was lying quietly. When she glanced up, she suddenly realised that she was the only adult left in the room. 'My God, aren't you tiny?' she heard herself whisper as she lightly touched the silky fair hair that covered the baby's head. 'But it looks as if you are well cared for,' she murmured. She fingered the lace that edged the neck and cuffs of the pretty pale pink dress the baby was dressed in. Two tiny hands were held up in the air, the fingers uncurling to show minute finger-nails and the baby opened her eyes. Gently Dee laid her forefinger against the tiny cheek. The skin was as soft as silk, and as she withdrew her finger, the baby grasped it tightly. The sight of the tiny fingers wrapped around Dee's own was too much. The tears pricking at the back of her eyes were threatening to overflow. She would never have admitted it, but from that moment she was lost. Moving away from the cot, she thought the sweet smell of baby soap and talcum powder would linger with her for some time to come.

The two nurses beckoned for Dee to join them in the office where Jeffrey Brent was already

427

seated. As she sat down, Kathleen told her that she and Lynn had a few tasks that couldn't wait, but that she could stay as long as she liked and if she wanted to see the baby again before she left, that was quite in order. Then the two of them left, closing the door to the office very quietly.

The silence was eventually broken by Delia. 'Is this some kind of special nursery? I only ask because it doesn't even remotely resemble a hospital.'

Jeffrey, whose job demanded that he always act the diplomat, said, 'Money speaks all languages.'

'Are you telling me this is a private nursery?'

'You don't need me to tell you, you've guessed.'

'In your opinion, was it really necessary for this baby?'

'First off I would say yes, it was. She was born prematurely, she then developed pneumonia and her chances of survival were not promising. By the time her health had improved there were no places available in any of the adoption agencies and she was too young to be sent to an orphanage.'

'Is my husband picking up the bills?'

'I'm sorry, Delia, but like a good many more questions that you've fired at me, I am not in a position to be able to answer that. As I told you earlier, those kind of questions you must put to Mr Underwood himself.'

To herself Dee muttered, 'And what makes you think I won't?' But it was said without bitterness, because during the short while she had stood beside that cot and stared down at that wee baby, her whole attitude to the situation had changed completely.

40

It was the last day of November. It had been a long, aggravating wait until at last Delia had been informed that she could once again visit her husband in the Queen Victoria Hospital in East Grinstead.

Jodie had offered to keep her company. 'I know I won't be allowed to come in with you to see him, but as you are only allowed to stay with him for a short while, I thought I could have a look around the shops, and when we meet up later we could maybe have dinner before driving home.'

Dee had accepted Jodie's kind offer gratefully.

The weather had turned really bad. For the past twenty-four hours it had been snowing, not pure white pretty snow but more like sleet most of the time, and the roads were in a mess. Jodie was driving, and she turned to Dee, commenting, 'If it freezes tonight on top of all this slush, there'll be a few problems. I'm glad that you're able to see Derrick today, though. This has been quite a big operation he's gone through this time, hasn't it?'

'Well, in regard to his speech I was told it was most important, but I have learnt not to expect too much. At least he is able to see more now, though nothing like perfect sight, still unable to read, and that fact really does annoy him. Still, whatever, it will be great to see him today.'

'I spent last evening with Laraine,' Jodie said,

changing the subject. 'She is swamped with work. Could fill her time at Shepperton Studios if she so wished. I think she sees her future lying in television. She asked that you tell Derrick that she is thinking of him. I still feel so sorry for her. Rick was too young to die. It wasn't fair on her or on Adele and Annabel, but outwardly they do all appear to be surviving well.'

'Nobody ever said life was going to be fair,' Dee murmured sadly as Jodie drove through the gates of the hospital.

'It's just one thirty,' Jodie said, looking at her wristwatch. 'What time shall I come back to pick you up?'

'Shall we say four o'clock? If I should be turfed out before then, there is a very nice waiting lounge just off the main entrance and I'll go and sit in there.'

'That sounds OK. Dee, have a nice visit, but don't get upset if things are not as great as you would wish.'

'All right, Jodie dear, I'll do my best.' The two friends stood for a few moments locked into each other's arms before going their separate ways.

As Dee passed through the corridors, she unbuttoned her long mackintosh. Beneath it she was wearing a purple calf-length dress which she knew made her look glamorous, and so it should, it had cost Derrick the earth when he had helped her choose it in a posh shop in Singapore. 'Happy memories,' she murmured. Maybe he wouldn't be able to see her properly, but with his one hand he might be able to touch her and to hold her, then he would know that she had made the effort.

Bob Patterson opened the door in answer to her knock and his face was beaming with a wide smile which told Delia that Derrick must have come through well from this last operation.

Wonderful! He was on his feet coming across the room towards her. She still had her gloves on and was struggling to take them off, but she managed to say, 'Hello, darling, how are you?'

'I'm a whole lot better. How are you?'

She couldn't believe it. His statement hadn't been perfectly clear but it was no longer a mangled selection of words. She glanced at Bob and he gave her a thumbs-up.

Now she was sitting down and stretching her neck to look up at her husband. She couldn't understand why she had the urge to cry. She didn't feel sad, rather pleased and mostly happy, although she didn't need telling that Derrick was still a long way off being fit and well. His forehead and the top of his head were still heavily bandaged, and the whole of one side of his face was red raw and wrinkled. She had to lower her gaze for a moment during which she stared at her own hands and dared herself not to let a single tear fall. She looked up at him again. His top lip was back in the right position, or was it a new one? It certainly looked fuller. His lower lip was nice, a different shape.

'Well, are you going to pass judgement?' There was no jest in his question.

'Are those ruby lips substantial enough to allow you to kiss me?' Dee had answered a question with a question.

Derrick sighed, but only very softly. 'Afraid not,

431

but please, darling, take my hand.' He was holding out his right arm, and it was only then that she noticed the padding in place just below his left shoulder. She stood up, and very gingerly Derrick took hold of her right hand and gently brought it to his mouth. When Dee felt his lips touch the skin on the back of her hand, it was all too much. The floodgates had burst. She flopped back down on to her chair and cried as she had never cried before.

'Guv, I'm gonna leave you two to it. I'll be back later with a tray of refreshments.' Bob Patterson was being the soul of discretion.

When the door had closed, Derrick went to his locker and came back offering Dee a handful of tissues. 'Here, wipe your face, and please, Dee, try not to get so upset. I really am greatly improved.'

Feeling guilty for having done exactly what she'd promised herself she wouldn't, she rubbed at her wet face and then ran her fingers through her hair. When she had calmed down, they both sat down on the side of the bed and Derrick again took hold of her hand. 'You've had a lot of worry piled on your shoulders and all I can do is apologise,' he said.

'No need,' she quickly told him. 'John came to see me; he made sure that I understood all the facts and the circumstances.'

'Good old John, he came through when I needed him most.'

Derrick was speaking very slowly, and it sounded to Dee as if every word he uttered needed a great effort. It was as if he had a boiled sweet stuck to the roof of his mouth. That fact alone warned her to be wary of how she answered.

As if reading her thoughts he said, 'I've been thinking about the best way to rearrange our lives.'

He had said *our lives* and that alone gave Delia new hope. 'Oh, that sounds intriguing.'

'Well, a lot depends on you, Dee. With Christmas almost on us I might be able to come home for a short stay. You probably wouldn't be able to share a bed with me, but could you stand a man with parts missing sleeping in your bedroom? You could find an old single bed, couldn't you?'

She knew he was trying to make her laugh, but with the best will in the world she couldn't. Once again she had the urge to cry, not with sadness this time but with utter relief.

Derrick said, 'Being together in our own home will give us a chance to talk things over. Every decision has to be made with the full consent of both of us. There is so much at stake here, and no matter what we decide, the outcome will affect not only our lives but other people's as well.'

He already sounded very tired and she didn't want him to continue to talk. At the same time she was fully aware that he had been trying to approach the fact that he had a baby daughter lying in a nursery in London. Why was he approaching it in such a roundabout way? Why couldn't he just broach the whole thing? Bring the subject out into the open and tell her what his private thoughts were on the matter? Was it because he felt embarrassed? If that was the reason, she wished that somehow she could let him know that she wasn't exactly comfortable with the situation either. She definitely hadn't enjoyed having to listen to his brother recount the details.

His voice was very low now as he asked, 'Delia, how have you been in yourself?'

She almost blurted out, *lonely, and sick and tired of having my thoughts go round and round in my head.* Instead she said, 'Missing you like hell.'

He nodded his head towards her. 'I'm very familiar with that feeling. Middle of the night and when I wake up in the morning, it is still the first thing I do, reach out my hand, feeling for you.' He bent his head towards her now before he asked, 'And have you been living in that big house all on your own?'

'Well, darling, where else would I be but in our beautiful house? You have so much to look forward to. You have yet to spend your first night under your own roof.'

Dee had been sitting on Derrick's left side, where the empty sleeve was hanging. Now she got up and took herself to what she was now referring to in her mind as his good side.

Derrick's eyes lit up and he tried hard to smile. 'Thank God for that,' he murmured as he placed his right arm around her waist and tucked her in close to his body. 'I've been half afraid you might fear being near me, even find the closeness repulsive.'

Dee closed her eyes and sucked in a deep breath, and it was a minute or two before she could bring herself to answer him. 'I thought we vowed to love each other for better or for worse. If it were me that had been caught in that explosion, would you have considered my wounds repulsive to look at?'

'No. No, I didn't mean to upset you. And I'll say

it now, I am so looking forward to coming home, though I don't consider that house even partly belongs to me. Since I blotted my copybook and made that young woman pregnant, I think of it as yours by rights. That's the least I can do, and I'd be happy to transfer it wholly over to you any time you say.'

'First off, Derrick, I'm so relieved that you've brought the question of the baby out into the open, but I am going to ask you to leave that subject for the moment and let us get this matter of our house settled. You dare to talk about making me the sole owner! You'll do no such thing. It's great news that you may be with me and the boys for Christmas. Without you I wouldn't even have thought about putting up any decorations. But I know that will not be the end of it. Of course your connection with this hospital will have to continue for many a long day. We both know that. But Marine House will be our home. I have come to love living there, and you will too. With all the frontage there is nothing to stop you buying a boat and keeping it on your own doorstep. I haven't been able to tell you before, but your brother John helped his two boys to buy a boat, and at the moment that is always berthed on our property. It works both ways, you know, especially at weekends. Reggie and Lenny do well at the fishing, and our two love nothing better than to go to sea with their cousins. Folk come to buy the fresh fish, and their mates are always around. Then there's Richard's twin girls: they spend a lot of time with me, and when the weather is fine those two are proper water babies. So, my darling, can't you see, all that I'm lacking is to have you at home.'

Now it was Dee's turn to pick up his one good hand and bring it up to lay the palm against her own cheek. Her voice barely audible, she was babbling on and on. 'Derrick, you are my dearest, dear husband, and all I want is to have you back home where you belong.'

When no sound came from him, Dee was suddenly frightened. She had talked her bloody head off! Never stopping to think whether she was tiring him out or not.

She got up from his side, where she had been nestling so comfortably, and went over to the window, where she stood with her back to him. Rising slowly, he went to her and put his hand on her shoulder, turning her round. 'Oh, my dear, for God's sake, you're not crying again!' Abruptly now he took his arm away and blurted out, 'What can I say to you, Delia? Will you please stop crying, I just can't stand to see what I've done to you.'

'You've done nothing to me,' came her quick answer. 'I understand about the baby, I would have to be almost inhuman not to. I'm sorry, I'll make sure you don't see me cry again.'

He came back towards her. 'You don't understand… Oh, God Almighty, give me strength! All right, we'll play it your way. I'll come home for two or three days over Christmas and we'll see how that goes. I've talked it over with Dr Wilkinson and a couple of his colleagues, and they tell me I will need quite a bit more patching up in the months to come. They aren't going to bother about a new arm, not at the moment, because the stump hasn't yet healed properly, but when they do, I hope they fix me up with a decent one. It would be nice if it could at least look natural.'

A loud rapping on the door ended the conversation, yet a couple of minutes ticked by before Bob Patterson entered the room carrying a heavily laden tray. When he went to put it on a side table, Derrick said, 'Bring it over here, please, Bob, we'll both of us manage fine sitting on the couch.' The covers were lifted from the plates and bowls and Delia said, 'What a lovely spread, a real cream tea.'

'Shall I pour the tea for you?' Bob asked, setting the cups down on to saucers.

'No, I can do that,' Dee told him, smiling.

'Very well, I'll leave you to it. Anything you need, guv?'

'No, I'll buzz you if I make a mess of things, but please thank the kitchen staff for me, they've done us proud.'

Watching Derrick use a fork, Delia thought it was marvellous, and was grateful that it was his right hand and arm that he still had intact. Suddenly she noticed his teeth, they appeared to be perfectly all right even though the skin around his mouth looked very tightly stretched.

Right now she felt better than she had for a long time. She couldn't wait to tell Martin and Michael that all being well their father would be coming home for Christmas.

Then a sudden thought struck her. Their boys had their own homes now and their girlfriends. That didn't matter. At least for Christmas Day the gathering would be held in Marine House. Hers and Derrick's future home. It didn't have to be a rowdy day, just being with loving family and friends, enjoying good food and excellent wine, the one day would be enough. If, on the other two days that Derrick would hopefully be at home, there should only be Derrick and herself, well, that would suit her fine.

That might just turn out to be the right time for both of us to sit down and discuss what the future is going to hold for that tiny baby girl, who like it or not, happened to be the daughter of Derrick James Underwood.

All too soon it was time for Delia to say goodbye, yet she wasn't unhappy, in general terms she would say it had been a good visit.

She loved the nearness of Derrick as with his one arm he hugged her close, this was what she was missing so much, but this time she managed to hold back her tears until she was outside his room.

So Derrick Underwood was coming home for the Christmas holiday. It seemed that friends and family all had different views on the situation.

Most were happy both for him and for Delia, and his mother especially was over the moon. Those who had misgivings had the sense to keep their thoughts to themselves.

All the arrangements had been made. Derrick would be brought home to Marine House by ambulance, with a paramedic travelling with him. The same arrangements would be made in reverse when he was due back at East Grinstead.

It was Christmas morning. Delia rubbed her eyes and sat up in bed. Leaning over the side, she stretched out an arm, as she always did, to flick the curtains back so that she was able to watch the sea. With her arm in mid-air, she realised that the curtains were already wide open and the sun was shining on a very frosty white morning. She jerked her head around so quickly her neck felt the twinge.

Twin beds had been set up in her lovely big bedroom, and there, as large as life, was Derrick. His pillows were propped up behind his head and he was sitting there smiling at her. 'Morning, Mrs Sleepy Head,' he said, now grinning broadly. 'I've been up since six o'clock. I made it to the bathroom but I didn't think I ought to try out the stairs, not without someone being with me. I did speak to you when I opened the curtains, but you merely grunted and hid your head beneath the bedclothes.'

'Oh Derrick,' she exclaimed, climbing out of her bed and moving over to his. 'Did you manage all right?'

'Just about,' he told her, then added quickly, 'but I am glad that Martin offered to come this morning and help me to bath and dress.'

As if on cue, they heard the key in the front door lock and Martin's cheery voice calling out, 'Merry Christmas, you two.'

While Martin was attending to his father, Dee had a bath and dressed herself in a silk two-piece suit that had also been bought while she and Derrick were in Singapore. She was hoping it would bring back many happy memories.

Looking around the house, she was more than pleased with what she had accomplished. The Christmas tree in the hall was brightly decorated with shiny glass baubles and masses of silver tinsel. Around the foot were heaped the presents for every member of the family and also for a good number of friends and neighbours. Jodie and Laraine had both popped in last night, each bringing a boxful of gaily wrapped parcels.

On the dot of eleven o'clock, Michael and Danny arrived bringing with them enough wine and spirits to ensure that today's visitors would go home at the end of the day feeling quite merry. By twelve o'clock the house was ringing with love and laughter. Both Derrick and Delia had been feeling very apprehensive as to how Adele and Annabel would feel about being around their uncle, but their fears were totally unfounded. Both girls showed their deep affection in a tender, loving way. Jodie's two boys, Lenny and Reggie, were more robust with their warm-hearted teasing. 'Suppose when you take up residence, Uncle Derrick, we'll have to cough up rent for having our boat on your seafront?'

Everyone laughed when Derrick replied, 'I've already started to calculate how much the back rental amounts to.'

Even John had turned up with a bag of presents, and nobody had made a comment when he made a great fuss over his mother and was even affectionate in his greeting towards Jodie.

'Christmas was never like this when we were abroad.' Derrick smiled up at his wife as she handed him a small whisky. She had been given a strict diet sheet as to what he could eat and drink. She sat down beside him and Derrick immediately moved nearer to her and placed his arm around her shoulders. She eased herself into him and buried her face in his good shoulder, and they clung together like that for quite a few minutes. Now it was Derrick's eyes that were brimming and his voice was thick and low as he said, 'I do love you so much, Dee, and I feel so lucky to be here today.'

Christmas lunch was as you'd expect it to be with so many people contributing.

When the dirty dinner plates and vegetable tureens were stacked up in the kitchen alongside the enormous carcass of the turkey and the remains of a leg of pork, Jodie carried in two Christmas puddings flaming with burning brandy. Laraine followed with mince pies, brandy butter, coffee and liqueurs.

Later, Adele and Annabel, armed with paper sacks, picked up the torn wrappings from everyone's presents and the crackers that had caused so much laughter. A sudden hush fell over the room as Dee asked her father to see to the television, and everyone settled down to watch the Queen's speech.

The afternoon was split into two groups, those who wanted to be outside on the beach kicking a football about and those who just wanted to throw a few more logs on the big open fire that was burning in the lounge and settle down for a nice snooze.

By nine o'clock that evening folk were being considerate, getting ready to leave. It had been a long day for Derrick and for Mrs Underwood senior. Several of the guests, including Marian, were going back to Jodie's house in Epsom to spend the rest of the holiday there. Dee had half-heartedly offered to accommodate some, but all had tactfully refused.

Martin and Michael with their two young ladies had stayed behind. The boys had walked one each side of their father going up the stairs, there to help him undress and to put on his nightclothes. Now even they had left and the house seemed silent.

Dee banked down the open fire and put the fireguard in place, then lowered the setting on the central heating clock before taking a last look around the room. It had been a really lovely day and she did feel relieved. The only worry was that not a soul had mentioned the baby. Perhaps that was for the best, she told herself, but to her mind discretion was being carried too far. All right, today had not been the time for that kind of discussion, but it couldn't be put off for ever. Pushing that thought to the back of her mind, she wearily climbed the stairs.

Derrick was propped up on his bed, his legs stretched out in front of him.

'Lovely day, wasn't it?' he said as she undid the buttons on the top half of her silk suit. 'Come and sit on this bed with me,' he laughed as her skirt fell to the floor.

'Are you sure you want us to be that close? Aren't you tired out?'

'You're talking too much.'

How was it she could feel so awkward with her own husband? As she did as he asked, she squeezed her eyes shut and took a long, long breath in. There were so many conflicting feelings

442

running through her body, she couldn't bring herself to look at him as he loosened his dressing gown. 'Don't you think we ought to talk about this?' she asked quietly.

Derrick didn't answer. She felt his hand move over her bare shoulder and down to her breast, which gave her a lovely little thrill. Then he took his hand away and snapped open the hook of her bra. Now he was exploring her body with his one hand, as if he was reminding himself of how they used to make love.

Her own response was shy and hesitant.

'I'm sorry if I'm being clumsy.'

'No, no, you're not, but wait a minute, please, let me take the rest of my clothes off.' Suddenly she felt like a proper woman once again. Derrick had managed to stir up all those long-denied feelings. It was the same for him, she needed no telling. Naked now, she gently positioned herself on to him, and more easily than she had thought possible he was inside her. It was a shock; it had happened without any difficulties.

Dear God, thank you, she was almost sobbing. She was his wife, she had no need to feel guilty, she was hoping against hope that she could be everything he had been longing for.

Later, he lay still, dazed but looking very happy. As for herself, she'd been touched and she had touched him, and she felt good, even though her heart was still banging like a drum in a marching band.

Derrick stirred himself enough to lift his hand and stroke it down her cheek. 'Darling, I feel I want to say thank you. Does that sound stupid?'

Dee pushed herself up to look down at him. His eyes were closed, his face relaxed. The expression of pure satisfaction on it made her want to jump off the bed, get down on her knees and thank God.

Her husband still belonged to her. They needed each other. They loved each other.

Then they lay wrapped together as much as was possible, and as the night ticked away Derrick felt his wife begin to drift off to sleep. He managed to free his arm from around her shoulders and reached down to pull the bedclothes up over them both.

Dee cuddled in, murmured something. Then slept.

Beside her, Derrick closed his eyes and gave a sigh of relief into the dark as he lay listening to the sea lapping the shore. She hadn't refused him, there had been no signs of repulsion, he thought; rather the reverse, in fact: they had come together as they always had, unconditionally, with love.

Epilogue

In the end no adoption order had been needed. It had been proved without a doubt that Derrick Underwood was the true father of the baby girl who had been abandoned in Hammersmith Hospital.

Delia had really put herself about. With the help of Jeffrey Brent, she had made three visits to Derrick's daughter. It hadn't taken long for her to decide that this child was not going to be fostered out and neither was she going to be put up for adoption. The baby's mother had done her best. Her principles had led her to bring her unborn child to England and to leave her with the scrap of paper that would lead the authorities to her father. That young woman hadn't been in a position to do much else. But I am, Delia had decided.

Eighteen months later, on the first Sunday in June, a christening was held in the old church in Rye at which a curly-haired, blue-eyed little girl was given the names Ann Kathryne Underwood. Judith Underwood and Laraine Underwood were her godmothers, John Underwood and Michael Connelly her godfathers.

The party held later at Marine House was the talk of the town.

As Baby Ann toddled from one aunt and uncle to another, her mother and father stood holding hands and watching. 'Derrick, just look at her, she is so beautiful and so sweet-natured. If anything were to happen to us, there would be no need to worry over the future for our daughter. Just look at them all! She has two grown-up brothers, grand-parents, and enough aunts, uncles and cousins to keep her happy for the whole of her lifetime.'

Derrick looked down at his wife. 'Dee, I have loved you from the moment I walked into Jodie's house to find you minding Lenny and Reg. You were just sixteen and I couldn't wait for you to grow up. And now, after all that has happened, I'll never be able to make you realise just how much you mean to me.'

445

Dee didn't know how to answer that, so she simply said, 'I love you too. Derrick, you are my whole life.'

There was a sudden commotion down at the end of the garden, and seeing that Baby Ann was in the centre of it, her parents went to find out what was happening. Adele and Annabel were laughing and Michael and Danny were trying to keep a straight face. Ann caught sight of her parents and immediately called out, 'Daddy, show Martin and Michael your new hand.'

Derrick dropped down on to his knees. Wrapping his good arm around his little daughter, he said, 'Of course I will, my darling, but why do you want me to?'

''Cos they don't believe you're wearing it, but I don't tell fibs.'

'Well we'll soon settle the pair of them,' her father said, standing up and rolling up the shirtsleeve of his left arm to proudly display his new arm and hand. As he flexed the fingers, the applause that went up from every guest was unrestrained.

A smiling Baby Ann was now being held in her mother's arms while her father pulled his sleeve down. Then, as Dee put her daughter down, the five of them stood together: Derrick, Dee, Martin, Michael and Baby Ann.

Michael Connelly said, 'Hold it, smile, all of you,' as he snapped away at his camera.

And everyone present smiled and agreed that they looked exactly what they were.

A very happy family.

The publishers hope that this book has given you enjoyable reading. Large Print Books are especially designed to be as easy to see and hold as possible. If you wish a complete list of our books please ask at your local library or write directly to:

Magna Large Print Books
Magna House, Long Preston,
Skipton, North Yorkshire.
BD23 4ND

This Large Print Book for the partially sighted, who cannot read normal print, is published under the auspices of

THE ULVERSCROFT FOUNDATION